A PRACTICAL GUIDE TO
EVANGELISM
HOW TO WIN AND KEEP NEW MEMBERS

2ND EDITION

Balvin B. Braham

A Practical Guide to Evangelism
How to Win and Keep New Members by **Balvin B. Braham**

This book is written to provide information and motivation to readers. Its purpose is not to render any type of psychological, legal, or professional advice of any kind. The content is the sole opinion and expression of the author.

Copyright © 2021 **Balvin B. Braham**

All rights reserved. No part of this book may be reproduced, transmitted, or distributed in any form by any means, including, but not limited to, recording, photocopying, or taking screenshots of parts of the book, without prior written permission from the author or the publisher. Brief quotations for noncommercial purposes, such as book reviews, permitted by Fair Use of the U.S. Copyright Law, are allowed without written permissions, as long as such quotations do not cause damage to the book's commercial value. For permissions, write to the publisher, whose address is stated below.

ISBN: 978-1-956461-00-8

Printed in the United States of America.q

22901SW 107 Avenue

Miami Florida, 33170

Contents

Foreword 5
Endorsements 8
Preface 11
Acknowledgements 14

PART 1—MOBILIZING YOUR CHURCH FOR EVANGELISM

Chapter 1: God's Call to Every-Member Evangelism 16
Chapter 2: Getting Your Church into Growth Mode 24
Chapter 3: Planning for Success 41
Chapter 4: Lifestyle Evangelism 53

PART 2—STRATEGIES FOR SUCCESSFUL EVANGELISM

Chapter 5: Digital Evangelism 78
Chapter 6: Evangelistic Visitation 93
Chapter 7: Evangelistic Small Groups 111
Chapter 8: Public Evangelism 131
Chapter 9: Preparing for a Public Evangelistic Campaign 149
Chapter 10: The Public Campaign 179

PART 3—EVANGELISM CONTEXT

Chapter 11: Evangelizing the Upper Class 195
Chapter 12: Planning and Implementing Effective Family Evangelism .. 217
Chapter 13: Planning and Implementing Effective Women's Evangelism 227
Chapter 14: Planning and Implementing Effective Men's Evangelism 243
Chapter 15: Planning and Implementing Effective Youth Evangelism 254
Chapter 16: Planning and Implementing Effective Children's Evangelism 270
Chapter 17: Planning and Implementing Effective Health Evangelism 281
Chapter 18: Evangelism in Educational Institutions 292

PART 4—DISCIPLESHIP AND NURTURE

Chapter 19: A Discipleship Paradigm 301
Chapter 20: How to Effectively Nurture New Believers 309
Chapter 21: For the New Believer 330

Appendix A: Planting New Churches 346
Appendix B: Reaching Non-Christians 351
Appendix C: Prayer Breakfast for Ex-Adventists 354
Appendix D: Fund-Raising for Evangelism 357
Appendix E: Bible Surfing 359
Appendix F: Bible Search Engines 361
Appendix G: Other Bible Study Methods 363
Selected Bibliography 369

Foreword

THE GROWTH of societies continues on an explosive path, and many individuals live with little heed to the Word of the Lord and little commitment to the faith of Jesus. Church growth is not keeping pace with the annual increase in population in each society, and the gap continues to widen. The gospel must not only be preached as a witness (Matt. 24:14). It must also be preached to gather new believers (Matt. 28:18–20). The church must find creative and innovative strategies to arrest and engage people's attention and secure their commitment to Jesus.

While most people in today's society demonstrate little apparent interest in the church and the gospel of Jesus, it is also evident that many who are members of the church are indifferent to our Lord's command to "go . . . and make disciples" (Matt. 28:19). It is also true that in some cases, interpersonal relationships among church members as well as the quality of the worship services do not inspire people to feel exuberant about their membership in the church. These realities do not enhance the growth of the church.

The objective of departmental ministries to win new believers to Christ and consolidate them in the faith is not clearly understood or practiced in many churches. This is possibly due to the fact that some leaders do not have the necessary resources or are not sure how to proceed. Numerous arguments have proposed using need-based ministries as an entering wedge for presenting the gospel and influencing others to accept Christ. However, much more can be accomplished by actually practicing this dimension of evangelism.

In order to contextualize the gospel for greater evangelistic effectiveness, there is a need for deliberate investigation of the needs of both the local congregation and the wider community to be evangelized. For this reason, appropriate survey strategies and survey instruments are essential for greater success in evangelism.

If a wider cross section of the members of the church were to become involved in evangelism, this would be a powerful response to the prayer Jesus asked the disciples to pray when He sent them two by two into the mission field. "He told them, the harvest is plentiful, but the workers are few. Ask the Lord of the harvest, therefore, to send out workers into His harvest field" (Luke 10:2, NIV).

Small groups ministries are a vital means of addressing this issue of engaging more laborers in the field and nurturing new believers. Through this ministry, more members can identify, develop, and utilize their spiritual gifts in leading souls to the Lord. As effective as this approach is in some territories, there is always the need to improve it and to implement it in other areas in order to achieve extraordinary success in closing the gap between the number of members and non-members in each community.

However, as effective as small-group ministry may be, it cannot eclipse or take the place of public evangelism. Rather, it should complement it. Before every public evangelistic activity, there should be small group initiatives that address the needs of the community and attract and prepare individuals to be receptive to the preaching of the gospel.

Those involved in public evangelism should not proceed without thorough preparation and consideration of all the areas that need to be addressed in order to achieve success. In order to obtain the best results, we must heed Jesus' counsel: "Suppose one of you wants to build a tower. Won't you first sit down and estimate the cost to see if you have enough money to complete it? For if you lay the foundation and are not able to finish it, everyone who sees it will ridicule you" (Luke 14:28, 29, NIV).

It is the pastor's responsibility to guide the church in devising strategies to care for those who are newly adopted into the faith. Ellen White said: "Preaching is a small part of the work to be done for the salvation of souls. God's Spirit convicts sinners of the truth, and He places them in the arms of the church. The ministers may do their part, but they can never perform the work that the church should do. God requires His church to nurse those who are young in faith and experience, to go to them, not for the purpose of gossiping with them, but to pray, to speak unto them words that are 'like apples of gold in pictures of silver' " *(Testimonies for the Church,* vol. 4, chap. 7, p. 69). While the Church must care for new believers, these individuals must be taught it is their responsibility to safeguard their salvation and eternal destiny. As new members of the faith, they must take deliberate steps to maintain their new relationship with the Lord and the church.

A Practical Guide to Evangelism: How to Win and Keep New Members by Dr. Balvin B. Braham is a relevant and useful resource for the church. It is rare to find a book that covers all the essentials mentioned above. However, this book does just that. It is nearly a complete guide. Every pastor needs a copy because it presents realistic insights on how to mobilize the laity and organize the church for evangelism and discipleship of new members. It provides pastors with innovative ways in which they can plan and execute personal and public evangelism and explains how to consolidate those who newly accept the faith.

This book provides the Children's, Youth, Family, Women's, Men's, Health, Education, and Personal Ministries departments with specific approaches on how they may plan and execute evangelistic outreach based on the goals and objectives of these departments. In an engaging way, it presents innovative means of executing small groups ministries in the church. It is an excellent resource for every small group leader and member. New church members will find this book helpful as it educates them on what to do to remain committed to the faith. It is truly a book for every leader and member of the church!

Dr. Israel Leito.
Former President of the Inter-American Division

Endorsements

"DEAR READER, the book that you have in your hands is a valuable contribution for meeting the challenge of finishing the task of preaching the gospel in this generation. It identifies the working forces of the church and integrates them into what we could call a total strategy with the intention of moving the local church to action to take ground away from the enemy of the salvation of souls. It gives a call to action from the perspective of public evangelism and from the perspective of internal evangelism, all so that the church member will become the main focus and motivator of the strategy that this work presents. Bringing souls to the feet of Jesus and keeping them active in the task at hand is the Purpose of this valuable work. I totally recommend it."

Dr. Filiberto Verduzco, treasurer of the Inter-American Division

Evangelism is the mission of the whole church, not solely a task for a department of the church. This book pulls together the entire local church— all members, departments, boards, and services—to cooperatively engage in the mission of leading others to Christ."

Dr. James Daniel, field secretary and associate Stewardship director of the Inter-American Division

If you are reading this recommendation, it is because you have this exceedingly valuable material in your hands. Don't let the opportunity to read, use, and practice the principles that are expounded here pass you by. I consider this book to be a fantastic contribution to the church in the twenty-first century. This book is not a mere manual of procedures or methods for evangelism that begins on a certain date and finishes in forty or fifty days; it is a simple way of looking for a true enabling to be more efficient as a disciple of Christ. The idea of the small group is a lifestyle and not just a strategy or method; this is clearly explained in chapter 5 of this material. The idea has been effectively captured that the basis of Christian effort is in the small group. Each missionary act should occur their; each training effort should pass through that filter. We must remember: 'The formation of small companies as a basis of Christian effort has been presented to me by one who cannot err' (*Testimonies for the Church,* vol. 7, chap. 3, pp. 21, 22). This is the most categorical way to say that every human effort must pass through the small group. This is the reason for which the proposition of making disciples through this means is a novel idea and works for capacitating the members of the church and moving them to action."

Pastor Melchor Ferreyra, Sabbath School and Personal Ministries director of the Inter-American Division

A Practical Guide TO Evangelism: How to Win and Keep New Members written by Dr. Balvin B. Braham. The content of this book is useful for this time. Its concepts are enjoyable and well founded and I am certain that using these tools will strengthen the reader's convictions with the result of carrying out more effective strategies in soul winning. Every church leader at every level and every lay worker should have this book in their library. It will be of great blessing for carrying out the mission of proclamation that God has placed in our hands.

Dr. Erwin A. González, Publishing Ministry director of the Inter-American Division

A Practical Guide TO Evangelism: How to Win And Keep New Members by Dr. Balvin B. Braham casts a new vision for evangelism in the Inter-American Division and beyond. This book emphasizes the application of the new knowledge, skills, and attitudes that are necessary to achieve the delicate balance between quantitative and qualitative growth at all levels of the church. It will spark renewed passion among pastors and lay people for public evangelism and the consolidation of new members."

Pastor Samuel Telemaque, director of the Office of Adventist Mission and associate director of Sabbath School and Personal Ministries of the Inter-American Division

"Are you dreaming about youth involvement in evangelism? As a young person, are you seeking to be better equipped for evangelism by being on the front line, sharing your faith with a contemporary generation? In your hand you have the right tool! A Practical Guide TO Evangelism: How to Win and Keep New Members by Dr. Balvin B. Braham is a timely resource. The author has provided new and practical ideas for helping all the youth of your church to better implement an evangelistic youth strategy. How about a task-force-based vision? Read this book; it is transformative for youth ministries!"

Louise Nocandy, associate director of Youth Ministries in the Inter-American Division

"Chapter 12 of this book covers important foundations for youth evangelism. Whether you have a small or large youth group, you will find this chapter loaded with practical tools for youth evangelism."

Dr. Baraka G. Muganda, former Youth Ministries director (1995 2010) of the General Conference

"If you are one who is passionate about the second coming of Christ for His church and anxious to participate in the fulfillment of the mission by taking the gospel to everyone, everywhere, then this book is for you. Its step-by-step method utilizes a fresh approach to ministry in a postmodern world and should prove to be a valuable resource in your hands, either as an instructor, an inexperienced gospel proclaimer, or an experienced practitioner in the gospel ministry. The times demand such an approach as is outlined in this volume."

Pastor Leon Wellington, vice president of the Inter-American Division and former president of the then West Indies Union Conference of Seventh-day Adventists

Preface

A CONSIDERABLE AMOUNT of evangelistic innovation and creativity takes place in churches around the world.. However, and churches always have the need for new approaches that will increase soul winning and enhance discipleship while cultivating qualitative growth. A Practical Guide TO Evangelism: How to Win And Keep New Members is a treasure of fresh ideas for pastors, elders, local church leaders, small group leaders, and church administrators and departmental directors at the division, union, and local-field levels, as well as for every member of the church, including all who are newly baptized.

This book will strengthen the efforts of and provide empowerment for: 1) those at all levels of church organization who strategize for evangelistic impact in urban, suburban, and rural areas; 2) those who actually organize and execute evangelistic initiatives at the level of the local field; 3) those at various levels of the organization who are actually responsible for organizing and executing evangelistic initiatives in the church; 4) all who are responsible for strategizing for the nurture and consolidation of church members; 5) all who are tasked with cultivating the qualitative growth of the local church; 6) all who are responsible for organizing and leading small groups in the local church; 7) church members who are interested in participating in outreach ministries in their communities; 8) all pastors and lay members who are involved in the evangelistic preaching of the gospel; 9) all who serve as Bible workers and Bible instructors; 10) all those who provide training in evangelism and discipleship.

For soul-winners to be truly effective, they need to have a biblical understanding of evangelism, understand the dynamics of their local congregation, and be familiar with the community and its needs. Furthermore, they must develop and implement effective strategies to meet those needs, share the gospel message, obtain decisions, and confirm and strengthen the faith of those who choose to follow Christ.

For this reason, this book adopts a comprehensive approach to evangelism. In part 1 you will learn how to get the local church engaged and ready for soul-winning endeavors and how to plan a continuous cycle of evangelism. Part 2 explains specific strategies for reaching people and gaining decisions for Christ, including how to plan, prepare, and execute a public evangelistic campaign. Part 3 applies these various strategies to the various departments and ministries of the church, suggesting ways in which every church member can be involved in sharing the gospel with all classes of people, thus enabling total member involvement in the evangelistic mission of the organization". Finally, since the objective of evangelism is not just to add members to the church but to prepare people for the Second Coming, part 4 focuses on conserving the results of evangelism, nurturing new believers in the faith so that they will become firmly committed disciples of Christ.

The strategies presented in this book focus on community action. This is an avenue through which to attract and engage the attention and interest of those in need of a saving relationship with the Lord and to encourage them to make a commitment to Christ. It is a novel resource that is relevant not just for bookshelves in libraries, but as an effective working tool that all Christians need. As you read its chapters, you will encounter ideas that will generate a brainstorm with which you can attack specific issues of evangelism and discipleship for which you desire more effective approaches.

This book will inspire you to think critically and impart skills to others in nurturing ministries, outreach, church growth, and discipleship. As you take in the concepts presented, you will find great value in contextualizing them to the needs of your territory by adapting, modifying, and even improving them as necessary. All twenty-one chapters along with the appendices will motivate you to do additional inquiry in order to broaden your horizons and knowledge base on this vital subject.

Only through the work of the Holy Spirit can true success be attained in leading souls to Christ. With much prayer, Bible study, and dependence on the Holy Spirit, pastors, elders, evangelists, department and ministry leaders, Bible instructors, church members, and new converts who apply the principles of this book will obtain great results in souls won to the kingdom of heaven. Enjoy the journey with this practical guide as you devote your life and service to the Lord and His children!

Acknowledgements

IT TOOK MUCH TIME, sacrifice, research, recall, and deep thinking to write this book. However, the Lord made it possible. I am indebted to Him for the realization of this evangelistic resource. It is about Him and was achieved through His enabling. As is obvious, this book is dedicated to the Lord and to His cause. May His work continue to grow!

Among those who shared in the sacrifice that made this publication a reality are my darling wife Ann and our beloved daughters, Shavannie an Attorney-at-Law and Julaine, a Medical Doctor. I thank them for their enduring patience and ability to be happy and courageous even in moments of divided attention. Their prayers, encouragement, and support motivated me to reach the finish line. They are truly wonderful, and I applaud and cherish them for being outstanding!

Pastor Israel Leito, former president of the Inter-American Division has done more to inspire this publication than he will ever know. By enabling me to coordinate the evangelistic strategies of the church in the Inter-American Division, he provided me with a vantage point that enriched my thought process and provided much practical experience, helping to make this book such a relevant evangelistic resource for the church.

The evangelistic passion that pastor Peter Joseph of the South Bahamas Conference exudes, along with his pulpit ministry, significantly influenced me to embark upon this project. I am greatly appreciative of the motivation he provided me to make this book a reality.

I highly treasure the contributions of Pastor Garfield Blake, Mrs. Shirnet Wellington, Margaret Daniel, Pastor Jeff Jefferson and Alfonso Veloza Harvey for the time and effort they dedicated to read the manuscript and offer grammatical and other suggestions.

Part I
Mobilizing Your Church for Evangelism

1

God's Call to Every-Member Evangelism

GOD CREATED human beings upon the earth for His glory (Isa. 43:7), for good works (Eph. 2:10), to have a personal relationship with Him (Acts 17:26–28), and to be holy and blameless before Him (Eph. 1:4). The entrance of sin frustrated God's Plan. Since then, the natural inclination of human beings is to resist God (Gen. 3:1–8). Before the world was even formed, God had made provision to restore humanity to His original design (1 Pet. 1:18–20, Rev. 13:8). To bring about this plan, He gifts, enables, and commissions those who accept the invitation to proclaim the everlasting gospel of Jesus (Eph. 4:11, 12; Acts 4:29; Mark 16:15). Thus the Holy Spirit, working through the testimony of His human agents, works to restore human beings to a state of holiness in which they demonstrate good works and live in readiness for the full and final restoration to the Edenic state. "God could have reached His object in saving sinners without our aid; but in order for us to develop a character like Christ's, we must share in His work. In order to enter into His joy—the joy of seeing souls redeemed by His sacrifice—we must participate in His labors for their redemption" *(The Desire of Ages, chap. 14, p. 142)*.

In the book of Acts, Luke provided an impressive account of how those who were thus gifted and enabled acted spontaneously, networked skillfully within their community, strategized aggressively, deliberately infected each other with enthusiasm, and harmoniously and intentionally proclaimed the gospel of Christ (Acts 2; 4:32–37; 5:12–6:7). Equipped by the Holy Spirit, they functioned effectively in their evangelistic role, and on a daily basis they saw scores of individuals embrace an intimate relationship with the Lord.

For centuries, pastors of all nationalities, cultures, and ethnicities have proclaimed the gospel of Jesus to both large and small gatherings of people. As they contemplated the expanding gap between those who accepted the gospel of Christ and those who continued to live without a Christian commitment, many pastors concluded that their effectiveness was less than what the Lord desired. Many began to wonder if they were using the right strategy, and as a result, they searched for new ways to evangelize and fulfill the gospel commission.

Joseph Kidder explains that since the 1970s, a concept has emerged among some pastors that in order to achieve greater results, they must renounce the traditional model of ministry and instead become visionary leaders whose role is to cast a vision and change the culture and structure of the church. To achieve this goal, they advocate that pastors should serve as chief executive officers (CEOs) of their congregations in order to achieve church growth. In this role, they are to function as charismatic leaders to whom people will gravitate. Unfortunately, this method results in building up megachurches in many cases rather than a servant community fulfilling the mandate of Christ.

In the medical community, there is a list of medications that all health care institutions are expected to have on hand at all times to be dispensed to patients by medical professionals as needed. These medications are known as VEN drugs—that is, *vital, essential*, and *necessary* drugs. Without these basic medications, an institution is not equipped to handle patients' basic health issues, and it is therefore not providing effective health care to the community.

Similarly, a church pastor who is called by God to do effective spiritual ministry should also have a VEN list of *vital, essential*, and *necessary* duties to be fulfilled. These duties include teaching and preaching the Word of God; caring for church members through visitation, counseling, and comforting; officiating at church ceremonies such as the Lord's Supper, baptisms, weddings, and funerals; conducting board and business meetings; and addressing other needs of the congregation.

Fulfilling these VEN duties in the local congregation sometimes becomes so overwhelming that the pastor neglects the *vital, essential, and necessary* duty to be the church's ambassador to the community and—by working with the members—develop an effective evangelism program for the church. Christian believers have the special privilege of extending God's kingdom by inviting those who have not made a commitment to Him to do so, and the pastor must lead in this mission.

To those who engage in this work Jesus gives the assurance of His power to equip them for effectiveness. In John 15:7 and 8, Jesus said, "If you remain in me and my words remain in you, ask whatever you wish, and it will be done for you. This is to my Father's glory, that you bear much fruit, showing yourselves to be my disciples" (NIV). Referring to Jesus' promise of His continuing presence in the Great Commission of Matthew 28:18–20, Ellen White said:

> Christ's last words to His disciples were: "Lo, I am with you always, even unto the end of the world," "Go ye therefore, and teach all nations." . . .
> To us also the commission is given And to us also the assurance of Christ's abiding presence is given. (*Evangelism*, sec. 1, p. 15).

Evangelism and soul winning is a *vital, essential*, and *necessary* duty, not only for the pastor, but for the entire congregation. In 1 Peter 2:9, the Apostle Peter, addressing the entire community of believers within the Christian faith, said: "But you are a chosen generation, a royal priesthood, a holy nation, His own special people, that you may proclaim the praises of Him who called you out of darkness into His marvelous light" (NKJV). This passage describes the priesthood of believers, a concept that does not conform to the CEO model of church leadership advocated by many who have a postmodern worldview. Ellen White emphasized the importance of soul winning as a duty for all Christians when she said, "The work above all work—the business above all others which should draw and engage the energies of the soul—is the work of saving souls for whom Christ has died. Make this the main, the important work of your life" (*Messages to Young People,* chap. 69, p. 227).

The writings of Ellen White are replete with quotations that impress upon the mind the urgency of extending the gospel commission. "We are now living in the closing scenes of this world's history. Let men tremble with the sense of the responsibility of knowing the truth. A world, perishing in sin, is to be enlightened. The lost pearl is to be found. The lost sheep is to be brought back in safety to the fold. Who will join in the search?" *(The Review and Herald, July 23, 1895).* In another place she said, "Evangelistic work, opening the Scriptures to others, warning men and women of what is coming upon the world, is to occupy more and still more of the time of God's servants" *(Evangelism,* sec. 1, p. 17). "Let us now take up the work appointed us and proclaim the message that is to arouse men and women to a sense of their danger. If every Seventh-day Adventist had done the work laid upon him, the number of believers would now be much larger than it is" (*Testimonies for the Church,* vol. 9, chap. 2, p. 25).

Empowering Ministry

As part of their *vital, essential,* and *necessary* duties, God has called pastors to a two-fold ministry. Firstly, they are to nurture those who comprise the community of believers. When Jesus reaffirmed Peter's call to the gospel ministry in John 21:15–17, He asked him to "feed My lambs" and "tend My sheep" (vv. 15, 16). Of this occasion, Ellen White said: "His work had been appointed him; he was to feed the Lord's flock. He was not only to seek to save those without the fold, but was to be a shepherd of the sheep" *Acts of the Apostles,* chap. 51, p. 515).

Secondly, pastors are to equip and engage the believers in ministries that influence those who do not know Jesus to accept Him as their Savior.

> The best help that ministers can give the members of our churches is not sermonizing, but planning work for them. Give each one

something to do for others. Help all to see that as receivers of the grace of Christ they are under obligation to work for Him. And let all be taught how to work. Especially should those who are newly come to the faith be educated to become laborers together with God. If set to work, the despondent will soon forget their despondency; the weak will become strong, the ignorant intelligent, and all will be prepared to present the truth as it is in Jesus. They will find an unfailing helper in Him who has promised to save all that come unto Him. *(Testimonies for the Church,* vol. 6, chap. 4, p. 49)

The pastor has broad biblical authority to develop the laity for evangelism. The Apostle Paul in counsel to Timothy, a young minister of the gospel, said: "The things which you have heard from me in the presence of many witnesses, entrust these to faithful men who will be able to teach others also" (2 Tim. 2:2, NASB). In its fundamental design, the church is unlike other human institutions. It is an organism that has Christ as its Head and every member— endowed with spiritual gifts— functioning as ministers. The pastor must help the members identify their spiritual gifts and utilize these gifts within the church and the wider community. A healthy, active, vibrant church is one in which the members discover, develop, and utilize their spiritual gifts.

Pastors should be proactive in providing leadership that equips church members for service, primarily for evangelistic activities. Christian Schwartz, through the program Natural Church Development, studied churches all over the world. The study revealed numerous characteristics that are common in growing churches, regardless of size or denomination. Empowering leadership is one of those characteristics. The term empowering leadership refers to a leader who helps build up the confidence and competence of others by sharing a compelling vision, helping others get caught up in that vision, and helping them use their talents and abilities to bring about the vision. According to Schwartz, this happens when leaders equip, support, motivate, and mentor members rather than acting as superstars. Russell Burrill also supports this concept of pastors providing empowering leadership within their congregations, articulating that leaders should spend time discipling others and delegating, by which the energy invested in others will be multiplied many times.

The Need for More Workers

Matthew the Evangelist gave us a synopsis of Jesus' compassionate and mission driven ministry, saying: "Then Jesus went about all the cities and villages, teaching in their synagogues, preaching the gospel of the kingdom, and healing every sickness and every disease among the people. But when He saw the multitudes, He was moved with compassion for them, because they were weary and scattered, like sheep having no shepherd. Then He said to His disciples, 'The harvest truly is plentiful, but the laborers are few. Therefore pray the Lord of the harvest to send out laborers into His harvest' " (Matt. 9:35–38, NKJV).

To fulfill the evangelistic mission of the church, Jesus' instruction to the disciples was to get more people on board. A need to expand the number of active workers to fulfill the gospel commission is as present a reality today as it was in the time of Christ. We may have a global church with millions of members, yet there is still a need for more workers. We may have a local church with thousands, hundreds, or scores of members, yet we need more people who are willing to take the gospel to the multitudes. Ellen White said:

> In such a time as this, every child of God should be actively engaged in helping others. As those who have an understanding of Bible truth try to seek out the men and women who are longing for light, angels of God will attend them. And where angels go, none need fear to move forward. As a result of the faithful efforts of consecrated workers, many will be turned from idolatry to the worship of the living God. Many will cease to pay homage to man-made institutions, and will take their stand fearlessly on the side of God and His law. (*Prophets and Kings,* chap. 13, p. 171)

Mobilizing the Members for Action

Pastoral involvement in evangelism is not optional. It is the most important activity for each pastorate and should be foremost on the annual schedule for both the pastor's personal ministry activities and those of the church members. To this end the pastor must mobilize the members for action. Addressing pastors, Ellen White said, "Prepare workers to go out into the highways and hedges. We need wise nurserymen who will transplant trees to different localities and give them advantages, that they may grow. It is the positive duty of God's people to go into the regions beyond. Let forces be set at work to clear new ground, to establish new centers of influence wherever an opening can be found. Rally workers who possess true missionary zeal, and let them go forth to diffuse light and knowledge far and near" (*Testimonies for the Church,* vol. 9, chap. 12, p. 118).

The involvement of lay forces is strongly emphasized in the Spirit of Prophecy. Of Ellen White's numerous statements on this matter, here are two examples: "In our churches let companies be formed for service. In the Lord's work there are to be no idlers. Let different ones unite in labor as fishers of men. Let them seek to gather souls from the corruption of the world into the saving purity of Christ's love" (*Evangelism,* sec. 5, p. 115). "All who receive the life of Christ are ordained to work for the Salvation of their fellow men. For this work the church was established, and all who take upon themselves its sacred vows are thereby pledged to be co-workers with Christ" (*The Desires of Ages,* chap. 86, p. 822).

Many more members must be motivated and mobilized to participate actively in evangelistic ministry. As part of this mobilization, pastors are to prepare church members spiritually for evangelistic engagements, organize evangelistic campaigns—which may be presented by the pastor, lay members, or guest evangelists—organize small groups, implement community-outreach initiatives, establish annual evangelistic goals, and facilitate evangelistic activities through departmental initiatives within the local church. Succeeding chapters of this book provide tools for carrying out this evangelistic endeavor.

Review and Discussion
- *For what purpose does God give spiritual gifts?*
- *What special privilege does God give to those who believe in Jesus?*
- *For whom is the call to evangelism and soul winning a "vital, essential, and necessary duty"?*
- *What is the concept of empowering leadership?*
- *How can this concept increase the effectiveness of a pastor's evangelistic ministry?*

2

Getting Your Church into Growth Mode

The Church: The Body of Christ

THE CHURCH is the body of Christ. He is its Head (Eph. 1:22, 23), and its members are interdependent on each other. The baptized members of the body have symbolically partaken of the death, burial, and resurrection of Christ (Rom. 6:3–11) and are therefore a new creation living a new life in Christ Jesus (2 Cor. 5:14–17; Rom. 6:13; Gal. 2:20; Col. 3:4). According to the Apostle Peter, the members of the body of Christ are called to a priestly function and have direct access to God, their heavenly Father (1 Pet. 2:9). Therefore, through their deeds and lifestyle (Rom. 12:1, 2; 2 Cor. 6:16), they must declare—to all those with whom they come in contact—the redemption that they have freely received from the Lord.

To be a member of the body of Christ is a high calling (Phil. 3:14), and through the gifts of the Holy Spirit, members are called to a lifestyle of ministry (1 Cor. 12:4–7, 27–28; Eph. 4:11–16; Gal. 1:15–16). For the body to function effectively, church leaders and pastors must take intentional measures to ensure that policies, actions, and programs converge to fulfill the mission of the body and prepare the members to live that lifestyle in readiness for the kingdom of God.

Sharing the Christian Faith

The command of Jesus in Matthew 28:18–20 must be understood as a corporate responsibility and an obligation for every believer. Therefore, church members must be organized and trained to fulfill this commission. Ellen White offered this inspired counsel: "In a special sense Seventh-day Adventists have been set in the world as watchmen and light bearers. To them has been entrusted the last warning for a perishing world. On them is shining wonderful light from the word of God. They have been given a work of the most solemn import—the proclamation of the first, second, and third angels' messages. There is no other work of so great importance. They are to allow nothing else to absorb their attention." (*Testimonies for the Church,* vol. 9, chap. 2, p. 19). The urgency of the gospel demands that Christ's ambassadors not wait to be approached. Rather, as the sent ones, they must be proactive in going to those who need an improvement in their understanding of their faith relationship.

Empowered by the Holy Spirit, every member of the church is obligated to reach out to others by precept and example and help them accept Christ and enjoy the salvation that He is ready and waiting to impart. It is the responsibility of the organized church to educate every member, imparting skills to them and providing initiatives that will enable them to work for the salvation of others. Ellen White suggested that each member of the church should do the work for which they are best adapted. She said that the members should put their energies into the cause of Christ and work harmoniously in extending the gospel commission (*Pastoral Ministry,* chap. 26, p. 154).

The Value of Lay Ministry

Lay members have unique opportunities to witness for Christ as their personal associations bring them into contact with a wide variety of people. They may encounter people who are going through times of transition and are thus more receptive to the gospel of Jesus, which brings them hope and assurance of a better and brighter future. Likewise, the poor, the hungry, the sick, prisoners, the physically challenged, victims of various kinds of abuses, delinquents, and the emotionally ill are all in need of specialized ministry. The bereaved, divorced, and separated, as well as the unemployed and those facing other kinds of abnormal life situations, all need to be reached and connected to the love of Christ and told of the possibilities available in Jesus.

Some church members have specific capabilities that enable them to connect with these persons, and they should be both trained and encouraged to do so. For example, where qualified individuals are available, the church or an appropriate facility within the community can serve as a counseling center in which church members with appropriate training provide Christian counseling to people in the community, making referrals when necessary to those who are properly equipped to handle specialized situations. Likewise, with proper guidance and encouragement, many members can develop their own social media ministry. Others are very gifted in the area of hospitality and should be encouraged to employ this gift to reach others with the love of Christ.

Ministers and church leaders, as well as the various ministries involved in evangelism, should inspire and motivate church members to unleash their creative and innovative skills and abilities in order to carry out evangelistic activities that will result in souls won to Christ. To this end, endeavor to develop, promote, and utilize evangelistic resources in your church that will empower church members in their evangelistic outreach. Seek out and provide opportunities for collaboration and training for the benefit of each member. Facilitate interactions among the members of the local church or within the church district. Assure the members that they can count on the support of the leadership of the church, which is there to aid them in achieving their maximum potential.

A Lay-Training Institute

Pastors should establish a lay-training institute in every church or church district. The purpose of such an institute is the ongoing training of lay members in order to equip them for effective outreach ministry. To provide for this training, recruit spiritually committed volunteers who possess gifts, experience, or professional training that make them competent to train others in different areas of outreach and ministry. The following two statements express Ellen White's support for lay training institutes in our churches:

> Many would be willing to work if they were taught how to begin they need to be instructed and encouraged. Every church should be a training school for Christian workers. Its members should be taught how to give Bible readings, how to conduct and teach Sabbath-school classes, how best to help the poor and to care for the sick, how to work for the unconverted. There should be schools of health, cooking schools, and classes in various lines of Christian help work. There should not only be teaching, but actual work under experienced instructors. Let the teachers lead the way in working among the people, and others, uniting with them, will learn from their example. One example is worth more than many precepts. (*The Ministry of Healing*, chap. 9, p. 149)
>
> The work of winning souls to Christ demands careful preparation. Men cannot enter the Lord's service without the needed training, and expect the highest success. The architect will tell you how long it took him to understand how to plan a tasteful, commodious building. And so it is in all the callings that men follow.
>
> Should the servants of Christ show less diligence in preparing for a work infinitely more important? Should they be ignorant of the ways and means to be employed in winning souls? It requires a knowledge of human nature, close study, careful thought, and earnest prayer, to know how to approach men and women on the great subjects that concern their eternal welfare. (*Gospel Workers*, sec. 3, p. 92)

Three Categories of Church Members

Working with Christian churches in the United States, Gallup conducted a study using its ME^{25} Membership Engagement Survey. Published in March 2013, this study identified three categories of congregants in the average Christian church: the *engaged*, the *not engaged*, and the *actively disengaged*. Engagement is the sense of personal connection that church members feel with their congregation.

Three Categories of Church Members

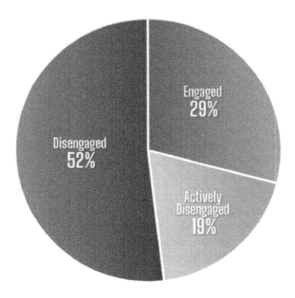

The *engaged* congregants, who comprise 29% of the church membership, are those who have a strong psychological and emotional connection to their church. These members experience dramatically higher levels of spiritual commitment and life satisfaction and are fully involved in the life and mission of the church. They spend more time in community service, are up to ten times more likely to invite others to the services of the church, and give two to three times more in financial contributions to their congregation. They are motivated by their growing faith and sense of belonging.

The *not engaged*, 52% of the membership, are those who are "part of the crowd." Although they regularly attend the services and activities of the church, they tend to be connected to the organization socially rather than rationally or emotionally. These disengaged members are less involved in giving, serving, and inviting others to the services and activities of the church. Often they are simply satisfied with their church because of what it provides to them. It would not be difficult to imagine this category of congregants becoming engaged if proper attention and focus were given to them in order to improve their involvement in the life of the church and the wider community.

Lastly, the survey identified 19% of the congregants *as actively disengaged*. These individuals can be divided into basically two groups. Those in one group attend church services infrequently but consider themselves members of the faith. Those of the other group may attend regularly, but they are consistently antagonistic to almost everything about the church. They are the most likely to be a negative influence in the church.

In seeking to equip a congregation for what Ellen White calls "the joy of service in this world and . . . the higher joy of wider service in the life to come" (*Education,* chap. 1, p. 13), a pastor must be aware of what kind of church members comprise the congregation. In order to evaluate a congregation's level of spiritual engagement, the church board, under the pastor's guidance, may appoint a team to carry out the survey in Table 1, which has been designed to measure member engagement in the context of a local Seventh-day Adventist congregation:

Table 1: Indicators of Member Engagement in a Local Adventist Church

No.	Indicator	Yes	No
1.	I feel a deep love for my church and a strong sense of community with other church members.		
2.	My personal relationships with other church members draw me closer to Christ.		
3.	I enjoy the companionship of those within my church even more than my friendships with others.		
4.	I appreciate the leadership provided by the pastor, elders, and other leaders of my church.		
5.	I enjoy attending worship services at my church because I find them inspiring and edifying.		
6.	I enjoy studying and discussing the Sabbath School lesson.		
7.	I strongly identify with my church's teachings.		
8.	As a matter of personal conviction, I endeavor to follow the lifestyle standards promoted by my church.		
9.	I believe my church provides a spiritual environment that is conducive to personal preparation for the second coming of Christ.		
10.	I am personally motivated by the influence of my church community to live in preparation for the second coming of Christ.		
11.	I find personal fulfillment in developing and utilizing my talents and spiritual gifts in the church.		
12.	I feel like the church community genuinely appreciates my contributions.		
13.	I consider it a privilege to help support my church through my financial stewardship, even when this requires personal sacrifice.		
14.	I enjoy participating in the outreach ministries of my church.		
15.	I am enthusiastic about sharing the principles of my faith with others.		
16.	I am eager to invite my friends to go to church with me.		

Key for determining the category of each member:
1. Engaged   9–16 Yes responses
2. Not engaged   5–8 Yes responses
3. Actively disengaged 0–4 Yes responses

Some pastors spend a lot of time doing evangelism and addressing the congregation as a whole, yet they know very little about the individual members of the congregation. This is understandable in large congregations; however, this provides a reason for establishing small groups and enlisting the participation of elders and other church leaders in nurturing and caring for the members. The Sabbath School also plays a vital role in this nurturing ministry. When pastors spend more time visiting and interacting with church members in small groups and in social activities, members will become more engaged in the life of the congregation and will progress in their spiritual growth.

Growing the Church

When ministers and church members combine their efforts to increase or deepen the quality of church life and when they extend their interests beyond the circumference of the immediate church family to others, the church grows. There are two essential dimensions of genuine church growth: (1) qualitative growth and (2) quantitative growth.

Whereas quantitative growth has to do with the increase of the church's membership and the geographical expansion of its influence, qualitative growth refers to the way the church's members live out their salvation in Christ. This is seen through the deepening of spiritual and social interactions between members as they connect with each other through love, tolerance, patience, forgiveness, happiness, acceptance, mercy, peace, care, compassion, and kindness. When the members of a congregation demonstrate a desire to be present at church and to participate in the various worship services and activities, and when they develop a genuine sense of community among themselves, qualitative growth becomes a reality.

The challenges that many churches experience with quantitative growth are closely related to the qualitative state of the congregation.

New members will be attracted to a church that demonstrates qualitative wellness. A church that exudes love, care, and concern for people and helps them achieve their maximum potential is a community that people will want to be a part of. It is the quality of life and the relationships within the community—both with God and with other church members—that matter. When people feel like they belong and are accepted and that their social, spiritual, emotional, and cognitive needs are met, they will not only stay, but will bring others with them; and as a result, the church will grow.

Four Dynamics of Church Growth

Spiritual → Team → Congregational → Outreach

Four Dynamics of Church Growth

Whether a church is located in an urban, suburban, or rural area, in order for it to experience qualitative and quantitative growth, four important dynamics must be considered:

1. **Spiritual dynamic:** This refers to the quality of the worship services, which focus on the Divine and enrich the spiritual life of each worshipper. This includes preaching, teaching, prayer, Bible study, music, praise, thanksgiving, confession and forgiveness, dedication, and reverence. Leadership,

preparation, and participation are necessary in all of these aspects to ensure quality in both form and content.

2. **Team dynamic**: The church is a community of believers in which each person possesses unique spiritual gifts. Organization of various team ministries should be encouraged and fostered to draw out these spiritual gifts for the edification of others. Through small groups and the various departments of the church, members work together to execute the mission plans, programs, and strategic initiatives of the church.

3. **Congregation dynamic:** Healthy and stimulating relationships between members within the church form an important aspect of fellowship, helping members to bond with each other as a community of believers. Social activities, constructive efforts to resolve conflict, and inclusive planning and decision making help to foster such relationships.

4. **Outreach dynamic**: The church must make itself relevant to the community. Members must be intentional about living their Christian faith to the glory of God. People want to see Christ, and church members are His ambassadors. Mingling with others and touching their lives on a social level is a powerful way to represent Christ in the community. Through both individual acts of kindness and group initiatives, members of the church show care and compassion for their fellow human beings. By addressing the material and social needs of the community, the church makes the gospel more attractive and enhances its own image in the community. When combined with Bible studies and the public proclamation of the Word of God, such initiatives yield great results in decisions for Christ.

Discovering the Needs of the Local Church

In order to effectively address the four dynamics mentioned above and promote qualitative church growth, conduct the survey provided in Table 2. This survey will ascertain the needs of the congregation, the capabilities of the members, and the deficiencies that should to be addressed. The information acquired will provide guidance for improving spiritual nurture and member involvement through worship services, training, and outreach events and initiatives.

Depending on the size of the church, the survey may be conducted formally or informally. In either case, appoint a committee to carry out the data collection process. This may be the Personal Ministries Council or another committee specifically appointed for the task. The members of this committee will determine the time frame for collecting the data as well as the demographics of the group to be surveyed. They will also select responsible individuals to administer the survey. Finally, they will analyze the collected data and present their findings and recommendations to the pastor and church board. The church board should then carefully consider the report and take appropriate action. The board will determine who will be responsible for the implementation of any initiatives, establish a timeline for their development and completion, and determine an appropriate evaluation mechanism to monitor their progress and effectiveness.

A Healthy Church

The health of a church is one of the pre-requisites for it to grow. People are interested to become members of a church that not only demonstrates signs of health but in fact is healthy. Both leaders and members in cooperation with the Holy Spirit are responsible for creating it. Pastors and elders must assume the primary role of leading the membership to the creation of such a community. They should seek to enable the members through the following six imperatives.

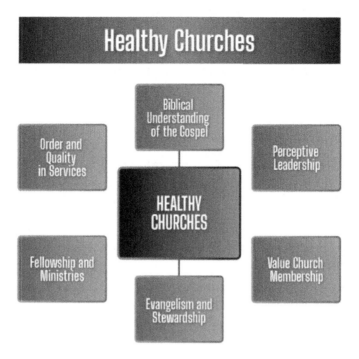

Imperative #1: Members have a biblical understanding of the Gospel in the life of believers

- They understand the life and ministry of Christ.
- They know who is the foundation of the Church.
- They understand the process of salvation.
- They understand the influence of the gospel in the life of believers.
- They know about the transforming power of the gospel.

Imperative #2: Perceptive leadership

- Leaders who have the ability to influence others in the direction of the kingdom.
- Leaders who ensure that conflicts are resolved in a timely manner.
- Leaders who give a sense of direction and keep the members informed.

- Leaders who listen to members and others.
- Leaders who allow for the total participation and inclusion of members.
- Leaders who are genuine examples or models of the way members should deport themselves.
- Leaders who embrace creativity and innovation.

Imperative #3: Members value their Church membership
- They know what are the prerequisites for becoming a member.
- The value of the vows they took at the time of their baptism.
- They know what it means to have membership in the Church.
- They are Committed to the cause and mission of the Church.
- They submit and subscribe to full participation in the life of the Church.
- They possess and demonstrate a sense of ownership and belonging to the Church.
- They embrace and demonstrate total surrender to Christ.
- They are serious about the kingdom and demonstrate it in their lifestyle.

Imperative #4: Members have a biblical understanding of evangelism and stewardship
- They are able to differentiate between evangelism and stewardship.
- They know what the bible says about evangelism and stewardship.
- They know what is the role of each member in the evangelism and stewardship program of the Church.
- They know what is the value of evangelism and stewardship to the Church.

Imperative #5: Members value the fellowship of others and ministries of the Church
- They demonstrate love for each other and to those outside their community of faith.
- They demonstrate compassion in service to each other and those of the wider community.

- They are involved in sharing their material and spiritual blessings to others.
- They demonstrate care for the needy, suffering and less fortunate.
- They express warmth and are welcoming to others.
- They make time to deal with the interests and needs of others.

Imperative #6: There is order and quality in the services of the Church

- People learn based on the nature, content and delivery mode of teaching and instruction in the Church.
- Members are discipled to grow and serve socially, spiritually and otherwise.
- Planning is a visible element in the execution of the elements of the worship service.
- Worshippers understand and demonstrate reverence during the services.
- The ministry of the Holy Spirit is emphasized and embraced.
- Everyone respects and values others.

Review and Discussion

- *Name and explain how the six imperatives for a healthy Church could transform and revitalize your local congregation.*
- *What is the church's mission and who is to carry it out?*
- *How can ministers and leaders empower church members to win souls to Christ?*
- *Suggest at least three ways in which your church could increase the number of engaged members and decrease the number of those not engaged or actively disengaged.*
- *Discuss the difference between qualitative and quantitative church growth.*
- *How active is each of the four dynamics of church growth in your church?*
- *Suggest at least one improvement that your church could make in each of these four areas.*

Table 2: Survey of Local Church Needs

Name of Church:	
Name of survey-team member:	
Number of members in local church:	
Group being surveyed. 1. Adult males. 2. Adult females. 3. Young men. 4. Young ladies. 5. Boys and girls	
Age range of survey group: 1. 10-15. 2. 16-25 3. 26-35. 4. 36-45. 5. 46-55. 6. 56+	

Spiritual Dynamic

1.	In which of the following areas would you lie to see your church improve? 1. Preaching. 2 teaching. 3. Prayer. 4. Bible study. 5. Needs-based ministries. 6. Worship services
2.	How would you suggest improving the areas you have chosen?
3.	What ministries would you change or improve in the church?

Team Dynamic

4.	How strong is the spiritual leadership in the church? 1. Very strong. 2. Strong. 3. Weak. 4. Very weak. 5. Poor
5.	How would you rate the spiritual life of the members? 1. Very strong. 2. Strong. 3. Weak. 4. Very weak. 5. Poor.
6.	What percentage of the membership do you believe are active disciples? 1. 10% 2. 20% 3. 30% 4. 40%. 5. 50%

7.	Would you be available to assist in carrying out some of the plans programs, and initiatives of the church? 1. Definitely. 2. Likely. 3 Not likely. 4. Definitely not.
Congregation Dynamic	
8.	How spiritual are the relationships between the members of the church? 1. Strongly spiritual. 2. Spiritual. 3. Somewhat spiritual. 4. Not spiritual.
9.	How well are the conflicts usually resolved in the church? 1. Excellently. 2. Satisfactorily. 3. Not satisfactorily. 4. Very Poorly.
10.	Does the leadership listen to the members? 1. Always. 2. Usually. 3. Sometimes. 4. Never.
11.	Does the leadership make the members feel that they belong and are accepted? 1. Always. 2. Usually. 3. Sometimes. 4. Never.
12.	How motivated are the members to participate in the life of the church? 1. Strongly motivated. 2. Motivated. 3. Somewhat motivated. 4. Not motivated.
Outreach Dynamic	
13.	Does the church have the activities that address the material and social needs of the community? 1. Yes. 2. No
14.	How effective are the community-needs activities of the church? 1. Very Effective. 2. Effective. 3. Ineffective. 4. Very Ineffective.
15.	Does the church have the activities that address the spiritual needs of the community? 1. Yes. 2. No.
16.	How effective are the spiritual-needs activities of the church in the community? 1. Very effective. 2. Effective 3. Ineffective. 4. Very ineffective.
17.	How effective are the soul-winning activities of the church in the community? 1. Very Effective. 2. Effective. 3. Ineffective. 4. Very Ineffective.
18.	What specific activities would you like to see implemented to address the spiritual needs of the community?

19.	What resources are needed for this initiative to be successful?
20.	What specific activities would you like you see implemented to address the material and social needs of the community?
21.	What resources are needed for this initiative to be successful?
22.	What groups in your community would you be comfortable to work with socially or spiritually?

3
Planning for Success

CHRIST CALLS His followers to evangelistic ministry in their communities, and accordingly He has blessed them with the necessary gifts and abilities to fulfill His will. He is ready and waiting to enable them to be used as His instruments in this soul-saving endeavor. However, success in evangelism comes as the result of joint effort between Divinity and humanity. Therefore, those involved in evangelism and soul winning should do their part to ensure that every aspect of planning and preparation is properly attended to. Thus, in preparing for the implementation of evangelistic initiatives, they must ascertain the needs of the community, determine appropriate strategies, acquire the necessary resources, and establish detailed plans for the execution of the initiatives. Finally, they should evaluate the effectiveness of the initiatives in order to facilitate future planning.

The Evangelism Action Committee

In order to facilitate the planning process, each congregation should have an Evangelism Action Committee (EAC). The Personal Ministries Council of the church exists to organize and equip members for outreach ministries; accordingly, this council could be expanded to serve as the Evangelism Action Committee. The pastor should chair this committee with one of the committee members designated as vice chair. The committee should have specific objectives and annual goals to be achieved. The objectives of the Evangelism Action Committee include the following:

1. To develop an Evangelism Master Plan for the church. This includes establishing the short, medium, and long-term evangelism and soul-winning vision for the church.
2. To recruit, train, and deploy members of the church for soul winning.
3. To provide soul-winning resources to the members of the church for effective implementation of evangelistic initiatives.
4. To communicate the evangelistic initiatives of the church to the members in order to create awareness of the outreach activities of the church.
5. To create awareness among members of their actual performance in the area of evangelism and soul winning in comparison to expectations.
6. To evaluate soul-winning initiatives and membership performance and advocate for changes or improvements to these initiatives.
7. To provide motivation and incentives for member participation in the soul-winning initiatives of the church.
8. To determine, implement, maintain, and supervise effective initiatives for the nurture and conservation of new believers.

Departmental Evangelistic Initiatives

Each department of the church exists to fulfill certain functions. Foremost among those functions are soul winning and the nurture of church members. This book provides a very useful and relevant resource specifically to the Family, Women's, Men's, Children's, Youth, Health, and Education Ministries of the church for organizing and executing soul-winning initiatives.

Thom Rainer and the Billy Graham School of Mission, Evangelism and Church Growth did a survey of formerly unchurched individuals in the United States who eventually accepted Christ. In this survey, 43% responded that family members were influential in their decision to accept Christ, a fact that provides a powerful argument for family evangelism. Within this group, 35% said that their wives influenced them to join the church. This result gives relevance to women's evangelism. While 9% of men influence their wives to accept Christ, men are also able to speak the language of men that women cannot; thus, they have unique opportunities to be effective in men's evangelism. Furthermore, the study showed that children's and youth ministries were influential with 25% of those who had accepted Christ. In addition, Ellen White wrote in *The Ministry of Healing* that "people need to see the bearing of health principles upon their well-being, both for this life and for the life to come" (chap. 9, p. 146), and she described the health message as the right arm of the gospel (see *Testimonies for the Church*, vol. 6, chap. 27, p. 229).

The church's soul-winning mission encompasses all of these ministries. Therefore, each of these departments should cultivate an intentional evangelistic vision. To this end, each department may establish it's own evangelism task force. This task force, working in cooperation with the Evangelism Action Committee of the church, investigates community needs in its particular area of ministry and determines strategies, goals, and objectives for the department's evangelistic initiatives.

Of course, it is not practical for a church to conduct seven different evangelistic campaigns every year, but the various ministries can collaborate to carry out an effective evangelistic program that involves every member of the church. The Evangelism Action Committee should coordinate this interdepartmental evangelistic collaboration. Accordingly, a leader or member from each of these departments should serve on this committee. In strategizing for the evangelistic year of the church, the Evangelism Action Committee determines the number of campaigns to be held each year and which combination of ministries will be involved in each campaign. Regardless of which departmental ministries are conducting the evangelistic program, the Sabbath School and Personal Ministries Department is usually involved since it is directly responsible for the evangelistic activities of the church.

In order to stay focused on the objectives to be reached, the Evangelism Action Committee and the departmental task forces

involved in evangelistic initiatives should carefully answer the following questions:
1. What specific evangelistic objectives does this committee or task force have?
2. In what specific soul-winning initiatives is this committee or task force involved?
3. What are the targeted demographic groups for these initiatives?
4. What do we need to know about these groups before executing these initiatives?
5. How many people are needed to execute these initiatives?
6. What strategy are we using to educate the members of the church about these initiatives?
7. Who will be responsible for this education process?
8. When will this education process begin and how long will it last?
9. How will we recruit the necessary personnel to carry out these initiatives?
10. Who will be responsible for this recruitment?
11. When will recruitment begin, and how long will it last?
12. What training will be necessary for the participants?
13. Who will provide this training?
14. How long will the training last?
15. What part will each participant play in the execution of these initiatives?
16. What resources will be required for the execution of these initiatives?
17. How will we obtain these resources?
18. Who will be responsible for obtaining them?
19. By what date should all of the resources be obtained?
20. When should execution of the initiatives begin?
21. What is the time frame for the implementation and completion of the initiatives?
22. How are the initiatives to be evaluated?
23. Who will be responsible for conducting this evaluation?

The Problem of Continuity

Continuity of is one of the most common challenges that churches face in the implementation of ministry initiatives. Often, a leader of a particular church department gets inspired to execute a certain initiative, but before the initiative is properly understood—and often when it has nearly reached the point of producing the desired outcomes—it is abandoned, changed, or allowed to disintegrate. Leaders must be intentional in allowing evangelistic and soul-winning initiatives to develop and produce the desired results.

The sigmoid curve shown in Figure 1 illustrates the typical life cycle of both natural and man-made systems, initiatives, and programs. At the beginning, they develop slowly. As they mature, they start to grow exponentially. Eventually, they reach a plateau and growth ceases. From there, they begin to decline until they become nonexistent.

A church's evangelistic initiatives are subject to this same cycle of growth and decline. In many cases, leaders allow evangelistic initiatives to die before they even get to the point of exponential growth. Other initiatives achieve exponential growth but are then allowed to plateau and decline prematurely. It is essential to plan for continuity in outreach initiatives in order to achieve and maintain exponential growth. This requires sufficient time, resources, and communication as well as an intentional leadership strategy.

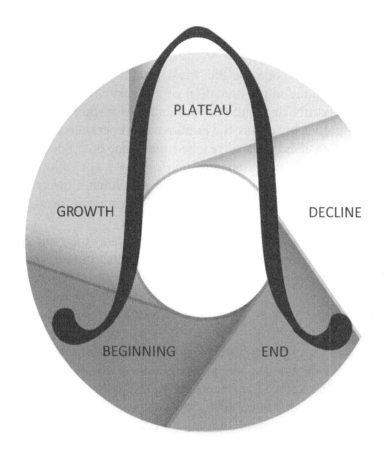

Figure 1: The sigmoid curve illustrates how living, social, and organizational entities rise and fall.

A Continuous Leadership Cycle

In order to ensure the continuity of evangelistic initiatives, it is important to establish a continuous leadership cycle of assessment, *analysis, planning and outcomes determination, execution,* and *evaluation.* The pastor, the Soul Winning Action Committee, and the departmental evangelism task forces should make provision for this five-step process before beginning an evangelistic initiative. Figure 2 illustrates these five steps

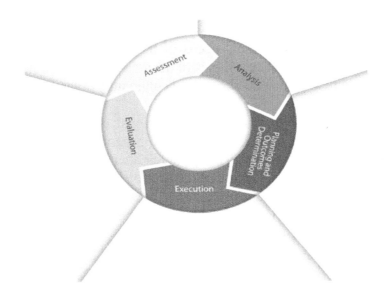

Figure 2: Leadership-Development Process in Evangelism

1. *Needs Assessment of the Territory to Be Evangelized*

In order to determine the best strategies that will lead to effective outcomes, intentional assessment should precede evangelistic initiatives among any people group. The purpose of this assessment is to determine strengths, weaknesses, opportunities, and threats. The assessment should be comprehensive in order to address all current needs of the targeted population. It should also systematically monitor specific and relevant issues on an ongoing basis in order to determine what changes have occurred within the community and what adjustments are necessary to maintain the relevance and effectiveness of the initiative.

The following is some of the information that this assessment process should ascertain: Is this an urban neighborhood? If so, is it downtown, inner city, inner urban residential, or outer urban residential? If it is a suburban community, is it inner suburb, metropolitan suburb, or a rural settlement at the edge of a metropolitan area. In the case of a small town or rural area, how large is the population, and what are the primary economic activities and the material and social needs of the residents? In any case, information about the boundaries of the area will be valuable. Also try to acquire information about local community organizations and their leaders.

It is important to know the generational composition of the territory as well as the interest that each generational group has in religion. The table below depicts church attendance in the United States according to generation as revealed by research conducted by Thom Rainer. This data is useful to the local church community for determining appropriate evangelistic and soul-winning strategies.

Table 1: Church Attendance by Generation		
Generation	**Birth Years**	**Percentage Who Attend Church**
Builders	Before 1946	51%
Boomers	1946–1964	41%
Busters (X)	1965–1977	34%
Bridgers (Y)	1977–1994	29%

Community leaders and those who have been familiar with the area for many years are one of the best sources for useful information about the community. In order to take advantage of this resource, contact these individuals and ask them to participate in the survey found in Table 2, which has the objective of discovering the material, social, and spiritual needs of the community and determining the best strategies to address those needs.[1] This survey may be conducted by either the Evangelism Action Committee or a departmental evangelism task force. Although it is based on the needs of urban areas, it may be modified to fit other contexts as well.

---

[1] Appendix B provides strategies specifically for working among non-Christian groups and communities.

Table 2: Survey of Community Needs	
Name of church:	
Name of survey-team member:	
Geographical area:	
Population of geographical area:	
Number of Adventist churches in geographical area:	
1.	What are the dominant religious groups in your community? **1.** Christian **2.** Jewish **3.** Muslim **4.** Others _____
2.	What are the dominant denominations of Christian churches? **1.** Reformed **2.** Presbyterian **3.** Baptist **4.** Methodist **5.** Adventist **6.** Pentecostal **7.** Catholic **8.** Anglican **9.** Mormon **10.** Others _____
3.	What are the principal employers in your community?
4.	How would you describe the average economic level of your community?
5.	What ethnic groups are represented in your community? **1.** Latin American **2.** African American **3.** Afro-Caribbean **4.** Caucasian **5.** Native American **6.** Jewish **7.** Asian **8.** Middle Eastern **9.** African **10.** Others _____
6.	What language groups are represented in your community? **1.** English **2.** Spanish **3.** French **4.** Portuguese **5.** Chinese **6.** Korean **7.** Arabic **8.** Others _____
7.	In what ways could our church connect socially with the different demographic groups within your community?
8.	In what ways could our church connect spiritually with the different demographic groups within your community?
9.	What are some of the specific needs of the families in your community?

1. *Analysis*

In analysis, the leadership of the church uses the information obtained in the assessment stage to determine the gap between the current realities in the community and the outcomes desired by the church. This analysis includes identifying the problems that exist for the church in relation to the implementation of a specific evangelistic initiative. Be sure to address problems that do not currently exist but could possibly exist in the future. Finally, determine if the church and the targeted group are ready for the initiative under consideration.

2. *Planning and Determination of Objectives*

In the planning stage, we combine and utilize the results of assessment and analysis to develop the plan of action for the evangelistic initiative. Identify the possible response of the residents within the targeted territory, and determine how those who are responsible for the evangelistic action will address this anticipated response. Consider methods, resources, time frame, and follow-up for the proposed initiative. Determine the territory that will be the focus of the initiative, the needs of that territory, the specific initiative to be implemented, and the number of people needed to carry out the initiative. Recruit and train the necessary personnel, and find ways to address the material, social, and spiritual needs of the community.

3. *Execution*

Execution is the implementation of the evangelistic plan with all of its specific elements. These could include public evangelistic campaigns; training for effective soul-winning; organization of small groups evangelism; strategies to transform the church into a nurturing, family-friendly community; lay training for how to plan and execute a successful evangelistic campaign from start to finish; use of technological resources in evangelism; empowerment of members to improve the church's image through needs-based community ministries; and equipping of members to serve as Bible workers and to carry out evangelistic visitation.

4. *Evaluation*

It is important for the leadership process to include evaluation of the effectiveness of the assessment, analysis, planning, and execution of the various evangelistic initiatives. This includes determining if the desired outcomes of the evangelistic initiatives have been achieved. Evaluation also considers what was done correctly and what could be improved in the future. Finally, determine what should be addressed in the ongoing decision-making process and what follow-up initiatives should be implemented.

Review and Discussion

- *Identify five of the functions of the Evangelism Action Committee.*
- *Explain the relationship between the Evangelism Action Committee and the departmental evangelism task forces.*
- *Based on the process illustrated by the sigmoid curve, how would you evaluate the continuity of the evangelistic initiatives in your church?*
- *Suggest three ways to ensure continuity in evangelistic initiatives in your local church.*
- *Describe the five phases of the leadership development process as it applies to evangelism.*
- *What are some characteristics of your community that would be important for evangelistic planning?*
- *In which department do you wish to contribute to the outreach ministry of your local church? What makes you choose this department?*

4
Lifestyle Evangelism

Evangelism is a lifestyle preoccupation of every member of the Christian Church. It is the intentional effort of believers to internalize the gospel, experience personal transformation and through the empowerment of the Holy Spirit, exemplify Christ likeness as a way of life. The Apostle Paul describes the process of this transformed lifestyle accordingly; "Be not conformed to this world; but be ye transformed by the renewing of your mind, that ye may prove what is that good, and acceptable, and perfect will of God" Romans 12:2. The renewal of the mind produces reformation in the way people live, interact and serve. Resulting from this renewal, they influence others through deliberate means, to accept Jesus as their Savior and become disciples of Christ. The outcome, disciples beget disciples. Let's consider the need for and process of making disciples

Theological Reflections

The current world in which we live is considered the evil age that is comprised of the lust of the flesh, the lust of the eyes, and the pride of life (cf. Gal. 1:4; 2 Cor. 4:4; Eph. 2:2; 1 John 2:15–17). This is placed in contrast to the age to come that will be glorious, devoid of every strain of evil (cf. Isaiah 65:17-18; Matthew 19:28; 2 Peter 3:13; Revelation 7:917; 21:1-5). Followers of Christ face the challenge of contending with these two ages at the same time. Through the influence of present daily realities, much of which is masterminded by the evil one, combined with sinful human nature, they are coerced each moment to conform to the distractions of the present evil age. Such coercion masks the fullness of the actual revelations about the age to come and encourages apathy and spiritual indifference. The Apostle Paul in his counsel in Romans 12:2 exhorts them "not to continue to be like the changing, fallen world system (the old age of rebellion) of which they are still physically a part, but to be radically changed into the likeness of Christ. Such change will result in people whom Ellen White in the book Education describe as experiencing the joys of service in this life and living in expectation of the higher joys of wider service in the life to come.

In his counsel **"do not be conformed to this world"** (Romans 12:2a NKJV), Paul employs the present passive imperative form of the verb with the negative article to call on believers in Christ to stop the behaviors of conformity to the present evil age. In another place he said; "I can do all things through Christ who strengthens me" (Philippians 4:13). This is assurance that all can live the ideal life in this present age; which is the life of transformation. He said; "but be ye transformed by the renewing of your mind" (Romans 12:2b NKJV). This life of transformation is placed in opposition to the life of conformity to this world and is humanly possible only through Divine aid. Ellen White said; "Nothing but the grace of God can convict and convert the heart; from him alone can the slaves of custom obtain power to break the shackles that bind them. It is impossible for a man to present his body a living sacrifice, holy, acceptable to God, while continuing to indulge habits that are depriving him of physical, mental, and moral vigor" {CTBH p. 10}.

Paul emphasizes in Romans 12:1-15:13, the expression of faith, righteousness that amplifies the concept of the transformed life. He accentuates the notion that Christianity is a way of life and that the Christian life is an obedient response to the grace of God. This response is manifested in true meaningful worship (Romans 12:1–2), which consists of total self-surrender and vital participation in church life or the life of the Christian community. In this sense, Christians should recognize their dependence upon God and one another (Romans 12:3–5) and should use the gifts, which God gives them through the Holy Spirit for the good of others (Romans 12: 6–8) and practice real love in all personal relationships (Romans 12: 9–21).

By his appeal to **"Be transformed"** in verse 2, Paul extends a call for Christians to dedicate their whole life to God. As believers are transformed in their minds and conformed to the image of Christ through the power of the Holy Spirit (Titus 3:4-7), they will develop an abiding relationship with Him (Mark 3:13-15), be able to discern the righteousness of Christ (Malachi 3:17-18), participate actively in the mission of Christ (Matthew 28:18-20), communicate in wholesome ways within the faith community (Ephesians 4:29), and actively seek to nurture others in the faith (John 15:16). Only through spiritual renewal can believers do the will of God (1 Thessalonians 5:16-18). This transformed life is a catalyst that attracts others who are in conformity to this evil age or the world to Christ. In that regard, evangelism is a lifestyle rather than an activity, event or a program.

Evangelism and the Christian Life

Paul considered evangelism an integral part of human life experience. He itemized the gifts of the Holy Spirit, evangelist being one, Ephesians 4:11 and concluded that was not the area of Timothy's giftedness. However, he still challenged him to "Do the work of an evangelist, fulfill your ministry" 2 Timothy 4:5. There is something significant about evangelism. It is the central work of the Christian's life. Whether or not believers in Christ have such a gift they are expected to do the work of an evangelist in order not to lose their passion to see lost souls rescued.

The origin of Evangelism is rooted in three Greek words (Sam Chan, 2018):

euangelion	gospel	to describe what is said (Mark 1:14–15)
euangelistes	evangelist	to describe the person who is telling the gospel (Acts 21:8; Eph. 4:11)
euangelizo	to proclaim the gospel	to describe the activity of telling the gospel (Rom. 10:15).

The word gospel is derived from the Anglo-Saxon term god-spell, meaning "good story," a rendering of the Latin evangelium and the Greek euangelion, meaning "good news" or "good telling." The gospel means "good news". When someone is in possession of good news, the natural inclination is to tell it to everyone. The transformed life automatically tells the good news or evangelizes. Chan says' "Evangelism is our human effort of proclaiming this message—which necessarily involves using our human; communication, language, idioms, metaphors, stories, experiences, personality, emotions, context, culture, locations" (page 14). Every Christian proclaims the good news or the gospel as a way of life.

Five Principal Goals or Components of Lifestyle Evangelism

1. Spiritual Connectedness
2. Soul Winning
3. Equipping for Service
4. Conserve and Disciple
5. Building Relationships

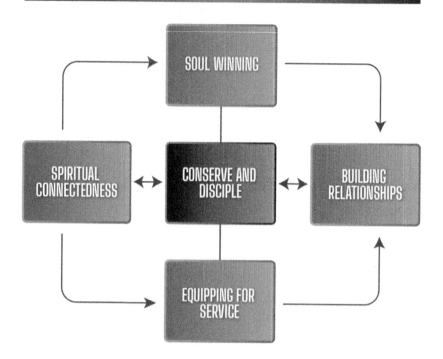

The five components or goals of lifestyle evangelism are interdependent and are simultaneously practiced individually or executed by the members of the Church. Spiritual renewal that is manifested through lifestyle evangelism is a progressive growth experience. Paul said; "But grow in grace, and in the knowledge of our Lord and Savior Jesus Christ. To him be glory both now and forever. Amen" 2 Peter 3:18. For believers to grow in Christ, they need to submerge themselves in spiritual knowledge, which requires establishing daily routines. Additionally, they should acquire cognitive, attitudinal and other skills and values to inform their actions. Hence, this necessitates some form of training. Personal spiritual growth inspires consciousness to the need for others to accept Christ and obligates the believer to be personally involved in acquiring the requisite human relations and other functional skills to connect with others socially and eventually to help them to develop commitments to Christ and to maintain such commitment.

Spiritual Connectedness

This component of lifestyle evangelism involves the believers' ongoing relationship with the Divine. It is connecting on the vertical which requires intentional and continual efforts on the part of the believer. This intimate relationship is developed and fortified by study of the Bible and reading of the Spirit of Prophecy and other inspirational writings and sustained prayer initiatives. The knowledge acquired through study, reading, association with other believers, faithful participation in personal, family and corporate worship experiences (Hebrew 10:25) must intentionally be a part of the believers' life. Such encounters lead to shadowing the righteousness of Christ which is the epitome of the life of the Christian.

A special study of the Righteousness of Christ should be the quest of every believer in order to become like Him. "See how great a love the Father has bestowed on us, that we would be called children of God; and such we are. For this reason, the world does not know us, because it did not know Him. Beloved, now we are children of God, and it has not appeared as yet what we will be. We know that when He appears, we will be like Him, because we will see Him just as He is. And everyone who has this hope fixed on Him purifies himself, just as He is pure" (1 John 3:1-3).

Churches or communities of faith should be intentional about providing special studies of the Righteousness of Christ to update and refresh the knowledge base of their members on an annual basis. To ensure that it gets done as part of the churches' annual spiritual education program, an elder may be assigned the responsibility to coordinate this important initiative meant for the spiritual growth of all members. Someone may also coordinate prayer initiative to ensure it is specially prepared and attended to as an essential aspect of the life of the Church and each believer. How interesting it could be to have daily or weekly prayer sessions in each home, or selected location in each neighborhood to invite and attract the participation of both members and non-members of the Church to participate in these small group spiritual growth encounters.

Through the spiritual connectedness initiatives, all participants are assisted to focus on their personal need for spiritual transformation, faithfulness and participation in the Mission of Christ, whereby the Holy Spirit can truly accomplish the work in them and use them in service to others. "When He came into the house, His disciples began questioning Him privately, "Why could we not drive it out?" And He said to them, "This kind cannot come out by anything but prayer" (Mark 8: 28-29).

In addition to focusing on the righteousness of Christ and focus on prayer initiatives, studying the fundamental bible doctrines as mentioned in Chapter 21 of this book will also serve to build the spiritual connectedness of believers. The Apostle Paul said; "Study to shew thyself approved unto God, a workman that needeth not to be ashamed, rightly dividing the word of truth" (2 Timothy 2:15). Equipping believers for growth in their spiritual relationship with the Lord includes assisting them to manage all the resources that the Lord has made available to them. "Do not fear what you are about to suffer. Behold, the devil is about to cast some of you into prison, so that you will be tested, and you will have tribulation for ten days. Be faithful until death, and I will give you the crown of life. 'He who has an ear, let him hear what the Spirit says to the churches. He who overcomes will not be hurt by the second death" (Revelation 2:10-11).

Equipping for Service

This includes all the didactic approaches for building relational skills and to address specific opportunities for effective connecting, reaping and consolidation of members. Through this important lifestyle evangelistic component, all believers should explore their strengths and growth areas in order to utilize their strengths in a meaningful way to increase their faithfulness to the Lord and to participate in His cause. As they consider the various mission opportunities in the church, and identify areas of interest to participate, they should seek training to develop competencies, skills, concepts and principles in order to effectively participate in the mission. "About this we have much to say, and it is hard to explain, since you have become dull of hearing. For though by this time you ought to be teachers, you need someone to teach you again the basic principles of the oracles of God. You need milk, not solid food, for everyone who lives on milk is unskilled in the word of righteousness, since he is a child. But solid food is for the mature, for those who have their powers of discernment trained by constant practice to distinguish good from evil" (Hebrew 5:11-14 ESV).

It is ideal for a survey to be done of the local congregation and any community to be evangelized by the congregation. Survey of the church members will determine what the needs of the congregation are, what the members are able to execute and what deficiencies need to be tackled. Dependent upon the size of the church, the survey may be conducted formally or informally. The community survey will determine the social needs to be addressed and how best to initiate and develop programs to address the spiritual needs of residents. "For which one of you, when he wants to build a tower, does not first sit down and calculate the cost to see if he has enough to complete it?" Otherwise, when he has laid a foundation and is not able to finish, all who observe it begin to ridicule him," (Luke 14:28-29).

Every ministry within the church should identify projects to be undertaken to fulfill aspects of the Mission both within and outside the local congregation and especially in connecting with those outside the faith. They should promote such projects and solicit participation of members. Members who are recruited to participate in such projects should be trained. When individuals are trained, they should be assigned to specific responsibilities based on their training so that they are able to utilize their skills in the work of the Lord. Pastors and directors of ministries should create training modules and ensure that qualified trainers are available to impart knowledge, skills and values to members in order for them to effectively participate in the mission.

Each training module should be contextualized to the mission activity to be addressed. Members should also be trained how to conduct Bible studies with others and how to initiate and develop evangelistic interests. Ministry leaders within the organization or local church should be involved in helping with identifying mission projects and in preparing training materials relevant to such projects. They should make themselves available to assist the pastors and other identified trainers to fulfill the task of equipping members for service. Every level of the organization and the local congregation should have established dates each year for the training of pastors, other employees and members to execute the established mission projects. The essence of equipping is to provide the requisite support to members to live and participate in Evangelism as a lifestyle.

Building Relationships

Building relationships is the deliberate, contextualized approaches to establishing mutual and amicable relations with others. The approach is to initiate contact with others on a social level that leads to friendly relations, working together to achieve specific goals and the eventual study of the Word of God. Principally, this is about preparing self and others to constructively address life's issues, share light moments, engage in support initiatives and assist in dealing with lifestyle and other social issues. Solomon said; "The fruit of the righteous is a tree of life, And he who wins souls is wise" Proverbs 11:30. When social relationships are established between believers and non-believers, the path is created for dialogue that leads to amicable discussions on a range of subjects. John MacArthur said; "while spontaneous evangelistic conversations should be a part of every believer's life, the majority of gospel presentations take place within the framework of existing relationships" *Evangelism*, p.166.

This Relationship building component is about a) helping others deal with their social, physical and emotional issues, b) encouraging others to take interest in spiritual matters and assume intimate relationship with the Lord. "Now after this, the Lord appointed seventy others, and sent them in pairs ahead of Him to every city and place where He Himself was going to come. And He was saying to them, "The harvest is plentiful, but the laborers are few; therefore, beseech the Lord of the harvest to send out laborers into His harvest..." Luke 10:1-2).

Every field and local congregation should determine the best possible method to attract the attention of individuals outside the faith and determine how to build friendly relationships with them. For effectiveness, the members should be trained for this initiative. Each one should intentionally have at least two persons with whom they are in social interactions and relation building. At least one should be a member of the church, the other should be a non-member. The member shall be the one with whom to share at the faith level and serve as a witnessing associate. The non-member shall be the prospect to be evangelized. Every effort should be made under the direction of the Holy Spirit to rescue the non-member into the body of Christ and membership of the Church. As soon as the non-member becomes a member, another non-member should replace that person, while keeping the relationship with the new member in order to assist in conserving and discipling the individual for the kingdom.

Transition from just social interactions and building of relationship should be intentional. Every member should be in the business of sharing or talking about their spiritual relationship by telling their stories and then inviting the prospect to an experience with the Lord. When individuals get to the point of accepting you as a person, they will most likely be willing to enter into spiritual conversation. Through such conversation the door is opened to present or share the gospel because they are willing to listen. This leads them to express on-going interest in the things of God that ultimately lead them to the knowledge and acceptance that the gospel requires a change on their part. Doing Bible studies with those with whom relationships are established will be an intentional aspect of this relationship building stage. Such studies will definitely build their knowledge of faith and encourage them to assume closer relationships with the Lord with a view to developing personal spiritual commitment with Him. .

It is important for Church pastors and leaders to have organization in place to assist the members through this process of building relationships with others. There should be appropriate and sufficient materials and resources provided as well as mentoring and coaching in order to ensure success in the process. Before every evangelistic campaign for soul winning is held, proper and well prepared and executed relationship building initiatives should be intentionally executed. Every member of the church should be invited and trained to participate in relationship building initiatives on an annual basis. Through well executed relationship building initiatives, before any soul winning campaigns are held, persons will already be prepared to make decisions for the Lord.

Soul Winning

This includes all the evangelistic activities, both personal, and public that motivate individuals to find security in Christ and make decisions to accept Him as their Savior and become members of the Church and citizens of the Kingdom of God. Pastors and lay preachers have major responsibilities in organizing themselves and members of the Church for effective personal and public evangelism which are intended to reap souls for the Kingdom. Public evangelism is the most effective method of speaking to and persuading both small and large groups of individuals to Christ in a single experience. Preachers need to spend time to qualify themselves to conquer their fears and engage in this divine activity. The Old Testament makes it evident that God used His mouthpieces in public proclamation to declare His messages. Jesus proclaimed the message publicly and did so in collaboration with His followers.

The Apostles also were involved in public evangelism and the mandate is given to all believers likewise. Preachers must determine that by the grace of God they will claim the Power of the Holy Spirit, prepare themselves and their teams, and go forward to proclaim the gospel through public evangelism. Effective evangelistic invitations that produce good results depend on persistent prayer, personal and field preparations, clear content, clear language, and clear directions. Preachers must be decisive, bold and fearless to extend the invitation to others.

Each congregation should determine a time each year to conduct intensive soul winning or proclaim and reap impacts. The place where these special impacts will be held should be determined at least one year in advance and intensive relationship building initiatives conducted by the members to adequately prepare people for decision making during the Proclaim and Reap phase. These may also be held as evangelistic apprenticeship training initiatives conducted to achieve greater effectiveness in soul winning.

The Proclaim and Reap training should cover relevant topics that will enable pastors/evangelists to connect with their congregants through preaching, connect the people to Christ, present testing truths, address the social and spiritual needs of congregants, present hope and reap decisions for baptisms. Ideally, these Proclaim and Reap campaigns should be for duration of two or more weeks. This provides the opportunity for the presentation of a series of fundamental subjects to be covered from the Word of God. However, each local context must determine the decision making process.

The Annual Proclaim and Reap or Soul Winning Campaigns are held for both members of the Church and non-members. The intent is to baptize a significant number of persons who are ready and at the same time, depending on the context, may provide apprenticeship training for:

i. District/Church pastors of the zone, region or local field
ii. Ministerial Students in training
iii. Prayer Coordinators
iv. Lay Evangelists
v. Lay Bible Workers
vi. Conference employed Bible Workers
vii. vii. Lay Witnesses
viii. Technology in Evangelism Providers

Reaping a large number of persons in one campaign or within a specified period of time is something to be celebrated. Ellen White said; "Let us now take up the work appointed us and proclaim the message that is to arouse men and women to a sense of their danger. If every Seventh-day Adventist had done the work laid upon him, the number of believers would now be much larger than it is" (*Testimonies for the Church,* vol. 9, chap. 2, p. 25). Effective soul winning is the combined efforts of everyone who is a members of the community of faith.

It is certainly a call to total member involvement. "All who receive the life of Christ are ordained to work for the Salvation of their fellow men. For this work the church was established, and all who take upon themselves its sacred vows are thereby pledged to be co-workers with Christ" (The Desires of Ages, chap. 86, p. 822). Jesus made it very clear, that human efforts in soul winning must not be devoid of the divine agency; "Behold, I send the Promise of My Father upon you; but tarry in the city of Jerusalem until you are endued with power from on high" Luke 24:49.

The Annual Proclaim and Reap Campaign may be carried live through technological means from a principal site. Technology has removed boundaries and social media and other digital platforms create the possibility for a wide cross section of persons to be reached with the gospel through the same series. It may even be rebroadcast on numerous basis. Collaboration among pastoral districts and other organizational entities make success a greater possibility.

Conserve and Disciple

This includes the social and spiritual activities deliberately administered to disciple new members into the advent faith providing them affirmation, love, assurance and support. Also, by equipping them to effectively share their faith with others thus influencing them to accept Christ as their Savior. In John 15:7 and 8, Jesus said, "If you remain in me and my words remain in you, ask whatever you wish, and it will be done for you. This is to my Father's glory, that you bear much fruit, showing yourselves to be my disciples" (NIV). John 15:16-17; "You did not choose Me but I chose you, and appointed you that you would go and bear fruit, and that your fruit would remain, so that whatever you ask of the Father in My name He may give to you. This I command you, that you love one another" (NIV).

Every soul winning or proclaim and reap initiative shall be associated with a special method to conserve and disciple all the newly baptized members as part of the planning process. The special laid out Conserve and Disciple program should have individuals specifically assigned to execute it. The needs of individuals are not all identical so it is important to contextualize the Conserve and Disciple initiative to Unions, local fields and communities. However, it is important to have initiatives planned to provide assurance, affirmation, love and support to each of the new believers. Three entire chapters in this book have dealt with aspects of this important subject of conserve and disciple.

Attrition in churches is not confined to new members. There are persons in the Church for many years, even decades that apostatize for various reasons. In order to address this issue, Conserve and Disciple programs should be arranged to address the needs of all members. The various ministries of the Church that are expected to plan and initiate conserve and disciple programs are:

i. Children's Ministries to conserve and disciple children
ii. Youth Ministries to conserve and disciple young people
iii. Sabbath School to conserve and disciple all members through study initiatives
iv. Women's Ministries to conserve and disciple women
v. Men's Ministries to conserve and disciple men
v. Family Ministries to conserve and disciple couples
vi. Ministerial Association to conserve and disciple pastors and their family

Lifestyle Evangelism and the Ministries of the Church

Each ministry is expected to embrace the lifestyle evangelism initiative of the church and participate actively in order to fulfill the general mission of the organization. Each director or ministry leader should determine which one or a combination of the five components would formulate the foundational initiatives of their ministry. They should establish achievable goals in such areas, and mobilize the participation of the laity towards the realization of such.

Each major program or congress of each department or Ministry of the Church should have a dimension in which non-members of the church are invited to participate in aspects of the lifestyle evangelism program especially the relationship building that impacts individuals on a social level. For example, all congresses should have the participation of non-members doing community impact initiatives along with the members, and participating in other aspects of the program according to organized plans. Through observations and participation, it is expected that these non-members will develop interest in the Church, the beliefs of the church and membership in the Church

Example of a Mission focus program

Where it is anticipated that 2,000 Adventist young people participate in a pathfinder camporee, provision shall be made for an additional number of non-Adventist participants. This program should be well marketed to youth groups within the community to have them participate as observers. They will participate in the relationship building or contact and share community initiatives that will be associated with that camporee to fulfill social needs within that community where the program will be held. The camporee directorate will determine in what other areas of the program they may be programmed to participate. All members should be aware that this is a mission initiative where non-members of the church are present with the expectation that they will all deport themselves as true witnesses of Christ by embracing inclusiveness.

Similar organization shall be in place to accommodate non-Adventists in congresses planned by the Women, Children, Health, Family, Communication, Men's, Youth, Education, Publishing, Personal Ministries, Stewardship, Religious Liberty and Sabbath School Ministries.

Some Evangelism Methods

There are numerous methods that may be utilized to achieve the objectives of evangelism. With choice, members are able to determine the best approaches that are compatible with their interest and passion and which provide them the kind of inspiration to engage in influencing others to Christ. The listing below highlights some of the methods with brief explanation of how they may be executed. None of these may be complete in themselves and a combination of two or more may ensure effectiveness.

1. Natural Lifestyle Evangelism
   a. Live right, a life compatible with the Gospel of Christ as enunciated in Scripture and people will see, admire and choose to model the gospel as you live in a practical way.
   b. Admiration of the life you exemplify will influence others to ask you about God.
2. Servant Evangelism
   a. It emphasizes showing love through helpfulness, as a way to open doors to evangelism.
   b. By helping others deal effectively with their issues and situations, opportunities are created to share the gospel with them.
3. Events Evangelism
   a. It capitalizes on the momentum of public interests that are existent
   b. It capitalizes on the gathering of crowds, large or small and utilizes it to share relevant messages of the Gospel.
4. Neighborhood Evangelism
   a. It generates personal home and individual contact with others especially new ones.
   b. It embraces the opportunity to meet people in homes or common, public or private areas to share the gospel.
5. Street Preaching Evangelism
   a. It is an approach in which the gospel message is shared with people as they pass by along the street.
   b. It does not necessarily need invitation as there is a ready audience – those who are passing along on their personal errands.
   c. It can lead to opportunities for one-to-one evangelism.
6. Tract Evangelism
   a. It is a simple and versatile method of personal evangelism. Just share a tract with someone who comes into your space.

b. It is ideal for situations where conversation is not feasible.

c. By having a variety of tracts, it is possible to share varying gospel topics.

7. Conversational evangelism
    a. It involves sharing the gospel in normal, everyday conversations with those to whom you converse on a normal basis.
    b. This can occur over the phone, in a store checkout line, at the office if permissible, at a sporting event, on a travel (airplane) or other human encounter.

8. Relational or friendship evangelism
    a. It is personal evangelism – talking to others about Christ.
    b. A variety of tools can be used, tracts, the Bible, etc.
    c. Can be done by anyone

9. Public Evangelism
    a. A large group of individuals are able to hear the message at the same time and given an opportunity to respond.
    b. Multiple persons are able to collaborate in sharing the gospel.

10. Small Groups Evangelism
    a. Members who do not have the skills to do the personal witnessing get the task done within the group setting.
    b. Relationship is built with the prospect making it easier for the person to want to accept the gospel.

11. Children's Home Evangelism
    a. An organized team or group of persons strategically visit children homes on a weekly or bi-weekly basis.
    b. The visiting teams or groups take donations and assist with nutrition, hygiene and other physiological, social and spiritual needs of residents in the facility.

12. Confinement Evangelism
    a. An organized team or group of persons strategically visit confinement centers on a weekly or bi-weekly basis.
    b. The visiting teams or groups take donations and assist with nutrition, hygiene and other physiological, social and spiritual needs of the residents in the facility.
    c. Confinement evangelism deals with persons in prison, shut-in elderlies, homes of the age, adult care centers, and persons in reformed institutions, rehabilitation facilities, etc.

13. Digital Evangelism
    a. Organized group of members who use social media to share the gospel with the unchurched and people of other faiths
    b. All group members should have at least one social media account WhatsApp, Facebook, Instagram, YouTube, etc.

14. Health Evangelism
    a. Organized group of members with healthy lifestyle interest and passion enlisted to connect with persons within the community to share their faith.
    b. Conduct health expos which will include some of the following activities and more: Video clips on healthy lifestyle practices, health literature, preparing healthy foods, lectures on lifestyle issues, health screening – vitals, Harvard test – exercises, healthy juices, data collection, etc.
    c. They will utilize health evangelism materials including health evangelism bible lessons to achieve desired outcomes.

15. Family Life Evangelism
    a. Organized group of members with the passion to influence and enhance healthy family lifestyle.
    b. They will utilize family life evangelism materials including family life bible lessons to achieve desired outcomes.

16. Reconciliation Evangelism
    a. A team or group of individuals organized and equipped to contact ex-members and influence their reconnection to the faith.
    b. It utilizes specialized approaches to identify the former members and have them re-engaged with the church through, contacting, listening, empathizing, acknowledging, assuring, praying,

Empower Active Members

All active members of the church should be identified and be part of a special program in which they receive discipleship training to participate in the lifestyle evangelism training of the church based on their passion, interest, spiritual gifts, talents or competencies. Each ministry involved in Conserve and Disciple under the guidance of the Pastor and other designees of the church should coordinate efforts for effectiveness. Every active member should be encouraged to determine the category of mission in which he or she will be involved and where necessary, they should be trained to participate. The following are some areas of classification in which active members of the church may be involved in Mission Initiatives:

- Prayer Coordinator
- Evangelistic Preaching
- Bible Knowledge Educator
- Small Groups Leader
- Social Relationship Builders
- Social Projects Financial Contributor
- Evangelistic Projects Financial Contributor
- Materials and Resources Developers
- Technology Services Provider
- Contextualized Ministries participants
- Evangelistic Witnessing Team Leader
- Clinching Decisions for Baptisms
- Inactive Members Re-engage coordinator
- Special Needs Care Givers

Re-engage Inactive Members

All inactive members of the church should be identified. After ascertaining the cause of their inactivity by intentionally engaging with them in dialogue, efforts should be made to address their needs and/or concerns. Where necessary, these individuals should be referred to persons within the Church or relevant professionals, who are able to address their issues. The church leadership should designate persons who are gifted with the skills, tact and art of persuasion and who are confidential, to address their area of need or concern. In the process of engaging these inactive members, they should be encouraged to participate in the lifestyle evangelism initiatives of the church, especially the spiritual connectedness. The goal of this re-engage initiative is to restore them to the column of the active members.

Appreciation and Recognition

"And behold, I am coming quickly, and my reward is with me, to give to every one according to his work. [13] I am the Alpha and the Omega, *the* [a] Beginning and *the* End, the First and the Last. Blessed *are* those who [b]do His commandments, that they may have the right to the tree of life, and may enter through the gates into the city" Revelation 22:12-14. Ultimate reward is given by the Lord. However, it is a natural part of human behavior and motivational expectation to give and receive rewards. Pastors and other ministry leaders should devise special appreciation and recognition program for members who have fulfilled their commitments in the lifestyle evangelism program of the Church. This may be an annual banquet, a formal dinner or some other representable activity. At that occasion, representatives from other levels of the organization should be in attendance to express the sentiments of appreciation to the members on behalf of the wider or other levels of the organization. Award pins and certificates may also be presented to member for their meaningful involvement in the mission.

Evaluating Progress

To periodically assess and adapt the initiatives to ensure they are as effective as they can be is important. Evaluation is a process that critically examines a program. According to Patton (1987) It involves collecting and analyzing information about a program's activities, characteristics, and outcomes. Its purpose is to make judgments about the program, to improve its effectiveness, and/or to inform programming decisions. Evaluation actually helps to identify areas for improvement and ultimately to realize goals more efficiently. It enables leaders to demonstrate success or progress of programs or initiatives and to be able to communicate the impact to others, which is critical for public relations, participants' morale, and attracting and retaining support from current and potential participants. Below are some forms that may be utilized to collect data and facilitate effective evaluation of the lifestyle evangelism program.

Identifying active and in active members for empowerment and re-engagement

No	Mission Classifcation	No. of Active Members	No. of Inactive Members	Comments
1	Number of members			
2	Prayer Coordinators			
3	Evangelistic Preachers			
4	Bible Knowledge Educators			
5	Building Social Relationships			
6	Social Projects Financial Contributors			
7	Evangelistic Projects Financial Contributor			
8	Materials and Resources Developers			
9	Technology Services Providers			
10	Contextualized Ministries participants			
11	Evangelistic Witnessing Team Leader			
12	Providing Support Services in Evangelistic Witnessing			
13	Clinching Decisions for Baptisms			
14	Develop and Produce Required Materials and Resources			
15	Inactive Members Re-engage coordinator			
16	Special Needs Care Givers			

Assignment of members for Relationship Building and Soul Winning

No	Name of Members	Area of Participation	Special Project
1			
2			
3			
4			
5			
6			
7			
8			
9			
10			
11			
12			
13			
14			
15			
16			

Ministry Projects Execution Form

No	Name of Ministry	Name of Project	Duration (Date)	No. of Participants
1				
2				
3				
4				
5				
6				
7				
8				
9				
10				

Review and Discussion

- *Define lifestyle evangelism and explain how it is achieved.*
- *How is Paul's counsel in Romans 12:2; "Do not be conformed to this world" and "be transformed by the renewing of your mind" relevant to evangelism?*
- *Explain and differentiate the Greek words that formulate the root for "Evangelism".*
- *Identify and explain the five principal goals or components of lifestyle evangelism.*
- *Develop an evangelistic program for your church or region including the five principal components of lifestyle evangelism.*
- *How would you evaluate effectiveness in your lifestyle evangelism program?*
- *Differentiate between active and in-active members of your church and develop a vision for evangelizing the community that involves both groups of members.*

PART II
STRATEGIES
FOR SUCCESSFUL EVANGELISM

5
Digital Evangelism

What is Digital Evangelism

Digital evangelism is the strategic integration of various digital tools, online technologies and channels into the mission of sharing the gospel of Jesus with others, and soliciting their commitment to become disciples of Christ and members of a faith community.

In Luke 8:1-11 we discover that a sower does not limit himself to a particular type of soil; he farms on the rocky, thorny, fertile and less fertile. In these closing hours of earth's history, gospel sowers are expected to be present on every soil type utilizing the best or most relevant farming methods. Christ's message must be proclaimed to all or as many people as possible. Digital evangelism is a potent approach. Technology provides the opportunity for connecting with a global audience.

Ellen White said; "New methods must be introduced. God's people must awake to the necessities of the time in which they are living. Some of the methods used in this work will be different from the methods used in the past; but let no one, because of this, block the way by criticism" (*Testimonies For the Church* Vol. 6, p. 96-97).

Through digital evangelism gospel proclaimers are able to accomplish multiple evangelistic objectives. Five of these principal objectives are:

1. To reach people beyond geographical and cultural borders and develop relationship with them.

2. To equip all those who are reached with relevant and potent knowledge, resources, services, acts of kindness, compassionate care, support and assistance.
3. To rescue and assimilate into the community of believers, all those who have developed conviction to live in a saving relationship with Christ.
4. To retain those who are rescued into the community of faith , through doctrinal instructions and sharing of norms that assist them to develop the culture and lifestyle of the community of faith.
5. To disciple the believers to become committed and active members, who participate in the mission of Christ and serve fellow human beings.

To achieve these five goals (objectives) of digital evangelism, there needs to be a combined or collaborative effort on the part of members who proclaim the Good News of Christ through digital channels.

The effective utility of practical technological means to reach, equip, rescue, retain and disciple people in the faith of Jesus, will greatly help the church to become a larger and more dynamic community of faithful Christian believers.

Executing Digital Evangelism in Phases

Phase 1

The Phase of intentional Planning and Strategizing

This is the phase in which the digital witnesses develop the vision. During the intentional planning and strategizing phase, the requirements listed below are carefully dealt with.

- Establish a collaborative or digital evangelism committee
- Put a prayer coordination process in place
- Appoint technicians
- Identify online resources and broadcast platforms to be utilized
- Appoint bible knowledge mentors
- Choose marketing specialists
- Determine the target audience
- Select the delivery platforms
- Identify and acquire the required technological resources
- Determine the leadership team and training needs and schedule
- Choose the social media and other online platforms that members will use to connect with target audience (and what strategy and training is needed) for online preparation
- Define the online resources that are prospect focused (such as Bible Studies, etc.)
- Establish the execution date and strategy
- Develop the prospect response mechanism and distribution and follow up procedure
- Define contingency plans if a system failure or glitch is encountered
- Set in motion the internal communications and Total Member Involvement onboarding strategy.
- Craft a digital promotion plan to reach prospects
- Determine budget for the campaign

Phase 2

The phase of Mobilizing and Total Membership Involvement

In this phase, every member of the Church with a social media account is invited to connect with one or more persons who are not of their faith that they would like to see saved in the Kingdom of God. They should invite them to connect to a designated bible study platform and do the recommended bible lesson series. Upon completion of each of the lessons, the member may engage in a review or just to have a conversation with the student about the lessons. It could be from just, how was the lesson? To engage in a discussion.

At the end of the series of online bible lessons study, the member should try to secure a decision from the student concerning a total commitment to Christ. The member may refer the student to a bible knowledge mentor in the church or invite the student to a digital or online evangelistic program that is planned or in progress. The member should share all the possible credentials for the student to connect and become engaged in such online campaign. A part of the special highlight at the end of the bible study should be a graduation ceremony where certificates will be distributed to students.

To make the graduation meaningful, it is important that each local church makes it a major evangelist initiative by inviting many persons within their localities to take the bible course. Persons who are not able to navigate the technology to complete the lessons, can have a member of the Church sign up for them and do the study with them directly, by calling and studying with them by phone or by face-to-face means where possible.

Members can download the lessons or they may utilize lessons made available to them through their local church. Completing a bible lesson series before an online evangelistic campaign is one of the most potent ways of preparing individuals to make decision for Christ during the actual public digital campaign. It is a major pre-digital evangelism preparation initiative to have people ready to make decision for the Lord and be baptized as members of the body of Christ.

Online Platforms For Digital Evangelism

Social Media and other online evangelism channels continue to explode with the regular and periodic development and accessibility of additional platforms. The ability to connect, communicate and receive messages are made easier and easier. Some of the platforms and digital means that are available for use are:

i. WhatsApp	ii. YouTube
iii. Twitter	iv. Instagram
v. Television	vi. Radio
vii. Facebook	viii. Tik-ToK
ix. Snapchat	x. Cable
xi. Messenger	xii. WeChat
Xiii. Tumblr	xiv. Viber
xv. Pinterest	xv. LinkedIn

Phase 3

Conducting the Online Campaign

The Collaborative Evangelism team shall coordinate, give leadership to and promote the program to achieve the goal of this online evangelism program. The team shall organize graduation ceremonies, details for the online evangelistic program, promotion and execution of the actual proclamation aspect of the campaign.

At this point, the team must ensure that the essentials for executing the program listed below that should have been determined during the phase of intentional Planning and Strategizing are actually arranged. Combined with the others, all must now be placed in motion.

1. Essentials for Execution of the program
   i. The date and duration of the Campaign
   ii. The online or digital evangelist
   iii. The technical assistants and assistance needed
   iv. The media through which the program will be broadcasted

v. Distribution of the names and contact information of all the persons who registered beforehand by taking the bible lessons, to selected persons or bible knowledge mentors for follow-up with them.
vi. The personnel who will contact and follow-up with each of the prospects daily, during the campaign, in order to take decisions.
vii. Develop the program and assign personnel for the nightly or daily meetings during the campaign.
viii. Invite all the members of the churches to pray for this evangelistic initiative.

2. Suggestions for Promoting the program:
 i. Advertisement campaign in the churches.
 ii. 30 second promotion on social media
 iii. Short dynamic dialogue between two or more members/yout
 iv. Use of the church's official media, TV, radio, website
 v. Involve persons on social media in the church to promote.
 vi. Teasers – 30 seconds promotions announcing that something is going to happen (build expectations).

3. How each local Church will participate
 i. Establish Bible studies goal
 ii. Execute the Bible study plan
 iii. Promote the online campaign
 iv. Secure commitment of each member to invite someone to watch or listen the presentations during the actual campaign meetings
 v. Develop an online evangelism response database with a response card or code.
 vi. Make the response card or code available to all church members
 vii. When the preacher makes the call and gives instructions for completing the response card, all members send the card or the code to their invited listeners.

Thom Rainer unearthed through research, that pastors and their preaching were the most influential elements in people's choice of accepting Christ and a church. In calling disciples Mark wrote of Jesus, "He appointed twelve, so that they would be with Him and that He could send them out to preach (Mark 3: 14 NAS). The twelve were with Him, they observed what He did and then, He sent them out to do what He had done. His preaching served as the primary example for His followers then and is similarly relevant for preachers today, irrespective of the method or channel that they use to convey the message.

Preaching that reach unbelievers effectively in an online campaign and lead them to acceptance of Christ and association with a local congregation must satisfy the following: 1) biblically based Christ-centered content, 2) preacher that is genuine or authentic, 3) emboldened and inspired by the Holy Spirit, 4) message that is relevant to unchurched or uncommitted listeners, 5) illustrations that capture attention and engaging, 6) energetic and dynamic delivery of the message, and 7) appeal that is persuasive.

Jesus, Peter, and Paul connected with the people they sought to reach by going to them. Their sermons were not like the public oration of their day. They were relevant to the lives of their listeners. They treated the people with respect as they proclaimed the word and spoke in ways that the listeners clearly understood. They dealt with issues that were of interest to their hearers and touched their lives in a direct manner. Online preachers must be similarly relevant.

Online preaching requires that the preacher deliberately connects with the mind and heart of listeners to help them understand the message and the spiritual truth that it brings. That is an appeal to the cognitive and affective dimensions of the human psyche. This connection begins with demonstration of identification with the listeners, respect for them and appreciation of their acceptance to connect. Paul summarized his approach toward people, "Though I am free from all [men], I have made myself a slave to all, so that I may win more" (I Cor. 9: 19 NAS). Jesus demonstrated respect to people that possibly no one else in his culture at the time would have done. Consider the following: the woman caught in adultery, a Samaritan woman spurned by people of the community in which she lived who was forced to draw water in the heat of the day (John 8:1-11), tax collectors (Mark 2:13-17), lepers (Luke 17:11-19), prostitutes (Luke 7:41-44), and officers of the Roman army (Matt. 8: 5-14).

How to Increase Audience Engagement in Your Digital Campaign Meetings Audience Engagement in digital evangelism campaign meetings is the growth of attention, interest, knowledge and participation or connection of individuals in the actual campaign events. When the people comprising the audience are engaged, they automatically share their experience and knowledge with others and motivate those within their sphere of influence to access the program likewise.

Audience engagement could be negative, positive or average. If it is negative, people may not connect regularly and they may speak unenthusiastically about the program that will not be inviting to those who have not yet accessed it. It might even discourage some of those who have. In the case of the average, the listeners will not be eager to return and may not seek or invite others to access the program. Positive engagement is what all online gospel proclaimers' desire. The positively engaged talk about the program with passion, enthusiastically share their experience to whomsoever they meet, cannot wait for the next occasion and invite others to connect.

To increase the audience engagement in your digital campaign meetings the following should be considered:

1. Get as many guests as possible to register
2. Assemble a digital campaign kit and send it to invitees or participants
3. Find a way to foster personal connections
4. Provide solutions to everyday challenges
5. Present keys to future satisfaction to people
6. Pose key questions and ask the people to respond
7. Create a reaction sheet for them to respond to
8. Feature real-time illustrations during the meetings
9. Ask listeners to submit questions in comments or through a chat tool
10. Respond to questions
11. Offer special recognitions and appreciations

12. Share personal experiences
13. Highlight important characteristics about the audience or current issues
14. Show visual images that are compelling.
15. Elaborate on what is at stake for the listeners.
16. Provide humorous observations or anecdotes
17. Explain to listeners how the subject being presented relate to them
18. Solicit the involvement of the audience by making the topic immediate, personal, and local to them

Phase 4

The Phase of Retention

A program of between six and twelve weeks of online conservation should be held to instruct and guide the newly baptized believers in their new found relationship with Christ and the community of believers. The chapters on; How to Effectively Nurture New Believers and For the New Believer, provide in-depth information on how to nurture and consolidate them in the faith.

Summarized 18 Steps in Digital Evangelism
1. Establish the development and execution team
2. Develop the vision
3. Communicate with the church members and get them involved
4. Determine a date for the preparation and launch a massive bible study campaign
5. Develop a broad database of people studying bible lessons
6. Determine a date for the actual rescue campaign
7. Promote for and invite people to connect and receive the message
8. Determine and or develop a customized digital platform or portal to share and access specific information
9. Get members to share the live campaigns – do watch parties
10. Conduct the actual campaign

11. Have an online consultation space or chat room or call center for after the meeting reflections
12. Assign prospects to teams and small groups through some electronic or social media platforms
13. Follow-up daily with the prospects
14. Arrange for and baptize those who are prepared and ready
15. Provide retention program for the baptized
16. Have a follow-up program for the non-baptized
17. Engage the members of the Sabbath school units or small groups

Suggested items for the digital campaign kit
1. Bible lesson series
2. Campaign note pad
3. Campaign logo 4. Campaign pins
5. Campaign caps, shirts, patch, stickers, etc.
6. Campaign posters and brochures
7. Campaign promotional videos

Online Witnesses

Engaging members of the Church as online witnesses is an important aspect of digital witnessing. Churches may develop a Web of Online Witnesses (WOW). This is a group of church members who commit themselves to maintain strong online presence and through their knowledge and use of all possible forms of digital and technological tools, influence others to a) practice healthy lifestyle habits, b) accept Jesus as their Savior, c) participate in the life and mission of the Seventh-day Adventist Church and d) join the Web of Online witness.

Each Online Witness is expected to be a social relationship asset with a growing number of followers and shall determine and utilize an online platform on the open web as the major tool that provides the menu of topics in their niche to influence followers.

Online Witness may collaborate with other Online Witnesses to challenge each other in the number of followers they will have and the number that make actual decisions in relation to the four stated objectives.

Churches should recruit and organize the Witness around common themes. They may even have them to register and receive special credentials. They may be required to update their membership periodically and may be ranked, based on the number of followings that they have. Online Witness shall be involved in blogging and shall make regular posts on relevant topics that are posted on the selected platforms. It is expected that they will generate large followings of enthusiastic, engaged people who pay close attention to their views.

Witnesses may choose to influence according to various niches such as:

1. Answers to frequently asked bible questions
2. Bible Study Topics
3. A selected television Series
4. A Place of Worship and Fellowship
5. Video Sermons
6. Christian Media Ministries
7. Facebook Interest Group
8. Adventist YouTube Channel

Online Witnesses may be classified accordingly:

1. Mega-OW– Those who influence 100 or more followers on the social networks.
2. Macro-OW– Those who influence between 50-99 persons
3. Micro-OW– Those who influence between 20 – 49 persons
4. Beginner-OW– Those who influence between 1-19 persons.

Other Areas of Importance

1. Rules and process for blogging
2. Providing video content
3. Podcasting
4. Social posts only
5. Mega-OW may be featured on the website of the Church or some other strategic places in the domain of the Church.

Conclusion

"Digital evangelism is a technological strategy that utilizes all forms of digital and social media channels to share the gospel of Jesus and solicit responses of those who are connected to make commitment for Christ and membership into the community of faith. This approach is one of the "New methods" introduced by church leaders to lead people to Christ as people awake to the necessities of the time in which they are living. Ellen White said; "The work of God in this earth can never be finished until the men and women comprising our church membership rally to the work and unite their efforts with those of ministers and church officers" Gospel Workers, p. 352. Effective digital evangelism that leads many souls to Christ and membership in the local church community is the sum total of combined efforts between members and leaders.

Digital evangelism should achieve at least five goals through the collaborative effort of members who are digital proclaimers of the Good News of Christ. By utilizing all relevant and practical technological means to reach, equip, rescue, retain and disciple people in the faith of Jesus, the result will be a church of faithful disciples. Executing this type of effective digital evangelism may be achieved through intentionality. Digital proclaimers of the Good News must be aware of the available social media platforms for accessing the online Evangelistic campaign and how to engage in using them.

It must not be forgotten or overlooked that after ever digital evangelism campaign meetings, there must be intentionally planned and executed retention programs to nurture the newly baptized person in the faith through instructions in the doctrinal teachings of the bible and the culture and practice of the faith.

The summarized 18 steps in digital evangelism, how to increase engagement in the digital campaign meetings and suggested items for the digital campaign kit are among the essential elements to be studied, understood and embraced in order to achieve success in the program.

Form for organizing your digital evangelism team

	Names	Ministries
Collaborative Evangelism Committee Members		
Date of the Campaign		
Description	Name	Contact Information
Evangelist		
Prayer Coordinator		
Technical Assistants		
Bible Instructors		
Nightly Program Coordinators		
Marketing Coordinators		
Other Info.		
Other Info.		

Review and Discussion
- *What is digital evangelism?*
- *What are some of the goals of digital evangelism?*
- *Explain or define each of the goals of digital evangelism mentioned.*
- *Identify and explain the four phases of digital evangelism covered in this chapter*
- *Name ten steps of digital evangelism and explain the significance of each*
- *Describe the phase of preaching in the online campaign*
- *What is audience engagement in digital evangelism and how can you build it?*
- *Prepare a complete ready to be implemented digital evangelism program for a local church or region*
- *Explain the Web of Online Witnesses and develop a complete ready to be implemented online witnesses program for your local church.*

6
Evangelistic Visitation

THERE ARE numerous stories all across the globe of how the planting of Seventh-day Adventist congregations and the significant growth and expansion of the church is largely due to personal contacts between church members and those outside the faith. These personal evangelism encounters have brought hope and conviction to millions of people who are now living in anticipation of the Second Advent.

Pioneering Adventism in the Inter-American Division

In 1879, Pastor John N. Loughborough—an Adventist missionary from the United States of America who was residing in Southampton, England— and William Ings—a colporteur in the same city—sent a box of books and tracts to Haiti with no specific addressee. This literature reached the hands of an Episcopalian missionary, who in turn shared the literature with other Protestant missionaries. A Baptist missionary distributed the publications within his congregation. When Henry Williams and his wife—a young Jamaican couple in the congregation— studied the literature, they began keeping the Sabbath as the day of rest and sharing what they had learned with others. In 1892, after more than ten years, Pastor L. C. Chadwick visited them for the first time. He baptized them, and they became the first Seventh-day Adventists in the Inter-American Division.

Henry Williams and his wife continued their evangelistic activities across Jamaica, and their influence spread throughout the Caribbean region. There were people on other islands and in other countries who also participated in evangelistic visitation and literature distribution. This contributed to the growth of Adventism in the territory. As the membership grew, the General Conference provided leadership for the work in the territory with the West Indies Union Conference, which was created in 1906. Subsequently, the Northern Latin American Mission was created in 1914. In 1922, The General Conference organized the Inter-American Division with 8,146 members in 221 churches distributed between 3 conferences and 10 missions. By 1924, the membership in Inter-America had grown to 11,670 members worshipping in 229 churches. It reached a membership of 3.6 million by 2012, and the growth continues today. A primary factor of this growth is the evangelistic visitation carried out by the laity.

Pioneering Adventism in the South American Division

A certain harbor worker in New York had a desire to send some Portuguese literature to "the neglected continent" of South America, so he placed it in the hands of a sea captain who promised he would give it to someone in Brazil. When the captain was about to return to New York, he remembered his promise and tossed the bundle of literature unceremoniously onto the dock from which his ship was already departing. A storekeeper from the state of Santa Catarina carried home the literature, which he used as wrapping paper in his grocery. One of his customers, a drunkard, used the paper to fill some cracks in his kitchen wall. While leaning against the wall one day, he began to read. The more he read, the more he felt impressed that he had found what he had been searching for. He became the first convert to Adventism in the country of Brazil. He began doing evangelistic visitation, and today that tiny lay ministry has reaped a bountiful harvest. Millions are rejoicing in the Adventist faith, and personal visitation continues to be one of the most important activities of the church in the South American Division.

Inspired Support for Evangelistic Visitation

Inspiration places great emphasis on the one-to-one evangelistic method. "The work of Christ was made up largely of personal interviews. He had a faithful regard for the one-soul audience. From that one soul the intelligence received was carried to thousands" (*Testimonies for the Church,* vol. 6, chap. 13, p. 115). Christ's followers employed this same method of preaching the gospel. Acts 8:26–40 relates how Philip's one-to-one interview with the Ethiopian eunuch resulted in this important government official accepting Jesus.

The story of the Samaritan woman in John 4 powerfully illustrates how Jesus' use of evangelistic visitation and one-to-one personal contact led a whole town to come to the saving knowledge of Christ. In The Desire of Ages, Ellen White wrote:

> The Saviour did not wait for congregations to assemble. Often He began His lessons with only a few gathered about Him, but one by one the passers-by paused to listen, until a multitude heard with wonder and awe the words of God through the heaven-sent Teacher. The worker for Christ should not feel that he cannot speak with the same earnestness to a few hearers as to a larger company. There may be only one to hear the message; but who can tell how far-reaching will be its influence? It seemed a small matter, even to His disciples, for the Savior to spend His time upon a woman of Samaria. But He reasoned more earnestly and eloquently with her than with kings, counselors, or high priests. The lessons He gave to that woman have been repeated to the earth's remotest bounds.
>
> As soon as she had found the Saviour the Samaritan woman brought others to Him. She proved herself a more effective missionary than His own disciples. . . . Through the woman whom they despised, a whole city was brought to hear the Savior. (chap. 19, pp. 194, 195) Evangelistic visitation that is modeled on Christ's approach yields great success, and it is still indispensable

to God's people as they engage in witnessing. Ellen White wrote, "For years I have been shown that house-to-house labor is the work that will make the preaching of the word a success" (*Evangelism,* sec. 13, p. 433). Thus she asserted that "it is not preaching that is the most important; it is house-to-house work" (*Gospel Workers,* sec. 10, p. 468). "In almost every community there are large numbers who do not listen to the preaching of God's word or attend any religious service. If they are reached by the gospel, it must be carried to their homes" (*The Ministry of Healing,* chap. 9, p. 144).

Carrying Out Evangelistic Visitation

Believers in Christ must be proactive in equipping themselves to reach others and share their faith. To equip oneself for the task of evangelistic visitation, it is essential to spend much time in personal prayer and Bible study. It should be the desire of every sincere Christian to have a more meaningful prayer life and a deeper personal Bible study experience to enrich their spirituality (1 Thess. 5:17; Col. 4:2; 2 Tim. 2:15). Jesus' prayer life is a model for all believers. Like Jesus, each one should find a suitable time, place, and method for prayer. They should pray with expectancy, believing that the Lord will answer. Prayer and study of the Word should constitute a way of life that precedes and accompanies evangelistic visitation.

Evangelistic home visitation is done with a specific intent: to influence souls to Christ. There are various types of evangelistic visitations that one may engage in; however, in this section, we will focus on only three types:

(1) *new-interest* visits, (2) *sequel* visits, and (3) *decision* visits. Where an individual begins with a new-interest visit, the natural progression will be to advance successively to the follow-up (sequel) stage and eventually to the decision stage. Every believer should have the desire for evangelistic visitations to culminate in decisions for Christ.

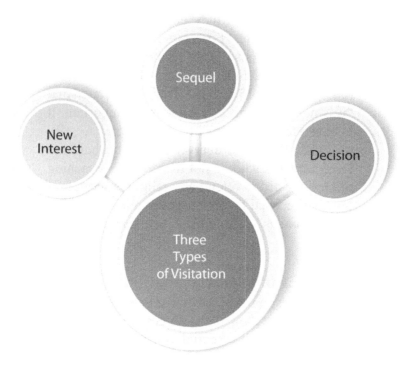

Figure 1: Types of Evangelistic Visitation

New-Interest Visits

New-interest visits are those that believers make to persons with whom they have not had a one-to-one relationship and whom they desire to influence to Christ. Initiating this kind of visit does not require the believer to focus directly on salvation issues, but rather to build a social relationship and eventually shift attention to the spiritual mission. This will require the believer to engage in return visits. Believers should not only be concerned with leading those with whom they are familiar to Christ, but should endeavor to reach strangers as well. The first step in carrying out new-interest visits is to develop a new-interest contact list. Present the names on this list in prayer to the Lord and ask for His guidance in how to contact and influence these persons to begin an intimate walk with Him. While praying for these persons, look for the right opportunity to initiate the visitation process. Also be ready in case the Lord provides an inadvertent encounter.

Now that you have settled on whom you want to visit, you need to determine an appropriate time and place. If you are unsure or timid about initiating the visit, you could ask someone who is experienced in evangelistic visitation to accompany you. However, this is your project with the Lord, and you have asked for His guidance and are assured of His presence, so you need to go forward in faith. If you choose to go with someone who is experienced, ask them to coach you in how to initiate the conversation and conduct the visit. It is important to always remember that the methods of others might not be tailored to your personality and way of working, so you should always endeavor to find your own approach.

People love to talk about their family, children, and career, so take advantage of this opportunity to establish a personal connection. If you know of a special occasion in the life of the person you want to visit, it would be a good idea to use that occasion as an opportunity to initiate the visit. If it is New Year's Day, pay them a new-year visit. If it is their birthday, anniversary, or graduation, take the opportunity to wish them well in that special moment of their life and thus initiate the contact. You may even want to take a gift if possible. Give gifts that will interest and delight the person. If children are involved, magazines, storybooks, or tapes with uplifting, Christian stories are examples of gifts that both adults and children can appreciate.

Other occasions that might offer an opportunity to initiate a visit include a new arrival to the family, a situation of bereavement, or other situations of significance in the person's life. A significant development in the community, society, or world could also provide such an opportunity. In this technological age in which people are busily attending to their personal lives and other interests, initial contacts may be made through e-mail, letter, phone call, text message, or social media. Sending a message through someone you know could work as well. For example, on your behalf, in your absence, a friend may say to the prospect: "I know someone gifted in social networking who would love to meet you someday. How about I introduce you to each other?"

This initial contact could provide an opportunity to build an acquaintance and begin to cultivate a strong social bond. Continued dialogue could lead to the opportunity to introduce discussion about God's providence. Then you could take advantage of opportunities to engage in joint efforts for the benefit of others. As acquaintance grows into social bonding, the way may open for you to introduce biblical subjects or even for the prospect to initiate discussion on some point of faith. Do not let such an opportunity slip away. Be vigilant and alert for every window of opportunity to get to your objective! Whenever an opportune time comes, invite the prospect to a church program. This could be a special musical program, holiday celebration, church-sponsored community project, or social activity.

How to Initiate the Spiritual Aspect of the Conversation

There are numerous questions and experiences that you can utilize to introduce and follow through with the spiritual aspect of a new interest visit. A natural transition may arise from the actual situation or conversation. This may create an avenue for alluding to the time and energy that people invest in choosing and developing their careers and relationships with others, often to the neglect of their spiritual lives. A relevant question in a situation like this could be, "How do you think people should attend to their spiritual growth?" If there is a case of tragedy, a negative experience, or even a positive outcome to a difficult situation, a relevant question might be, "How has your concept of God been affected by this experience?"

Conversation with the person might also lead to the following: "We've talked about many things, but we've never spent much time talking about religious things. If I may ask, where are you right now in your spiritual journey?" You could even ask the question, "What is your personal concept of God?" You could also initiate a spiritual conversation by saying, "Could I share with you a little about my personal relationship with the Lord?" Another question that could be used to create a conversation is: "Have you had the personal experience at some point in your life of accepting the Lord as your Savior?"

Other leading questions could be: "May I share with you how I reached this point in my Christian journey?" "Do you believe spiritual values influence the way you function in your marriage, or do they affect your perspectives toward life and work?" "If you could be sure that there's a God, would you want to know Him personally?" Or, "If you could know God personally, would you want to?" "What do you think about your faith?" "Have you made that exciting discovery of knowing God personally?" "How often do you go to church?" "Would you like to spend some time together to discuss the basic essentials of our Christian beliefs?" "Can we take some time to discuss some important issues in life?" "Do you think we should allow faith to have a greater influence in our lives?" "How about if I share with you some of the basic beliefs of my faith so that you can determine if this is what you're looking for?" "Many people say they are Christians. What does it mean to you to be a Christian?" "Have you ever had a discussion with someone about how to strengthen your faith?"

Other Ideal Ways to Connect with People

Invite the person to your home for a friendly visit. Tell them how much you care about establishing a friendship or some kind of social relationship with them. During your visit, it would be good to offer a relevant prayer at some point. This could be an important witness to your faith. If necessary, invite—or ask them to invite—other families, friends, and acquaintances to participate in some meaningful activity.

If you are unsure of what you could do on such an occasion, try singing some songs or watching a Digital Recording with an interesting, spiritual message that can stimulate conversation. Serving a meal may add to the fellowship. It could also provide an opportunity to introduce the subject of healthful living. A family outing or other recreational activity could also be a good activity to capture attention, hold interest, build a relationship, and establish a transition to discussing more transcendent subjects and matters of faith.

The Sequel Visits

So the new-interest visits have gone well, the transition has taken place, and now dialogue has begun regarding spiritual issues. Or this might be a case in which a person has been referred for visits due to their interest in discussing a particular point of faith. They may have attended a religious meeting and responded to a call, and the purpose of the visit will be to continue discussion. It may even be that they have indicated their desire to follow Jesus, thus the need for a sequel visit. Ellen White said, "The interest awakened should be followed up by personal labor—visiting, holding Bible readings, teaching how to search the Scriptures, praying with families and interested ones, seeking to deepen the impression made upon hearts and consciences" (*Evangelism*, sec. 13, p. 438).

Visiting a Person Who Is Missing from an Evangelistic Series

Persons who have shown interest in an evangelistic series may have missed some nights. This sequel visit serves the purpose of updating them on the central message of each topic they have missed and obtaining their response on the subjects presented. Some printed materials on the subjects in question may be presented to them. This visit also helps to encourage their return to the meetings. If there is some difficulty that has kept them away, then where possible, offer some assistance to resolve the situation and get them back to the meetings.

It would be good to inform them of the title the preacher will present at the next meeting. When introducing the title for the next meeting, always present the subject as something to be anticipated and not to be missed. Express regret if they indicate their unavailability to attend, find out which date would be better for them, and assure them that you will give them an update on the central points of the message. However, never leave without getting their commitment on the next date that they will be available to attend. Assure them that you will be following up to ensure that they stay informed and to help them return to the meetings.

As a Follow-up during an Evangelistic Series

When prospects respond to a call in an evangelistic meeting and express a desire to know more, it is time for a sequel visit. This gives the visitor an opportunity to prepare for the visit. This evangelistic visit should be properly planned to share biblical information with the prospect. If you know of any specific point of concern that the prospect has, make sure to research that point and have appropriate answers ready. One of the goals of this visit is to get the prospect to the point of being ready to make a decision to follow the Lord in baptism.

The purpose of this visit is specifically evangelistic. If a series of meetings has occasioned this follow-up request, review with the person the main points of the messages presented and provide answers to any questions they may have. If they do not have any questions, then have them answer some questions regarding essential doctrinal positions. Use relevant Bible passages to reinforce these concepts. A series of Bible study lesson guides would prove very useful in this endeavor. A sample pledge card is listed below that can serve as a guide for important doctrinal topics that should be covered in these sequel visits.

General Advice for Making Sequel Visits

The request for a visit may not come as the result of a planned evangelistic series, but rather through an interest created through some kind of personal contact. It may even be the result of the prospect's own initiative due to a variety of factors. A series of Bible study lessons can be one of the best tools to ensure a systematic order of witnessing and responding to particular needs. It is always important to ensure that the person's questions are answered satisfactorily.

There is always a need for support, which is why Jesus sent the disciples in teams or small groups. Choose your team wisely. If you and the members of your team are faced with questions that you do not feel competent to answer, tell the prospect that you do not think you can answer their questions or concerns adequately. Let them know that there is someone who can address their concerns more effectively and that you will be inviting that person to the next meeting in order to adequately address the subject. Ask their permission to bring that person to the next meeting. If it is a question that you can address but need time to research, let them know that you will need some time to study the topic a little more and that at the next meeting you will provide the response.

Do not waste time arguing over points of disagreement. "Here is a lesson for all our ministers, colporteurs, and missionary workers. When you meet those, who, like Nathanael, are prejudiced against the truth, do not urge your peculiar views too strongly. Talk with them at first of subjects upon which you can agree. Bow with them in prayer, and in humble faith, present your petitions at the throne of grace. Both you and they will be brought into a closer connection with heaven, prejudice will be weakened, and it will be easier to reach the heart" (*Evangelism*, sec. 13, p. 446).

There are times during these visits when social, emotional, or physical issues are unearthed that need to be addressed before the prospect can be led to make a decision for Christ. In such cases, if you cannot address the issues, refer the person to a competent professional who can guide them through the situation. Always be careful not to get into areas in which you are not competent. Let professionals do their job. If you make a referral, you should stay in contact with the prospect. Developing strong bonds can aid them in the process of dealing with the issues and will help them be comfortable to join the faith.

Decision Visits

When a prospect has been engaged in dialogue regarding issues involving their eternal destiny and the time comes for them to make a specific decision to follow the Lord in baptism, it is time for the decision visit. This visit may or may not follow previous new-interest and sequel visits, but the person is now at the point of making this decision that is so important for their eternal destiny. This visit should focus specifically on that purpose.

Determine quickly where to expend your efforts. If the visit is during an evangelistic campaign, is this person a prospect for this harvest or a future harvest? Keep your focus on those who are ready to make an immediate decision for baptism. There are those who are disposed to making the decision but, because of various situations, are not prepared to do so. Place these on the future harvest list. Do not abandon them, but rather keep in touch, letting them see, feel, and know that you have a genuine interest in them. Have others from the church visit them during this time. There are also those who are prepared but are not disposed to make this decision. You may need to ask for the assistance of persons to whom they could be more inclined and who would be more effective in securing their decisions. The decisions of those who are both disposed and prepared should be secured immediately.

Be mindful that arguing with a prospect is never an ideal approach. When a person is at the point of making a decision, they may look for ways to evade it. Recognize this, move on, and try not to engage in an argument that could divert attention from the mission at hand. At this point, Bible studies should only be done where absolutely necessary in order to clear up doubts or address specific issues. This is a moment when a battle for minds is raging, so prayer should be without ceasing. Give the prospect a commitment card and a covenant card to sign. Personally writing their name, signature, and planned date of baptism will help create a sense of obligation to the decisions they are making.

The commitment card covers specific doctrinal positions. It can serve as a guide for church members who are witnessing to prospects about the important doctrinal points that should be considered leading up to the covenant. Form A contains a sample commitment card that can be contextualized as needed.

Form A: Sample Commitment Card

My Personal Commitments

Name: _____ Date: _____

I have studied, accepted, and believed the doctrine of God:

1. The Word of God
2. The Godhead
3. God the Father
4. God the Son
5. God the Holy Spirit

Signature: _____

I have studied, accepted, and believed the doctrine of man:

6. Creation
7. The Nature of Man

Signature: _____

I have studied, accepted, and believed the doctrine of salvation:

8. The Great Controversy
9. The Life, Death, and Resurrection of Christ
10. The Experience of Salvation
11. Growing in Christ

Signature: _____

I have studied, accepted, and believed the doctrine of the church:

12. The Church
13. The Remnant and Its Mission

14. Unity in the Body of Christ

15. Baptism

16. The Lord's Supper

17. Spiritual Gifts and Ministries

18. The Gift of Prophecy

Signature: _____

I have studied, accepted, and believed the doctrine of the Christian life:

19. The Law of God

20. The Sabbath

21. Stewardship

22. Christian Behavior

23. Marriage and the Family

I have studied, accepted, and believed the doctrine of last things:

24. Christ's Ministry in the Heavenly Sanctuary

25. The Second Coming of Christ

26. Death and Resurrection

27. The Millennium and the End of Sin

28. The New Earth

Signature: _____

The covenant card is a signed agreement that the prospect has made a final decision to submit his or her life to the Lord and seal that decision with baptism on a specified date. It also signifies a pledge to become an active disciple of Christ and a member of the church. A sample covenant card is provided in Form B.

Form B: Sample Covenant Card

My Personal Covenant With God

My name is: _____

❏ I have accepted Jesus as my personal Savior and decided to become a Christian.

❏ I have wandered from Jesus, but I choose to wander no more. I hereby give myself fully to Him.

❏ I have been a follower of the Lord Jesus, but I have now accepted the additional biblical truth of the seventh-day Sabbath and have decided to live in harmony with the whole truth of Scripture.

❏ Recognizing that complete obedience is my responsibility, I covenant to be baptized.

Date of my baptism: _____

My address: _____

My phone number: _____

Signature: _____ Date: _____

How to Get Decisions to Follow the Lord

People usually make decisions based on how valuable the decision will be to them. They consider risks and measure them against the reward that will be obtained. Usually, at the moment of decision, numerous distractions become prevalent. The prospect who is about to make a decision for the Lord has to determine how that decision will ultimately be of value, especially if something very dear will have to be given up in the process. The devil usually orchestrates attacks and discouragements at these times, especially from persons with whom the prospect is closely connected. For this reason, prayer should have a prominent part in the visit.

There is an important place for the expression of emotion when making decisions. The Christian believer who seeks to influence decisions in the evangelistic visit should enthusiastically express the joy of the gospel. Let the prospect feel the joy and happiness that comes when the Spirit of the Lord is moving, and make them feel at liberty to express that emotion.

However, the prospect should not wait to experience a certain emotion. Making decisions is more than just a feeling. It is a calculated and intentional review of the facts presented and a conscious action in response to truth. If emotion were the only basis for making a decision, many who today are committed to following the Lord would never have made their decision.

Those involved in influencing evangelistic decision making have to provide information about the rewards and value of the decision to be made compared to the factors that cause resistance. The prospect must be encouraged to look to the greater value. Show them what will provide the best long-term result, and urge them to choose eternal reward over temporary satisfaction.

Depending on emotion may keep the person in a prolonged state of procrastination because, while they are able to recognize truth and the best course of action, they may have a challenge with value-based decision making. The decision may not feel good or seem appealing, and the wise option may appear bleak.

Cognitive control plays a major role in the decision-making process. Prospects have a problem with hoarding or maintaining, which is placing excessive value on a particular relationship or something else that is important to them. This does not provide incentives to sever ties and initiate new relationships. These people are inclined to choose immediate gratification over delayed reward. To overcome this tendency, they must take the necessary cognitive control to shift their attention away from that which they are hoarding. They need to learn to be adventuresome, take a leap of faith, and trust the Lord to fulfill His promises and carry them to new heights in their religious experience.

The Art of Persuasion

To get decisions for Christ, you must depend upon prayer. Divine power is a major influence in making decisions. However, we must also prepare ourselves with a knowledge of how human beings behave and what influences their actions. The art of persuasion is fundamental to the process of helping people make decisions.

To obtain decisions for Christ, you must persuade individuals to love and serve the Lord. Aristotle, the ancient Greek philosopher, taught that one could persuade individuals to action through a combination of *ethos, pathos, and logos*. *Ethos*—from which the word "ethics" is derived—has to do with the character of the one who is witnessing to the prospect. Thus it includes everything about you as the messenger: your personal appearance, demeanor, trustworthiness, and so on. *Pathos* has to do with the emotion, passion, feeling, and confidence with which you present the message. Logos is the logic, reasoning, and arguments with which you present the truth. Those who are involved in gaining decisions for Christ should consistently employ all three of these elements of persuasion.

Review and Discussion

- *What biblical and Spirit of Prophecy support is there for one-to-one evangelistic visitation?*
- *List at least five things that believers in Christ can do to equip themselves for effective evangelistic visitation.*
- *Identify and differentiate between the three types of visitation discussed in this chapter.*
- *Mention three ways in which a church member can initiate a new-interest visit.*
- *In your evangelistic visitation, when would you use a personal commitment card instead of a personal covenant card?*
- *Explain the relevance of ethos, pathos, and logos in evangelistic visitation.*

7
Evangelistic Small Groups

EFFECTIVE ORGANIZATIONS are comprised of individuals or members who are organized in small teams or groups that work harmoniously to achieve specific goals. An evangelistic small group is a team of generally seven to ten members of the church who commit themselves to working with each other to achieve specific evangelism and soul-winning objectives. All who accept Jesus as their personal Savior automatically become members of the body of Christ and of the royal priesthood of God? They all receive spiritual gifts through the empowerment of the Holy Spirit and are therefore obligated to share their faith (1 Pet. 2:9). Through evangelistic small groups, members are able to identify and nurture their spiritual gifts and employ them in fulfilling the gospel commission through both personal and corporate initiatives. Witnessing is beneficial to those who participate in it, for they are personally transformed into the likeness of the Savior as they engage in acts of witnessing that lead others to Christ.

Biblical Foundation for Evangelistic Small Groups

The Abrahamic covenant was rooted in a community setting. God decided to establish His people as a recognized community through which salvation history would unfold (Gen. 12:1–3). For effectiveness and as a model, Jesus worked with a group of twelve disciples and transformed them from just a collection of individuals into a community of Christians. He shared meals with them, walked with them, and established strong bonds with them. He mentored them, called them His friends and ministered with them (John 15:12–17).

The biblical view of God portrays Him as a relational Being who operates within the context of community. He leads through relationships and achieves desired outcomes through processes that He undertakes through a community or group of servants. All Christians are His servants, and as such, they are empowered by His Holy Spirit. Therefore, they should organize themselves to do ministry for Him.

The Four Components of an Evangelistic Small Group

Every evangelistic small group should include four essential elements: *devotion, nurture, community, and mission.*

Devotion is the element of believing in a Higher Power and acting based on a value system that goes beyond mere self-interest. This is essential for the effectiveness of the group. Devotion has to do with the time members dedicate to studying the Word of God together for understanding and personal spiritual growth. During this time, they engage in prayer dialogue in which they spend time just talking about what prayer is, how to pray better, how God answers prayer, and the assurance that prayer brings. During this time of devotion, they encourage and help each other to improve in their prayer life. They study different types of prayers and how to offer them. Special emphasis is given to faith and the relationship between faith and prayer. How to accept and give forgiveness both inside and outside the group is also an important topic to discuss. The group will determine the amount of time to be spent in devotion. This element could consist of a song, prayer, and discussion of the main devotional feature, followed by another prayer.

Nurture is basically everything that is done in the group. Devotion, community, and mission involvement are all aspects of the nurturing initiative. When people are active in working for others spiritually, socially, and physically, they are actually being nurtured in the process.

However, nurture also includes addressing the specific needs of individual members, whether material, social, spiritual, or otherwise. It is this nurturing ministry that makes participation in evangelistic small groups so powerful, as each participant is being directly and indirectly ministered to through the various interactions within the group.

Community has to do with the activities that the members of the group are engaged in—both individually and corporately—to address the needs of those outside the faith. Every small group should be engaged in community initiatives. These do not have to be organized by the group itself, but could instead be organized by the Evangelism Action Committee or one of the departments of the church. Each small group may be involved as an avenue for executing these community-outreach initiatives.

Mission refers to the group's specific evangelistic activity to influence, inspire, motivate, and train those outside the faith to accept Christ as their Savior, become His disciples, and unite with His church. Simply by inviting others to participate in the devotion of the group, the members are involving themselves in mission. Conducting Bible studies with them, praying for them, and visiting them in their homes to encourage them spiritually are also mission initiatives in which small groups can participate. When members of the group invite others to attend any evangelistic program of the church, including weeks of prayer, evangelistic campaigns, the Sabbath service, or any other gospel oriented program, the group is participating in mission activities.

The Sabbath School and Small Groups

The Sabbath School Action Unit is a standard small group that is organized in every church. According to Ellen G. White, "The Sabbath school, if rightly conducted, is one of God's great instrumentalities to bring souls to a knowledge of the truth" *(Counsels on Sabbath School Work,* chap. 4, p. 115). According to the Sabbath School and Personal Ministries Department of the General Conference, the Sabbath School Action Unit is a "plan set in operation to organize, equip, and mobilize the church to accomplish its mission and to give support to new members and to active long-standing members." The following is a description of such a Sabbath School:

> It is a place with a warm, caring atmosphere, where new and older members feel the spiritual and emotional support and encouragement they need in meeting the complexities of daily life. It is a place where missing class members are first cared for, where the class outreach leader then leads out as all share the joys and challenges they met in sharing Jesus during the week in accordance with their class outreach plan.
> Finally, it is a place where prayer lists are updated, where soul winning training is conducted that is appropriate to the outreach needs of the coming week, and where total participation in the discussion of the lesson takes place as it is applied to life and witnessing opportunities that week.[1]

Ideally, the Sabbath School Action Unit rightly organized and executed fulfills the required needs of devotion, outreach, community and mission. However, due to the amount of time required to effectively fulfill all four components of the small group program, it may be beneficial to organize voluntary small groups apart from the Sabbath School Action Units. In this case, all who are willing to contribute time, resources, influence, talents, and effort should be involved in organized small groups. However where such small groups are organized, there must be no effort to eclipse the function of the regular Sabbath School Action Units in the local church.

Small Groups Organizing Committee

In order to promote, organize, and establish small groups in the church, a Small Groups Organizing Committee may be appointed. This committee should be chaired by the pastor or someone designated by the pastor, and the leaders of each small group should be committee members.

---

[1] Sabbath School and Personal Ministries Department of the General Conference of Seventh-day Adventists, "Cool Tools for Sabbath School Action Units," (Silver Spring, MD: Sabbath School and Personal Ministries Department of the General Conference of Seventh-day Adventists, 2009),

http://www.sabbathschoolpersonalministries.org/site/1/ leaflets/Action%20Units.pdf.[1]

The responsibilities of the committee include:
- Promoting and organizing small groups.
- Motivating the leadership of each group.
- Defining strategies for small group ministries.
- Receiving periodic reports on the progress of each group.
- Training and empowering group leaders and members.
- Assisting group leaders in the training of group members.
- Evaluating the performance and effectiveness of each group based on the defined objectives of the group.
- Attending to all other administrative functions of the small groups.

Establishing Small Groups

Various methods may be utilized to establish small groups, including leader oriented and member-oriented approaches. In the leader-oriented approach, the Small Groups Coordinating Committee selects the small group leaders and recommends their names to the church board for approval. The group leaders then select between seven and ten members for their groups and present the selected names to the Small Groups Coordinating Committee for approval. In the *member oriented* approach, the Small Groups Coordinating Committee divides the interested members into groups of between seven and ten persons. The members of each group then select a leader from among themselves and present the name of the leader to the Small Groups Coordinating Committee for approval. Both of these approaches can also be used to form small groups that consist of members who live within a specific area of the community, members who possess a common interest, or members who have a similar profession, skill, or training.

With either method, the members of the newly formed small group select additional officers—such as secretary and treasurer—as they deem necessary. The group then determines the following:
- Purpose of the group.
- Specific initiatives and activities to be engaged in.
- Geographical area in which to concentrate group initiatives.
- Time and place of meeting.
- Best methods for accomplishing the group's mission.
- Goals to be achieved in a specified period of time.

Form A: Small Group Organization and Membership

Name of church: _____

Name of ministry group: _____

Date of organization: _____ _____

Name of group leader: _____

Telephone: _____ E-mail: _____

Secretary: _____ Telephone: _____

Treasurer: _____ Telephone: _____

Other group members   Telephone

_____

_____

_____

_____

Coordinating committee's comments:

Signature_____ Date _____

Stages in Small Group Development

For a small group to be effective, leaders must be intentional in helping members understand their various roles and functions as they learn to work together. Every group goes through distinct stages of development, so new groups are different from those that are mature. In new groups, members have to get to know each other, clarify tasks to be accomplished, and divide responsibilities. In his book *The Leadership Experience*, Richard Daft states that groups of all types go through five developmental stages: *forming, storming, norming, performing, and adjourning.*

Figure 1: Five Stages of Group Development

Forming

This is the stage of the initial organization of the group. All the members are on board, getting acquainted with each other, and receiving orientation for the tasks to be accomplished. At this stage, members decide on the purpose of the group, time of the meetings, and group officers as well as establish agendas, set ground rules, and explore friendship possibilities. It is important for the leader to facilitate interaction and communication among members of the group and help them feel comfortable to establish relationships with each other.

Storming

In this stage, personalities emerge more clearly, and conflicts are likely to surface. Differing perspectives and opinions on how the group should function, how rules should be interpreted, and what exactly the group should be doing are common. Disunity and lack of cohesiveness may become pronounced. For the group to achieve effectiveness, it must overcome these challenges. The leader must play a pivotal role at this stage, helping members work through uncertainties and conflicting perceptions in order to find common values and agree on a shared mission.

Norming

In this stage, conflicts are resolved, and unity and harmony become visible within the group. Roles are clearly defined and understood. The function of each individual is accepted as the members learn to accept each other. The leader must continue to emphasize and facilitate openness and communication, making sure that roles are clarified and that desired outcomes are foremost in the minds of all.

Performing

During this stage, the major emphasis is on the accomplishment of the mission and purposes of the group. Each member has developed commitment to the goals of the group and is self-motivated. Frequent interactions take place, and efforts are coordinated. The interest of the group takes precedence over personal interests, and practical accomplishments take place. Effective leaders focus attention on effective performance of tasks and help the group to achieve self-management. During this stage, the group does what it was organized to do.

Adjourning

Groups should not be organized for eternity. There must come a time when the group adjourns so that new groups can be established. When groups are organized to serve endless purposes, members lose interest, and participation becomes sparse or even nonexistent. Therefore, when the objectives have been achieved, the group should be adjourned.

There should be celebration among the members that they organized themselves, achieved their objectives, and are now ready to dissolve. At the celebration function, members look back through the different stages, identify successes and failings, determine what could have been done differently for greater effectiveness, express gratitude for the participation of each individual, give special recognition and awards, and rejoice with the souls that have been won to the truth through the ministry of the group.

Members of the Small Groups Coordinating Committee may be present at the adjournment to participate in the celebration. They could make their own observations and encourage the members of the group to prepare themselves to participate when reorganization takes place.

Function of Small Group Leader

Small group leaders should be baptized members of the church who model Christian discipleship. They should have a regular devotional and prayer life, possess good relations with others, be of relatively good physical and emotional health, be actively involved or willing to participate in the activities of the church, and have a strong commitment to the mission of the church. They should ensure that appropriate plans are in place for the group and see that group meetings include the elements of *devotion, nurture, community, mission*. They serve as shepherds to the members, helping them commit to the purpose of the group. They should meet with each member individually to encourage their spiritual growth and their involvement in the activities of the group and the church at large. They should mentor others to serve as coleaders of the group, encourage regular church attendance by each member, and pray regularly for the members, initiatives of the group, and general programs and administration of the church. Leaders should be foremost in the development and communication of the vision and purposes of the group. Evaluation of the effectiveness of the group should also be of vital interest to them.

Establishing Cohesion in Small Groups

A small group needs cohesion to function effectively. This is facilitated by the participation of all the members. To ensure that all are on board in building such cohesion, the leader should take an active presiding role, asking key questions to establish this essential group dynamic. The responses to the questions should be recorded and discussed, and a consensus or majority vote should be reached in each case. These questions include:

- Who should be the officers of this group?
- What specific objectives do we wish to achieve as a group?
- What are your expectations of the group?
- When should the group meet?
- How often should the group meet?
- Where should the group meet?
- Based on your experience in other group contexts, what should we avoid?
- Are there any specific tasks to which you would like to commit that will contribute to the success of the group?
- How long should this group last?

The leader should arrange for the responses to these questions to be printed and should give a copy to each of the members. This document will constitute an agreement or covenant between the members of the group. It would be ideal for each group member to sign this covenant. The secretary of the group could collect and archive a signed copy of the covenant from each member.

Training for Small Group Leaders

The effectiveness of any group is dependent upon the quality of its leadership. Too often groups fail because their leaders are not adequately trained for the task. The list below mentions some topics that should be covered in the process of equipping small group leaders. This process should provide for both theoretical and practical training.

- Biblical Philosophy of Small Groups
- The Real Effectiveness of Small Groups
- The Small Group as a Loving Community
- Leadership Styles
- Group Dynamics
- Conflict Management and Resolution
- Leading Discussions: Formulating and Using Discussion Questions
- Leadership and Listening
- Developing Relationships among Group Members
- How to Conduct Effective Meetings
- Leading throughout the Five Stages of a Group
- How to Lead Effective Bible Study Sessions
- Expectations of Small Group Members
- Conducting Group Evaluation
- The Art of Persuasion: Getting Others to Participate
- Promoting Reconciliation
- The Spiritual Life of a Group Leader
- The Four Components of an Evangelistic Small Group
- Establishing a Shared Vision for the Group
- How to Establish the Group Atmosphere

Important Skills for Effective Group Leaders

- *They listen carefully*. In order to understand what is being communicated, group leaders must focus carefully on what speakers are saying. As part of careful listening, the group leader must be attentive to the voice and observe the body language of the speaker. These provide important keys for

knowing how to respond to the speaker, as well as for capturing the intended message and utilizing it for the benefit of the group.
- *They mirror speakers.* In mirroring, leaders restate what speakers say in order to ascertain that the content and feelings being communicated are correctly understood.
- *They inquiry and simplify.* Leaders ask questions and try to simplify what speakers are saying. They do this to ensure proper understanding for the benefit of the entire group.
- *They encapsulate.* Leaders condense or compress what speakers say so that the most important points are understood.
- *They support and inspire.* Some group members are timid. Others have various anxieties and fears. Leaders should help all group members deal with these fears, anxieties, and timidity so that they can participate actively in the group.
- *They establish a positive atmosphere.* Group atmosphere is important for success. This has to do with the mood in meetings. Leaders may establish an atmosphere that is formal, boring, stern, or trivial, or they may cultivate a supportive, friendly, and accepting environment.
- Other important skills for group leaders include: modeling desired behaviors; self-disclosure; using the eyes to scan for nonverbal cues as well as to draw out or cut off members or speakers as necessary; using tone of voice to energize the group; and using this energy to get the group engaged.

Mistakes Leaders Should Avoid

Over the years, persons who have led groups have discovered reasons why some leaders do well while others don't. Ed E. Jacobs and his associates, drawing from the wealth of their counseling experience, share valuable information on the reasons why some group leaders fail. These reasons corroborate what I have discovered through years of interacting with and leading groups. These mistakes include:
- *Not planning.* The best way to ensure that a meeting will be valuable to the members is to plan.

- *Trying to cover too much.* It is better to present one or two topics properly than to superficially skim over multiple topics. It may be wise to arrange the topics in a series in order to complete a topic and ensure that the greatest possible benefits are obtained.
- *Focusing on irrelevant matters.* Activities, topics, and exercises should be selected based on the interest of the members. The interest of a wide cross section of the membership should be considered, rather than that of just a few individuals.
- *Poorly managing time and program order.*
- *Not planning an interesting beginning.*
- *Vague planning.*
- *Lack of flexibility.*

Dynamics within Effective Small Groups

Proper use of time in the group addresses the normal routine of the meetings as well as special traditions and celebrations that affirm members, connect them together as a team, and add creativity and humor to the regular schedule. Agree upon the time to be spent together in group activities and clarify what should be expected in group meetings. If certain people are allowed to dominate conversation and use too much time, this may discourage others from attending. People are busy; therefore, they do not have much time to spend in situations of monologue or individual dominance. They want to ensure that their time is spent wisely. In effective evangelistic small groups, members spend time together sharing, accepting, and blending ideas, as well as developing initiatives and executing plans.

Leadership in a small group should be dynamic in order to ensure that members are committed to fulfilling their responsibilities. The leader should ensure that each member receives the encouragement, training, and resources they need to fulfill their responsibilities. To ensure high performance, carry out a periodic assessment of group performance, recognize improvements in performance, ask members for suggestions on how to improve, and propose improvements that are not mentioned in these suggestions.

Appropriate materials or resources should be provided for the use of the group. Someone in the group should be responsible for procuring and distributing the materials that the group determines are necessary to fulfill the established purposes and mission of the group. If the church is responsible for providing such materials, the person in charge should know whom to contact. If the group itself is responsible, then there should be a clear understanding within the group of the procedure to be utilized in procuring such materials or resources.

Relationships in the group are important for effectiveness and productivity. The leader should make an effort to help members work together as a team. Indicators of a strong team include: members who demonstrate care and concern for each other, regular attendance at group meetings and activities, and achievement of desired outcomes.

Involvement of each member of the group is an essential aspect of achieving success. Encourage all members to participate in the principal activities of the group. Everyone should feel at liberty to share relevant knowledge and information and to participate in discussions. Members should also be encouraged to bring visitors or prospects to the group, and all members should help these visitors adjust and feel accepted.

A climate of trust in which members work toward shared goals through self-sacrifice, persistence, and loyalty is vital for proper group function. Leaders and members should work together to cultivate an environment of trust and dependability. All should develop a sense of belonging along with a sense of accountability to others.

Effective communication patterns in the group include clear, open, and affirming speech and consistent, empathetic listening. These lead to constructive conflict management and problem solving. They contribute to the comfort of both members and visitors within the group and influence people's decisions on whether to remain a part of the group or not. If participants feel free to contribute to discussions, this will help to establish an atmosphere of warmth and belonging. Make an effort to recognize the suggestions of everyone. If there is a disagreement, look for a solution that satisfies the entire group as well as the individuals who have the difference of opinion.

Small Groups and Prayer

Evangelistic small groups should serve as nurturing environments where members are discipled and deployed for service. Prayer is a major ingredient in the effectiveness of small group activities. The effectiveness of small group members in their personal life and service to others depends on their persistence in prayer. In Colossians 4:2 Paul says to "continue steadfastly in prayer." This persistence in prayer should become a way of life for Christians. In Acts 12 we see the power of group prayer, which led to Peter's release from prison.

Some members may be concerned that they will not be able to converse with others on a level that will be acceptable or that will impress. It is important for them to remember that witnessing is not about impressing others. If they endure in prayer, the Holy Spirit will take full control of their lives and elevate their conversation to the point that they will make sense to those with whom they are interacting (Col. 4:6).

Small Groups and Spiritual Gifts

A spiritual gift is a special endowment of abilities or attributes given by the Holy Spirit to all believers with the purpose of unifying and building up the body of Christ. Spiritual gifts cannot be earned, won, or merited. A distorted concept of spiritual gifts infested the church of Corinth. Some members had inflated ideas of their personal importance because they thought they possessed more public and more spectacular gifts from the Holy Spirit than others. Some coveted the gifts exercised by others. Thus the gifts that were supposed to unite the body of Christ became a cause of division among them. The schism gave rise to the need for the Apostle Paul to address the question of spiritual gifts. He emphasized that the way the gifts of the Holy Spirit are intended to function is analogous to how the body and its various parts function (1 Cor. 12:12–26; Rom. 12:4).

In 1 Corinthians 12:14–21 he emphasized that each member must be involved, or else the body will not function optimally. In this interdependent relationship, every member is needed and has a job to do (vv. 27, 28). Ellen White said:

> To every person is committed some peculiar gift or talent which is to be used to advance the Redeemer's kingdom. All God's responsible agents, from the lowliest and most obscure to those in high positions in the church, are entrusted with the Lord's goods. It is not the minister alone who can work for the salvation of souls. Those who have the smallest gifts are not excused from using the very best gifts they have, and in so doing their talents will be increased. None should mourn because they cannot glorify God with talents which they never possessed and for which they are not responsible. (Testimonies for the Church, vol. 4, chap. 61, p. 618)

Each member should identify their gifts and utilize them within the church body. The small group is an ideal setting to help members identify, nurture, and use their spiritual gifts. In this group setting, members should be given intentional opportunities to examine, experiment, and explore options to discover their spiritual gifts.

Identifying Spiritual Gifts in a Small Group

Each member of the group should pray earnestly for the aid of the Holy Spirit. Then as a group, read Romans 12:1–13, 1 Peter 4:8–11, and 1 Corinthians 12. Make a list of all the spiritual gifts mentioned in these texts and perform the following exercises:

1. Discuss what each passage adds to each person's understanding of the proper use of the gifts of the Holy Spirit.
2. Identify which of these gifts each member thinks other members of the group possess. Some members may possess gifts that are not included in the passages studied. Try to identify these gifts too.

3. Each group member should indicate whether or not they acknowledge the gift or gifts attributed to them by the other members of the group.
4. If any member of the group does not confirm the gifts attributed to them by other group members, they should indicate what they think is their gift.
5. Make a list of the spiritual gifts that each member of the group possesses.
6. Assign tasks to each member of the group based on their identified spiritual gifts.
7. Where necessary, give training to help individuals develop confidence in using their gifts.
8. Determine as a group what gifts can be utilized to fulfill desired outcomes.
9. Spiritual gifts surveys may also be used to help members identify and confirm their gifts.

Small Groups and Bible Studies

Small groups may use Bible studies for devotion, nurture, or mission. For any of these purposes, similar methods may be employed. If a specific book of the Bible is to be studied, the different members of the group could be assigned specific sections to read and study. They should observe main themes, repeated words, main characters, and important divisions. They could also look up the historical background of the book in Bible commentaries, dictionaries, or encyclopedias. When the group meets to study, each person could present the segment assigned to them. If a Bible lesson is used to conduct the study, a similar approach could be taken, assigning specific questions to individuals for them to research ahead of time. When the group meets, each person presents or responds to the question assigned to them. This makes the study participative and dynamic. A variety of different Bible study methods are provided in the appendices.

Helpful Suggestions for Small Group Bible Study

1. Use the introduction to get the members excited about the study.
2. Build curiosity to attract their interest.
3. Avoid an anticlimax by not giving away the central truth at the beginning of the discussion but rather focusing the thoughts of the members on the subject being discussed.
4. Review past studies to ensure continuity or to show completion of and transition between topics.
5. If the study is on a book or chapter of the Bible, prepare observations on each paragraph.
6. Examine the significance of each observation.
7. Create a title for each paragraph.
8. Ask what meaning the passage has for each participant.
9. Where relevant and applicable, help people get personally into the scene of the passage by asking questions like: "What do you hear?" "What does it sound like?" "What do you see?"
10. Provide information about the background of the passage when necessary.
11. If using a study guide, focus carefully on the significance of each question.
12. Identify the main theme of the lesson or passage.
13. Based on this theme, write out the purpose of the specific study.
14. Show how each question or paragraph fits into the theme.
15. Spend enough time on each passage or question for each person to understand it clearly.
16. Formulate short, clear questions that relate to observation, interpretation, and application.
17. Questions, observations, and interpretations should facilitate moving smoothly through the passage or lesson.
18. Consider the sequence of the questions or observations, making sure that each one leads to the next.
19. Make note of the most important questions so that if time runs out, you can make sure that they are covered.

20. Discuss what truth God is asking each one to practice based on the message of the passage.
21. Consider what significance the central truth of the study has for the lives of each person in the group.
22. During preparation, at the beginning of the study, and throughout the study, there should be much prayer. Stop at points during the study and ask God to enlighten each mind before going forward. When a question or passage seems difficult and everyone seems locked in a state of uncertainty and confusion—pray!

Evaluation of Evangelistic Small Groups

Each group should perform a periodic evaluation, which should be based on specific performance targets. The strengths and weaknesses of the group should be considered. The Small Groups Coordinating Committee should prepare an evaluation sheet to be used by each group for defining performance success, team spirit, and developmental needs within the group. The results of this evaluation should be utilized to guide the future direction of the group and improve its effectiveness in the fulfillment of the four components of d*evotion, nurture, community,* and *mission.*

Review and Discussion

- *Identify and define the four components of an effective small group.*
- *Describe the function of a Small Groups Organizing Committee in the local church.*
- *Explain two methods or approaches that may be used to establish small groups.*
- *Mention two characteristics of each of the five stages of a small group.*
- *What important role does the leader play in the organization and implementation of small groups?*
- *How important is prayer for the effectiveness of small group members?*
- *Mention five ways to help small group members identify and use their spiritual gifts.*

8
Public Evangelism

JESUS sat beside Jacob's well in Samaria and viewed the vast fields of wheat ready to be reaped. As He sat there, He also saw the many people who came to the well for water. He discerned in them the need for more than just literal water. They needed a deep spiritual experience that would result in an eternal infilling. Looking upon this scene, He said to His disciples, "Look, I tell you, lift up your eyes, and see that the fields are white for harvest" (John 4:35). The reaping of the harvest is an apt illustration that characterizes the evangelistic task to be done in reaping souls for the kingdom of God. Like the ripened wheat, the people needed to be reaped; that is, they had to be won to the truth of the gospel.

As He sent the seventy disciples to do evangelistic ministry, Jesus used this same analogy to refer to the need for more workers for the task of reaping: "The harvest is plentiful, but the laborers are few; therefore pray earnestly to the Lord of the harvest to send out laborers into His harvest" (Matt. 9:37, 38). The Lord is calling for harvesters who will serve in various lines of evangelistic ministry and discover the possibilities of public evangelism.

Ellen White gave the following inspired counsel regarding the importance of the public proclamation of the Word of God: "We should make efforts to call together large congregations to hear the words of the gospel minister. And those who preach the Word of the Lord should speak the truth. They should bring their hearers, as it were, to the foot of Sinai, to listen to the words spoken by God amid scenes of awful grandeur" (*Evangelism,* sec. 6, p. 119).

Public evangelism is the Holy Spirit–filled proclamation of the gospel of Jesus through public preaching. This message includes the divinity, incarnation, ministry, death, resurrection, ascension, intercession, and Second Advent of Jesus. It involves publicly teaching the origin, progression, and destiny of the world and its inhabitants. Public preaching is the presentation of the good news—through verbal and nonverbal means—in which an invitation is extended for the hearers to accept and commit to the message.

The message of public evangelism proceeds from the inspired Word of God, in which we find the written deposit of heavenly teaching for human beings of every nation, kindred, tongue, and people. The gospel does not consist of a system of man's thoughts or actions. Therefore, the Bible is the only source from which we preach. Only there do we find the objective authority against which all Christian teaching must be measured.

Public Evangelism in the Bible

Public preaching is ubiquitous in Scripture, and this fact speaks to its permanence and irrefutable effectiveness as a compelling method of communicating the gospel to the world. It is not a human invention, but rather a God-ordained ministry. Throughout the ages, God has always had representatives who have publicly proclaimed His messages.

Josephus and Clement were among the historians who argued that Noah publicly preached repentance to the people of the ancient world. Peter also lent his voice to the popular idea that Noah preached to his generation. He said, "[God] did not spare the ancient world, but preserved Noah, a herald of righteousness, with seven others, when he brought a flood upon the world of the ungodly" (2 Pet. 2:5). When the nation of Judah was on the verge of being overrun by the Assyrians, God needed a spokesperson who would publicly proclaim His message. He called Isaiah to make this public proclamation. "And I heard the voice of the Lord saying, 'Whom shall I send, and who will go for us?' Then I said, 'Here I am! Send me' " (Isa. 6:8). Jesus began His public ministry in Nazareth—with public evangelism.

He read the prophecy of Isaiah 61:1 and 2 and announced to those assembled in the synagogue that He had come to fulfill that prophecy. He acknowledged that the Spirit of God had anointed Him to evangelize the poor, to proclaim freedom for the prisoners and recovery of sight for the blind, to release the oppressed, and "to proclaim the year of the Lord's favor" (Luke 4:18, 19). He lived an evangelistic ministry, and public evangelism was a major part of it. He drew reference to His own public evangelistic acts when He sent John's disciples to take a report to their master about Jesus' ministry. "Go and tell John what you hear and see: the blind receive their sight and the lame walk, lepers are cleansed and the deaf hear, and the dead are raised up, and the poor have good news preached to them" (Matt. 11:4, 5). Once when Jesus was about to depart to a new territory He said, "I must preach the good news of the kingdom of God to the other towns as well; for I was sent for this purpose" (Luke 4:43).

Luke 8:1 says that Jesus "went on through cities and villages, proclaiming and bringing the good news of the kingdom of God. And the twelve were with Him." Here we find Jesus practicing public evangelism in company with others. He preached to thousands of people and fed them as well (Matt. 14:13–21). Luke 9:6 says, "And they departed and went through the villages, preaching the gospel and healing everywhere." He proclaimed the gospel in the temple as well, in spite of confrontation with the religious authorities. "One day, as Jesus was teaching the people in the temple and preaching the gospel, the chief priests and the scribes with the elders came up and said to Him, 'Tell us by what authority You do these things, or who it is that gave You this authority' " (Luke 20:1, 2).

The purpose of public evangelism is to get a response from people. In Luke 16:16 we read, "The Law and the Prophets were until John; since then the good news of the kingdom of God is preached, and everyone forces his way into it." Jesus sent His disciples, and by extension all believers, to proclaim the gospel and call for decisions, giving them the assurance of His perpetual presence with them (Matt. 28:18–20).

In Acts 14:1 we find that the Apostle Paul would begin his evangelism in Gentile cities by building connections within the Jewish community. His evangelistic preaching occurred in synagogues with an assembly of people. Thus it constituted public evangelism. He performed public evangelism in many different places: Pisidian Antioch (Acts 13:14–44), Thessalonica (Acts 17:1–3), Berea (Acts 17:10), Athens (Acts 17:16, 17), Corinth (Acts 18:1, 4), and Ephesus (Acts 19:1, 8).

Paul concentrated his public-evangelism efforts on new territories where the gospel had not yet been preached. "I make it my ambition to preach the gospel, not where Christ has already been named, lest I build on someone else's foundation, but as it is written, 'Those who have never been told of Him will see, and those who have never heard will understand' " (Rom. 15:20, 21). Similarly, to the Corinthian church he wrote: "We do not boast beyond limit in the labors of others. But our hope is that as your faith increases, our area of influence among you may be greatly enlarged, so that we may preach the gospel in lands beyond you, without boasting of work already done in another's area of influence" (2 Cor. 10:15, 16).

The Pastor and Public Evangelism

For pastors, organizing themselves, lay workers, and the church for effective public evangelism is a major responsibility. Success in public evangelism is not a dream or a fortune that is stumbled upon; public evangelism is hard work. Many pastors shy away from it because they do not feel they are ready for the work that is involved. However, preachers must never forget that Jesus promised to be with them all the way. He provides divine empowerment for success to those who are willing to make the necessary effort to do proper planning and organization for public evangelism.

I believe that most pastors have an intense interest in soul winning. However, many are reluctant to hold public evangelistic meetings because they have a fear of failure. Some are not prepared for the work that is involved. In many cases, preachers focus on small groups and other types of personal evangelism instead of planning and organizing effective public evangelism. Small groups and personal evangelism are important, as are all the various methods utilized in soul winning. Ellen White said that diverse methods should be employed in this work (See Evangelism, sec. 4. p. 70; sec. 5, pp. 105, 106). However, this does not call for abandoning the most effective method to capture and arrest the attention and interest of large groups of people in one location, presenting the good news and acquiring large numbers of decisions at the same time. If we are going to have multiplied results in soul winning, we must spend much more time planning and devising methods to execute more effective public evangelism.

There is a place for "star evangelists." There are those who have received a special gift from the Holy Spirit in this area. Many pastors have the potential to become star evangelists, but they are either unaware of their gift or too timid to go forward and develop it. Some may suspect that they possess this gift, yet they are doing nothing about it. However, there are also many who are aware that they possess it and are also actively using it. Every pastor should discover if they possess it so that they can cultivate and utilize it to save souls and thus bring honor and glory to the Lord. Many who have the gift may never be considered star evangelists, but they have the gift and should utilize it.

Many pastors are waiting for a star evangelist to assist them before they will conduct a public evangelistic campaign. However, they should take note of Paul's counsel to Timothy: "But you, keep your head in all situations, endure hardship, do the work of an evangelist, and discharge all the duties of your ministry" (2 Tim. 4:5, NIV). Even if Timothy thought he did not have the gift of an evangelist, Paul counseled him to do the work of an evangelist, to be involved in the proclamation of the gospel. Every pastor is called to proclaim the good news, to do the work of an evangelist. There is no need to wait for a star evangelist to come along. As human beings, we do not win souls. It is Christ working through the Holy Spirit who wins souls (*Testimonies to Ministers,* chap. 5, pp. 144, 145). Pastors are to place themselves at the foot of the cross, where the Holy Spirit can take charge of their lives and use them. The pastor's most urgent concern regarding public evangelism should not be whether or not it will be successful, but rather the prayer, "Lord, I give myself to You. Use me according to Your will and for Your glory."

According to Ezekiel, it is the responsibility of God's messengers to warn the nations of coming judgment, even for the sake of their own salvation. "If I say to the wicked, O wicked one, you shall surely die, and you do not speak to warn the wicked to turn from his way that wicked person shall die in his iniquity, but his blood I will require at your hand. But if you warn the wicked to turn from his way, and he does not turn from his way, that person shall die in his iniquity, but you will have delivered your soul" (Ezek. 33:8, 9). Public evangelism is a life-and-death matter, and all pastors are called to personally proclaim the message and prepare their churches to be involved.

Those who have been involved in the life-saving efforts of public evangelism and have given it their all, experiencing the infilling of the Holy Spirit and sharing the joy of seeing souls brought to Jesus, can extol its virtues. They are intrinsically motivated to keep planning, organizing their churches, training their members, and engaging in public evangelistic campaigns.

For those who are not yet involved, "Oh, taste and see!" (Ps. 34:8). The high and sacred call to the gospel ministry is a call to the public proclamation of the gospel. It is the pastor's job, and it is a sacred privilege. The work of preaching the gospel and saving souls for the kingdom of God must be finished, and public evangelism is one important method among many to accomplish it. It is a method designed by God, and He will use it to His ends through the pastor and lay evangelistic team.

Myths about Public Evangelism

Many who do not engage in public evangelism have devised or believed various objections to it. Very often, they do so to justify their own actions or omissions rather than on the basis of authenticated facts. These myths and objections include: "Public evangelism does not work." "We have done it before or have seen others do it, and there was no success." "Those baptized through public evangelism do not stay in the church." "Public evangelism is too expensive." "It is too time consuming, preachers are busy, and there are easier methods." "Now is not a good time for public meetings."

"People do not come to such meetings." "Postmodern people are not interested in listening to Bible-based presentations." "People are too busy to attend meetings every night." "The distinct message of the Seventh-day Adventist Church is too offensive for public proclamation." "Public evangelism disturbs the entire program of the church, and it is more difficult to get things back in order afterward."

Some compare the number of baptisms to the amount of money spent for the campaign and say it was not worth it. Others say that satellite evangelism, radio evangelism, Internet evangelism, and social media evangelism have made public evangelism irrelevant. All of these attempts to find plausible arguments for not doing public evangelism are simply "broken cisterns that can hold no water" (Jer. 2:13).

The Truth about Public Evangelism

Public evangelism works! It is the essential method by which the Three Angels' Messages are carried to the world by the Seventh-day Adventist Church. Through public evangelism, people encounter the hope of eternal life. Thus, it works for people who are seeking for something better. It works for those who are looking for meaning in life. Quite simply, it works! Public evangelism is not an either-or to personal evangelism. Personal and small groups' evangelism are complementary to public evangelism. They prepare the way for public evangelism so that the public campaign can be shorter and more effective. Public evangelistic efforts gather in the harvest where personal efforts have been insufficient. There are many who have completed Bible studies, developed relationships in the church, and even started attending church, but they have never been baptized. However, when public evangelism is conducted, they commit their lives to Christ, are baptized, and become members of the church. Public evangelism works!

Moreover, the argument that those who join the church through public evangelism do not stay is not corroborated by facts.[1] A study in one conference in the United States indicated that out of every two people who leave the Adventist Church, almost one is someone who was born and raised in the church. The study also showed that new converts brought new energy and passion to the local congregation and inspired new growth within the church.

Public evangelism is just as alive and powerful today as it ever has been. We must not accept the myths and objections against it as valid arguments for abandoning it. Patriarchs and prophets did public evangelism; Jesus did public evangelism; the apostles did public evangelism; and it is still—and will continue to be—relevant in the 21st century. It is not human effort acting alone that brings power to public evangelism. It is the cooperation of the human with the Divine that makes the difference. The hour is late, Christ wants to come, and the harvest is ripe, but the laborers are few. Public evangelism is a powerful tool to reach hundreds of people with the gospel at the same time.

Public Evangelism Takes Time

Gone are the days when evangelistic campaigns would continue for twelve weeks. Thousands of souls were reaped through those campaigns. The preachers would prepare the soil, sow the seed, reap the harvest, and nurture the believers in one single campaign.

In many societies it would be difficult to pursue the same course today, and indeed, greater preparation allows for shorter campaigns to be successful. However, to limit public evangelism to only one week does a serious disservice to the proclamation of the gospel. Experience has shown that in such a short campaign, precious little is done to reap all those who would be ready to say yes to the invitation. Also, the one-week campaign does not allow for the presentation of the full range of the distinctive truths of the gospel.

At least fourteen messages should be presented in order to cover the basic doctrines of the church. This also gives individuals more time to develop a personal connection with Christ and the members of the church. Do not be carried away by objections and fear. Give public evangelism more time for prayer, Bible instruction, developing relationships, and clinching decisions.

---

3. Monte Sahlin, "Net Results,"*Adventist Review,* September 7, 2000, 16, http://archives.adventistreview. org/2000-1541/1541story1-3.html.

Public Evangelism Is Expensive

In the 21st century, everything comes with a price. Almost everything that exists costs something for someone. However, based on the perceived value of goods and services, people often overlook cost and indulge. Value matters! Proclaiming the gospel through public evangelism can be very costly. However, the salvation of lost souls that comes as a result of this proclamation is priceless; and for this reason, in Matthew 24:14 and 28:18–20, Jesus commissioned His church to preach the gospel to those who do not know Him. Therefore, the church must invest liberally in the fulfillment of this mission in full confidence that God will bring success to the efforts of His people.

Regarding an occasion when the church demonstrated insufficient ambition in evangelism, Ellen White said:

> I am convinced that we might have had a good hearing if our brethren had secured a suitable hall to accommodate the people. But they did not expect much, and therefore did not receive much. We cannot expect people to come out to hear unpopular truth when the meetings are advertised to be held in a basement, or in a small hall that will seat only a hundred persons. The character and importance of our work are judged by the efforts made to bring it before the public. When these efforts are so limited, the impression is given that the message we present is not worthy of notice. Thus by their lack of faith our laborers sometimes make the work very hard for themselves. (*Evangelism*, sec. 12, p. 422)

It is the responsibility of every church member to contribute to this lifesaving mission. Ignoring the call to finance public evangelism is equivalent to the situation described in Haggai 1:4 and 5: "Is it a time for you yourselves to dwell in your paneled houses, while this house lies in ruins? Now, therefore, thus says the Lord of hosts: consider your ways." Just as we care for our own material needs, we must also provide for the proclamation of the gospel.

In some places only 34–40% of church members return tithe, a portion of which is used to finance the evangelistic activities of the church. In some places the percentage is even less. What contribution does the other 56–60% make? Can those who faithfully return tithe to the Lord say that they have done enough and that they are willing to do no more for the proclamation of the gospel? Is the Lord stingy and ungenerous with His children? Does He close His providing hand in reluctance to bless them?

In *The Acts of the Apostles,* Ellen White wrote: "Money, time, influence— all the gifts they have received from God's hand, they will value only as a means of advancing the work of the gospel. Thus it was in the early church; and when in the church of today it is seen that by the power of the Spirit the members have taken their affections from the things of the world, and that they are willing to make sacrifices in order that their fellow men may hear the gospel, the truths proclaimed will have a powerful influence upon the hearers" (chap. 16, p. 71).

Many churches have allowed many other things to divert attention and funds from the all-important task of proclaiming the gospel publicly. In some places, the church is on the verge of losing, if it has not already lost, its sense of urgency toward its soul-winning mission. Public evangelism is an integral part of the fulfillment of that mission and must remain so. The church, therefore, must find an effective way to finance public evangelism.

Greater sacrifice on the part of many church members will be necessary to finance public evangelism. Every church should have a public evangelism budget. The members of the church should, in arranging their own personal budgets, set aside an amount for public evangelism. That portion should be presented to the church as an offering for evangelism. Each level within the organizational structure of the church should have an evangelism budget from which funds for evangelism are distributed appropriately to the constituency.

Innovative means should be devised to raise funds for public evangelism. Ellen White said: "I am greatly encouraged to believe that many persons not of our faith will help considerably by their means. The light given me is that in many places, especially in the great cities of America, help will be given by such persons" (*Evangelism,* sec. 2, p. 40). The church should implement special strategies to collect funds from such individuals. Public evangelism projects should form part of the annual offering cycle of every church. A special offering for public evangelism should be collected once or twice each quarter in order to acquire money for this vital aspect of the church's mission. The appeal for this offering should emphasize the importance of public evangelism. Additional fund-raising suggestions can be found in chapter 8 and appendix D.

How to Increase Attendance at Public Evangelistic Meetings

Great attendance at public evangelistic campaigns does not happen by chance; it requires deliberate planning. There are many reasons why the twelve-week campaigns of previous years were so successful. Aside from the novelty of the tent and the nightly convergence of a crowd in the community, the length of the campaign provided time for the meetings to grow night after night. One- or two-week campaigns, however, do not provide so much time for growth. Thus they must begin at capacity with prospects who have been well prepared. It is here that pre-campaign activity becomes important.

Some churches and evangelists print and distribute thousands of promotional flyers and hope that this will bring great attendance. However, people are far more accustomed to receiving printed materials today than in previous years, and most are no longer attracted by flyers. In fact, they may even be able to make flyers themselves that are more attractive. Often, instead of serving as a motivation to attend the meetings, flyers actually act as a deterrent.

Getting the members of the church engaged and working is the best way to build attendance at an evangelistic campaign. Members should be passionate about the campaign and committed to bringing their friends. They should have their prospects ready and arrive with them at the beginning of the campaign. If every member commits to bringing at least one person to the meetings, the attendance will not disappoint.

Building momentum for an evangelistic campaign takes time. The pastor cannot do it alone. The church as a whole must work as a team through prayer, organization, training, promotion, advertisement, and physical preparations. There must be less reliance on printed materials and greater emphasis on recruiting members to participate. The energy for getting good attendance at the meetings is dependent upon the work of the Holy Spirit and the active involvement of the church members.

How to Attract and Hold Attention

An engaging presentation of the message as well as interesting program features play a vital role in attracting the attention of the attendees and influencing them to return. Furthermore, when people are cognitively and emotionally engaged with the message, they are more likely to make positive decisions to accept and live in harmony with it. Ellen White made the following observation:

> In the cities of today, where there is so much to attract and please, the people can be interested by no ordinary efforts. Ministers of God's appointment will find it necessary to put forth extraordinary efforts in order to arrest the attention of the multitudes. And when they succeed in bringing together a large number of people, they must bear messages of a character so out of the usual order that the people will be aroused and warned. They must make use of every means that can possibly be devised for causing the truth to stand out clearly and distinctly. (*Testimonies for the Church,* vol. 9, chap. 12, p. 109)

In conducting public evangelism, it is important to be aware of the different styles in which people learn. A learning style is a person's preferred way of learning. It has nothing to do with how intelligent the person is or what skills they possess. It has to do with how each brain works most efficiently in acquiring, assimilating, and decoding new information. There is no such thing as a good or bad learning style. Different people have different learning styles, and some are able to benefit from more than one. Neil Fleming's theory identifies four different styles of learning:

Learning Styles

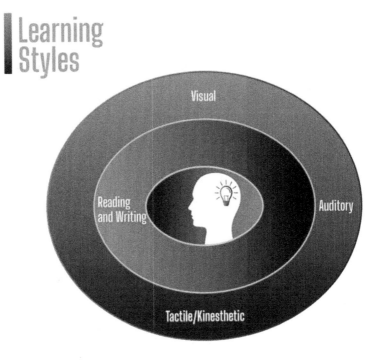

1. *Visual*: Visual learners do best with information that is presented visually. Use visual aids and illustrations such as videos, maps, charts, and diagrams to enhance the learning experience of this group. Visual learners tend to use mental images when trying to remember something.

2. *Auditory:* Those who belong to this group learn best when information is presented in an auditory or oral-language format. They find audio recordings to be beneficial. When trying to remember something, they can often "hear" the way someone told it to them or the way they previously said it out loud. They learn best in a listening speaking exchange.

3. *Reading and Writing:* These individuals learn best when information is presented in a written-language format. To capture their interest, use a projector to list the essential points of the presentation, or provide an outline that participants can

use to follow along. Magazines, books, and other written materials are also beneficial for this group.

4. *Tactile/Kinesthetic:* These persons learn best through tangible, hands-on experience. They prefer to learn through active participation and exploration. They benefit from practical demonstrations and activities that involve movement and physical contact.

The extent to which preachers are able to effectively communicate their messages depends to a great degree on how well they appeal to the learning styles of their listeners and capture their attention. In order to provide cognitive and emotional satisfaction for all the listeners, make sure that each evangelistic presentation and program incorporates some of the basic elements that appeal to each learning style. "Let every worker in the Master's vineyard, study, and plan, devise methods, to reach the people where they are. We must do something out of the common course of things. We must arrest the attention. We must be deadly in earnest. We are on the very verge of times of trouble and perplexities that are scarcely dreamed of" (*Evangelism,* sec. 6, pp. 122, 123). Succeeding chapters in this book include ideas and program features that may be used to arouse interest and appeal to various learning styles.

Preach to the Times

"Those who will study the manner of Christ's teaching, and educate themselves to follow His way, will attract and hold large numbers now, as Christ held the people in His day When the truth in its practical character is urged upon the people because you love them, souls will be convicted, because the Holy Spirit of God will impress their hearts" (*Testimonies for the Church,* vol. 6, p. 57).

Public evangelism is about preaching the gospel of Jesus. He must be the central focus of each meeting. Christ is the message that we proclaim. Proclaim Him! Jesus is always relevant. In your preaching, make Him relevant to each individual listener.

Many are questioning the meaning of the crises in the world and in their lives. Some are depressed by the incessant bombardment of distressing news reports in the media. They go to bed with anxiety and wake up with it too. The living conditions of many are less than desirable. Their physical experiences are daunting. Their income is far below their economic needs. Some who are affluent in this world's goods feel an inner void. There is still something missing.

The preacher must speak to the crises of the times but must present solutions that surpass those offered by politics, science, and philosophy. Scientists, sociologists, environmentalists, and engineers all make predictions. They look into the future and forecast what will soon come to pass. However, only the public evangelist, founded upon the Word of God and empowered by the Holy Spirit, can clearly navigate the gloom, chaos, and darkness and speak hope to those in despair. Preachers must take their hearers beyond the hopelessness, despair, and destruction of this world to that brand-new world that is on the horizon. The gospel message must be proclaimed with a sense of freshness.

George Washington Burnap said, "The three essentials for happiness in this life are something to do, something to love, and something to hope for." The gospel provides us with these essentials. Therefore, it is the solution that we must proclaim through public evangelism. Ellen White said: "We are under obligation to declare faithfully the whole counsel of God. We are not to make less prominent the special truths that have separated us from the world, and made us what we are; for they are fraught with eternal interests. We are to proclaim the truth to the world, not in a tame, spiritless way, but in demonstration of the Spirit and power of God" (*Testimonies to Ministers,* chap. 17, p. 470).

As the preacher preaches to the times, the message must be simple and have clear content, language, and direction. Do not make it confusing or exclusive. The message of the crucified and risen Lord must be presented in such a way that the people can understand it. There is power in the cross of Christ. Present this power to the people for them to grasp.

Let the people see clearly where they stand before the Lord and admit that they are sinners, then explain the provision Christ has made for them. Give them the opportunity to accept Him who died on the cross for their sins. He paid the price with His shed blood.

He arose from the dead. His resurrection offers the promise that they too will be resurrected. Through repentance, their sins will be blotted out and they will receive renewal from the Holy Spirit.

Preach with Power

The preacher must proclaim the message with power and conviction. Ellen White said: "Now, just now, we are to proclaim present truth, with assurance and with power. Do not strike one dolorous note; do not sing funeral hymns" (*Evangelism,* sec. 7, p. 180). She also said: "When these truths are given their rightful position in God's great plan, when they are presented intelligently and earnestly, and with reverential awe, by the Lord's servants, many will conscientiously believe because of the weight of evidence, without waiting for every supposed difficulty which may suggest itself to their minds, to be removed" (*Evangelism,* sec. 6, p. 122).

"Those who present the truth are to enter into no controversy. They are to preach the gospel with such faith and earnestness that an interest will be awakened. By the words they speak, the prayers they offer, the influence they exert, they are to sow seeds that will bear fruit to the glory of God. There is to be no wavering. The trumpet is to give a certain sound. The attention of the people is to be called to the third angel's message. Let not God's servants act like men walking in their sleep, but like men preparing for the coming of Christ" (ibid., p. 119).

Preach the Doctrinal Truth of the Church

Evangelistic proclamation must answer the ultimate questions of life. The preacher must focus on the doctrinal truths of the church that so often are not dealt with in regular worship services. Present these doctrines with proper sequencing so that the deepest questions of life are answered. The Sabbath and Creation, the origin of evil and the fall of humanity, the Cross and the assurance of salvation, the state of the dead and the resurrection, the sanctuary doctrine and the investigative judgment, the second coming of Christ and the creation of a new heaven and a new earth—these are to be preached for the listeners to understand. Through all these presentations, they should be able to discern God's saving actions to redeem humanity and restore His dominion on earth

Preach Repentance and Conversion

Each sermon in the public evangelistic campaign provides an opportunity for the preacher to inspire and motivate the hearers to a closer relationship with Christ. The resulting spiritual growth should be progressive until the individual surrenders all to Jesus and accepts baptism. Each presentation in effective public preaching should focus on conversion. Very eloquently, Ellen White stated: "When the Spirit of God takes possession of the heart, it transforms the life. Sinful thoughts are put away, evil deeds are renounced; love, humility, and peace take the place of anger, envy, and strife. Joy takes the place of sadness, and the countenance reflects the light of heaven." Acceptance of Christ leads to true repentance and conversion.

Call for Decisions

Greg Laurie tells about how he was just a two-week-old Christian when he was dragged into witnessing on a California beach. He was a starry-eyed convert with hardly any training. He hadn't even memorized the tract he was handing out. He walked up to a middle-aged woman and asked if he could talk to her about Jesus. Then he read the tract to her. When he got to the point where it asked the question, "Is there any good reason why you should not accept Christ?" she said, "No." Suddenly he froze. Not knowing what to do, he told her to close her eyes to pray while he frantically searched the tract for a prayer to read. He had not planned on being successful. As they were praying, he was sure it would not work. She was not going to become a Christian. But when they finished, she opened her eyes and said, "Something just changed inside of me." And he said, "Yeah, something just changed inside of me, too." The experience of leading someone to a decision for Christ had lit a fire in his soul, and he kept inviting people to accept Christ from that moment.

In public evangelism, the preacher must intentionally call for decisions. Effective evangelistic invitations that produce good results depend on clear content, clear language, and clear directions. Make it clear to the people what you want them to do. Ask them to raise their hand, stand, come forward, complete a response card, or indicate their response with some other gesture, clearly explaining *why* you are asking them to do so.

Dwight L. Moody shared an experience of how he once preached the gospel in a public meeting but did not give an invitation. When he closed, he asked the people to think about the message for the next week. However, that very night the Great Chicago Fire broke out. Many of the people who had been at the meeting that night died. From that day forward, he determined never to tell people to go home and think about the gospel. He would ask them to make a decision every time he preached. The preacher must be decisive, bold, and fearless to extend this invitation.

Review and Discussion
- *Why are many pastors and lay members reluctant to conduct public evangelistic campaigns?*
- *List three myths and three truths about public evangelism.*
- *Discuss the effect that the duration of an evangelistic campaign has on its success. For at least how many weeks should a campaign be conducted?*
- *What are the best ways to secure good attendance at public evangelistic meetings?*
- *Suggest some effective methods to acquire funding for public evangelism.*
- *Identify four principles that an evangelist should consider when preparing for public evangelistic preaching.*

9
Preparing for a Public Evangelistic Campaign

EVANGELISM is not an activity or an event. It is a lifestyle of the church that is lived by the members. There is no single approach that can be considered the only approach that has led to proven success. Rather, it is necessary to contextualize the method used in order to effectively address local needs. Even the most experienced and astute evangelists can glean ideas from others to increase their efficiency and success. This chapter and the next explain a plan for evangelism that will improve results in member involvement and soul winning. The words of Christ assure success in this endeavor: "I chose you and appointed you that you should go and bear fruit and that your fruit should abide, so that whatever you ask the Father in My name, He may give it to you" (John 15:16). Furthermore, in Isaiah 55:11, the Lord promised, "So shall My word be that goes out from My mouth; it shall not return to Me empty, but it shall accomplish that which I purpose, and shall succeed in the thing for which I sent it."

Whenever we invade Satan's territory to win souls, we can be certain that he will attack and will do so viciously. We must therefore plan and prepare wisely for battle. As Brian Tracey explains in his Six-P formula, "proper prior planning prevents poor performance." Success is not measured by what we begin but by what we complete, and we must make sure that everything is done with diligence, efficiency, and order for the results to be lasting. Ellen White said: "God is a God of order. Everything connected with heaven is in perfect order; subjection and thorough discipline mark the movements of the angelic host. Success can only attend order and harmonious action. God requires order and system in His work now no less than in the days of Israel. All who are working for Him are to labor intelligently, not in a careless, haphazard manner. He would have his work done with faith and exactness, that He may place the seal of His approval upon it" (*Patriarchs and Prophets*, chap. 33, p. 376).

Integrated Evangelistic Initiative

A combined-ministries evangelistic initiative is an approach in which diverse ministries of the church collaborate to achieve a shared evangelistic objective. Through this process, leaders of each ministry willingly make personal and departmental interests secondary to a shared interest of growing the kingdom of God and the local church. The collaborating ministries define the mission and strategy together, and each ministry commits personnel, time, and other resources for the execution of the initiative. Figure 1 illustrates this collaboration. The center of the diagram represents the evangelistic activity to be executed, while the converging ministry labels show how each department collaborates to execute the initiative.

The Evangelistic Year in Five Phases

To achieve evangelistic success within a given year, prudent planning is essential. Conference leaders, pastors, and ministry leaders must be deliberate in their planning and organization. Dividing the evangelistic year into distinct phases enables proper budgeting and assignment of resources, allows members to organize themselves for participation in the evangelistic initiative, and provides an established order for evangelistic achievement. Proper organization opens the way for the Holy Spirit to perform extraordinarily in the life of each believer, just like He did in the early church.

The evangelistic cycle in the local church should include spiritual renewal and empowerment for discipleship. While there is a degree of overlap between different phases, the five distinct phases to be established are: (1) recruitment and training, (2) revival and inspiration, (3) community outreach, (4) reaping, and (5) celebration and nurturing. While the following paragraphs propose a specific annual schedule for these five phases, this schedule should be adapted to fit the local context.

Recruitment and Training

This phase could go from September to November. This is the time to recruit the volunteers needed to carry out the various aspects of the evangelistic initiatives of the church. Among others, these include lay evangelists, Bible workers, and small group leaders, as well as coordinators for music, prayer, health programs, social activities, and social media ministries.

Conferences, pastors, districts, and local churches should also conduct training programs to equip pastors, lay leaders, and church members to carry out their various roles.

Figure 1: Integrated Evangelism

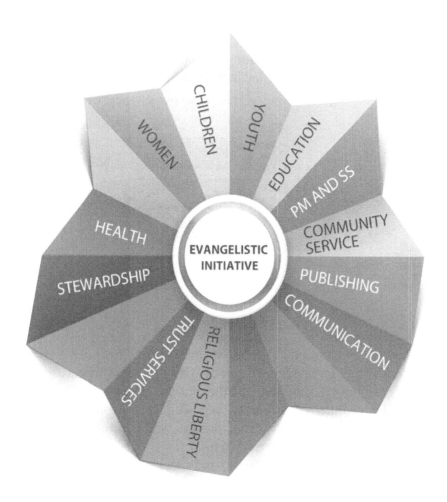

Community Outreach
October through March could be the time for Bible studies and community initiatives with the widest possible involvement of church members. However, since community initiatives and Bible studies should be an ongoing activity, this could be seen as a period

of intense operations to deepen social contacts with the members of the community and connect them with the church.

Reaping

This phase could include the months of January through May. This does not preclude evangelistic reaping at other times throughout the year, especially since Bible studies and community initiatives are ongoing and not everyone is ready to make a decision at the same time. This phase should combine all the most effective evangelistic strategies, engaging the members in close collaboration and concentrated effort to reap souls for the kingdom through what the Apostle Paul calls "the foolishness of preaching" (1 Cor. 1:21, KJV).

Celebration and Nurturing

In this phase, which could be carried out between May and August, new believers are welcomed into the fellowship of the church and spiritually nurtured. They are also immediately integrated into the evangelistic life of the church. The elements of this stage may include discipleship festivals, educational programs, and an educational package for new members. Other possible discipleship initiatives are addressed in chapter 17.

The Planning Meeting

It is advisable to have an evangelistic-planning meeting to set the agenda, determine the way forward, and establish procedure for an upcoming evangelistic campaign. Below are listed some considerations that the church may need to address, depending on its specific plans and circumstances. This list will be especially helpful for organizing large, multi-church evangelistic programs.

1. Personnel considerations:
    a. Churches that will be participating
    b. Campaign-coordinating committee (Evangelistic Action Committee in a single-church campaign)
    c. Evangelist
    d. Bible workers

e. Ushers
   f. Prayer-team members
   g. Campaign treasurer
   h. Other campaign committees and personnel
   i. Accommodations for evangelist and Bible workers
   j. Training for personnel
2. Dates for the following:
   a. The entire campaign (from intense field preparation to reaping and conservation of new believers)
   b. Meetings of the various committees
   c. Church and community-needs surveys
   d. Community-action initiatives to be executed
   e. Spiritual initiatives to be executed
   f. Public campaign
3. Field preparation:
   a. Territorial zoning for Bible workers
   b. Evangelistic visitation by church members
   c. Community-service activities
   d. Bible correspondence school
   e. Personal Bible studies
   f. Use of social media ministry
   g. Advertisement and promotion of the public campaign
4. Material considerations:
   a. The site for the public campaign
   b. Adequate seating for the congregation
   c. Musical equipment
   d. Audio-visual and public-address systems
   e. Other technological resources

    f. Production of sermon recordings and outlines
    g. Transportation
    h. Refreshments
    i. Financial expenses of the campaign
    j. Any other necessary resources

5. Programming considerations:
    a. Nightly features and program outline
    b. Musical program
    c. Use of drama
    d. Use of appropriate video clips
    e. Personal testimonies
    f. Story time or children's program
    g. Distribution of sermon recordings and outlines
    h. Day-time community activities
    i. Sabbath program
    j. Baptism

6. Follow-up plan for new converts:
    a. Reception and celebration
    b. New-believer orientation
    c. New-believer education package
    d. Mentorship program
    e. Integration into small groups and ministries

Field-Preparation Responsibilities

Every Church Member

Every member of the church should identify at least two persons whom they would like to see give their lives to Christ. They should be intentional about this mission and add these names to their own evangelistic prayer list. They should endeavor for these prospects to attend the social and spiritual activities organized by the church. Whenever the evangelistic campaign begins, they are to bring these prospects to the meetings.

Members must keep abreast of the progress of the visitors and pay attention to how they are enjoying the meetings. They should ascertain what concerns or questions their prospects may have and arrange for Bible workers to visit them. Members should also be supplied with decision and covenant cards that they will eventually utilize to secure decisions from their prospects.

Sabbath School Action Units and Small Groups

Each member should share the names on their evangelistic prayer list with the leader of the Sabbath School Action Unit or small group in which they are involved, who should add these names to the evangelistic prayer list of the group or unit. This list should include the name, address, and telephone number of each prospect that the group is presenting to the Lord in prayer, as well as the name and contact information of the member who submitted the name. The Evangelistic Action Committee will supply the form that leaders of Sabbath School Action Units and small groups will use for this list. Every week, during either Sabbath School or the small group meeting, there should be a brief progress report on the contacts being made. The names of individuals should not be mentioned in these report sessions. It is sufficient to just refer to the progress of the personal, evangelistic contact with that person.

Form A: Sample Evangelistic Prayer List for Sabbath School Action Unit or Small Group

**Mountainside Seventh-day Adventist Church
Evangelistic Prayer List for Sabbath School
Action Unit (or Small Group)**

Name or number of unit/group: _____

Name of unit/group leader: _____ Contact # _____

Unit or Group Member	Prospect	Phone or E-mail
1. _____	(a) _____	_____
Phone _____	(b) _____	_____
2. _____	(a) _____	_____
Phone _____	(b) _____	_____
3. _____	(a) _____	_____
Phone _____	(b) _____	_____
4. _____	(a) _____	_____
Phone _____	(b) _____	_____
5. _____	(a) _____	_____
Phone _____	(b) _____	_____
6. _____	(a) _____	_____
Phone _____	(b) _____	_____
7. _____	(a) _____	_____
Phone _____	(b) _____	_____
8. _____	(a) _____	_____
Phone _____	(b) _____	_____
9. _____	(a) _____	_____
Phone _____	(b) _____	_____
10. _____	(a) _____	_____
Phone _____	(b) _____	_____

Evangelistic Action Committee

Each Sabbath School Action Unit or evangelistic small group will provide a copy of its list to the Evangelistic Action Committee, which should compose a master evangelistic prayer list for the church and convene evangelistic intercession forums on a regular basis. The purpose of these forums is to pray intentionally for the persons whose names are on the evangelistic prayer list. A sample of a master evangelistic prayer list for the church is shown on the next page. The Evangelistic Action Committee will keep a copy of this master list for use in evangelistic planning. A copy should also be given to the prayer team, pastor, evangelist, Bible workers, and Bible school coordinator.

The Prayer Team

There should be a designated prayer team with an appointed leader, assistant leader, and secretary. Before the campaign begins, the prayer team will meet every Sabbath morning and at other times according to convenience in order to present the names of the prospects to the Lord. Their prayer should be, "Lord give us these souls and supply their needs according to Your good will and purpose." Members who are having difficulties getting through to their prospects or whose prospects are having challenges may share these issues with the prayer team in order to petition the Lord for solutions. The team should present the campaign to the Lord in prayer continuously. They should pray about all the aspects of the organization and execution of the pre-campaign, campaign, and post-campaign.

The role of the prayer team is very important to the effectiveness and success of the campaign. Team members should be chosen early and trained for their tasks so that they can begin to function far in advance of the beginning of the campaign. This team may be selected from the churches, departments, small groups, or Sabbath School Action Units that are involved in the campaign. Team members should be baptized, fully committed individuals who love the Lord, love to pray, believe in prayer, love people, and desire to see souls come to the Lord. They should be people who know their duties and are willing volunteers. They should have their own experiences of answered prayers, as well as the assurance that there is nothing more powerful and important than prayer in gaining decisions for the Lord, resolving issues and disputes, and facing life's challenges.

The Church Pastor

The church pastor is the program director—or in the case of a departmental or interdepartmental initiative, one of the program directors—and as such, is an integral part of the total execution of the plan. The pastor leads, supervises, and supports, ensuring that the required training and resources are available to execute the program from start to finish. Even if someone other than the pastor is conducting the campaign, the pastor must take responsibility for preparing the field and overseeing the campaign.

Form B: Sample Master Evangelistic Prayer List for the Local Church

The Mountainside Seventh-day Adventist Church
Master Evangelistic Prayer List

Name of Prospect	Phone or E-mail	Church Member
1.		
	Phone	
2.		
	Phone	
3.		
	Phone	
4.		
	Phone	
5.		
	Phone	
6.		
	Phone	
7.		
	Phone	
8.		
	Phone	
9.		
	Phone	

The pastor will divide the territory into zones and assign a zone to each Bible worker, providing them with a prospect list for the zone that corresponds to them. This list is taken from the master evangelistic prayer list and includes the names, addresses, and telephone numbers of prospects who are receiving or have already completed a series of Bible lessons. A comprehensive prospect list should also be provided to the evangelist if this is someone other than the pastor.

Bible Workers

It is important to secure Bible workers for the campaign as early as possible. Each Bible worker should set goals with respect to the number of persons they expect to influence for baptism. They report directly to the pastor. Bible workers may be volunteers, or they may be paid. They should be experienced with the art of persuasion so that, through prayer and dependence upon the Holy Spirit, they will be able to influence prospects to make decisions to follow the Lord and be baptized. They may utilize the commitment card provided in Form A of chapter 4. Thus they would basically be reviewing the subjects that were already presented and addressing the subjects that have not yet been covered.

Working with the prospect list given to them by the pastor, the Bible workers will follow up with the mature prospects within their respective zones. To obtain information about these prospects, they should contact the members who are working with them. The Bible workers will also generate their own lists of prospects, which they will share with the pastor, who in turn will share them with the Evangelistic Action Committee and prayer team for record keeping and prayer.

Bible School Coordinators

A small group of between three and seven members (depending on the size of the church) should be selected and trained to serve as Bible school coordinators. They should receive a copy of the master list of prospects to guide them in the fulfillment of their responsibilities, which include:

• Procuring the correct number of Bible lessons for the prospects.

- Determining who should receive the lessons.
- Staying in contact with both members and prospects for follow-up.
- Staying in contact with the leaders of the Sabbath School Action Units and small groups regarding the progress being made with the program.
- Distributing the lessons to the members for them to conduct the studies with their prospects.
- Receiving completed lessons to ensure that they are properly graded, recorded, and returned to the prospects.
- Keeping accurate record of all the lessons distributed and returned.
- Arranging the graduation and certification for all the persons who have completed the lessons.
- Giving progress reports and information about the graduation and certification of the students to the conference Bible school director (if there is someone with that designation).

Evangelistic Mingling: Preparing the Field for effective Soul Winning

We are living in a rapidly secularized culture in which many classify themselves as post–Christians, non-Christians, religious nones, agnostics, spiritual but not religious, and atheists among others. However, there remains a growing number of believers in Christ (Christians). Fruit bearing, which is influencing the non-committed into a committed relationship with Christ, is the mandate of Jesus to His believers (John 15:5-7, NKJV). Evangelistic mingling is a crucial pretext to fruit bearing. It is all the programs, activities and initiatives that are initiated to reach people, build relationships with them and influence them to engage in Christ centered activities that lead to personal surrender to Christ and decision to become members of the community of the Christian faith.

On the other hand, Evangelism includes the message, the method, the medium, the occasion and the audience. In this section it is important to highlight four essentials for evangelistic mingling which are growing in intimacy with the Supernatural, having community members talking about what the Church members are doing, engaging with the community to satisfy human needs and influencing the community to hope for something. A seven-point process towards achieving effectiveness in evangelistic mingling is also relevant.

Growing in Intimacy with the Supernatural

In Mark 3:14 Jesus called the disciples to Himself on a mountain and there ordained them to abide with Him. Situated in that abiding relationship, He commissioned them to preach and do ministries, addressing human needs and alleviating suffering. In mobilizing His followers for ministry He said, "I am the vine, ye are the branches: He that abideth in me, and I in him, the same bringeth forth much fruit: for without me ye can do nothing. If a man abide not in me, he is cast forth as a branch, and is withered; and men gather them, and cast them into the fire, and they are burned. If ye abide in me, and my words abide in you, ye shall ask what ye will, and it shall be done unto you" (John 15:5-7, NKJV). These texts signal the importance for each believer to experience a growing intimate relationship with the Supernatural. This is a conscientious and deliberate communion with Him that enables relational closeness and spiritual growing.

Ellen White magnified Jesus' example in Ministry of Healing p. 143 "Christ's method alone will give true success in reaching the people. The Savior mingled with men as one who desired their good. He showed His sympathy for them, ministered to their needs, and won their confidence. Then He bade them, 'Follow Me.'

To achieve this intimate growth with the Lord, 'ongoing members' evangelization programs are essential ingredients for pastors, church leadership and ministry leaders to establish in order to create the environment and motivation for members to engage in such spiritual mingling. These include engaging the members in all the core values of discipleship (worship, fellowship, outreach, evangelism, stewardship, sacrifice and love) that strengthen their up reach, in reach and outreach aptitudes.

Some of the organized initiatives that position members to enjoy the intimacy of interacting with the supernatural are weekend spiritual revivals, Daniel and Revelation seminars, doctrinal bible studies, personal and group prayers, spiritual retreats where people camp in the Word, well planned weekly worship services in the church and continuous motivation for members to engage in family worship. Mingling with the Supernatural is foundational to the abiding relationship that Jesus calls each disciple to experience. Sharing the joy of personal abiding, inspires members to participate in the mission of the church within the local community and farther a field where possible. Bearing much fruit results naturally from interacting with the Supernatural.

Have community members talking about what the Church is doing

As members mingle and enjoy what the Lord is doing for them and in their lives through their interactions with Him, they develop a growing desire and anxiety to be involved in personal and organized activities that improve the image of the Church in the community. They are not content with a church that is just domiciled in the community, being neither salt, light nor leaven. They are more content with a church that is actively doing things that benefit residents, but more so, a church that works with the community to address human needs while contributing to community development. This kind of collaboration and social partnership inspires residents and entrepreneurs within the community to engage in dialogue or overt talks about the positive nature of the churches' impact within the community. People want to be associated with a church that is impacting lives and contributing to community development.

In the book *Growing Young*, the authors talk about "a Church for the city" (page 235), that young people and others could imagine themselves joining. It is that church that incarnates Jesus in its community through the members' active involvement in social justice initiatives in the surrounding neighborhoods. A young lady who was moved by the involvement of the Church in the community and who is now a member of the church said; "I love that I met these people at a festival. I didn't need to be looking for Jesus or a Church to find them. They were out there doing their thing as opposed to a lot of churches that try to get you to come to their events in the church building" (p.235).

She said that the primary focus of the Church at the festival was not to promote its services, but to make its city a better place. The associate pastor of a mega church on the island of Barbados who became a Seventh-day Adventist said she was moved by the intelligence of the young people of the Seventh-day Adventist Church who were active in their community and were willing to do programs for her radio station, though she was not a member of their Church. As she listened to them she said she was moved and wanted to know more about what they believed. She eventually became a member of the Seventh-day Adventist Church with her radio and television ministries of over twenty million listenership globally.

Engage with the community to satisfy human needs

People have a plethora of emotional/mental, social and physical needs. They are living with expectations of overcoming these needs and are hopeful that persons who can help will take them into consideration. When they are convinced that God's intervention can make a difference, they will be drawn to mingle with or serve the Supernatural, the God of Host. It is a part of the fundamental responsibility of the church to assist them in finding solution to their issues. Jesus spoke to His believers about how to be proactive in addressing their needs Matthew 25:36-44. It must be emphasized that the church's primary motive for addressing their socio-emotional needs is not in exchange for church membership. It is because this is a part of God's plan to "… send rain on the just and on the unjust" Matthew 5:45.

In his book *Building a people of power,* Robert Linthicum describes one of the responses that a church gives to its community; *the church with the community,* in which the church does not ignore the needs of the community to focus on its own parochial interest. Instead it works with principal players within the community based on assessed needs and devise solutions as an incarnational approach in addressing community needs. It is a partnership approach that invites residents to participate with the church or the church joins residents in providing authentic outreach ministry to alleviate community needs.

Influence the community to hope for something

When the members of the church are effectively and genuinely engaged in mingling or interacting with the supernatural and addressing needs within the community people will be influenced to develop expectations of other possible impacts that could satisfy their personal interests. In this case, the church's soul winning impact will not only be centrifugal, where members carry the gospel out to others based on the command of Jesus in Matthew 28:19-20. It will also be centripetal, where people come to the center of action the church, as originally intended by God when he said; "2 And it shall come to pass in the last days, that the mountain of the LORD's house shall be established in the top of the mountains, and shall be exalted above the hills; and all nations shall flow unto it. 3 And many people shall go and say, come ye, and let us go up to the mountain of the LORD, to the house of the God of Jacob; and he will teach us of his ways, and we will walk in his paths: for out of Zion shall go forth the law, and the word of the LORD from Jerusalem" (Isaiah 2:2-3).

This anticipated response in Isaiah was in harmony with God's centrifugal force of witnessing emphasized in His promise to Abraham in Genesis 12:1-3. This text demonstrates, God did not intend his blessing to reside only with Abraham and his immediate family. He blessed Abraham to be a conduit through whom "all the peoples of the earth will be blessed." The New Testament corroborates the centripetal effort of witnessing where the believers, after Pentecost, lived in loving community, fellowshipped with each other, engaged in sacrificial giving and attracted (centripetal) their neighbors (see Acts 2:42-47). Resulting from their spiritual and social mingling, the Lord added "to their number daily those who were being saved" (Acts 2:47). The centrifugal witnessing mode (disciples going outward) was also pronounced as the followers put into action Jesus' Great Commission (Matthew 28:19-20) and His announcement in Acts 1:8, "…and you will be my witnesses in Jerusalem, and in all Judea and Samaria, and to the ends of the earth"

Christians must be involved in both the Centripetal and centrifugal witnessing modes. The people of the community will talk about what the church is doing as the members genuinely mingle with the supernatural, with each other and with others of the community. As they see transformation of lives and feel the impact of the Church influencing social change in the society, not only will they talk, they will conceive the Church through positive lenses hence, improved image of the Church in the community. As their curiosity heightens, rather than waiting to be approached, some will initiate the process by seeking to become associated with the Church. Those who do not come must be reached. Both the centripetal and centrifugal gospel forces complement each other in winning the world to Christ. Ellen White said; "God could have reached his goal of saving sinners, without our help; but in order for us to develop a character like that of Christ, we must participate in His work. In order to enter into His joy the joy of seeing souls redeemed by his sacrifice we must participate in His work for their redemption". *The Desire of Ages,* chapter 14, p. 120.

How to achieve effectiveness in evangelistic mingling
1. Put in place an evangelistic mingling committee
2. Recruit and engage visionary and resourceful members on this committee.
3. The committee should propose a list of mingling options on how members may interact with each other and with the residents of the wider community to realize the following objectives:
    i. To motivate the members to interact with the Supernatural
    ii. To achieve initiatives that will enable residents of the community to talk about what the church is doing to improve services and amenities to residents within the community
    iii. To organize and mobilize the church members to do things for and with the residents of the community.
    iv. To influence residents of the community to develop the expectations and desire to associate with the church
4. Determine how each option will function and the implementation details

5. The Church Board should consider the options and take actions on the most practical, relevant and achievable.
6. Persons should be recruited, trained and deployed to implement the initiatives.
7. Evaluate the processes and projects and take relevant action.

The centripetal and centrifugal dimensions of witnessing are biblical patterns that the Church must effectively utilize to impact the secularized cultures of this century and beyond. We must be intentional and deliberate in addressing human needs while, not as an exchange, give them the opportunity to make a decision for Christ. Evangelistic mingling is essential to soul winning. Our missionary creator and Savior is ready to guide us as a Church to be both centripetal and centrifugal as we engage to realize the promise to Abraham; "that all the families of the earth might be blessed through him!"

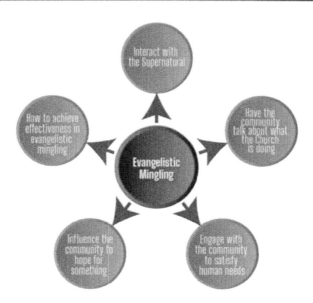

Field-Preparation Activities
Community-Empowerment Projects

Initiatives that meet material and social needs strengthen the image of the church and provide opportunities to establish relationships with individuals in the community. As explained in chapter 3, each departmental task force involved in the campaign should investigate the needs of the community in its particular area of ministry, whether that be women, men, youth, children, or health. After the needs are analyzed, the task force could organize a community-development day, inviting members of both the church and the community to participate in a project that will benefit the local community. Specific suggestions for community initiatives for each departmental ministry are provided in chapters 9–14. Some of the community initiatives in which the church can engage include:

- Health clinics
- Christian counseling services
- Food distribution
- Clothing distribution
- Ministry to the blind and disabled
- Reading classes
- Language classes in multi-cultural communities
- Music lessons
- Computer literacy classes
- Classes in arts and crafts
- Training in various sports
- Tree planting
- Community cleanup
- House repairs and construction
- Community-action campaigns against drug use, domestic abuse, and pornography
- Establishment and dedication of anti-crime monuments in volatile communities
- Lifestyle and temperance parades
- Community leaders' town hall meetings hosted by the church
- Unity concerts in the community
- Gender-roles conferences

Community-Outreach Forums

To further address community needs in its area of ministry, and as a transition to addressing the spiritual needs of individuals, each task force involved in the campaign should conduct an outreach forum.

A neutral location where people will feel free to attend—such as a school, community center, or home—is ideal for such a forum, although the local church may be used as well. The number of seminars to be presented in this forum will depend upon the needs of the local area, as revealed by the results of the community-needs survey conducted by the departmental task force.

Advertise these seminars through face-to-face contacts, the local community bulletin board, e-mail, text messaging, Facebook, Twitter, or other electronic communication, and local newspaper, radio, or television. Those involved should invite others to participate in these forums, especially those who are on their evangelistic prayer list. These may be family members, relatives, friends, coworkers, schoolmates, or neighbors. Those who invite others to participate in these forums should themselves be present at the forums.

If appropriate and possible, serve some refreshments. Select the best available presenter who will be able to get and hold people's attention and impart valuable material in the content of the presentation. Have one or two people give a personal testimony that will be relevant to the topic. Be sure to conclude each forum with a spiritual nugget. At the conclusion of each forum, the topic, date, and venue for the next should be announced.

A graduation ceremony may be held for all who participate in these forums, with appropriate certificates issued to those who complete them. This graduation could take place at the church or at the commencement of the public campaign.

Bible Studies

After the conclusion of the outreach forums, or whenever the prospects have matured through personal contact, the members should initiate Bible lessons with them. If some members are not confident in their abilities to conduct Bible studies, they should invite other members of the church to join them in administering these lessons. The studies could also be done in a group setting where people discuss the questions and write the correct answers.

The Bible school coordinators, in cooperation with the Evangelistic Action Committee, will provide lessons to the members for this purpose. These lessons may be printed or electronic, or they may be delivered via social media. The prospects are to study the lessons weekly until they have completed the series. Make sure to have a diverse selection of lessons available so that the same series is not used repeatedly. Some prospects will complete more than one series of lessons before making a commitment to follow the Lord.

At the opening night of the campaign, a graduation may be held for those who have completed the lessons. Those who have not yet completed them at the beginning of the campaign may receive their certificates at other times during the campaign or at a special program at the church to recognize their commitment and completion of the lessons.

Evangelistic Fellowship Day

The Evangelistic Action Committee, or the departmental task forces involved in the campaign, should plan a recreational or educational excursion or a fellowship day at the church or some other venue. Church members will invite their friends and evangelistic prospects to this activity, which could take place around the time the prospects complete the fourth or fifth Bible study lesson.

One of the features of the day could be a review of the Bible lessons completed so far. That way the prospects would be able to share intelligently in the discussion. The day could also include singing, preaching the Word, personally introducing the prospects to various members of the church, and providing an opportunity for individuals who so desire to meet in a prayer circle with the members of the prayer team. It may or may not be the best time to promote the campaign; however, it would be good for the evangelist to be present as the guest speaker. The purpose of this activity is to broaden the scope of relationship building and to showcase for the prospects what the Seventh-day Adventist Church offers to individuals and families.

Social Impact Projects Form

Each ministry will determine and develop its approach to address human needs, improve the image of the Church in the community, connect people to Christ and secure decision for the Kingdom of God and the Church. This form provides a template for the ministries of the church to utilize to comprehensively recruit and equip leaders and members in the process of executing specific social projects in the community.

Guide for teams in Preparation of the territory for soul winning

Description	Response	Comments
Objectives of the project/activity		
Target group to be benefited by the project/activity		
Time frame for the project / activity (beginning and closing dates)		
Persons needed as participants to execute the project/activity		
Number of participants needed to execute this activity		
Method of recruiting participants		
Type of training needed for each participant or team leader		
Date for the training		
Person(s) who will conduct the training		
Materials or resources that are needed for the implementation		
Where will this activity be implemented?		

Bible Counselors Preparation Plan

For effectiveness in the function of the Bible Counselors, it is important that they be organized and trained to fulfill their roles. The information provided in this section outlines the process in organizing this essential group of mission workers to execute their function and to secure the greatest possible number of souls for the Kingdom of God.

1. The territory of the Evangelistic campaign shall be divided into zones based on the size of the territory
2. The Bible Counselors are divided into teams and assigned to zone. Counselors may be:

   a. Pastors

   b. Ministerial Interns

   c. Theology Students

   d. Trained lay bible counselors

   e. Committed and competent lay members of the Church
3. Each zone shall have a Pastor or Elder assigned who will provide leadership and motivation to the team in order to achieve the established desired outcome for the zone
4. Each zonal team shall have regular meetings to assess progress and formulate strategy as may be deemed necessary.
5. Each team needs to answer the following questions (see the table below Bible Workers Preparation Guide which is similar to the questions listed here):

   i. Name of the campaign.

   ii. Venue of the campaign.

   iii. Number of churches involved in the campaign.

   iv. How many people are in the prayer team?

   v. Number of active members in the church within the campaign zone

   vi. Number of non-active church members within the church or zone

   vii. Number of SDA children and adolescents in the church or zone

viii. Number of SDA young people between 16 and 35 years within the church or zone.
ix. Number of SDA ladies within the church or zone x. Number of SDA men within the church or zone.
x. Number of regular visitors who attend the church within the community or zone
xi. Number of active small or life groups within the Church or zone
xii. What is the strategy of the team to connect and share with non-members?
xiii. What social projects are being conducted within the community or zone?
xiv. Number of non-Adventists that are actively involved in doing bible studies
xv. Number of visitors from the zone that are attending the meetings
xvi. What are the means of transportation from the zone for people to attend the meetings?
xvii. How many persons are prepared to be baptized from the zone or life groups?
xviii. What is the visitation schedule of each team?
xix. What is the retention and consolidation plan for the new members?

Guide for teams in Preparation of the territory for soul winning

In order to prepare for any evangelistic campaign, each team must be engaged in social activities. Such activities must be conducted as mentioned before, in order to:

i. Attract the attention of persons in the community.
ii. Mingle with people on a social level.
iii. Improve the image of the church in the community.
iv. Permit people of the community to have positive things to say about the church
v. Enhance their desire to be associated with Seventh-day Adventists
vi. Address some of the social, physical, emotional and spiritual needs of persons in the community.

vii. Demonstrate that the Church has interest in the wellbeing of people in the community.
viii. Demonstrate that the Church is active and essential within the community.

The following questions are important to help each team organize for and prepare the field effectively before the campaign begins.

1. What specific evangelistic objective does the team have?
2. In what specific initiative or social project to win souls is this team involved?
3. In what specific demographic group will this team concentrate?
4. What does the team need to know about the demographic group to determine the type of initiative to be utilized in order to prepare them to make decisions for Christ?
5. How many persons are needed to execute this initiative?
6. How will team members be educated or trained to participate in the project or initiative?
7. When will the training of the participants and the initiative or project begin?
8. How will volunteers be recruited to participate in the initiative or project?
9. Who will be responsible for leading this initiative?
10. What role will each participant play in the project or initiative?
11. What resources are required for the execution of this project or initiative?
12. How will the resources be obtained?
13. Who will be responsible for obtaining them?
14. How will the effectiveness of this project or initiative be evaluated?
15. Who will be responsible for ensuring that the evaluation is carried out?

Bible Workers Preparation Guide

Nu.	Description	Response	Comment (if any)
1	Name of the campaign		
2	Venue of the campaign		
3	Number of churches involved in the campaign		
4	How many people are in the prayer team?		
5	Number of active members in the church within the campaign zone		
6	Number of non-active church members within the church or zone		
7	Number of SDA children and adolescents in the church or zone		
8	Number of SDA young people 16 precampaign 35 years within the church or zone		
9	Number of SDA ladies within the church or zone		
10	Number of SDA men within the church or zone		
11	Number of regular visitors who attend the church within the community or zone		
12	Number of active small or life groups within the Church or zone		
13	What is the strategy of the team to connect and share with non-members?		
14	What social projects are being conducted within the community or zone?		
15	Number of non-Adventists that are actively involved in doing bible studies		
16	Number of visitors from the zone that are attending the meetings		

17	What are the means of transportation from the zone for people to attend the meetings		
18	How many persons are prepared to be baptized from the zone or life groups?		
19	What is the visitation schedule of each team?		
20	What is the retention and consolidation plan for the new members?		

List of Bible Counselors

Nu.	Description	Team Leader	Other team member
1	Name		
	Telephone		
2	Name		
	Telephone		
3	Name		
	Telephone		
4	Name		
	Telephone		
5	Name		
	Telephone		
5	Name		
	Telephone		

Review and Discussion
- *What scriptural assurance do church members have that success will attend their soul-winning endeavors?*
- *Explain your understanding of an integrated evangelistic initiative.*
- *Identify the five phases of the evangelistic year and describe the activities to be executed in each one.*
- *Name three items to be addressed in each of the six areas of consideration in the evangelism-planning meeting.*
- *Briefly explain each of the seven areas of responsibility in the field preparation process.*
- *How would you execute the four field preparation activities?*
- *Devise an effective plan for procuring, distributing, collecting, and keeping record of field preparation materials such as Bible lessons in your church.*

10
The Public Campaign

AFTER APPROPRIATE PREPARATION has been completed, a reaping campaign should be held. This campaign may be held in a church, tent, or rented facility and should last two weeks or more, depending on the precampaign preparation that has been done. It may be conducted as a midweek series, weekend series, or full-week series. The theme will correspond with the primary ministries that are involved. This public campaign should be a spiritual encounter that attracts souls to Christ, motivating them to live in readiness for the Second Advent and encouraging them to make their decision for baptism.

Campaign Finance

Fund-Raising

Campaign financing is a costly endeavor and is becoming more costly. Organizers must be very innovative to ensure that they secure adequate funding to execute the initiative effectively and lead souls to the Lord. A fund-raising committee should be appointed to plan, organize, and execute special activities for obtaining additional funds to offset expenses. The following list contains several fund-raising suggestions. Additional methods can be found in appendix D.

- Collecting a nightly offering.
- Distributing recorded messages (as previously explained).
- Asking for contributions from those using the campaign's transport services.
- Conducting a special fund-raising drive among church members.

- Conducting a campaign bake sale, garage sale, or market day.
- Offering refreshments or other products for sale at the nightly meetings.

Treasurer

In the case of a multi-church campaign, it will be necessary to choose a campaign treasurer. If only one church is involved, the church treasurer could fulfill this function. The campaign treasurer's duties include the following:

- Preparing a budget for the campaign based on all income and expenses and obtaining authorization from the church board or the campaign coordinating committee.
- Ensuring where necessary that a checking account is opened in the name of the campaign so that all financial transactions can be completed using checks.
- Collecting all financial contributions for the campaign and depositing all funds to the campaign account.
- Ensuring that all financial receivables for the campaign are collected.
- Making authorized disbursements of funds.
- Ensuring that all expenditures are made according to budgetary allocation or official authorization by the board or the campaign coordinating committee.
- Ensuring that all authorized campaign expenses are paid.

Advertisement and Promotion

Church members should bring those whom they invited to the outreach forums or who have started or completed the Bible lessons. Thus these individuals will have already been introduced to the essential doctrines of the church and the basic concepts of salvation. However, if some prospects did not participate in the forums or Bible studies, this should not discourage church members from inviting them to the public campaign.

The Communication Department, or a specially appointed promotion team, will be responsible for advertising the campaign using billboards, posters, and television and radio advertisements, handbills distributed in the targeted area, social media, and other means. A vehicle-mounted public-address system can be used to promote the campaign while driving through the community. Each week, elders, departmental leaders, and others should promote the campaign in the participating churches.

Community Service

Appoint a team to be responsible for community services in connection with the campaign. This team will collect, launder, and package clothing to be distributed to the needy. It will also be responsible for keeping extra changes of clothing at hand for individuals who request baptism without prior notice. The territory should be divided between different volunteers, who will work with the needy and carry out community service visitation.

Daytime Activities

Daytime outreach activities, preferably at the meeting site, will facilitate special community initiatives that train people to develop skills, attitudes, and critical thinking and that provide other forms of empowerment. This personal and community empowerment enables individuals to further appreciate the results of accepting the Lord as they experience lifestyle changes in areas other than the spiritual dimension. A committee should be appointed to coordinate these activities. The responsibilities of this committee include:

- Planning the daytime activities to be conducted.
- Finding and selecting instructors for each activity.
- Procuring the equipment, materials, and resources required to execute the program.
- Arranging the graduation (and certification where applicable) of those who have satisfactorily completed the training program.
- Where possible, working with other institutions to offer training.
- Promoting the program and enrolling people in training.
- Arranging for media coverage of this aspect of the program.

These training programs can be offered at the campaign site or another appropriate location. They consist of short, structured courses for which people will receive certification at the conclusion of the campaign or shortly thereafter. Some programs may be continued after the campaign, and they may begin before the campaign as well.

These initiatives demonstrate that the church adopts a holistic approach to people's lives and is not only concerned with spiritual matters. Some of these programs can be conducted in cooperation with vocational schools or other organizations that can grant certification upon satisfactory completion of training. The objectives of these programs can include helping individuals acquire a livelihood, teaching optimal use of equipment or devices, providing basic life management training, or improving people's social adjustment and enjoyment. The following are some examples of areas in which training could be offered:

- Mediation and conflict-resolution techniques
- Marriage enrichment
- Effective parenting
- Parenting for prospective parents
- Child care
- Caretaking of the elderly
- Managing personal finances
- First aid
- Reading
- Writing
- Languages
- Use of computers
- Use of the Internet
- Use of social media
- Health
- Cooking
- Dressmaking and tailoring
- Knitting
- Craft making
- Gardening
- Farming

- Construction
- House painting
- Welding
- Crime control and management
- Driving
- Popular sports
- Swimming

Material Considerations for the Campaign

Transportation

There should be a transportation coordinator and transportation team, which should include representatives from each church that is participating in the campaign. The coordinator ensures that transports are provided on designated routes every night to take people to the campaign. A contingency plan should be in place in case one of the transports cannot run. There should be someone on each transport who is responsible for maintaining order. The coordinator receives and records the money collected on each transport (if required) and turns it over to the campaign treasurer, keeping accurate records of the number of times each transport runs and ensuring that the owner of each transport is paid.

Security and Maintenance

There should be a security and maintenance leader who is responsible for the following:
- Protection of the meeting site, including all equipment and valuables.
- Cleanliness of the meeting site and surrounding areas at all times.
- Accessibility of proper water and sanitation facilities.
- Coordination and security of vehicle parking.

Technology

Volunteer electricians and technicians should be found to attend to the following technical aspects of the campaign:'

- Ensuring that the campaign facility is properly wired and lit and that it has reliable electrical service.
- Obtaining an adequate mixing board, microphones, amplifiers, speakers, computer, projector, screen, and video equipment.
- Ensuring that all equipment is properly installed and operated.
- Coordinating the recording and broadcasting of the campaign on cable television, radio, Internet, and other social media.
- Obtaining the necessary personnel to facilitate such broadcasting.

Digital Technology Coordinators

Volunteers should be chosen to coordinate the digital recordings. They are to record the sermons in the campaign, collect orders, and distribute the recordings through the best possible means. This may be used as a source of income for the campaign budget. Alternatively, when possible, the recordings could be distributed as a courtesy. Members may purchase them to distribute as well, and this could become a special media ministry for some members.

Decoration

Select a team to be responsible for beautifying the campaign site for the evangelistic occasion. This team will obtain attractive floral arrangements for the nightly meetings and Sabbath services. As needed, they will also choose appropriate material from which to make and install drapes in the platform area.

Team Responsibilities during the Campaign

The Prayer Team

As previously indicated, the prayer team should consist of an adequate number of baptized, committed church members. These individuals should be willing, spiritual, and responsible and must have the success of the campaign at heart. The team should meet before each nightly meeting to petition the Lord for His guidance in every aspect of the program. If the leader of the prayer team has to be absent one night, the assistant leader should lead out. As often as possible, the pastor, evangelist, and other members of the evangelistic team should join the team for this special time of prayer.

During each meeting, the team should pray for the evangelist, church members, visitors, persons requesting special prayer, all team members, and any other relevant matter. When people submit their names at the altar or in the prayer box, these names should be presented to the prayer team to petition the Lord on their behalf. Those with special needs who so desire may be brought to the team for special prayer. During the appeal each night, the team is to plead with the Lord to move upon the hearts of individuals to yield to the promptings of the Holy Spirit and make their decision for baptism.

Arrange the place in which the prayer team meets so as to be free from distractions. The atmosphere of the room should give a sense of "holy ground." Visuals related to answered prayer and materials that focus on prayer or communication with the Lord are conducive to this end. There is no set way to create such an atmosphere. Rather, those in charge should use their creativity, allowing the Spirit of the Lord to guide them in arranging the room.

Make sure that each team member has the opportunity to participate. Specific nightly duties may be assigned to different team members with sufficient anticipation to adequately prepare. These duties could include selecting and reading a Scripture passage on a relevant topic, presenting a short excerpt from the Spirit of Prophecy, praying for the evangelist, praying for the guests, praying for those making decisions, organizing the room, etc. The team could also include other members of the church by assigning them various times throughout the day to pray for the success of the campaign.

Music

There should be a designated music coordinator for the campaign. This should be someone who has good organizational skills. They are responsible for ensuring that the musical program flows smoothly each night. This includes establishing a schedule of who is responsible for all musical duties in the campaign, including song service, special music, meditation songs, and appeal songs.

A praise team with an adequate number of capable persons should be selected. This team will serve as the evangelist's special singers who will be available every night and on Sabbaths. They should be able to motivate the congregation to sing. They are to prepare the songs that will be used in the song service each night. They must be punctual and ensure that their dress is modest and does not serve as a distraction to worshippers. They should rehearse together and also with the instrumentalists.

There may or may not be a choir made up of members from the church or churches involved in the campaign. Choir members must be on time and properly dressed. There must be no bickering among choir members. Their attitudes, deportment, and relationships must invite the presence of the Spirit of God. All selections should be well practiced so that the presentations are inspiring and Spirit-filled. Those who did not attend the rehearsals and are unfamiliar with the songs should not attempt to participate in the presentation.

The choir director, who may or may not be the music coordinator, is fully in charge of the choir, and the decisions of the director must be respected. However, dialogue is always the best way to ensure that people are not just in compliance but are happily committed. The choir director should be people oriented and inclusive and should set an example for the choir members in punctuality and dress.

Ushers

Ushers collect the offering, hand out gifts, hand out and collect quiz papers, and distribute other materials. They welcome attendees as they enter and also conduct the nightly visitor-registration program.

Select a coordinator and an appropriate number of ushers. They should show respect for each other and follow the directions of the coordinator. They should be courteous, genuine, friendly, and people oriented. They must be patient and relate to people in a Christ-like manner. It is important for them to dress modestly and in a way that identifies them as ushers.

Each usher will be responsible for a particular section of the congregation, and all ushers should take up their positions before the song service begins each night. They are to be vigilant and alert, assisting those leading out in the program as well as the members and visitors in the congregation. They must not congregate outside the meeting during the preaching.

Telephone Receptionists

Before, during, and after the nightly meetings, volunteers should be available to answer phone calls from those who are listening to the program over the radio or watching it through cable or Internet. Arrange to have temporary telephone lines connected to the meeting place if necessary, or use cell phones if that is preferred. The telephone number(s) should be made publicly available, and during the sermon, the evangelist should refer to the availability of persons to answer phone calls, inviting listeners to utilize this opportunity and make immediate contact. Through this avenue, prayer requests can be received, evangelistic visitation initiated, and decisions for Christ obtained. Use discretion in choosing volunteers for this important responsibility.

Health

The Health Ministries Council, or a combined task force in a multi-church campaign, will organize the health programming for the campaign. This includes scheduling doctors, nurses, and other health professionals to give lectures on relevant health topics. Health videos may also be used for these lectures. There should also be doctors or nurses available at each meeting in case there is a need for first aid medical attention.

Sabbath School

The Sabbath School plays an important part in the execution of the campaign. The Sabbath School Council, or a joint committee in a multi-church campaign, will decide in advance which churches, Sabbath School Action Units, or small groups will be in charge of the weekly programs during the campaign. These programs should be in keeping with the themes presented by the evangelist while at the same time incorporating the study of the weekly Sabbath School lesson. The Sabbath School program must not surpass its allotted time during the campaign.

Adventist Youth

The Adventist Youth Society should also participate in the campaign. The Adventist Youth Society leaders of the participating churches will cooperate to decide in advance which churches or groups will be responsible for each weekly Adventist Youth program during the campaign. Like the Sabbath School, the program should be in keeping with the themes presented by the evangelist.

Sabbath Celebration

A special celebration may be planned for one or more of the Sabbaths during the campaign. This may be the first time that many visitors and prospects are keeping the Sabbath, and this celebration provides an opportunity to make it a special day both for them and for all the members of the church. The pastor, evangelist, and coordinating committee must cooperate to ensure that every detail is properly attended to so that the day will be an ideal celebration of the Creator.

The celebration should include a fellowship meal after the church service. A designated hospitality team will be responsible for planning the menu, purchasing the necessary supplies, and preparing the food for this meal. Where necessary, they may solicit donations to provide for these meals. The meals should be very sumptuous and have a good variety of nutritious food. The ushers, along with other volunteers, will assist in serving these meals.

The church service may include a baptism or Bible school graduation. The Sabbath School and Adventist Youth Society may plan special programs for the morning and afternoon respectively. The celebration may extend from morning until sunset, but this will depend on what is most appropriate for the local context.

The Campaign Program

The manner of presentation chosen for a particular campaign will depend upon many factors: budget; availability of technology and

equipment; availability of trained, experienced, or knowledgeable personnel; size of attendance; and demographics of the congregation and territory. The following is a list of ways in which the messages can be presented to varying audiences:
- Satellite uplink series with one speaker.
- Satellite uplink series with alternating speakers.
- Local series with one speaker.
- Local series with alternating speakers.
- A duet or trio with two or three speakers preaching one sermon.
- Recorded messages on a DVD or some other type of digital media.
- Live transmission on cable television.
- Delayed transmission on cable television.
- Live or prerecorded Internet transmissions.

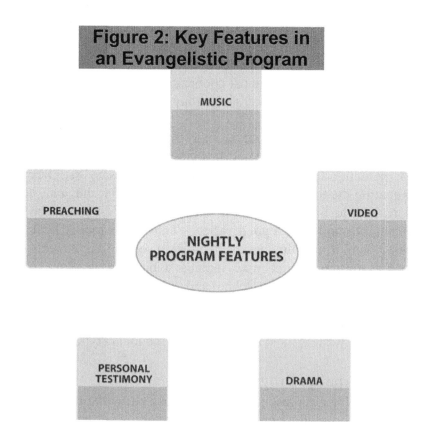

Nightly Features

Each nightly program of the public campaign will have a specific theme that is relevant to the target audience. Chapters 9–14 provide suggested themes that correspond with each departmental ministry. As a gift in connection with each theme, some of the attendees may be invited to attend a relevant enrichment program, seminar, or tour; special breakfast, lunch, dinner; or some other fellowship activity.

The campaign program should include special features that emphasize specific aspects of practical Christian living related to the chosen theme

Each feature should show how these matters take on a new significance when Christ enters a person's life. In the sermon, the evangelist will combine these issues of daily life with relevant Bible doctrines that demonstrate the love of God and create a desire in the hearts and minds of the hearers to accept Christ as their Savior.

As depicted in Figure 2, there are five key elements that should be present in each program in order to capture the attention of the varying minds in the congregation and gain decisions for Christ: (1) personal testimony, (2) drama, (3) video, (4) music, and (5) preaching.

Personal Testimony: A member of the church family could give a two-minute testimony that is relevant to the theme of the night. This could illustrate how the Lord is able to resolve difficult circumstances in our lives and use them for our best good. Personal testimonies are experience sharing moments that inspire and motivate others to recognize the power of the Lord in order to strengthen their faith in Him. All testimonies should be carefully planned to fit within the allotted time.

Drama: The drama each night—which should take no more than five minutes—will be related to the theme and may either reflect an ideal situation with a happy ending that results from depending upon the power of God, or a dysfunctional situation that is transformed by the Lord's marvelous intervention. The drama may come either before the message or at the end of the message as a preparation for the appeal.

Video: A short video clip that reflects the night's theme may be used to add interest to the program. It could highlight the theme by portraying either an ideal or dysfunctional situation, or alternatively it could feature church members who participated in an outreach activity that is relevant to the theme. This video must be carefully chosen, and the projection and sound should be of good quality.

Music: The songs should be related to the night's theme. There should be proper coordination between the preacher and those responsible for arranging the nightly music. The appeal song should be well chosen and appropriately rendered. The preacher may need to stop the singer at times to make appropriate comments as part of the invitation, and the singer and accompanist must be able to continue without interruption. Coaching is vital for this demanding responsibility, and it is important to recognize that not every singer is prepared to present a song of appeal.

Preaching: As an important representative of Christ, the evangelist brings everything together in the message in a way that magnifies Christ as the One who is all important. The message should connect Bible truth with the night's theme, using the drama and the other features of the program as a point of reference to invite individuals to accept Christ as their Savior.

Other Special Features

The following are other features that may be used on certain nights to vary the nightly routine, making the program colorful and unique:

- A special, uniformed parade led by the Pathfinders and Master Guides
- Graduations for students of the Bible school or community training programs
- Gifts related to the program theme
- Report on a community initiative
- Recognition of outstanding contributions
- Recognition of special achievements
- Short concert before the meeting
- Weddings

- Baptisms
- Health feature
- Career feature
- Youth feature
- Confession and forgiveness feature
- Children's corner
- Blessing of babies
- Blessing of marriages
- Special prayer for families
- Special prayer for women
- Special prayer for men
- Special prayer for children
- Special prayer for youth
- Special prayer for the bereaved
- Special prayer for healing
- Special prayer for businesspeople in the community
- Special prayer for the nation

Schedule of Nightly Program

To definitively determine the nightly schedule for all evangelistic campaigns would be unrealistic. Based on the local context, each church must choose the specific features to include and how much time to dedicate to them. In some places, two hours for the entire program from song service to benediction may be acceptable. In others, one hour and a half would be ideal. Thus, the following program outline serves as a suggestion:

- Recorded music before program
- Greeting and seating of attendees
- Song service: 10 minutes
- Opening hymn: 3 minutes
- Prayer: 2 minutes
- Welcome, recognitions, and announcements: 3 minutes
- Special music: 3 minutes
- Testimony feature: 4 minutes
- Offering: 4 minutes
- Presentation of special gifts: 4 minutes
- Video: 2 minutes

- Theme song: 3 minutes
- Sermon: 40 minutes
- Drama: 5 minutes
- Appeal: 8 minutes
- Benediction: 2 minutes

All the features of the nightly program must contribute to the message, capturing the attention of the people, holding their interest, and enhancing the retention of the concepts presented. The object of these meetings is to influence souls to Christ and gain positive decisions in response to the message that is preached from the Bible. Nothing must be allowed to create distractions that will interfere with this outcome.

Review and Discussion
- *Mention several ways to acquire adequate funding for a public evangelistic campaign.*
- *Identify and discuss some appropriate means for advertising and promoting a public evangelistic campaign.*
- *How relevant do you consider daytime activities in a public evangelistic campaign, and what are some activities that would be practical for your community?*
- *Mention and explain the function of any three material considerations for a public evangelistic campaign.*
- *Mention and define five team responsibilities that you consider most important for the execution of a public evangelistic campaign.*
- *What is a Sabbath celebration in an evangelistic campaign, and how can it be effectively executed?*
- *Discuss the various manners of presentation that can be used in a public campaign, and state which of these you consider to be most appropriate*
- *Identify the five nightly features of a public evangelistic campaign, and explain how they contribute to assimilation and recall of the message and how they influence people to make decisions..*

Part III
Departmental Evangelistic Initiatives

11
Evangelizing the Upper Class

IN the summer of 1998, I traveled from Montego Jamaica with a group of over 200 Pathfinders to the Inter-American Division Pathfinder Camporee which was held in Puerto Rico. The flight from Montego Bay was delayed. We arrived 30 minutes late in Miami and missed the connecting flight at 9:00am. The airline rebooked us on a confirmed flight that would leave Miami at 12:00 midnight, meaning we would be waiting for 14 hours in the Miami International Airport. We were subsequently told to go to the next gate to explore the possibility of travelling on stand-by on a flight that would leave within the next two hours.

Flights left every 2 hours from the Miami International to the International Airport in San Juan Puerto Rico on that day. Due to the number of persons travelling and primarily the thousands of passengers to the camporee, getting onto a stand-by flight was well-nigh impossible. After every two hours traversing from gate to gate, all efforts proved futile. At 12 midnight, we eventually boarded the flight on which we were confirmed. We celebrated when we arrived at our destination. Travelling on stand-by did not work. We made it on our confirmed flight.

People of all social classes must be encouraged and assisted to confirm their flights to the throne of God for that is the divinely intended destination of all human beings. Without a confirmed flight, travelling stand-by will most likely be futile. Accepting the gospel of Christ and making Him Lord of one's life is confirmation of the flight to the Kingdom. The followers of Christ are duty bound to be inclusive in the presentation of the gospel and must interpret it, make it applicable and communicate it to those of the upper class while doing similar to all other classes.

Revelation 7:9 says, "After this I beheld, and, lo, a great multitude, which no man could number, of all nations, and kind reds, and people, and tongues, stood before the throne, and before the Lamb, clothed with white robes, and palms in their hand." The destination of all human beings notwithstanding their social class, is the kingdom of God. Luke 19:10 "For the Son of Man came to seek and to save the lost." Ellen White said; "We talk and write much of the neglected poor; should not some attention be given also to the neglected rich? Many look upon this class as hopeless…Thousands of wealthy men have gone to their graves unwarned because they have been judged by appearance and passed by as hopeless subjects. But, indifferent as they may appear, I have been shown that most of this class are soul-burdened. There are thousands of rich men who are starving for spiritual food. Many in official life feel their need of something which they have not. Few among them go to church, for they feel that they receive no benefit. The teaching they hear does not touch the soul. Shall we make no personal effort in their behalf?" Testimony Volume 6, P. 78

Men and women in the highways and byways are to be reached. We read of Christ's labors: "Jesus went about all the cities and villages, teaching in their synagogues, and preaching the gospel of the kingdom, and healing every sickness and every disease among the people." Just such a work as this is to be done in our cities and villages, in the highways and hedges. The gospel of the third angel's message is to be carried to all classes {*Evangelism* p. 46}. The rich or the upper class in societies have not been emphasized much in our evangelistic strategizing and the result is clear, only a minute number of them are classified among those active in the community of Christ's believers.

The gospel must be contextualized and communicated to those of the upper class as well. John 1:14-17, tells us that the Word (*Logos*), which is the Organizing Principle of the universe, became flesh, incarnated Himself among the peoples of the world and provided them Grace that saves them from their sins (Matthew 1:21). John 1:29 said "behold the Lamb of God which taketh away the sins of the world." "The sins of the world" is a generic rendering of the condition of all human beings without regard to class, it is inclusive, and all are sinners. Salvation is available to people of every demographic group in society.

Social Classes

Social scientists have classified individuals within societies in hierarchical groupings based on wealth, educational attainment, occupation, income, status in a community or membership in a subculture or social network. The ranking of the social class structure is based on more than just how much money individuals have or do not have. It includes the clothes they wear, the music they like and the school they go to, among many other things. People's class has a strong influence on how they interact with others and who they are in reality. Those who seek to evangelize people of the upper must utilize evangelistic strategies based on clear understanding of their defining characteristics. Listening to their concerns, understanding their ways of viewing the world, and even learning their ways of communicating is essential to evangelistic effectiveness.

Defining the Upper Class

The phrase upper class denotes a group of individuals who are of the highest social status in society. They are considered the wealthiest and are above the working and middle class in the social hierarchy. People of the upper class have higher levels of disposable income and wield more control over the use of natural resources. The overall population of society is made up of a minimal percentage of upper class people however, they control a disproportionately sizable amount of the total wealth.

In a 2018 report from the Pew Research Center, it was reported that 19% of American adults live in households that are termed; "upper income". In the year 2016 the median income of that group was $187,872. Their annual household income then was more than double the national median. At that time, the national average was $55,775 after incomes were adjusted for household size. This class may be divided into two groups: lower-upper and upper-upper. Those with money made from investments and business ventures among other things are considered of the lower-upper class while the upper-upper class includes families who have been rich for generations.

In numerous cases, people of the upper class are more satisfied than others with their family life, their housing situation and their education. The research showed that among those who identify as being upper or upper-middle class, 53% have a bachelor's degree or more. Among middle-class adults, 31% have a college degree and among the lower or lower-middle class, only 15% are college graduates. Nearly one-in-five lower-class adults (18%) do not have a high school diploma. The study showed that only 29% say they frequently experience stress, compared with 37% of those in the middle class and 58% of lower-class adults. About four-in-ten adults (43%) say that upper class people are more likely than average Americans to be intelligent. The study showed that 42% of adults share the view that rich people are more likely than average Americans to be hardworking compared to 24% who say rich people are less likely than average Americans to be hardworking.

Some Religious Thought Patterns of the Upper Class

Many persons of the upper class are indifferent to spiritual things because they are more material than celestial focused. Some have a significantly different view concerning the nature and prowess of God and how He is involved in one's life than people of other classes. The upper class tends to embrace relativism, pluralism, religious nones or exclusivism.

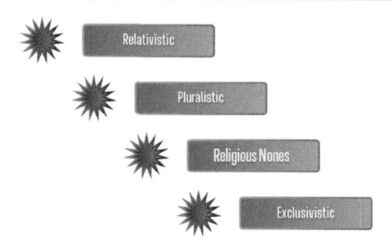

While these thought patterns are not unique to the upper class, they are common among a wide cross section of this demographic. Influenced by some of these predominant thought patterns, people within the upper class tend to *focus* on temporal concerns. Consequently, they tend to lack interest in discussions about the future and the mystical issue of life after death. Jesus addressed this tendency among the wealthy when he said; "And again I say to you, it is easier for a camel to go through the eye of a needle than for a rich man to enter the kingdom of God" (Matthew 19:24).

Relativistic Thought Pattern

Relativistic thought pattern is a philosophical outlook. It denies the claims that people do behave with objectivity. It asserts that truths or facts are relative to the viewpoint or perception of those concerned or the context in which they are evaluated. It embraces the concept that there are legitimate differences in moral judgments of people and cultures and holds that there are no absolute facts or truths regarding norms of beliefs, justification or rationalization because everything is relative. According to this thought pattern, there are no absolute truth, instead it is always relative to some particular frame of reference. Every person and situation determines what is truth therefore, truth cannot be objective, i.e. everyone can believe as they want to, which means there is no moral judgment. Common expressions of relativism include:

–Everything depends upon the concept, perspective or thoughts of the individual.

- *Each person is at liberty to do whatever is right for him or her.*
- *Everyone decides what is best for oneself and that is final.*
- *What is moral is defined and determined by what is acceptable* within a community. What is accepted as right in one community may not be considered to be right in another community.

Pluralistic Thought Pattern

Religious pluralism generally refers to the belief in two or more religious worldviews as being equally valid or acceptable. Pluralistic thinking in relation to truth proposes the notion that all considerations in all domains are true in exactly the same way. It proffers, that truth appears in more than one way and is not confined. It contends that there is no universal or common way of being true. Pluralism conflicts with monism that advances the notion that there is a one truth property that exist. In other words, it seeks to negate the idea of absolute truth.

More than mere tolerance, religious pluralism accepts multiple paths to God or gods as a possibility. One person puts it this way; "All roads lead to Rome…. Everyone uses a different motor vehicle but all arrive at the same destination… going to heaven is like that, if there is any such reality of a heaven".

Religious Nones

Religious unaffiliates are characterized as Religious Nones. They do not identify themselves with any religion. Over the last decade, this group continues to grow at a rapid pace around the world. Persons of the upper class and university trained are more likely to embrace characteristics of this community. About two-thirds of those who comprise this group say they believe in God. Over 50% express a deep feeling of connection with nature and the earth. More than a third classify themselves as "spiritual" but not "religious" (37%), and one-in-five (21%) say they pray every day. In addition, most religiously unaffiliated Americans think that churches and other religious institutions benefit society by strengthening community bonds and aiding the poor, however, they do not reckon themselves members in such communities. However, many are still willing to support the causes that they advance in respect of peace and social welfare of human beings.

Exclusivistic Thought Pattern

Exclusivists believe that there is only one way to salvation and to religious truth. Some of them even argue that it is necessary to suppress the falsehoods taught by other religions. They are motivated by the Holy Scriptures that teaches that, a) there is one God – Deuteronomy 6:5,
b) There is only one way to know God—through Jesus Christ, John 14:6; Acts 4:12, c) the Bible condemns other religions as following gods that are not really God. Reinforcing the biblical concept of One God, Joshua 23:16 says: "If you violate the covenant of the LORD your God, which He commanded you, and go and serve other gods and bow down to them, the LORD's anger will burn against you." Dogmatic exclusivism embraces three basic propositions that animate the Christian faith:

1. The Deity of Christ – John 1:1,14
2. The Substitutionary death of Christ for all human beings – 1 Corinthians 5:21
3. Salvation from Sin is derived only by Grace though Faith – Ephesians 2:8-9.

Idiosyncrasies of the Upper Class

Idiosyncrasies are distinctive or peculiar expressions, values, features or characteristics, likes or areas of interest of an individual, group or class of persons.

In the case of the upper class, there are certain peculiarities that need to be enumerated in order to create understanding and context to develop a strategy in evangelizing them.

The upper class is generally interested in:

Health reform and health practices	family-relationships
Wealth money and possessions	Education
Prestige – high station in life	Influence and
legacy Hoarding of resources	Focus on self

Perspectives and behavior patterns of most upper class people are:

i. They live within their means – many of them save up 20% or more of their income.
ii. Many avoid gambling.
iii. They read every day – about 88% read an average of 30 minutes a day.
iv. They spend less time in front of television screens and other monitors.
v. They are able to control their emotions compared to many of other classes.
vi. They volunteer depending on the context as deemed necessary.
vii. They work hard to achieve.
viii. They set goals and aspire to attain them.
ix. They avoid procrastination.
x. They talk less and listen more.
xi. They avoid toxic relationships.
xii. They persevere amidst severe odds.
xiii. They challenge and negate conventional opinions that are limiting.
xiv. They have mentors, coaches and special advisors
xv. They determine and know their primary objectives and purpose.
xvi. They create personal methods of achievements.
xvii. They network and maintain relationships.

xviii. They resist being pressured or controlled and value freedom and respect.

In order to effectively reach members of the upper class, the gospel worker or Christian witness needs to understand the mindset and idiosyncrasies of persons within that demographic group.

Ellen White said: "Let every worker in the Master's vineyard, study, plan, devise methods, to reach the people where they are. We must do something out of the common course of things. We must arrest the attention. We must be deadly in earnest. We are on the very verge of times of trouble and perplexities that are scarcely dreamed of" *Evangelism,* sec. 6, pp. 122, 123.

Wealthy Bible Characters who Loved the Lord

Very often, gospel workers and Christian believers neglect witnessing to the wealthy based on the concept that they are not interested in spiritual matters and are too difficult to engage. Nevertheless, the Bible is replete with examples of wealthy persons who were receptive to the message of salvation. Many of them were faithful followers of the Lord. This reality provides a frame of reference for Christian believers not to become disheartened in reaching out in witness to this group of individuals. Some of these wealthy and faithful in Scripture are:

- Abraham
- Isaac
- Jacob
- Joseph
- Lot
- Job
- Boaz
- Abigail
- Nabal
- David
- Solomon
- Hezekiah
- Dorcas
- Matthew

In Luke 19 we find Zacchaeus who before his actual conversion cheated and abused the poor but repented and made restitution after accepting salvation offered through Christ.

Barnabas (Acts 4:36-37), he sold some of the lands that he possessed and gave the proceeds to believers in Christ.

Lydia (Acts 16:13-15, 50), hosted the first church in her home in Europe. Cornelius (Acts 10:1-48), after and even before he sent in search of Peter concerning the Faith of Jesus, he was very generous to the poor.

Ethiopian Eunuch (Acts 8:26-40), he invited Phillip to explain the faith of Jesus to him then requested to be immediately baptized as he came to a pool that possessed sufficient water.

Philemon (Philemon 1), was the owner of slaves and a large number of properties. He forgave, both financially and morally, one of his slaves that ran away.

Joseph of Arimathea (Matthew 27:56-61; Mark 15:42-46 and Luke 23:50-53), who had pre-paid for his own tomb, donated it for the burial of Jesus.

The Roman Centurions (Matthew 8:5-13 and Luke 7:5), demonstrated kindness towards the Jews, paid to build a synagogue and demonstrated compassion for his servant that was sick.

Jesus' Approach in Dealing with the Wealthy or the Upper Class

Jesus was all inclusive in dealing with humanity. He embraced people of every class. "The Lord is not slack concerning His promise, as some count slackness, but is longsuffering toward us, not willing that any should perish but that all should come to repentance" 2 Peter 3:9. Jesus a) hanged out with the rich, b) welcomed and ate with sinners, c) attended to the sick, d) dined with Pharisees, e) invited rich officials to join him, f) took resources from the rich to support the mission and g) went to the house of the rich and dined. "Now it happened, as He was dining in Levi's house, that many tax collectors and sinners also sat together with Jesus and His disciples; for there were many, and they followed Him. And when the scribes and Pharisees saw Him eating with the tax collectors and sinners, they said to His disciples, "How is it that He eats and drinks with tax collectors and sinners?" When Jesus heard it, He said to them, "Those who are well have no need of a physician, but those who are sick. I did not come to call the righteous, but sinners, to repentance". Mark 2:15-17 NKJV.

Evangelizing the Upper Class

Is it possible to communicate the gospel to people who possess thought patterns which are not favorable to monotheism or rational objective truth? How can the believers in Christ witness to those who maintain a skeptical attitude towards the Bible and who are not motivated to organized religion? Believers in Christ must be concerned about these questions if they will effectively make in roads in the lives of these people when presenting the gospel.

Their mandate is not just to present the gospel but to influence them to accept Christ as their personal Savior and become members of the faith community.

To witness effectively to them, a contextualized approach is required. The success stories of evangelizing the upper class are not few and far. However, as we are told in Matthew 9:37, 38; "Then He said to His disciples, "The harvest truly is plentiful, but the laborers are few. Therefore, pray the Lord of the harvest to send out laborers into His harvest." The traditional public evangelism and other soul-winning methods used to evangelize the middle and working classes of individuals are not reaching the wealthy and upper class. Three important imperatives to observe when evangelizing the upper class are: enter their context, challenge their context and address their desire.

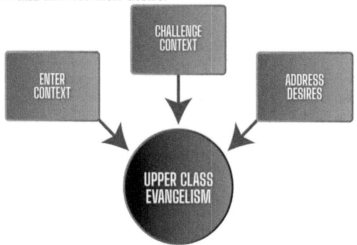

Enter the Cultural Context of the Upper Class
- Develop understanding of their values
- Put yourself into their place - empathize See Acts 17:16-34 (Paul in Athens)

Challenge the Cultural Context of the Upper Class
- Speak to the satisfaction and joys of this class
- Speak to the ignorance of the upper class
- What is it that they should know that they do not know?
- Paul spoke to the ignorance of the Athenians
- Always remember, according to Ellen White, new and different methods are to be employed to save different ones. (*Evangelism* p. 106).

To challenge the cultural context of the upper class is a difficult task to be achieved, but the gospel is the power of God. "For I am not ashamed of the Gospel of Christ, for it is the power of God unto salvation to everyone who believeth, to the Jew first and also to the Greek. 17 For therein is the righteousness of God revealed from faith to faith; as it is written: "The just shall live by faith." Romans 1:16-17.

Ellen White said: "The classes of people you meet decide for you the way in which the work should be handled."-- {*Evangelism* p. 106}. "Some of the methods used in this work will be different from the methods used in the work in the past; but let no one, because of this, block the way by criticism."--{*Evangelism* p. 129}

Address Characteristics of the Upper Class [Desires]

It is important for preachers to address characteristics of the upper class and clearly show them how the Gospel of Christ is relevant to their lives. By beginning with their needs such as - things they value, things that are unique and things that threaten - preachers immediately gain their attention. This group of individuals are not necessarily searching for truth. Instead, they are in quest of peace, well-being and greater satisfaction in this life. Seven considerations for contextualizing the gospel to the upper class are:

1. Most people of the upper class *believe in God*. They just have a more material focus than celestial; preachers should equip them to sense the presence of God and the importance of living with that consciousness every moment.
2. Many are *not knowledgeable about the Christian faith* so evangelists and preachers should avoid the use of stories and phrases that assume they have comprehension of the scriptures. Instead, teach them the basics of the gospel in a simple, clear and understandable manner.
3. Because many people of the upper class *like to share experiences of success,* evangelists and preachers should enable them to experience the success that the Gospel engenders through narrative and inductive preaching. Provide opportunities of success and faith sharing testimonies through multi-sensory approaches.
4. Many of them *do not sense the importance of Church* or a spiritual community in their lives. Evangelists and preachers should point out the value of a faith community as a support group and help them comprehend and experience such benefits on a personal basis.
5. Many upper class people are *family oriented* and relational so evangelists and preachers should reveal to them the origins, intentions and virtues of happy family and point them to the church as a spiritual family. They should help them to see how Christ and the Church offer practical assistance, counsel and resources for healthy relationships and the value of connecting meaningfully in relationships with Christians or the family of God.
6. Because many of them embrace a *pluralistic thought pattern,* evangelists and preachers should help them to recognize the inclusive nature of the Gospel and the distinctiveness of Christ and help them to repudiate the misconceptions of pluralism.
7. Since people of the upper class are *material oriented* and usually more pragmatic, evangelists and preachers should show them how the Gospel relates to the concerns of daily life and point

them to the possibility of experiencing a fringe benefit. That is, the joys of acquiring and living in this life and the higher joys of living eternally in the paradise of God.

Connecting with the Upper Class through personal experience

Sharing one's experience is fundamental to presenting the gospel of Christ to people of the upper class. Since the Relativists are accepting of everyone's point of view, this is a good place to begin. Similarly, since the Pluralists feel insulted to be told that they or anyone needs a better life, personal experience cannot be refuted with much success. It is sharing with them your personal stories that will capture attention and provide an opening to bring life-changing results. Since discussion may not necessarily result in the desired outcome, an advocacy approach, which is to intentionally propose your faith after sharing your personal experience will prove quite effective.

The opportunity to intentionally propose your faith will be made possible after relationship is established with the prospect. A strong reliance upon the Holy Spirit to drive home the truth into the hearts of people is crucial. Ellen White said, As human beings, we do not win souls.
It is Christ, working through the Holy Spirit who wins souls (*Testimonies to Ministers*, chap. 5, pp. 144, 145. In I Corinthians 3:6,7, the Apostle Paul said: "I have planted, Apollos watered; but God gave the increase. So then neither is he that planteth anything, neither he that watereth: but God that giveth the increase."

Many church people do not possess the academic preparation as many of the upper class and that makes it difficult for them to evangelize such educated, upper class. It actually is intimidating and is a source of temptation to become daunted by the thought that reaching the upper class is an impossible target. God already addressed that temptation in His communication to Jeremiah in Chapter 1:4-10 NKJV: "Then the word of the LORD came to me, saying: "Before I formed you in the womb I knew you; Before you were born I sanctified[a] you; I ordained you a prophet to the nations. Then said I: "Ah, Lord GOD! Behold, I cannot speak, for I am a youth." But the LORD said to me: "Do not say, 'I am a youth,' For you shall go to all to whom I send you, And whatever I command you, you shall speak. Do not be afraid of their faces, For I am with you to deliver you," says the LORD. Then the LORD put forth His hand and touched my mouth, and the LORD said to me: "Behold, I have put My words in your mouth. See, I have this day set you over the nations and over the kingdoms, To root out and to pull down, To destroy and to throw down, To build and to plant."

Gaining the Upper Class for the Kingdom

It takes the supernatural power of God to release those who are in Satan's grip (Matthew 17:21AV) and to open the eyes of those blinded to the light of the gospel (2 Corinthians 4:4). If God doesn't take the initiative in the life of the unbeliever, as He promises to do in response to our prayers, we are limited to human resources and human understanding. However, God will act in response to our specific prayers. He has always acted. We must go forward and be intentional in asking Him to rescue the upper class from the clutches of the devil into His Church and Kingdom.

Does this mean that evangelism to rescue the upper class with little or no prayer support will always fail? The answer is 'no'! God in His sovereign good pleasure may bring people to a saving knowledge of Jesus Christ despite our prayerlessness. The believer in Christ may in fact be instrumental in reaping where he has not sown (John 4:37-38). However, God's preferred method is to work through and with the human agents. Prayers and activities of the believer of the Church must not only be focused toward the needs of those within the community of believers. If the concerns for the upper class, part of those that God loves (John 3:16) is not considered – then the church or those engaged in the witnessing process will be: a) missing the opportunity that is made possible by God to see them saved in the kingdom; b) lacking in Christ-like vision and compassion; c) ineffective in building God's kingdom and will miss the joy of seeing God's power released and redemption of this group of His people come to Him.

Once there is an understanding of the way the upper class think, feel, reason, and make decisions, Christ's believers must proceed to proclaim the gospel to them. The goal of presenting the gospel to them is to influence them to make a decision for Him. To effectively present the gospel to them, the believer must address at least three of their central needs:

1. How to acquire
2. How to enjoy
3. How to keep

The truth must be presented within the context of these overarching desires of theirs. Paul gave them Jesus as the source of their eternal riches, the Messiah, whom they needed to acquire in their lives. He gave them Jesus whose presence brings assurance and abundance of security and satisfaction to enjoy. He gave them Jesus who is the eternal hope that they need to keep. When we read Acts 18:1-8, we note that Paul preached the gospel in Corinth and a vast number of people accepted Christ and were baptized. The church started out small and then grew to a large number. The motivation for evangelizing the upper class is not to achieve numbers, instead it is to:

i. Present the gospel which is the truth that they are to embrace.
ii. Present the gospel with clarity so they can assimilate it.
iii. Present the gospel with biblical accuracy so they can have a correct knowledge of Christ.
iv. Present Christ in His purity and righteousness, who is the Good News that they need to receive.
v. Invite them to accept Him as their personal Savior for in Him they find eternal life.

Five important considerations in presenting the plan of salvation

In presenting the gospel to the upper class be sure to explain to them five considerations of the plan of salvation that are important and attractive; a) Union with Christ, b) New creation, c) Adoption, d) justification, e) redemption. Explain to them how:

- Jesus brings redemption to those who are living with the consciousness of guilt
- Jesus accepts those who feel rejected by justifying them
- Those who may feel abandoned by circumstances are adopted in and by the love of a perfect and sustaining Father
- Jesus transforms into a new creation, those who feel hopeless irrespective of all of life's possessions.
- Jesus enables a life of union and intimacy with Himself to those who are lonely, stressed and depressed.

Preparation for the Presentation of the Gospel to the Upper Class
- Let it be a subject for continued and fervent prayers
- Employ prayer as a major aspect of the planning, and execution of the program
- Plan a two-year program to evangelize the upper class
- Connect with the people through appropriate social means – choose the approach
- Hang out with them as much as is possible through electronic or in-person means
- Approach them, do not wait for them to come to you

- Conduct special forums that address social needs within their context
- Select topics that will address their core values and success habits
- Plan a dinner conference with them to address health, social and economic topics like:
- stress management
- wealth acquisition
- wealth management
- partnerships
- Choose presenters who can connect with them
- Develop strategy to transition from social to spiritual conversations
- Eventually, do bible studies with them – use technology and face to face bible study with them
- Choose venue wisely where forums will be conducted in a way that is attractive to the upper class

Venue for Upper Class Evangelism

"The large halls in our cities should be secured, that the third angel's message may be proclaimed by human lips. Thousands will appreciate the message".--Letter 35, 1895. {Ev 75.2}

"The Most Popular Halls.--It requires money to carry the message of warning to the cities. It is sometimes necessary to hire at large expense the most popular halls, in order that we may call the people out. Then we can give them Bible evidence of the truth". --Manuscript 114, 1905. {Ev 75.3}

"I am convinced that we might have had a good hearing if our brethren had secured a suitable hall to accommodate the people. But they did not expect much, and therefore did not receive much. We cannot expect people to come out to hear unpopular truth when the meetings are advertised to be held in a basement, or in a small hall that will seat only a hundred persons. . . . By their lack of faith our laborers sometimes make the work very hard for themselves".--Historical Sketches, p. 200. (1886) {Ev 126.1}

Opportunities that digital evangelism provide for engaging the upper class

In an attempt to reach the upper class and relevantly witness to them, the believer in Christ must engage channels of communication to proclaim the message to them that will be effective. The technological revolution in communications has made it amazingly possible to package and deliver the message to them in an effective way considering their idiosyncrasies. Through Cyberspace, transmitting information costs almost nothing. Distance is irrelevant, and there is no limit to the volume of content that can be made instantly accessible. Chapter 5 that deals with digital evangelism provide practical and relevant information that can be contextualized in utilizing technology to reach the upper class.

A Step-by step Process for Effectiveness in Upper Class Evangelism

- Establish an Upper Class Evangelism Committee
- Perform demographic research on the upper class
- Provide orientation to the committee
- Develop a vision for evangelizing the upper class
- Identify alternative options and channels to reach them in their context
- Determine economic, social, health and lifestyle forums through which to connect with them
- Determine attractive venues to meet with them and conduct instructional sessions
- Select the team of persons that will work with the upper class
- Communicate with members of the team and all those who need to be in the know
- Train all participants to effectively fulfill their roles
- Establish and maintain program quality standards
- Promote and invite members of the upper class to specially organized forums
- Adopt the recommendations of the committee to:
    a. Enter the cultural context of the upper class

b. Challenge the cultural context of the upper class
   c. Address the central needs and characteristics of the upper class
- Present the Gospel
- Be consistent and on time
- Evaluate and make adjustments where necessary

Role of the Committee
1. Establish specific evangelistic objectives to reach the upper class
2. Determine specific initiatives to achieve the objectives
3. Determine the specific targeted group(s) for these initiatives
4. Determine what should be known about the targeted group(s) before execution of the initiatives
5. Determine how many persons are required to execute these initiatives
6. Determine what is the specific strategy to equip persons to execute the initiatives
7. Determine when the education process will begin and for how long
8. Determine who will be responsible for the education process
9. Determine how persons will be recruited to participate in the execution of these initiatives
10. Determine who will be responsible for the recruitment
11. Determine when recruitment will begin and how long will it last
12. Determine what training will be necessary for the participants
13. Determine who will provide the training to the participants
14. Determine what resources will be required for the execution of these initiatives
15. Determine how the initiative will be evaluated and by whom

Conclusion
A studied approach to evangelizing the upper class is an imperative of our time. For various reasons most of them are not being

impacted by the Gospel. Many believers in Christ do not know how to reach them and many are intimidated. Ellen White said that presenters who can connect with them should be chosen: "Workers of Intelligence to Reach Higher Classes—There has not been the effort made that should have been made to reach the higher classes. While we are to preach the gospel to the poor, we are also to present it in its most attractive light to those who have ability and talent, and make far more wise, determined, God-fearing efforts than have hitherto been made, to win them to the truth". *Evangelism*, p. 556.

In presenting the gospel to people of the upper class, method should not be emphasized above that which is essential, the use of scripture which is the lesson book. "Charmed by Scripture Truth—Men in high positions of trust in the world will be charmed by a plain, straightforward, Scriptural statement of truth". *Evangelism* p. 557. She said that the intelligent, and refined are altogether too much passed by because; "The hook is not baited to catch this class, and ways and methods are not prayerfully devised to reach them with truth that is able to make them wise unto salvation. Most generally the fashionable, the wealthy, the proud, understand by experience that happiness is not to be secured by the amount of money that they possess, or by costly edifices, and ornamental furniture and pictures. They want something they have not. But this class are attracted toward each other, and it is hard to find access to them; and because of this many are perishing in their sins who long for something that will give them rest and peace and quietude of mind. They need Jesus, the light of righteousness". *Evangelism* p. 556

To evangelize the upper class takes time, it requires a change in thinking and doing, it is not fishing among a new group by utilizing the same method that we utilize to the middle and working classes, instead, it is a different culture or lifestyle to be impacted with the gospel of Christ. It requires intentionally identifying persons to reach them, training these persons and deploying them. Without the inclusion and dependence upon the Holy Spirit it will be a daunting venture. With the Holy Spirit impacting minds and bringing convictions and the total involvement of the Divine triune combined with human efforts, success is assured.

Review and Discussion

- *What implication does Revelation 7:9 have for evangelizing the upper class?*
- *Name and explain at least three thought patterns of the upper class*
- *Identify at least 6 idiosyncrasies of the upper class and state how these may be utilized in an effective evangelistic approach to them.*
- *Identify any five wealthy bible characters and state how their experience in scripture can be utilized to shape a message that will be acceptable to the upper class.*
- *Identify three important imperatives to be considered when planning to evangelize the upper class and hoe gospel proclaimers may be guided by them.*
- *Name five considerations of the plan of salvation and state how they may be utilized to address human needs in the presentation of the gospel.*
- *Develop a complete ready to implement evangelistic plan to reach, equip, rescue and retain people of the upper class in the faith of Christ and the Church*

12
Planning and Implementing Effective Family Evangelism

GOD CHOSE to make the family a center of evangelism when He designated the family of Abraham as the means through which to bless all the families of earth. He said to Abraham, "I will make of you a great nation. . . . And in you all the families of the earth shall be blessed" (Gen. 12:2, 3).

The purpose of the Family Ministries Department in the local church is to disciple families. This mission should not be confined to the four walls of the church. Through family ministries, the church should go into the byways and hedges to proclaim the love of Christ by preaching and teaching the gospel of the kingdom of God. Family ministries in the church takes on new dimensions when families become focused on sharing this message, and through effective family evangelism, the church can take a significant step toward fulfilling the promise that the Lord made to Abraham.

Love in action is the engine that drives family evangelism. Through the gospel, families are to be restored to the condition that humanity possessed in the Garden of Eden. Therefore, Family

Ministries leaders should intentionally establish outreach initiatives and organize members to witness to those in their communities.

Family Life: A Powerful Witness

Dysfunctional family relationships are so prevalent in today's society that many are seeking a way out, either though divorce or by a reformation to restore functional family relationships. This provides an important opportunity for ministry. Paul says that the children of light are to confront the works of darkness with the power of Christ in order to bring those who are in darkness into the light (Eph. 5:11–14).

The family life of Christians should serve as a model for those who do not know Christ. According to Ellen White, "One well-ordered, well-disciplined family tells more in behalf of Christianity than all the sermons that can be preached. Such a family gives evidence that the parents have been successful in following God's directions, and that their children will serve Him in the church. Their influence grows; for as they impart, they receive to impart again" (*The Adventist Home*, chap. 4, p. 32). Christian family life thus becomes a powerful public witness. Furthermore, the apostles Peter and Paul both referred to the power of personal influence within the family (1 Pet. 3:1, 2; 1 Cor. 7:12–16). According to Neufeld, family life is to be a public act of Spirit-filled worship that is lived as to Christ (Eph. 6:5).

Field Preparation for Family Evangelism

In executing family evangelism, the Family Ministries Department of the church should emphasize the restoration of family relationships in both the community and the church. The Lord has declared: "Behold, I will send you Elijah the prophet before the great and awesome day of the Lord comes. And he will turn the hearts of fathers to their children and the hearts of children to their fathers" (Mal. 4:5, 6). Through family evangelism, families and individuals should be inspired to joyfully anticipate the coming of the Lord.

Each family in the church should be considered a Family Witnessing Cell that functions as a small group. According to this plan, each family will be actively engaged in the family-evangelism initiatives of the church. Every Christian has a family member, friend, coworker, or acquaintance who has not surrendered to the Lord and needs to be reached with the gospel of Christ (Matt. 28:19, 20; Acts 1:8; 1 Pet. 3:15). In order to evangelize these individuals, families in the church should begin by identifying them by name and praying for them. Through prayer, ask the Lord to change the hearts and open the eyes of those you desire to reach with the truth as it is in Jesus (2 Cor. 4:3–6). Ask Him to convict them of His love and of their need for salvation through Jesus Christ (John 3:16). Also request divine guidance and wisdom in order to effectively minister to these precious souls (James 1:5). In addition to praying, church members must live godly, Christian lives in their homes, at work, at school, in the community, and at church. Thus others will see the change God has made in their lives (1 Pet. 3:1–2).

Chapter 3 of this book explains the initial planning process for departmental evangelistic initiatives, and chapter 7 explains the various approaches and initiatives to facilitate social mingling, share the gospel, and ultimately help individuals make decisions for Christ. In family evangelism, these initiatives may include a Family Wellness Forum and a Community-Development Family Day. Specific suggestions for these activities are provided below. After each initiative, members of the church family should always follow up with the families of interest.

Family Life Evangelism

Dimensions of Family Ministries Evangelism

Family life evangelism prepares husbands, wives and children as well as prospective spouses and parents for wellness in family life, sharing of family and spiritual values as well as living in readiness for the Second Advent of Christ. There are five distinct dimensions of family life evangelism enumerated and explained in the foregoing sections.

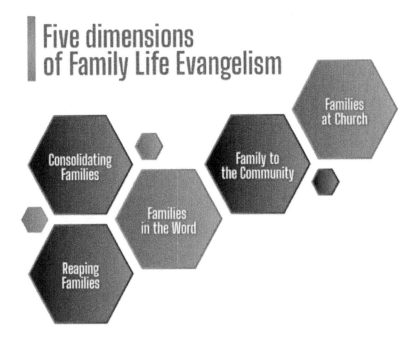

The Families at Church
One of the goals of this dimension of family life evangelism is to prepare family members of the Church to deal with their personal in-family relationship needs. The family ministries committee of the Church will seek to address this goal through effective planning and execution of specific initiatives. These shall address intimacy within the family, relationship wellness, vitalized, conventional and other types of relationships within marriage. Relevant strengths and growth areas in marriage and family relationships shall also be addressed. Other goals to be achieved through this dimension are:

building relationships and connection with the Lord, developing and embracing dynamics for living unitedly as Christian families, understanding how the families of the Church can work unitedly in the mission of Christ and the development of tools, resources and knowledge of their use to share the gospel of Christ to members of other families that are not of the faith.

The Family to the Community

1. This dimension of family life evangelism deals with contacting, connecting with, sharing skills and working together with families of other faiths or unchurched family members. Unchurched family members may be biological or non-biological. This dimension involves a partnership program in which the families of the church connect with them through various forums in which they develop social relationships, share skills, assist with personal and corporate family needs, engage in partnerships with resource persons in the community and address practical needs. Some of the needs addressed in this area, additional to those in listed below under the headings, Family Wellness Forum and Community Development Family Day as well as in the chapter on Field preparation are:
   i. Parenting
   ii. Economic.
   iii. Separation and Divorce.
   iv. Loneliness.
   v. Health.
   vi. Bereavement.

Families in the Word

Through the families in the Word dimension, families of the church who are equipped or trained in the families of the Church phase share their faith with families of other faiths or non-church families. They tell stories of how God works in their lives and do bible studied with them. This dimension is intended for spiritual equipping and helping other families to grow in love with the Lord and other members of the faith community. During this phase, families, pray together, and expect God's favors together. Family members accept the need for lifestyle changes and embrace of the Faith of Jesus. As the family members of the Church incarnate themselves with those of the unchurched community, a catalyzing effect will be realized in which the unchurched will sense the need for embracing: a) the righteousness of Christ, b) repentance, c) forgiveness and living in obedience to the commandments of God.

Reaping Families

This is the public evangelism dimension in which reaping campaigns are held to secure decisions for Christ and membership into the family of believers – the Church. Careful efforts should be made by members of the family life committee to plan and execute effective campaigns with the involvement of all the family members of the Church. **Chapters 3, 5 and 7 provide more detail on how this phase may be developed and executed.**

Consolidating Families

In this dimension, all the families that are won to Christ must be thoroughly instructed in the doctrines of scripture in order to grow in the Faith of Jesus. A program of at least 12 weeks should be designated for this. It should also help them to understand the new Spiritual family that they have become members of as well as the culture of this new community. Chapters 20 and 21 give full details on how such program may be developed and executed.

Family Wellness Forum

The following may be used as topics for Family Wellness Forums:
- How to Keep Your Husband or Wife Happy and Smiling
- The New Model for Parenting
- Relating Happily with Your Children
- Understanding Your Children's Generation
- Forgiveness in the Family
- Unconditional Love and Acceptance in the Family
- Effective Communication in the Family
- Speaking the Language of Love

- Best Recreational and Bonding Activities for the Family
- Surviving Economic Hardship in Your Family
- The Family in the Community
- Keeping the Family Together as a Team

Community-Development Family Day

Community-development projects could include:

- Repairing and painting the house of a needy person in the community. • Repairing a retirement home and providing services to the residents.
- Repairing an orphanage and providing services to the children.
- Repairing a school in the community.
- Distributing back-to-school supplies.
- Distributing eyeglasses to needy persons within the community.
- Distributing shoes to needy persons in the community.
- Hosting a blood drive.
- Organizing a community musical program.
- Building a bus shed for residents in the community.
- Participating in a park-development or tree-planting project.

Suggested Topics for a Family-Evangelism Reaping Campaign

A family evangelistic campaign emphasizes various family-life issues. Chapter 8 explains the details of carrying out a public campaign, including the various features of the nightly program.

Each program should include music, drama, video, testimony, and preaching that are related to the theme and its doctrinal emphasis. The following examples are some of the many themes that may be used in this series.

The Home Theme

This theme and all of its features focus on ideal home relationships that are in harmony with biblical principles including love, communication, family worship, Bible study, prayer, recreation, and living happily together. This contrasts with an undesirable home that has various challenges with interpersonal relationships, such as lack of conformity to biblical principles, antagonism between the parents, hostility among the children, domestic violence, and child abuse. Our future home in the kingdom of God is a strong emphasis of this theme. As a gift, some families may be invited to visit a home for a special tour or other fellowship activity.

The Husband, Wife, Children, and Parents Themes

On different nights, the home theme may be applied to specific members of the family, resulting in a husband theme, wife theme, children theme, and parents theme. These themes may focus on individuals from each group leading other family members to the kingdom of God.

Communication in the Family

The family theme can also provide the basis for a communication theme, which focuses on proper understanding, cooperation, and communication in the family as opposed to misunderstanding, poor dialogue, lack of feedback, and aggression. Areas of emphasis in this theme include communication between God and His children, communication within the church, communication within the family, and what communication will be like in the kingdom of God. The preacher invites family members to accept Christ into their lives and experience reform in their family communication.

Family Finance

The features and message of this theme, focus on the ideal way of dealing with family finances in harmony with biblical principles. These include living within available means, budgeting, spending wisely, showing restraint, seeking to improve family income, and living with contentment. Wise planning and faithful stewardship are major areas of emphasis in this theme. The preacher invites family members to accept Christ into their lives, budget wisely, spend wisely, and prepare for the great joys that the committed and prudent will enjoy in this life and the higher joys that they will experience in the kingdom of heaven when Jesus returns. As a gift, a few families may be invited to attend some seminars on family finance or to visit a bank or credit union.

The Good Neighbor

The features of this theme portray ideal neighborly relationships that are in harmony with biblical principles—such as compassion, communication, service, cooperation, recreation, spiritual understanding and dialogue, and living peacefully with neighbors—

in contrast to antagonistic and hostile relations between neighbors. This theme emphasizes coexisting with others both here and in the kingdom of God. The preacher invites family members to accept Christ into their lives and live in harmony with those in their home, church, school, workplace, and community.

Other Topics for a Family Evangelistic Campaign

Other themes in a family evangelistic series may cover family issues like love, conflict, recreation, renewal, forgiveness, suffering, bereavement, rules and discipline, joy and happiness, acceptance, and separation, as well as marriage and new additions to the family.

Review and Discussion

- *What are the five dimensions of family life evangelism and how do they contribute to improving the evangelistic activities of the local Church?*
- *What biblical and Spirit of Prophecy support can you provide to justify family evangelism in your church?*
- *Explain how a Christian family can exert a powerful influence in favor of the gospel.*
- *Mention three specific community initiatives—from either this chapter or other parts of this book—that you can implement as a part of family evangelism.*
- *Suggest ways in which to make a transition from these community-action initiatives to spiritual dialogue with prospects in preparation for a public evangelistic campaign.*
- *Explain how Bible doctrines can be integrated with family-life issues in a family evangelistic series.*
- *Use one of the other suggested topics to develop and plan a program to be used in a family evangelistic campaign.*
- *Suggest three program themes for a family evangelistic campaign that were not mentioned in this chapter.*

13
Planning and Implementing Effective Women's Evangelism

THE BIBLE MENTIONS numerous cases in which women were involved in evangelism and were instrumental in furthering the work of the gospel and winning souls for the kingdom of heaven. In the book of Acts we find multiple accounts of women who played active ministry roles in the early church.

Dorcas, or Tabitha, was a woman in the New Testament who was called a "disciple" (Acts 9:36). Mary of Jerusalem, John Mark's mother (Acts 12:12), was a wealthy widow whose house became the hub of the church's activities in Jerusalem, providing refuge and security for the believers during the intense persecutions of Herod Agrippa. Lydia, a wealthy businesswoman and apparently Paul's first convert in Europe, opened her home to Paul and Silas (Acts 16:14–15).

The rest of the New Testament mentions other women who fulfilled pivotal roles in ministry. In Philippians 4:2 and 3, Paul identifies Euodias and Syntyche as his fellow workers. This is a remarkable designation, considering that Paul also referred to Titus and Timothy as fellow workers (2 Cor. 8:23; Rom. 16:21). Paul classified Junia as "outstanding among the apostles" (Rom. 16:7, NASB), and this is likely a reference to her role as one commissioned by the church for special duties. In his list of fellow workers in Romans 16, Paul commended twenty-nine people for their missionary efforts, ten of whom were women.

Mark identified by name three women who witnessed the empty tomb and testified of the resurrection of Jesus. These were Mary Magdalene, Mary the mother of James, and Salome (Mark 15:40). Jesus appeared to them and the other women who were with them and personally directed them to proclaim His resurrection to the rest of the disciples. Angels also appeared to them with the same message and directive. This account is recorded in all four of the gospels. Indeed, every person who heard the good news of Jesus' resurrection received it through the initial testimony of women.

By sharing her testimony (John 4:28–30, 39–42), the woman of Samaria brought nearly her entire town to Christ. She invited the people, saying, "Come, see a man who told me everything I ever did. Could this be the Messiah?" (v. 29, NIV). The account says that many of the Samaritans of that town believed in Jesus because of the woman's testimony. Not only did she share her experience, she also urged all the inhabitants of the town to meet Jesus for themselves. They later testified that they believed, not just because of her word, but because they had met Jesus themselves and were convinced that He was the Messiah, "the Savior of the world" (v. 42). Thus, a woman evangelist led an entire city to experience personal faith in Jesus Christ. Clearly she was involved in public evangelism, considering that she influenced an entire town in such a short time.

Dwight L. Moody said that if this world was to be reached, he was "convinced that it must be done by men and women of average talent." Women played a decisive role in the great success of the early Christian church. Throughout history, their contribution has been vibrant and vital, and their work is still essential to the fulfillment of the church's mission. "In ancient times the Lord worked in a wonderful way through consecrated women who united in His work with men whom He had chosen to stand as His representatives. He used women to gain great and decisive victories. More than once, in times of emergency, He brought them to the front and worked through them for the salvation of many lives" (*Daughters of God,* chap. 6, p. 94).

Preparation for Women's Evangelism

Chapter 3 of this book explains the initial planning process for departmental evangelistic initiatives, and chapter 7 explains the various field preparation initiatives for an evangelistic campaign. In order for the Women's Ministries leaders of the church to organize an effective evangelistic outreach program, the participation of the women of the church is essential. Each woman should identify those whom she would like to reach with the gospel and add their names to the women's evangelistic prayer list. These names should be the object of daily intercessory prayer. Eventually, these prospects will be contacted and invited to attend the Women Connect Forums, which will be organized to address specific community needs. A genuine demonstration of Christ-like care and compassion is a vital aspect of these social-mingling efforts. After these activities, women from the church should always follow up with the prospects.

As part of the field preparation for women's evangelism, Women in the Community activities could be organized for women from the church and the community to work together on projects like the following:
- Making and distributing hot meals.
- Cleaning houses in the community.
- Beautifying public areas in the community.

Five Steps of Women's Evangelism

A complete cycle of women's evangelism includes five key steps: *modeling, teaching, encouraging, preaching, and coaching.* The first three steps are evangelistic activities in preparation for the preaching step, while the coaching phase is concerned with the nurturing activities that are necessary to consolidate the new believer in the faith.

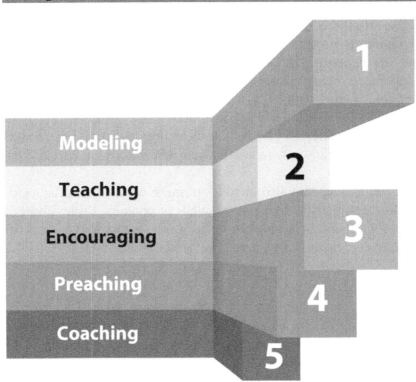

Figure 1: The Five Steps of Women's Evangelism

The Modeling Step

Modeling is the art or process of producing behavior that aptly represents the ideal. Through modeling, we draw attention to the original. Effectively reaching people with the gospel requires women to joyfully live out their salvation in Christ. When a Christian woman sincerely models the Christian lifestyle, she draws others to Christ through her influence as her life reveals Jesus as the true Model to be emulated. Ellen White said:

> God does not intend that your light shall so shine that your good words or works shall bring the praise of men to yourself; but that the
> Author of all good shall be glorified and exalted. Jesus, in His life,
> gave to men a model of character Our life must be hid with Christ in God, and then the light will be reflected from Jesus to us, and we shall reflect it upon those around us, not in mere talk and profession, but in

good works, and by manifesting the character of Christ. (*Our Father Cares,* p. 286)

The task force for women's evangelism should train the ladies of the church to model Christ-like attributes, behaviors, or emotions such as patience, tolerance, forgiveness, love, joy, happiness, acceptance, mercy, peace, and kindness. This will attract the attention of other women as well as children, youth, and men. It is important to develop these attributes as a genuine lifestyle phenomenon. They should not be mere dramatization but should rather characterize a woman's normal demeanor as a part of her everyday life.

The modeling step also includes training women to initiate and develop evangelistic interests as well as conduct Bible studies. Some should also be trained for leadership in the various aspects of the teaching, encouraging, preaching, and coaching steps.

The Teaching Step

The modeling step leads to the teaching step. The gospel commission given by Jesus includes "teaching them to observe all that I have commanded you. And behold, I am with you always, to the end of the age" (Matt. 28:19, 20). Ellen White said that as those who have received this commission, we are to be "dedicated to the work of making known the gospel of salvation. Heaven's perfection is to be your power" (*Testimonies for the Church,* vol. 9, chap. 2, p. 20).

Teaching takes place in Women Connect Forums, which are social activities that address specific needs of those within the wider community. These are conducted according to the guidelines in chapter 7 for community-outreach forums. In these forums social, vocational, paraprofessional, and other types of skills are taught. This training is provided for those on the prospect list through various activities, events, and seminars. Some of the topics that may be covered include:
- Cooking
- Baking
- Home decoration
- Weight management
- Exercise

- Woman: the spice of the family
- Sharing love in the family
- Handling the stress of parenting
- Single parenting
- Being a mother and a bread winner

In some neighborhoods, Sabbath afternoons are good times to conduct Women Connect Forums, depending on the type of training. In other cases, Sunday afternoon may be the best time. The results of the community needs surveys conducted by the Women's Ministries evangelism task force will help determine the best time to conduct these forums. Women Connect Forums may be held for one hour to one and a half hours once or twice each week according to what is most suitable.

The Encouraging Step

To know Jesus intimately should be the goal of every woman of faith. This intimate walk should inspire her to develop a passion to see others experience a similar relationship. Christian encouragement is an important part of helping others achieve this goal. Such encouragement should take at least two forms: (1) helping others deal with material, social, and emotional difficulties; and (2) encouraging others to take an interest in spiritual matters in order to develop an intimate relationship with the Lord. The women of the church should urge other women to participate in the Women Connect Forums and should find other means to help them deal with troubling and difficult issues in their lives. In order to give spiritual encouragement, women should share Bible knowledge with others and conduct selected series of Bible lessons with them, encouraging them to develop a closer relationship with the Lord.

Encouragement ministry is important because there are many ladies who are able to make initial contacts but do not possess the skills of encouragement or persuasion. As a result, they are not able to perform the necessary follow-up. Therefore, those involved in this encouragement ministry should receive names from other women of the church in order to work with them.

Encouragement is a gift of the Holy Spirit, yet it can be learned and cultivated. The evangelism task force of the Women's

Ministries Department should identify women who are interested in participating in the encouragement step of the women's evangelism plan. This group of women should be taught the best possible means of approaching others, attracting their attention, developing relationships with them, and encouraging them by attending to their material, social, emotional, and spiritual needs.

The Preaching Step

In the modeling step, women in the church are trained to model Christ like attributes, behaviors, and emotions, as well as to participate in various evangelistic initiatives. The teaching step provides various types of training to women in the community through the Women Connect Forums. In the encouragement stage, these women receive encouragement to deal with their material, social, emotional, and spiritual needs.

At the conclusion of these three steps, the task force for women's evangelism should make a list of prospects who are committed to living the faith of Christ. The names on this list should be presented to the pastor and Bible workers for continued prayer, visiting, and encouragement. Then comes the preaching step, in which the task force for women's evangelism will carry out an evangelistic reaping campaign, which should already have been planned.

Chapter 8 explains the details of carrying out such a campaign, including the various features of the nightly program.. Each program should include music, drama, video, testimony, and preaching that are related to the theme and its doctrinal emphasis. Practical life experiences should be used to present the spiritual message. The following examples are some of the themes that may be used in this series.

A Second Opportunity in Healthful Living

The features and message of this theme focus on a healthy lifestyle that is in harmony with biblical principles. Resources and programs on healthful living should be made available in connection with this theme. As a gift, some attendees may be invited to attend a healthy living enrichment seminar. In addition to a healthy lifestyle, the Second Advent is emphasized as the ultimate solution to all sickness.

Making Use of Informal Education

This theme highlights personal development through informal education. The authenticity of the Word of God forms the emphasis of the sermon and the other program features. As a gift, some attendees may be invited to participate in a Bible conference or other Bible-based activity.

Overcoming the Past

The centerpiece of the features of this program is the emergence of sin and its negative effects on the human race. Many people struggle to overcome addictions in their lives, and this theme is an opportunity to make relevant programs and resources available to such individuals. As a gift, some attendees may be invited to participate in an addiction relief activity.

Attending to Personal Priorities

The Ten Commandments as the transcript of God's character is the emphasis of this service and its features, which highlight important principles for personal and relational wellness. As a gift, some attendees may be invited to activities that highlight laws or principles governing health, security, safety, or happy family life.

Embracing Love

The love of Christ as revealed in His ministry, death, burial, resurrection, and ascension are the major emphases of this night's subject. The sermon and other features should focus on the love of Christ. As a gift, some attendees may be invited to a special function to watch a movie that illustrates this theme.

Forgiveness and Renewal

The features of this service focus on acceptance in Christ and baptism. It would be good to have a baptism as part of this theme in order to give the attendees the opportunity to witness such a service.

Those who are interested in baptism should be given the opportunity to express this desire.

Managing Your Personal Resources
The features of this theme emphasize proper life management, highlighting the importance of the wise management of one's time, talent, financial resources, relationships, and body. As a gift, some attendees could receive an invitation to visit a financial institution or successful company that can offer advice on sound financial management.

Living a New Life
The features of this service should focus on repentance and conversion. The emphasis of the sermon is experiencing a new beginning in Christ. As a special gift, some attendees may be invited to visit the local conference office in order to meet the conference officers.

Other Topics for a Women's Evangelistic Campaign
Other themes that may be covered in a women's evangelistic series include grace; the Holy Spirit; the life, death, and resurrection of Christ; growing in Christ; the state of the dead; spiritual gifts; marriage and the family; Christian behavior; Christ as our Intercessor; the millennium; unity in Christ; the mission of the remnant; and the new earth.

The Coaching Step

There will be persons who commit to following the Lord after the soul-winning activity is completed, and the task force for women's evangelism should have appropriate strategies in place to nurture these individuals. Chapter 17 provides suggestions of activities that may be utilized in this step. A team of both women and men should be selected, trained, and deployed to serve as spiritual coaches who are assigned to these new believers. Their responsibilities should be clearly defined, including a specific time frame in which to help new members transition into their new relationship with Christ and the church.

A Discipleship Growth Plan for Women

The Objectives

To inspire and motivate each female member of the church to continual personal growth in their devotion, fellowship, outreach, evangelism and stewardship lifestyle (See the chapter on discipleship).

Introduction

The mandate of Jesus to his disciples is found in Matthew 28:19-20; "Go therefore and make *disciples* of all the nations, baptizing them in the name of the Father and of the Son and of the Holy Spirit, teaching them to observe all things that I have commanded you; and lo, I am with you always, even to the *end* of the age."

Based on this text, discipleship making is the core responsibility of the Women Ministries of the Church. Five of the core values of Jesus' disciples are; Devotion, Fellowship, Outreach, Evangelism and Stewardship.

The design of this program is to engage each woman within the church to grow in these five primary areas as faithful disciples of Jesus.

Organization

The Women Ministries leader shall establish a discipleship committee comprising individuals who are *leaders of discipleship small groups*. The leaders of each of these small groups shall form their discipleship small group. Each group shall conduct initiatives designed to help each member fulfill the objective of this discipleship initiative.

Each small group may have a person responsible for each of the five areas of the discipleship core values. Other persons may be selected to be responsible for finance and as the secretary of the group. The secretary shall keep records, write notes and present reports.

A chief function of each small group is to train the members to fulfill their roles and participate in the various core values activities.

Members of the discipleship committee shall receive regular training in order to fulfill their roles.

Suggested activities for each core value of the discipleship program:

I. Discipleship Core Value – Devotion
Under this value, the women will be encouraged to:
- Attend weekly worship services
- Study their Sabbath School lesson
- Enhance their personal prayer life through ongoing prayer initiatives.
- Have daily family worship
- Read their bible that will inspire and motivate every member of the Church to develop a personal bible reading routine that will help them to increase their bible knowledge and apply the word of God to their personal life.
- Encourage the members to enhance their knowledge of the ministry and counsels of Ellen White and to make personal applications to their lives and ministry.
- Support and participate in the various spiritual programs and initiatives of the church.
- Study the following four doctrines of the church within a year;
    a. Doctrine # 10 The Experience of Salvation
    b. Doctrine # 11 Growing in Christ
    c. Doctrine # 12 The Church
    d. Doctrine # 13 The Remnant and its Mission
- Be engaged in any other initiative relevant to grow their spiritual life.

II. Discipleship Core Value – Fellowship
Under this value, the women will be encouraged to:
- Develop contacts and relationships with others on a social level that leads to friendly relations, and engage in various forms of

social interactions with individuals both within and outside the Church community.
- Be involved in one-to-one contact with others within the church, through organized social activities or personal encounters.
- Help both members and non-members to deal with their social, physical and emotional issues.
- To have at least two persons in their social relations at all times. One should be a member of the Church, the other should be a nonmember who is a prospect for church membership.
- Learn how to attract the attention of other individuals as mentioned above and build friendly relations with them.
- Participate in specific social activities organized by the group to get the women connecting with each other, building strong bonds and enjoy the Christian community.

III. Discipleship Core Value – Evangelism
Under this value, the women will be encouraged to:
- Share their faith and the gospel of Jesus—the good news of salvation—with others.
- Work with a team or a partner in sharing of the gospel to others.
- Determine the most appropriate time to be involved in evangelistic activities.
- Participate in the menu of evangelistic activities to share their faith that is determined by the group.
- Contribute to any special financial plan for the evangelistic program of the group
- Learn how to attract the interest and attention of non-Adventists and conduct bible studies with them.

IV. Discipleship Core Value – Outreach
This value deals with addressing material, social, and other needs of individuals in the surrounding community. Under this value, the women will be encouraged to:
- Participate in organized outreach ministries of the church or personal outreach endeavors.
- Address material, social, and other needs of individuals in the surrounding community.

- In Matthew 25:35-36 (NLT), Jesus described the *outreach* ministry of a disciple: "For I was hungry, and you fed Me. I was thirsty, and you gave Me a drink. I was a stranger, and you invited Me into your home. I was naked, and you gave Me clothing. I was sick, and you cared for Me. I was in prison, and you visited Me".
- Participate in organized Outreach that includes all these compassionate services
- Participate in other activities that relieve human suffering and satisfy human needs.
- Participate in relevant surveys within the church and the wider community to determine social and other needs and work to address such deficiencies.

V. Discipleship Core Value – Stewardship

This core value deals with all the gifts, talents, and other resources that the women possess that are given to them in trust and belong to God. The women are encouraged to use them wisely and appropriately to meet personal necessities, to further the cause of Christ, and to bless others. They are encouraged to:

- Sacrifice at least 8 hours weekly to participate in organized fellowship and outreach activities of the church
- Spend at least 45 minutes daily in prayer, lesson study, bible study and other inspirational reading
- Return their tithe and offering faithfully.
- Identify their talents and spiritual gifts and be encouraged to use them within the Church
- Live a life of faithfulness to the Lord in the way they manage their talents, time, resources and body temple and serve the church and others.

Worksheet for each Discipleship Group
Instructions

The leader of each small group shall lead out in this exercise to determine how the group will function. The following are some questions to be answered.

GROUP ACTIVITY #1

I. Name, of discipleship group leader: _____

II. Name and telephone number of each member:

_____ _____
_____ _____
_____ _____
_____ _____
_____ _____
_____ _____
_____ _____
_____ _____
_____ _____

III. Name group officers:

    Chairperson _____
    Secretary _____
    Finance Coordinator _____
    Devotion Coordinator _____
    Fellowship Coordinator _____
    Evangelism Coordinator _____
    Outreach Coordinator _____
    Stewardship Coordinator _____

IV. Name four specific Devotion initiatives that the group will do

_____
_____
_____
_____
_____

V. Name four specific Fellowship initiatives that the group will do.

_____
_____
_____
_____
_____
_____
_____

VI. Name four specific Outreach initiatives that the group will do.

_____
_____
_____
_____
_____
_____
_____

VII. Name four specific Stewardship initiatives that the group will do.

_____
_____
_____
_____
_____

Review and Discussion

- *Which female Bible characters were influential in their witness for Christ, and what impact did they have?*
- *List some of the questions that must be answered by the task force for women's evangelism. See chapter 3.*
- *Plan a Women Connect Forum that could be relevant and effective in your territory to prepare for an evangelistic campaign.*
- *How would you transition from a Women Connect Forum to a public evangelistic campaign?*
- *Explain how you would integrate Bible doctrines into any five of the suggested themes in a women's evangelistic campaign.*
- *Why do you think that women's evangelism would be effective in your church?*
- *What are some of the functions of the task force for women's evangelism? See chapter 3.*
- *Develop a complete, ready-to-implement plan that includes all five steps in a complete cycle of women's evangelism. See chapters 7 and 8.*

14
Planning and Implementing Effective Men's Evangelism

During Jesus' earthly ministry, "He went up on the mountain and called to Him those whom He desired, and they came to Him. And He appointed twelve (whom He also named apostles) so that they might be with Him and He might send them out to preach and have authority to cast out demons" (Mark 3:13–15). To initiate this men's evangelistic ministry, Jesus first called these apostles to be with Him. He is a God of relationship and wanted to have an abiding relationship with those whom He would commission for evangelistic duties. After the relationship was established, He sent them to preach and to have authority over satanic forces through the empowerment of the Holy Spirit.

The emerging men's ministries in the church has at least three foci: (1) to nurture men to fulfill their spiritual, social, and physical roles within the family, church, and society; (2) to lead others to Christ through outreach ministries and personal influence; (3) to equip men to live in readiness for the coming of the Lord. Thus, evangelism forms a central part of men's ministries. Men should be fully dedicated to proclaiming the gospel of Jesus and serving as catalysts to influence other men, as well as women, children, and youth, to accept Christ as their personal Savior.

Men's Evangelistic Growth Movement

The Men's Evangelistic Growth Movement (EGM) is an organized group of men in the church who demonstrate an interest in soul winning. They commit personal time and resources to evangelism and serve as catalysts to influence other men to participate in evangelism. They may be organized to function in small groups of between five and seven persons. The members of these small groups should be actively engaged in all the activities of the Men's Evangelistic Growth Movement. They are the men's ministries evangelistic team of the church.

Chapter 3 of this book explains the initial planning process for departmental evangelistic initiatives, and chapter 7 explains the various field preparation initiatives for an evangelistic campaign. A complete cycle of men's evangelism includes five key steps: *contact, connect, bond, proclaim, and support.*

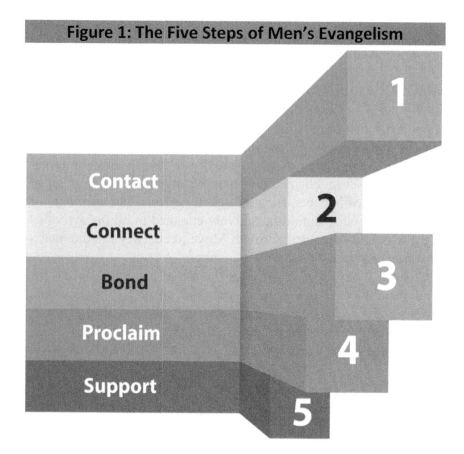

Figure 1: The Five Steps of Men's Evangelism

The Contact Step

In order to develop an effective men's evangelism program, the participation of the men of the church is essential. In the contact step, the men of the church identify those whom they, through the help of the Holy Spirit, would like to influence to the faith. These may be family members, relatives, friends, coworkers, schoolmates, or neighbors. The men add these names to their own evangelistic prayer lists and that of the task force for men's evangelism. They should look for the best time and approach to initiate contact with these persons.

Jesus' evangelistic strategy of one-to-one contact in Luke 10:1 and 2 has not lost its relevance. According to this plan, the disciples made initial contact with the people in preparation for Jesus' arrival in each town. Likewise, Christian men, either in small groups or individually, should make direct, personal contact with others in preparation for the preaching of the gospel. Contact may be spontaneous or intentional. Spontaneous contact takes place when a person inadvertently meets someone and initiates a conversation that leads to the development of a social relationship. This is one of the best ways to build a prospect list. It provides for a very smooth transition to faith sharing.

Intentional contact happens when, by design, members establish a prospect list of a determined number of persons. They should then dedicate time in personal prayer for these individuals while seeking ways to reach them with the gospel. These names should also be the focus of daily, intercessory prayer by all those who participate in the men's evangelism program.

How to Make Effective Contacts

Research has shown that when meeting someone for the first time, one only has about thirty seconds to make an impression. Within that time frame, the other person draws conclusions and decides whether or not to engage socially. This is instructive to men who are on evangelistic contact missions. Select the best possible time for the contact. Be very courteous in greeting the prospect and giving the person your undivided attention. If you know the name of the person, be bold in using it as part of your greeting. Identify yourself promptly, and state the reason for your visit. In your initial contact, you should never state that you are there to give a Bible study; and neither should that be your interest on an initial visit, unless the prospect is expecting you for such an occasion. Speak low and as softly as possible, but audibly so that the person does not have to strain to hear you or have to ask you to repeat yourself. Speaking in a lower tone conveys confidence and authority.

The contact phase is basically a greeting, introduction, and get-to-know you phase through which the prospect is introduced to you and made aware of your interest and ability to be of assistance in various ways. Highlight your professional, social, academic, vocational, handyman, or other skills in the contact phase. This will inform the prospect of areas in which you may be of service. After this initial meeting, an avenue should be established through which regular dialogue and collaboration can develop. To adequately establish the contact, it may be necessary to have more than one meeting with the prospect.

The Connect Step

Successful conclusion of the contact step will lead automatically into the connect step, which is the phase in which both parties begin to discuss common interests. At this stage, there is willingness to be engaged in common activities, which could be on a professional or social level. You become comfortable with each other by sharing interests, hobbies, ideologies, and ways of looking at the world. As a Christian, you should be sincere in modeling the Christian lifestyle and presenting Christ to the prospect. While still not preaching, your mannerisms and conduct should manifest the character of Christ in a way that commends you to the prospect. By being a genuine Christian, you live out salvation in Christ with joy so that the prospect can see Christ in your life.

The Bond Step

This is the step in which actual training is provided, information shared, and skills learned. This is done through Men's Collaboration Forums, which are conducted according to the guidelines in chapter 7 for community-outreach forums. The men should invite their prospects to attend these forums. They should attend the meetings themselves, as this will provide additional ideas or points for discussion to deepen the conversation and relationship with their prospects, thus leading to a stronger bond. After these forums, men from the church should always follow up with the prospects.

The following list suggests topics that may be presented in these forums according to the needs of the participants. Biblical and doctrinal studies should also be included in these forums using a selected series of Bible lessons.

- How to Keep Your Wife Happy and Smiling
- Managing Your Role as a Man
- How to Maximize Your Potential
- Balancing Work, Family, Pleasure, and Church

- Building Effective Social and Spiritual Relationships
- Overcoming Negatives and Building Positives
- Handling Stress and Making Progress
- Time Management that Pays Dividends
- Growing Your Wealth and Managing Wisely

During these meetings, men should intentionally cultivate patience, tolerance, forgiveness, love, joy, happiness, acceptance, mercy, peace, and kindness. These attributes are not the content of the gathering, but are the glue that holds the attention of the attendees and motivates them to attend. Care should be taken in the Evangelistic Growth Movement to train all participants to understand the objectives of the program, preparing them to anticipate and deal with situations that could frustrate these attributes in the forums. It is important to develop these attributes as a genuine lifestyle phenomenon. They should not be mere dramatization but should rather characterize a Christian man's normal demeanor as a part of his everyday life.

During this bonding phase, the men of the church could organize a Men's Community-Development Day to invite men from both the church and the community to participate in a project that will benefit the residents of the local community. Some examples of projects that may be undertaken as part of this initiative include:

- Repairing and painting the house of a needy person in the community. • Repairing a retirement home and providing services to the residents.
- Repairing an orphanage and providing services to the children.
- Distributing eyeglasses to needy persons in the community.
- Distributing shoes to needy persons in the community.
- Hosting a blood drive.
- Organizing a community gospel concert.
- Repairing a school in the community.
- Participating in a park-development or tree-planting project.

The Proclaim Step

The contact, connect, and bond steps are preparatory to the proclaim step, which consists of the reaping campaign. The campaign should include at least fourteen presentations and may be between two and four weeks. Bible lesson courses on the basic doctrines of the church have been completed, relationships between church members and prospects have progressed, and it is now time to reap the harvest of souls.

Chapter 8 explains the details of carrying out such a campaign, including the various features of the nightly program. Each program should include music, drama, video, testimony, and preaching that are related to the theme and its doctrinal emphasis. The following examples are some of the themes that may be used in this series.

Love Without Exception

This theme presents the grace of God that is available through Christ. The features and message highlight how the love of God goes searching for all, irrespective of how wayward, careless, and indifferent they have been. The drama should depict how this unconditional, divine love appears to people, offering them a relationship with God and a new life that is uplifting and enriching. As a gift, some individuals may receive a DVD or an invitation to watch a film or drama that highlights Christ's unconditional love.

Staying in Love and Going Home

The features of this theme focus on the second advent of Christ. The drama could depict Christ returning and taking home those who have committed their lives to Him or could depict various happy and healthy or unhappy and unhealthy relationships. The preacher could invite wives to bring their husbands to the Lord or invite men to bring their families to the Lord. As a gift, invitations may be given to a few men to participate in a specially planned event that will provide fellowship and the opportunity to discus the Second Advent.

Love, Lust, and Infatuation

The various features of this theme may describe the differences between romantic and benevolent love as well as lust and infatuation. The joys and pain associated with love could also be discussed. The message could highlight ten things that every woman should know about loving a man or that every man should know about a loving a woman. After these practical life issues are presented, they should be integrated with the biblical principles of the Ten Commandments, showing what God has put in place to enable amicable relationships in both the horizontal and vertical planes. The preacher should invite men in particular, as well as all those who are not committed to the Lord, to accept God's will and commit to keeping the Ten Commandments through the power of the Holy Spirit.

Living in the Shadows

This theme employs illustrations based on the deeds of men who live in the shadows. The doctrinal segment of the sermon relates these stories to the final judgment. The drama could depict the story of a man who was either acquitted or convicted or a biblical story involving the judgment. Gifts should emphasize freedom and liberty. The opening and closing comments should be about being acquitted in the judgment. The preacher invites men, women, youth, and children, both individually and as families, to accept Christ into their lives and thus avoid condemnation in the judgment.

Finding Abundance and Security in Life

In this theme, men are called to stand up and face trials with the knowledge that the Lord will take care of them. The various features use illustrations and testimonies related to trials in the areas of family, relationships, finances, job, health, security, immigration, education, and housing. This theme highlights the experience of the three Hebrew boys in Daniel 3 who resisted temptation when they were challenged for their faith in God and as a result, were miraculously delivered. The drama could reenact this experience. The sermon emphasizes that in spite of the trials that they have to face in life, like those three Hebrew boys, Christian men have a strong defense. The preacher invites men as well as other attendees to establish their faith upon the Word of the God and accept Christ into their lives.

Your Next Relationship

This theme deals with relationships that have turned sour, how to improve them, and how to avoid negative relationships in the future. These practical life issues will be used to illustrate the importance of a strong, committed relationship with the Lord that is sealed with baptism. The features of the program focus on how to handle social relationships in harmony with biblical principles such as living within one's means, showing restraint, and demonstrating forgiveness. This could include a testimony that highlights a specific area of relationship management. The drama could be a biblical story on baptism, and the opening and closing comments should be about being faithful to the baptismal vows. The preacher invites married couples, courting partners, and others to commit their lives to Christ and be baptized.

Time for Remodeling

Conversion is the biblical doctrine emphasized by this theme. The features highlight experiences in which individuals have experienced transformation. The drama could present the story of Nicodemus or a story about a man or woman who was preoccupied with physical transformation but then received spiritual transformation through an encounter with Jesus. The video could emphasize the difference between genuine, lasting conversion and temporary conversion in a time of crisis. The preacher invites men and other attendees to experience true and lasting transformation in Christ.

Clinical Procrastination

The message and features of this theme present the reality of procrastination, some of the reasons for it, some of its effects, and how to overcome it. One study asserts that one out of every five people suffers from clinical procrastination. This condition affects quality of life, work performance, and relationships, as well as present and future life goals. It can also affect a person's salvation. As an example of this, the drama could recount the experience of Felix in the book of Acts. A book on overcoming procrastination may be used as a gift for this theme. The sermon centers on a call to come out of Babylon, in which the preacher invites attendees to make the decision to accept Christ now rather than later.

Other Topics for the Men's Ministries Evangelistic Campaign

Other themes that may be covered in a men's evangelistic campaign include "Wall-to-Wall Happiness", "Living and Loving," "The Joys of Giving," "Living a Second Time," "Freedom from Captivity," "The Joy of a Second Chance," "Forgiving and Enjoying," "Defeat and Victory," "When Time Will Be No More," and "Real Acceptance."

Support Step

Those who have accepted Christ as their Savior will need to be integrated into their newfound faith. The task force for men's evangelism should have appropriate strategies in place to nurture and conserve those who commit to Christ. Chapter 17 provides some suggestions of activities that may be utilized in this step. A team of men and women should be selected, trained, and deployed to serve as spiritual-support guides, who will be assigned to new believers. Their responsibilities should be clearly defined, with a specific time frame in which to help new members transition into their new relationship with Christ and the church.

Review and Discussion

- *List some of the questions that must be answered by the task force for men's evangelism. See chapter 3.*
- *What are some projects that may be done on a Men's Community-Development Day in your neighborhood?*
- *Explain what a Men's Collaboration Forum is and how the men of your church can execute it effectively.*
- *Identify the five steps in the cycle of men's evangelism and briefly share what you would do to execute each step.*
- *Suggest any five themes that you would present in a men's public-evangelism campaign, and state what Bible doctrines you would integrate into those themes.*
- *Choose one of these themes and explain how you would perform the five nightly features in it.*
- *What are some of the functions of the task force for men's evangelism? See chapter 3.*
- *Develop a complete, ready-to-implement plan that includes all five steps in a complete cycle of men's evangelism. See chapters 7 and 8.*

15
Planning and Implementing Effective Youth Evangelism

THE GOSPEL COMMISSION has no age restrictions. Jesus was speaking to all those who would accept Him as Savior in any time, regardless of their age, when He issued the commission, "Go therefore and make disciples of all nations, baptizing them in the name of the Father and of the Son and of the Holy Spirit, teaching them to observe all that I have commanded you. And behold, I am with you always, to the end of the age" (Matt. 28:19, 20). "All who receive the life of Christ are ordained to work for the salvation of their fellow men. For this work the church was established, and all who take upon themselves its sacred vows are thereby pledged to be co-workers with Christ" (Desires of Ages, chap. 86, p. 822).

It is believed that when Jeremiah was given the task of delivering an unpopular, convicting message to Israel, he was only seventeen years old. He said:

> The word of the Lord came to me, saying, "Before I formed you in the womb I knew you, before you were born I set you apart; I appointed you as a prophet to the nations."
>
> "Alas, Sovereign Lord," I said, "I do not know how to speak; I am too young."

But the Lord said to me, "Do not say, 'I am too young.' You must go to everyone I send you to and say whatever I command you. Do not be afraid of them, for I am with you and will rescue you," declares the Lord. Then the Lord reached out His hand and touched my mouth and said to me, "I have put my words in your mouth. See, today I appoint you over nations and kingdoms to uproot and tear down, to destroy and overthrow, to build and to plant." (Jer. 1:4–10, NIV)

The Spirit of Prophecy is replete with instructions on the importance of young people's involvement in soul winning. "Youthful talent, well organized and well trained, is needed in our churches" (*Gospel Workers*, sec. 6, p. 211). She further stated, "The youth, if right, could sway a mighty influence. Preachers, or laymen advanced in years, cannot have one-half the influence upon the young that the youth, devoted to God, can have upon their associates" (*Messages to Young People*, chap. 63, p. 204).

The youth of the church, therefore, must rally to the following call: "Young men and young women, cannot you form companies, and, as soldiers of Christ, enlist in the work, putting all your tact and skills and talents into the Master's service, that you may save souls from ruin? Let there be companies organized in every church to do this work. Will the young men and young women who really love Jesus organize themselves as workers, not only for those who profess to be Sabbath keepers, but for those who are not of our faith?" (*Christian Service*, chap. 2, p. 34).

Many younger people have a negative conception of Christianity, a fact borne out by a study by Thom Rainer that showed that only 29% of those born in the United States between 1977 and 1994 attend church.1 At the same time, our church records show that about 70% of the baptized members of the church are age thirty or younger.

There are hundreds and thousands of young people in the church who could be involved in fulfilling the gospel commission. They are sharp, talented, and creative, and they have extraordinary and innovative skills. Such an army of youth is great news for the church. To have them idle, however, is not good news. They must be put to work. Ellen White said: "We have an army of youth today who can do much if they are properly directed and encouraged. We want them to act a part in well-organized plans for helping other youth" (*Testimonies to Ministers and Gospel Workers,* chap. 1, p. 32). To this end, these youth "must be taught how to labor for the Master. They must be trained, disciplined, drilled, in the best methods of winning souls to Christ" (*Gospel Workers,* sec. 6, p. 210).

Youth-Evangelism Resource Bank

Every district or local church should have resources available to empower the youth in evangelism and soul winning. These resources should include the following:
- Audio and video recordings of sermons
- Printed copies of sermons
- Sermon outlines
- Audio and video courses on sermon preparation
- Printed materials on sermon preparation
- Sermon-illustration materials
- Audio CDs on a wide range of topics
- Magazines and periodicals for research
- Encyclopedias
- Concordances
- Bible Dictionaries
- Computer with internet connection
- CD-ROM of Ellen G. White's writings

Preparation for Youth Evangelism

In order to lead others to Christ, young people should begin with themselves by seeking divine aid to live godly, Christian lives in their homes, at work, at school, in the community, and in the church. They thus demonstrate the life changes that they desire others to emulate.

Chapter 3 of this book explains the initial planning process for departmental evangelistic initiatives, and chapter 7 explains the various field-preparation initiatives for an evangelistic campaign. It is important

---

for the Youth Ministries Department to establish an evangelism task force to oversee this entire process. This task force should develop an evangelistic prayer list. The youth of the church should present the persons on this prayer list to the Lord in prayer every day. In their prayers, they should ask God to convict these individuals of His love and of their need for salvation and should ask Him for wisdom to be able to minister to them.

Youth evangelism may follow a five-step procedure of (1) *organization, (2) participation, (3) relationship building, (4) commitment, and (5) consolidation*. A rigid application of this procedure will not always be the ideal approach; rather, it is necessary to contextualize these methods according to what is most relevant and effective for the situation.

Figure 1: The Five Steps of Youth Evangelism

The Organization Step

This step begins with the appointment of the youth-evangelism task force. The objective of this task force is to provide every young person in the church with the opportunity to participate in youth evangelism. Its leaders should approach and encourage youth in whom they perceive the potential to be effective in soul winning, encouraging them to be involved in working for others. It is important to point out their abilities, gifts, and talents and share with them the evangelistic vision of the church. It is also helpful to talk to the parents about these observations in order to obtain their support for the involvement of their children in the youth-outreach ministries of the church.

Develop a list of young people to be equipped for the important spiritual task of soul winning. The members of the task force and other church members should present these names to the Lord in prayer each day. They should schedule meetings to build relationships with these young people and motivate them to become front-line disciples of Christ. They should encourage them to participate in and conduct evangelistic campaigns, Bible studies, Youth Contemporaries Forums, and other soul-winning activities. During the organization step, advisors, counselors, and guides for the youth-evangelism task force should be chosen to assist, support, and equip the youth in their evangelistic initiatives. The youth should be organized into mission teams based on the tasks that they will perform when the outreach endeavors begin. During the participation phase, they will receive instruction according to the objectives of their mission team.

Comfort Team

Some of those identified and motivated by the youth-evangelism task force may recruit other youth to form comfort teams to execute specific mission initiatives. These are small groups made up of persons who share a similar passion and whom the team leader feels comfortable working with. These teams should be organized according to the principles for establishing small groups presented in chapter 5. The task force coaches the team leader—according to their talents, gifts, training, and passion—to be the principal standard bearer in fulfilling the group's mission objectives and trains all the members of the team to execute their specific tasks.

The Participation Step

The actual equipping or training of the youth for evangelistic activities takes place in the participation step. The youth have already been organized into mission teams with stated objectives, and now they must be trained before they are sent. Some of the activities of this participation phase are explained below.

Bible Surfing Mission Team

This is a team that conducts Bible studies on doctrines and other biblical topics. Bible Surfing is explained in appendix E. The topics studied should be properly prepared with handouts, if possible. The members of the team first complete the selected lessons among themselves. They may demonstrate their Bible knowledge at youth programs in the church in order to build their confidence and motivate other members to participate in this ministry. Then they will present these studies to their evangelistic prospects. This team-study approach is beneficial in at least three primary ways:

1. Group members become conversant with the doctrines of the church.
2. As soon as they have studied a doctrine or topic, they have the opportunity to present it to other church members as well as evangelistic prospects.
3. Members who have a good command of certain doctrines present them to the prospects. In this way, church members are able to establish positive relationships with prospects so that whenever these individuals become members of the church, they will already have friends, allies, and confidants within the church.

Share-Your-Faith Mission Team

As a means of training the youth to witness to others, each young person is expected to find at least one member of the church to share their faith with during the week. The youth of this team will also work together to carry out evangelistic visitation. The information on new contact, sequel, and decision visits in chapter 4 can be utilized in training this team.

Sabbath Seminars

A Sabbath Seminar is a one-and-a-half-hour topical Bible study that is conducted by young people through the local Adventist Youth Society in cities, towns, villages, streets, and highways. This outreach program is designed to utilize the talents, interests, and influence of the youth of the church to impact lives and communities and attract individuals to the Seventh-day Adventist Church. Each church should conduct a Sabbath Seminar as part of its preparation for the public evangelistic campaign.

Youth Marshalls and guides should be appointed for each Sabbath Seminar. They will position themselves at strategic points within a certain proximity of the center of action of the seminar. There they will contact passersby and invite them to attend the discussion or presentation. They will then walk with the persons they have contacted to the center of action, stand with them, and help them get answers to their questions. They will obtain the names and telephone numbers or e-mail addresses of their contacts and give this information to the organizers, who will arrange for follow-up to be done with those interests.

The Sabbath Seminar may span a period of two to four weeks, covering issues taking place within the local community or society at large that affect youth, women, men, families, etc. The presenters will draw attention to the Bible's response to these issues. The topical presentation may utilize a lecture, audio-visual, or discussion format, or a combination these. Each seminar should be brief, not lasting for more than one and a half hours. There should be seminar leaders and assistants who will plan and execute the weekly program, which may consist of:
- Singing
- Prayer
- Topical presentation
- Bible application
- Conclusion

Youth-Evangelists Mission Team
This is a group of young preachers who are trained as gospel workers and sent to do ministry in other pastoral districts, communities, neighborhoods, cities, islands, or countries. Their mission is to (1) contribute to the growth of existing churches through evangelistic preaching, (2) plant new churches, (3) train others for qualitative and quantitative church growth.

Youth-Evangelism Equipping Retreats
These are weekend or weeklong series in which advisors, counselors, and guides dedicate exclusive time to training the youth to effectively execute their evangelistic tasks.

Youth-Preachers Academy
This is a program organized in each church or pastoral district to train young people to do sermon-preparation research, sermon preparation, sermon delivery, campaign organization, and campaign-team building. All those chosen to form a part of the Youth-Evangelists Mission Team will be enrolled in this academy to receive training.

The Relationship-Building Step

In this step, the youth engage in conducting a series of Youth Contemporaries Forums (YCF), which are conducted according to the guidelines in chapter 7 for community-outreach forums. These forums deal with practical issues affecting young people and provide an opportunity to carry out community projects. They could also include a youth excursion where young people from the church and the community go on a fun trip or educational tour together. The number of forums will depend upon the needs within the local area, as determined by the community-needs survey conducted by the youth-evangelism task force. A key element of these forums is to demonstrate the love of Christ. Working upon the heart, the Holy Spirit uses this practical love to bring conviction to the uncommitted. "The strongest argument in favor of the gospel is a loving and lovable Christian" (*Counsels on Sabbath School Work*, chap. 4, p. 100).

The purpose of these forums is to integrate faith with the development of specific competencies, which may include:
- Skills in sports (such as basketball)
- Exercise techniques (for therapy, health care, rehabilitation, restoration, etc.)
- Environmental stewardship
- Neighborhood crime watch
- Career selection
- Job acquisition
- Counseling and encouragement
- Overcoming addictions
- Use of technology
- Use of social media
- Foreign languages

It would also be good to organize a Youth Community-Development Day for the youth of the church and the community to work together on a project that will benefit residents in the local community. Examples of such projects include:
- Repairing and painting the house of a needy person in the community.
- Repairing a retirement home and providing services to the residents.
- Repairing an orphanage and providing services to the children.
- Repairing a school in the community.
- Distributing back-to-school supplies.
- Hosting a blood drive.
- Organizing a community musical program.
- Building a bus shed for residents in the community.
- Participating in a park-development or tree-planting project.

Satellite Groups

These are groups of young people who are trained to prepare the territory for evangelistic reaping campaigns. They will work in and around the area where the campaign will be conducted, creating interest in the upcoming campaign and preparing prospects. They will accomplish this by forming friendships with community members and distributing printed materials.

The Commitment Step

This step consists of the actual execution of the public reaping campaign, for which all previous activities were preparatory. There should be direct integration of relevant precampaign activities into the campaign itself. This may be accomplished by giving recognition to individuals for their participation in various aspects of these activities. Such recognition could be in the form of certificates, plaques, trophies, monetary gifts, articles of clothing, food baskets, fruit baskets, scholarships, and reading materials. This may be done throughout the duration of the campaign. There should be a schedule to inform people of which competencies or areas of concentration will be recognized nightly.

Chapter 8 explains the details of carrying out a public campaign, including the various features of the nightly program, as well as the various modes of presentation that may be used to make the messages available to both face-to-face and remote audiences. Each program should include music, drama, video, testimony, and preaching that are related to the theme and its doctrinal emphasis. The speaker should make use of the practical life experiences highlighted in the various features to present the spiritual message. The features of the meetings can include various emphases in which other departments of the church can participate. Thus, instead of the Youth Ministries Department working alone, the campaign is a joint departmental effort in which the young people carry out many of the leadership functions.

Presentation Styles

Chapter 8 explains several possible formats for presenting evangelistic messages. In addition to these methods, the reactive and thematic presentation styles can be particularly effective in youth evangelism. With the reactive style, the evangelist's presentation revolves around one to three questions posed by either the speaker or those in the congregation. The evangelist answers these questions from a biblical perspective. Thus, doctrines and the essentials of salvation can be presented in a way in which hearers are able to readily absorb and retain these concepts.

In the thematic style, on the other hand, the various elements of the campaign revolve around a selected theme. In the case of a youth evangelistic campaign, choose youth-friendly themes like "Family Life," "Relationship Building," "Practicing Healthy Communication Patterns," "God and the Internet," "Youth: Happy Followers of Christ," "God Includes Young People Too," and "Healthy Lifestyles for Youth."

Key Considerations for Leading Program Participants

Be genuine. Participants should be vulnerable and honest. Rather than trying to imitate others, they should be themselves. Everyone has their own unique qualities, and youth are interested in what is real. They will accept participants as they are but will be turned off when they recognize that someone is trying to imitate the mannerisms of others.

Be relevant. Young people are interested in practical messages. Use real-life experiences to illustrate spiritual truth. Covering up or shunning issues and situations that are unpleasant to talk about will not satisfy today's youth. Young people must know that they are expected to develop positive habits instead of destructive ones.

The truth of the gospel as it is in Jesus is always relevant. Preach it without apology, always exalting God's grace, which provides redemption and reconciliation in Jesus. The love of Christ will soften the hearts of all, both young and old.

Be stimulating. Employ current methods and approaches, including videos, music, drama, and personal stories. However, do not use these methods simply to entertain. Deal with life issues that touch the experiences of young people. Thus they will see the truth for themselves and be able to apply it to their own lives.

Those presenting each feature must demonstrate and emphasize love and compassion where applicable. Explain the principles of Scripture, even if this causes some to feel uncomfortable, which is often a necessary aspect of conviction. This is what the gospel is about: Grace finds sinners where they are, leads them to become conscious of their reality, and saves those who surrender. It instructs, saves, and enables.

Be relational. Participants should seek to identify with those to whom they minister. Presenting oneself as better or more perfect than others produces division and destroys attention and conviction. The gospel is not to be used to exalt oneself. Exalt Jesus; He makes the difference.

Social Media Usage in Youth Evangelism

The largest audience today is on social media and electronic devices. Organizers of a youth evangelistic series should arrange for the campaign to be broadcast live by Internet streaming or local cable television. The youth of the church should participate in a "Social Media Campaign for Christ" by inviting their friends and others through Facebook, text messaging, or other forms of electronic communication to participate in the evangelistic campaign. They should be innovative in their use of social media in order to invite friends to the campaign and ensure that those who do not come have access to the program.

A social media coordinator should be appointed as a member of the youth-evangelism task force. This individual should be very active in the campaign, reporting on the progress, connections, and responses of those who participate. The coordinator should have a list of social media guides who are participating in the social media ministry and a list of the interested persons whom these guides have contacted through their social media involvement.

Social Media Evangelistic Chat Room

The social media Evangelistic Chat Room is a designated area within the facility in which the evangelistic campaign is being held. From this Chat Room, participants transmit live snippets of the message through online posts, texts, tweets, and other relevant forms of social media. If possible, Wi-Fi should be made available in this area. Chat Room coordinators should be chosen to assist participants with technical support where necessary, as well as to ensure order and a worshipful atmosphere. The coordinators should register each person who enters the Chat Room. Each participant should complete an information form similar to the form below, which can be adapted to make it relevant to the specific evangelistic campaign. Relevant information from the form should be presented to the campaign evangelist, campaign coordinator, or Bible workers so that where necessary, follow-up can be performed to engage interested virtual worshipers to make decisions for Christ.

Social Media Evangelistic Chat Room Information Sheet

Name of participant _____
Meeting Date _____
Participant's e-mail address _____
Telephone #: _____
Type of device used _____
Social media used _____
Number of posts, tweets, etc. _____
Number of responses received _____

Name of Respondent	Contact Information	Interest ("Needs a phone call," "Desires a visit," etc.)

Consolidation Step

Those who accept a new life in Christ will need to be integrated into their newfound faith. This step is a postcampaign activity in which the church community works to consolidate new members through nurturing programs, while at the same time continuing to build relationships and study with those who have not been baptized. The youth-evangelism task force should have appropriate

strategies in place to execute this step. Chapter 17 provides some suggestions of activities that may be utilized. A new believers nurturing and support team should be organized to build relationships with new members and assist them in adjusting to their new life. This team should take into consideration the possibility that new believers will have some or all of the following needs:
- Physical needs (food, shelter, clothing)
- Job-related needs
- Immigration challenges
- The need to cope with family problems and other social challenges
- The need to be accepted by other members of the Seventh-day Adventist Church
- The need to accept the following realities:
  o I am now a Seventh-day Adventist.
  o I am no longer a member of my former faith with its beliefs and practices.
  o I now have a new spiritual community, with different doctrinal beliefs, to understand and embrace.

New members may be consolidated in the faith through participation and involvement. A mentor should be assigned to each newly baptized member. The mentor must be an experienced, baptized member of the Seventh-day Adventist Church who is in good and regular standing.

Mentors are to ensure that new members are given the opportunity to participate in the services of the church. They should find out what the new members do best, speak to the leaders of the corresponding ministries, and seek to involve the new members in the worship, outreach, and social activities of the church. They should invite them for a meal on Sabbath or another convenient time or make sure that other members invite them for dinner and fellowship.

A postbaptismal class in which motivational and faith-related topics are studied is essential. This class should be held at a time that is convenient for all. This will likely, although not necessarily, be during the class time of the weekly Sabbath School.

Review and Discussion

- *Mention six things that the youth-evangelism task force can do to ensure effective soul winning through youth evangelism. See chapter 3.*
- *What should be the relationship between the youth-evangelism task force and the Evangelism Action Committee of the church? See chapter 3.*
- *Name six resources that you would include in your youth-evangelism resource bank.*
- *List the five steps of the youth-evangelism cycle and discuss various activities that may be conducted in each step.*
- *Differentiate between a comfort team and a satellite group.*
- *Explain the difference between the reactive and thematic sermon-presentation styles.*
- *Provide examples that illustrate the four key considerations for those who have leading parts in the nightly evangelistic program.*
- *How would you use social media in youth evangelism, and what is the function of the Evangelistic Chat Room?*
- *Develop a complete, ready-to-implement plan that includes all five steps in a complete cycle of youth evangelism. See chapters 7 and 8.*

16

Planning and Implementing Effective Children Evangelism

JESUS ESTABLISHED no age requirement for individuals to begin their labors in evangelistic ministry. Josiah, one of the greatest reformers in the history of Israel, became King of Judah at the age of eight (2 Kings 22; 2 Chron. 34). When the book of the Law was found and brought to his attention, he read it; and through the knowledge he received, he led the nation to follow the Lord. Many often focus on children's lack of maturity and experience as a reason for excluding them from many activities. But on the contrary, Jesus said, "Let the little children come to Me and do not hinder them, for to such belongs the kingdom of heaven" (Matt. 19:14). And just as He has a place for children in His arms, He has a place for them in His service.

Children who participate in evangelism are instruments in the Lord's hands to reap His harvest. Isaiah declared, "The wolf will live with the lamb, the leopard will lie down with the goat, the calf and the lion and the yearling together; and a little child will lead them" (Is. 11:6, NIV). The Lord will subdue these most powerful and ferocious beasts under the control of children in the new earth, and through the Holy Spirit He uses children today in bringing the message of truth and salvation to all classes and conditions of humanity. For this reason, calculated and intentional efforts should be dedicated in the home, school, and church to involve children in soul-winning initiatives.

Preparing Children for Soul-Winning Ministry

Children's evangelism must be an integral aspect of the church's evangelistic program that is carefully, prayerfully, and delicately nurtured. Many churches have wonderful children who have a great potential to preach the Word of God and participate in other evangelistic activities to lead others to Christ. However, such children should not be immediately thrust into the pulpit or engaged in evangelistic activities just because they possess talents in such areas. It is little wonder that many children who have been called child evangelists never go on to fully develop their evangelistic aptitudes. They simply become frustrated as demands and expectations are placed upon them that they are unable to fulfill since they lack the necessary preparation.

Children's evangelism is a spiritual phenomenon. Therefore, children should not simply be praised, pushed forward to preach, and then passed by. Rather, teachers, mentors, and role models should empower and nurture them so that through balanced spiritual growth they may achieve their maximum potential. Most children who are involved in evangelism could be more effective in leading others to Christ, and many who have not been involved could do an excellent job as well.

In order to execute successful children's evangelistic efforts, it will be necessary to appoint a task force for children's evangelism. Chapter 3 explains the planning process the task force should follow, while chapter 7 explains the various field-preparation initiatives for an evangelistic campaign. There are five important phases that pastors and Children's Ministries leaders should follow in order to establish an effective program of children's evangelism and soul winning in the church: *(1) recruiting, (2) orientation, (3) training, (4) deployment, and (5) nurture.*

The Recruiting Phase

Pastors, Children's Ministries leaders, and the task force for children's evangelism should identify children who demonstrate an ability to perform well in evangelism. Leaders should approach these children individually, talk to them about the abilities, gifts, or talents they see in them, and share a vision with them of how they can contribute to the fulfillment of the mission of the church. They should also talk with the parents, seeking their permission and support to encourage and involve the children in evangelistic efforts.

It is important to develop a list of children to be equipped for this important spiritual task. Their names should be placed on a special prayer list, which the task force, members of the Evangelism Action Committee, and others within the church will present to the Lord in prayer each day. Mentors, coaches, and trainers for children's evangelism should also be selected during this phase of the program.

The Orientation Phase

Once the children along with their mentors, coaches, and trainers are recruited, the orientation phase should begin. Orientation establishes in the minds of the children the purpose for which they were recruited. In this stage, they are informed of the specific tasks to be accomplished, the purpose of these tasks, and the resources they will need. Explain how the initiative will benefit them as well as the persons they labor for and the church as a whole. Communicate to them what support will be given, what training will be available, what is expected of them, the various phases of the initiative, and the duration of each phase. Make sure that this phase of the initiative is adequately explained so that each participant fully understands the program in its entirety. Assign mentors, coaches, and trainers to the children who are participating, and organize the children into mission groups.

Mission groups are organized based on the specific mission tasks that they will engage in. The following are some possible types of mission groups: child evangelists, homework guides, Bible study instructors, community project leaders, birthday-celebration organizers, and seminar presenters. There should be trainers or coaches for each mission group, and each group should have a mentor, whose function is to serve as counselor, motivator, and organizer. The mentor will keep all relevant records for the group and accompany the children during training and in the execution of their mission activities.

Figure 1: The Five Phases of Children's Evangelism

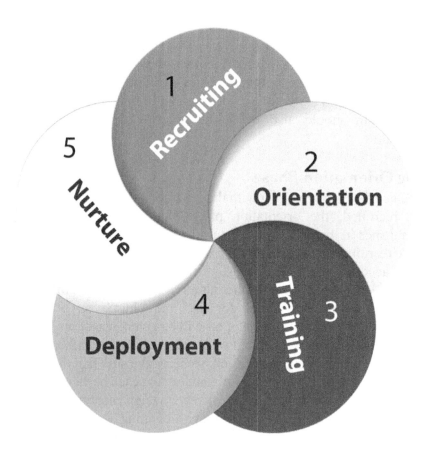

The Training Phase

Immediately after orientation, training should begin. The objective of this initiative of training children is to make them productive in evangelism in their own right, rather than to merely enlist them as helpers to accomplish the projects of others or to just stand in the pulpit and read sermons prepared by adults. Training children for evangelism does not happen overnight. Modeling, encouraging, coaching, and deploying children to fulfill various roles within the local church and the community requires time, strategy, resources, and patience.

Training should unleash children's creativity and help them improve in the ministry area for which they have a passion or interest. It should also motivate them to strengthen their commitment to the success of the ministry in which they are involved. When children are given the opportunity to work alongside someone who has experience in ministry, they will identify with that person, and through this connection they will develop a passion and a sense of ownership for the initiatives in which they participate. As they experience the Lord's blessings in their ministries, their confidence will grow.

Children should be trained to fulfill the specific mission tasks of their group. For example, if they are part of a Bible study group, they should be trained to conduct the Bible study, seek reactions, and answer questions. Trainers and coaches for those in the homework group should train the children to lead out in their group, teaching them leadership skills as well as building their self-confidence and developing their competency in their specialized area. Those in the child-evangelists group should be taught sermon preparation and delivery, as well as how to make effective appeals for individuals to accept Christ.

This training process should not end prematurely. Children must be given sufficient time to develop the necessary skills. A time of initial training should be dedicated to developing basic competency in the tasks of the mission group. After this initial training, coaches and trainers should continue to accompany the children as they begin to carry out these tasks.

The Deployment Phase

In the deployment phase, children become actively involved in community outreach activities. With the help of their mentors, each child involved in a mission group should develop a list of children or others whom they would like to reach for Christ. These may include family members, relatives, friends, schoolmates, or neighbors. Children should learn to pray for these individuals daily.

Child-to-Child Improvement Get-Together

Before conducting a public evangelistic campaign, the task force should organize a Child-to-Child Improvement Get-Together, which is conducted according to the guidelines in chapter 7 for community-outreach forums. This is a children's social-mingling initiative through which skills are taught, information shared, and understanding created based on the needs of the participants. Children lead out in these activities, and adults are present to provide support and encouragement and to ensure order.

Each child involved in a mission group should invite those on their prayer list to participate in this activity. Other children and adults in the church should also invite children to participate. Children who invite others should be present themselves, as the get-together is for their benefit as well. Their presence also provides support for those they invite and leads to deeper relationships and stronger bonds with these individuals.

Parents should be encouraged to accompany their children to this get-together if possible. This will help to maintain discipline and will provide an opportunity for them to develop relationships with members of the church. "Through the children many parents will be reached" (*Evangelism,* sec. 17, p. 584).

It would be good to include a short feature in this get-together to celebrate the recent birthdays of those invited to the program. Encourage those who are celebrating birthdays to invite their parents and friends to attend with them. A special children's church service may also be held at some point during the preparation for the public campaign. Invite all the participants in the Child-to-Child Improvement Get-Together program to attend along with their parents. The following are some of the topics that may be used for Child-to-Child Improvement Get-Togethers:

- How to complete school assignments correctly and on time.
- How to manage your time well.

- How to spend money wisely and save for the future.
- How to cope with hurtful experiences and move on happily.
- How to make good friends and keep them.
- How to enjoy family, school, church, and recreation.

These get-togethers may last between one hour and one and a half hours. They may take place once or twice each week or as often as is most convenient for the participants. They may be arranged in a series of between four and six weeks according what needs to be accomplished. Biblical and doctrinal studies should be included in these forums using a selected series of Bible lessons, and the task force for children's evangelism should make sure that appropriate follow-up with the prospects is carried out.

Community Projects

Each mission group should plan special days for the children to work on projects that will benefit the community or individuals with special needs within the community. The task force for children's evangelism should coordinate these activities in order to avoid conflicts and ensure effectiveness. These projects could include:
- Caring for the elderly.
- Providing services to children at an orphanage.
- Distributing food to the needy.
- Organizing a community musical program.
- Participating in community cleanup or tree planting.
- Performing a drama for the residents of the community that provides enjoyment and promotes good morals.

Children's Evangelistic Reaping Campaign

After the Child-to-Child Improvement Get-Togethers have achieved their objectives, the task force for children's evangelism should organize an evangelistic reaping campaign in which children who have received appropriate training will conduct many aspects of the program. Bible lesson courses on the basic doctrines of the church have been completed, relationships between church members and prospects have progressed, and it is now time to reap the harvest of souls. The campaign may last from one to three weeks or more, depending on what the local church determines will produce the best results. The messages presented should cover the essential doctrines of the church.

Chapter 8 explains the details of carrying out a public evangelistic campaign, including the various features of the nightly program. This program should be adapted to the needs of children. In order to capture the attention of the varied minds in the congregation, the service should include the following seven elements: *(1) stories, (2) humor, (3) video, (4) drama, (5) music, (6) sermon notes, and (7) preaching.* These elements should combine practical issues of daily life with related Bible doctrines, demonstrating the love of Christ and creating in the hearts and minds of the hearers the desire to accept Christ into their lives and make a commitment to live for Him.

Figure 2: Elements in a Children's Evangelistic Reaping Campaign

Stories used in sermons or as stand-alone features create powerful impressions on the mind. They provide object lessons and illustrations that capture the attention, clarify concepts, and reinforce important points of the message. They link causes with effects in narrative form, which is basically the way in which the brain thinks. They also provide a breather between two deep thoughts. Both adults and children will remember a story and its lesson long after they have forgotten the rest of the sermon.

Humor can be a great way to capture and hold the attention while at the same time presenting a spiritual message. Jesus frequently employed humor in His teaching, like when He referred to taking a plank out of one's own eye. It is important to only use humor appropriately and to do so with a smile so that the hearers will recognize it as humor.

Video is a powerful teaching tool. Children love to watch videos, and preachers should use video clips or pictures as visual illustrations in their sermons. This will increase the impact and effectiveness of the spoken words on the minds of the hearers.

Sermon notes provide an effective means of holding the attention of both children and adults and helping them to follow the message as the preacher presents it. These notes should provide the children with an activity that is relevant to the sermon and gives them the opportunity to put their response to the message in writing. This could include questions for them to answer while the preacher is speaking.

Music adds variety to the worship experience, inspires the soul, presents a spiritual message, and complements the sermon. The musical program must be carefully planned to help create a worshipful atmosphere rather than merely providing entertainment. Rightly chosen and presented, music helps the hearers to make a decision for Christ.

Drama draws the attention of both children and adults. It places indelible impressions on the mind as it depicts the outcomes of various situations, explaining abstract concepts in a tangible way and encouraging decision making. Bible stories can be dramatized to help bring out the spiritual message of the sermon.

Preaching should be clear and to the point. With a combination of stories, sermon notes, and humor, the preacher brings the message alive for children as well as adults. The sermon should incorporate all of the various program features as a means of reinforcing the message and clinching decisions for Christ.

The Nurture Phase

Training and deployment of children should not be a one-time event but rather should continue after the evangelistic campaign. The ultimate goal is nurturing the children of the church so that as they transition from childhood to adulthood, they will mature in the faith of Jesus and in their dedication to serving others. For this reason, mentors, coaches, and trainers should maintain their involvement with these children, encouraging them to keep participating and growing.

Those who accept the new life in Christ will need to be integrated into their newfound faith. The task force for children's evangelism should have appropriate strategies in place to nurture and conserve those who commit their lives to Christ. Chapter 17 provides some suggestions of activities that may be utilized in this step. Spiritual-support guides should be assigned to each new believer. Their responsibilities should be clearly defined, with a specific time frame in which to help new members transition into their new relationship with Christ and the church.

Review and Discussion

- *Establishing the task force for children's evangelism is one of the first things to be done in preparing for a children's evangelistic campaign. What is the function of such a task force? See chapter 3.*
- *List some of the questions that must be answered by this task force. See chapter 3.*
- *Name and explain each of the five phases in equipping children for evangelism and soul winning.*
- *How would you execute a Child-to-Child Improvement Get-Together, and what are some activities and topics you would include?*
- *Identify and explain the value of each of the seven elements to be included in each nightly program of the children's evangelistic campaign.*
- *Choose a theme, and outline how you would include all seven elements in executing that theme as one of the nightly programs of an evangelistic campaign.*
- *Develop a complete, ready-to-implement plan that includes all five phases in a complete cycle of children's evangelism. See chapters 7 and 8.*

17
Planning and Implementing Effective Health Evangelism

FOR MORE THAN 150 years, the church has been preaching the gospel of Jesus through health evangelism. An emphasis on healthy lifestyle is a cardinal feature of Seventh-day Adventist theology and lifestyle, and health education forms an essential part of the church's mission. Ellen White said: "The rich and wonderful provisions of the gospel embrace the medical missionary work. This work is to be to the third angel's message as the right arm is to the body" (Letter 256, 1903). Many local communities and wider societies have embraced and accepted these preventative-health principles that the church models.

Everyone wants better health, and they are willing to listen to anyone who can give them advice or heal their diseases. The Spirit of Prophecy contains the following counsel: "Gospel workers should be able also to give instruction in the principles of healthful living. There is sickness everywhere, and most of it might be prevented by attention to the laws of health. The people need to see the bearing of health principles upon their well-being, both for this life and for the life to come" (*The Ministry of Healing,* chap. 9, p. 146). Adventists must utilize all available technology, resources, and methods to enhance effectiveness in soul winning through health evangelism.

Health Evangelism in the Bible

During His earthly ministry, Jesus associated the work of public proclamation with that of healing: "And He went throughout all Galilee, teaching in their synagogues and proclaiming the gospel of the kingdom and healing every disease and every affliction among the people. So His fame spread throughout all Syria, and they brought Him all the sick, those afflicted with various diseases and pains, those oppressed by demons, epileptics, and paralytics, and He healed them. And great crowds followed Him from Galilee and the Decapolis, and from Jerusalem and Judea, and from beyond the Jordan" (Matt. 4:23–25). Jesus' disciples also participated in this combined ministry: "So they went out and proclaimed that people should repent. And they cast out many demons and anointed with oil many who were sick and healed them" (Mark 6:12, 13).

While Jesus' teachings were famous, His fame was the result not just of what He said but also of what He did. The word on the street was, "This Man speaks as One having authority" (see Matt. 7:29). But the healing work that He did attracted large crowds. His ministry was a blend of urgency, personal acquaintance, teaching, healing, preaching, and enabling. "The Savior made each work of healing an occasion for implanting divine principles in the mind and soul. This was the purpose of His work. He imparted earthly blessings, that He might incline the hearts of men to receive the gospel of His grace" (*The Ministry of Healing*, chap. 1, p. 20).

Through His healing ministry, Christ gave an example to His followers. The apostles and members of the early church embraced and adopted this example in their evangelistic ministry. Acts 5:16 says, "Also a multitude gathered from the surrounding cities to Jerusalem, bringing sick people and those who were tormented by unclean spirits, and they were all healed" (NKJV). The great fame of the apostles' preaching was due to the combination of healing with the preaching of the Word. As a result, thousands were converted.

Executing Health Evangelism

Chapter 3 of this book explains the initial planning process for departmental evangelistic initiatives, and chapter 7 explains various field-preparation initiatives for an evangelistic campaign. Successful execution of health evangelism includes six important pillars: *urgency, acquaintance, teaching, healing, preaching, and enabling.*

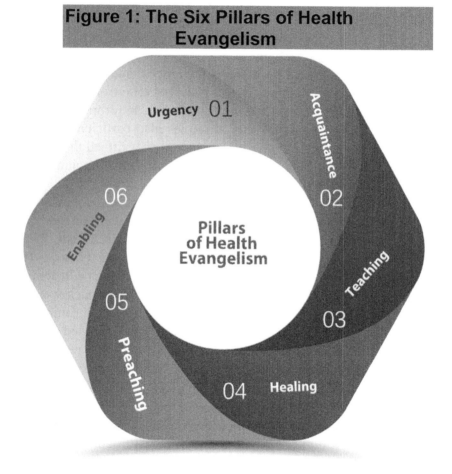

Figure 1: The Six Pillars of Health Evangelism

The Urgency Pillar

The purpose of this pillar is to create a sense of need for health evangelism among individuals within the church and the community and to determine a strategy to address those needs. To establish this sense of urgency, there should be a task force for health evangelism. After determining the health needs in the church and the community, the task force should recruit a team of healthy-lifestyle coordinators to develop and implement the health evangelism strategy. A major aspect of the outreach initiatives of this strategy should be Health Renewal Seminars. The number of seminars will depend upon the needs within the local area, as identified by the community-needs survey conducted by the task force.

The healthy-lifestyle coordinators will be trained to develop competency in managing health issues. This training should include salesmanship techniques that will help them to approach individuals with health issues and inform them about healthy-lifestyle programs. During this stage, each coordinator develops a list of healthy-lifestyle advocates, who are interested church members that will be participating in the health-evangelism program. The coordinators should conduct a general meeting with the advocates, explaining the program to be executed and soliciting their participation. They should then train each of their teams to engage in the initiatives of this program. Special trainers, as well as inspirational and motivational presenters, should be invited to meet with both coordinators and advocates for training at different times.

The Acquaintance Pillar

In the acquaintance pillar of health evangelism, healthy-lifestyle advocates identify persons from the community who are not members of their faith and begin to interact with them, as explained in chapter 4. Each advocate should identify acquaintances whom they would like to reach with the gospel. With these names, they will form an evangelistic prayer list, which they will present to the Lord daily, asking Him to bring these individuals into a closer walk with Himself. The advocates will seek to develop friendships with these individuals and will eventually invite them to participate in the Health Renewal Seminars, which form part of the training pillar.

The Healing Pillar

This pillar is the segment of the program in which actual interventions are carried out to alleviate human suffering.

Community-health days should be conducted periodically, providing health clinics for those with physical, mental, and emotional illnesses. Persons who arrive at these clinics should receive health screening from medical professionals. Professional counselors and psychologists should participate by attending to those with mental and emotional difficulties. These health-care professionals may appropriately integrate faith into each intervention that they perform. Prayer is an essential healing therapy and a powerful witnessing tool.

Healthy-lifestyle advocates who are not trained in the medical field should make themselves available to provide social and spiritual support to the sick in homes, hospitals, hospices, or any other institution where these patients may be. It is their duty to inform these persons of the health clinics that will be conducted and to help them to access this professional care. If the church is not conducting a health clinic when someone is in need of help, the healthy-lifestyle advocates should assist these persons in obtaining care from appropriate public or private institutions.

All healthy-lifestyle advocates should deploy themselves into the communities where they will work and form connections with individuals who are at risk or who have health issues. They will invite these persons to participate in the Health Renewal Seminars.

The Training Pillar

This step consists of the Health Renewal Seminars, which are conducted according to the guidelines in chapter 7 for community-outreach forums. These are training classes in the principles of healthy lifestyle and disease prevention. Training activities could also include an educational Health Renewal Tour for members of the church and the community.

The topics presented in Health Renewal Seminars will depend upon the needs within the local area, as determined by the community-needs survey conducted by the task force for health evangelism. These topics may include:
- Managing stress
- Quitting smoking
- Diet renewal

- Healthy lifestyle changes
- Cooking
- Exercise
- Weight management
- Nutritious baking
- Geriatric training

These clinics, seminars, workshops, and tours should be designed to attract individuals from all social classes, and they should expose the participants to some of the beliefs, practices, and humanitarian activities of the Seventh-day Adventist Church. This exposure will help prepare them to ultimately embrace the church's message. After the Health Renewal Seminars, healthy-lifestyle advocates and other members of the church family should follow up with prospects, using a series of health-related Bible lessons.

The Preaching Pillar

The urgency, acquaintance, healing, and teaching pillars are preparatory for the health-evangelism reaping campaign, which may last between two and three weeks or more and should include at least fourteen evangelistic themes. Bible lesson courses on the basic doctrines of the church have been completed, relationships between church members and prospects have progressed, and it is now time to reap the harvest of souls.

Chapter 8 explains the details of carrying out a public evangelistic campaign, including the various features of the nightly program. In order to capture the attention of the varied minds in the congregation, each program should include music, drama, video, testimony, and preaching that are related to the theme and its doctrinal emphasis. These features will provide practical examples of a positive Christian lifestyle. The sermon should combine these practical health issues with relevant Bible doctrines, demonstrating the love of Christ and creating in the hearts and minds of hearers the desire to accept Christ into their lives and make healthy lifestyle choices, both for this world and for eternity. The following examples are some of the themes that may be used in this series.

The Spiritual Cardiologist

Heart health is a major issue in health care. Thousands of people die every year from cardiac problems. People are afraid of developing heart conditions, and this results in a great demand for the services of cardiologists. A cardiologist is a physician who has obtained special training and skills in finding, treating, and preventing injuries and diseases of the heart and blood vessels. As a medical advisor, a cardiologist must understand a patient's social, economic, and family dynamics.

We each have a spiritual heart. Just like a bad heart leads to physical death, a bad spiritual heart leads to spiritual death. Jesus is the great Cardiologist. Not only is He a genius with regard to the physical heart, He can also diagnose and treat the spiritual heart and give the patient eternal life. This subject, rightly presented with relevant Bible texts, will capture the attention and interest of scores of persons in the congregation.

The features and message relate heart health to how Christ does not merely repair broken hearts but recreates them. The drama could depict a cardiologist saving someone's life as a result of the patient's choice to receive treatment. A member of the church family who has experienced a heart problem could give a brief testimony of how the Lord intervened in their situation. The preacher will invite individuals to choose Christ and accept the new heart that He offers them.

Spiritual Cancer

The presence of cancer indicates that there are deficiencies in a person's immune system, since when the immune system is strong, cancer cells are destroyed and cannot form tumors. These deficiencies could be the result of genetic, environmental, nutritional, and lifestyle factors.

Changes in lifestyle and diet, like supplements and exercise, can help overcome these deficiencies and strengthen the person's immune system.

Sin is like cancer. Both lead to death. Sin resides in our nature, and when our spiritual immune system is compromised, sin contaminates, circulates, dominates, destroys, and kills. Sin manifests itself and brings death in a multitude of different ways in today's world, including the following: sexual immorality, resulting in HIV/AIDS; gun violence, resulting in death and prison; and drug abuse, which leads to drunkenness, addiction, illness, and family violence, resulting in divorce, separation, and imprisonment. There is no human solution for this kind of cancer; the blood of Jesus is the only cure.

The various features and the message relate the effects of cancer to those of sin, focusing on the Savior as the solution for our spiritual condition. The video could feature a case in which a patient was cured from cancer, highlighting the role of the physician in their treatment. The preacher explains how we receive Christ's spiritual chemotherapy through daily exercise, prayer, Bible study, spiritual meditation, Christian fellowship, deliberate abstinence from sinful practices, trust in God, and dependence upon the Holy Spirit.

Health in Three Dimensions

This theme focuses on the doctrine of the Trinity. It illustrates this concept by presenting human beings as a unity of social, physical, and spiritual faculties, each of which affects the others. It is important to emphasize that health in all three of these dimensions is essential for true well-being. The various features and the message relate this principle of holistic wellness with the unity of the Godhead, explaining how the Father, Son, and Holy Spirit are each involved in the plan of salvation.

Heart Transplant

A literal heart transplant is the health emphasis of this theme. What diagnosis indicates the need for a new heart? How is the procedure performed? How must a person take care of a new heart? The features and message of this theme relate a heart transplant to the doctrine of baptism and the new heart that Christ offers to those who believe in Him. It would be good to include a baptismal service as part of this theme. A member of the church family should give a brief testimony about the joy experienced in submitting to Christ in baptism, and the preacher should invite attendees to take this important spiritual step.

Living with Healthy Hope

Sickness often leads to death. How we care for our bodies can help us avoid certain illnesses and prolong our lives. Nutrition is important for good health, and this theme will include practical counsels on nutrition that can help a person increase their longevity. However, death is still inevitable, although it does not have the final say. It is in this context that the resurrection becomes important. The features and message of this theme use principles of healthy living and proper nutrition to introduce the doctrine of the state of the dead and the resurrection. The drama could be a dramatization of the resurrection of Lazarus. The preacher invites the listeners to commit their lives to Christ and to live in anticipation of the first resurrection.

Overcoming Diabetes and Addiction

This theme presents real-life experiences with diabetes and describes the types, causes, diagnosis, and treatment of this disease. It also explains how different kinds of addictions can lead to diabetes and provides strategies for overcoming these addictions. The features and message of this theme relate overcoming diabetes and addictions to the biblical concept of conversion, highlighting the difference that conversion makes in the life of an individual through a personal encounter with the gospel of Jesus. The preacher invites individuals to overcome addictions by experiencing transformation in Christ.

The Milk and Honey Syndrome

The features and message of this theme focus on the judgment. It uses illustrations that describe individuals who are living only for the pleasures of this life. They abuse their bodies for pleasure and are only concerned with "milk and honey." This theme emphasizes the inevitable consequences of a lifestyle of indulgence.

The program will highlight the case of Belshazzar. While this wicked king was indulging in partying and merrymaking, the Lord wrote a message of judgment on the wall. The drama for this program may depict this occasion or another biblical story involving judgment. The preacher will relate the story to what will happen in the final judgment, inviting individuals to accept Christ into their lives and thus escape eternal condemnation.

We Shall Not All Sleep

This theme highlights the possibility of recovery from many conditions of impaired health. There may be numerous persons in the congregation who are ailing and are hoping for recovery. There should be a special prayer for healing for these individuals. However, they should be urged to continue with their current medical treatment since God works according to His will, not ours. The emphasis is on faith in God's ability to bring healing, and even if He does not choose to do so at the very moment we wish, we have the greater hope that Christ's second coming will bring total healing from all illness.

The features and message of this theme focus on the second advent of Christ, encouraging the people to be ready for that momentous event. A member of the church family could give a brief testimony about how they are motivated by this hope. A short video may be shown about someone who is suffering but still clings to the hope of deliverance at the Second Coming. The preacher will challenge the listeners to place their faith upon the Word of God, accept Christ as their Savior, and live in readiness for Jesus' imminent return.

The Enabling Pillar

Those who have accepted Christ as their Savior will need to be inte grated into their newfound faith. The task force for health evangelism should have appropriate strategies in place to nurture and conserve those who commit to Christ. Chapter 17 provides some suggestions of activities that may be utilized for this pillar. Healthy-lifestyle advocates should be selected, trained, and deployed to serve as spiritual-enabling guides, who will be assigned to new believers. Their responsibilities should be clearly defined, with a specific time frame to help new members transition into their new relationship with Christ and the church.

Review and Discussion

- *What are some of the scriptural and Spirit of Prophecy quotations that justify health evangelism?*
- *List five questions that the task force for health evangelism should answer in order to ensure effective soul winning. See chapter 3.*
- *What are the six pillars of health evangelism, and what does each entail?*
- *Select one theme for a program in a health-evangelism reaping campaign and demonstrate how you would execute the features of music, drama, video, testimony, and preaching. What biblical doctrine you would integrate into this theme?*
- *What special gifts would you provide for some of the guests in your nightly evangelistic program?*
- *Develop a complete, ready-to-implement plan that includes all six pillars in a complete cycle of health evangelism. See chapters 7 and 8.*

18
Evangelism in Education Institutions

MARK 16:15 records Jesus' commanded to His disciples, "Go into all the world and preach the gospel to every creature" (NKJV). In Matthew 28:20, we find that an integral part of this commission is "teaching them to observe all things that I have commanded you" (NKJV). These interrelated concepts of *preaching and teaching* could also be expressed as e*vangelizing and educating*. The goal of Seventh-day Adventist Christian education is evangelistic in nature; the salvation of souls is its compelling vision. Ellen White said, "In the highest sense the work of education and the work of redemption are one, for in education, as in redemption, 'other foundation can no man lay than that is laid, which is Jesus Christ' " (*Education*, chap. 4, p. 30). Teachers and professors in our institutions must prepare students for both the present life and the future life. As Ellen White states: "True education means more than the perusal of a certain course of study. . . .

It prepares the student for the joy of service in this world and for the higher joy of wider service in the world to come" (*ibid.,* chap. 1, p. 13).

Evangelism through Adventist education is a sacred obligation and a noble work that is entrusted to those who are commissioned to mold the minds of students, shape society, and advance the kingdom of God.

In order to carry out effective evangelism in the church's educational institutions, a task force for education evangelism should be appointed as explained in chapter 3. This task force will have the following objectives:

1. To deepen the spiritual life of each student and staff member.
2. To address the sociological needs of the students and their families, as well as others in the community.
3. To conduct evangelistic initiatives to baptize students and their family members, as well as others in the community.
4. To collaborate with the church to conduct evangelistic initiatives to reap souls for the kingdom of God.

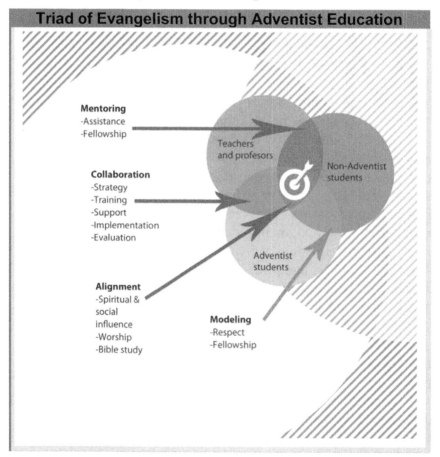

Triad of Evangelism through Adventist Education

The Triad of Evangelism through Adventist Education is an on-campus initiative to foster social and spiritual growth among teachers and professors, Adventist students, and non-Adventist students. By integration through association, non-Adventist relatives and friends of students are also impacted through this initiative.

The purpose of the *collaboration, modeling, and mentoring* dimensions of the triad is to achieve the desired outcome of spiritual and social alignment. This takes place when the Holy Spirit, teachers, professors, and Adventist peers influence students to accept Christ as their Savior and become members of the Seventh-day Adventist Church.

Collaboration

In this dimension of the triad, teachers, professors, and Adventist students are recruited and given orientation for the evangelistic program. They will demonstrate interest in the non-Adventist students' social and spiritual lives. The collaboration dimension should include:
- Strategy
- Training
- Support
- Implementation
- Evaluation
- Spiritual gifts discovery (as explained in chapter 5)
- Provision of resources
- Prayer for students and teachers
- Fellowship

Modeling

The modeling dimension describes how teachers and professors relate to non-Adventist students. They are to model Christ to these students, treat them with respect, and be intentional about fellowshipping with them. The teachers or professors also demonstrate interest in the students' spirituality and other areas of their lives as deemed necessary. They become personally involved

with the students so that through direct association and involvement they are able to make a significant impact on the students' lives. Some of activities that form a part of this dimension are:
- Conducting doctrinal Bible studies.
- Cultivating fellowship (sharing a meal on Sabbath or some other time).
- Organizing special prayer sessions.
- Distributing evangelistic literature.
- Carrying out community-outreach initiatives.
- Inviting students to evangelistic programs.
- Interacting with students during Week of Prayer.
- Visiting student's homes when necessary and developing relationships with their parents.
- Appropriately assisting students with material, social, and academic issues.
- Genuinely modeling Christian lifestyle practices.
- Inviting students as well as their family and friends to participate in faith influencing spiritual activities that are planned by the task force or institution.

Mentoring

The mentoring dimension consists of direct interaction in which Adventist students associate with non-Adventist students and identify with them personally. They eventually invite them to participate in church activities. Some of the activities that take place in these interactions are:
- Assisting other students with academics where necessary and possible.
- Conducting doctrinal Bible studies.
- Praying for the success of other students.
- Distributing evangelistic literature.
- Cultivating fellowship.
- Working together on community issues.
- Inviting non-Adventist students as well as their family and friends to participate in faith-influencing spiritual activities planned by the task force or institution.

Alignment

The center of the triad depicts the spiritual and social alignment that takes place in the life of non-Adventist students as the result of teachers, professors, and Adventist students intentionally interacting with them under the influence of the Holy Spirit. Everyone involved in these interactions experiences spiritual growth. Non-Adventist students become Disciples of Christ and committed Seventh-day Adventists, while teachers, professors, and Adventist students experience a closer walk with the Lord that deepens their evangelistic interest and effectiveness.

The results of alignment include:
- Acceptance of Christ
- Baptism
- Participation in corporate and personal worship exercises
- Continued doctrinal Bible Studies to nurture faith
- Participation in outreach activities both on and off campus
- Participation in various types of wholesome social activities in church and on campus
- Participation in various types of personal and corporate prayer initiatives
- Participation in various types of discipleship initiatives
- Organization and implementation of ministry projects that utilize spiritual gifts
- Distribution of evangelistic literature

Implementing Evangelistic Initiatives in the School

In order to fulfill the objectives of the Triad of Evangelism through Adventist Education, it is important to designate an evangelism coordinator for the school. Where there is a chaplain, this person would automatically fulfill this role. If there is no chaplain, a trustworthy church member who is committed to Christian education and knows how to get along with children may be asked to carry out this responsibility. However, it can be very delicate to bring in someone who is not employed by the school for this duty, so this matter must be considered according to the context of each school.

In order to fulfill the objective of deepening the spiritual life of each staff member, the coordinator—working with the conference education director and the local church pastor—should conduct spiritual enrichment services for the teachers. These services may take place at the beginning and end of each school term or school year.

The focus of the entire school program should be winning souls to Christ. It is essential to conduct at least one annual Week of Prayer in each school, whose purpose is to deepen the spiritual lives of both students and staff members. In addition, the daily worship in each school should be specially planned to fulfill the purpose of helping the students develop and strengthen their spiritual experience. Every subject in the curriculum should be taught so as to accomplish an evangelistic purpose, and Christian educators should always remember that they are training their students to be future missionaries.

There should be a combined prayer team of teachers and students as one of the standing committees of the school. The evangelism coordinator or another staff member may be tasked with leading this prayer team. The members should have a schedule for the meeting times. The duration and regularity of the meetings must be determined, and efforts must be made to keep this schedule as strictly as possible. The team will be tasked with praying for success in all the social, spiritual, and academic programs of the school and should consider the personal issues affecting students and their families.

The school's evangelism coordinator should collect the names and contact information of the parents and guardians of all students. The members of the prayer team will develop a prayer schedule, choosing a special time to pray for each one of these names. The students whose parents and relatives are being presented to the Lord in prayer each day may be invited to come forward and join the members of the prayer team. It would be good to inform each parent and relative about this prayer schedule and the day on which they will be prayed for. They may be invited to come to the school on that day, or they may send their special prayer requests. They could also connect through Skype or other some other form of electronic communication.

The church pastor, the chaplain or school evangelism coordinator, the class teacher, and other available church members should visit the parents of students in their homes or another suitable location. This provides an opportunity to talk with them about the progress of their children, listen to any concerns that they may have, and hold them up in prayer before the Lord. Those visiting should demonstrate that the school is interested in their personal welfare and is willing to do whatever is possible to assist them with any challenge that they face. This will help them to develop a bond with the members of the school and church, as well as to see the school and church as a great partner in helping them to train their children "for the joy of service in this world and for the higher joy of wider service in the world to come."

A parent-appreciation day should be held at the school once or twice each school year. This could take place on the Sabbath at the end of each Week of Prayer. Gifts may be given to parents and children on that day, and the program may include a baptismal service. The giving of these gifts should be limited to non-Adventist parents and children, since the soul-winning focus is on them. This will minimize large expenses in the planning and execution of these programs.

As relationships develop and bonds strengthen with students' parents and family members, avenues will open to conduct Bible studies with these individuals. These studies should cover the essential doctrines of the church and help the prospects to develop a deep love for Christ and commitment to the church.

Review and Discussion

- *Name the four objectives of evangelism through Adventist education.*
- *How could a task force for education evangelism function effectively in your school? See chapter 3.*
- *What elements constitute the Triad of Evangelism through Adventist Education?*
- *Explain each of the dimensions of this triad.*
- *What are some activities that teachers and professors can do with nonAdventist students to influence them to Christ?*
- *Identify and explain six things that Adventist students can do both on and off campus to influence non-Adventist students and others to accept Christ as their Savior.*
- *Develop a complete, ready-to-implement evangelistic plan for your educational institution.*

PART IV

DISCIPLESHIP AND NURTURE

19
A Discipleship Paradigm

REACHING OTHERS with the gospel of Jesus and inviting them to follow Him is central to the church's mission. However, evangelism involves much more than just bringing people into the church; it also includes nurturing and discipleship.

The word *disciple* is a translation of the Koine Greek word, mathetes. It refers to a pupil of a teacher or an apprentice to a craftsman. It carries the connotation of one who follows another. If we look at Jesus' ministry, we will see that His relationship with His disciples transcended the normal pupil-teacher relationship with which we are acquainted.

It prepares the student for the joy of service in this world and for the higher joy of wider service in the world to come" (ibid., chap. 1, p. 13).

We use the word discipleship very frequently in our churches, but sometimes one must wonder if we clearly understand what we are saying. Many people see discipleship merely as a program, a set of initiatives, or a series of tasks to be accomplished. Such a concept could lead us to perform all kinds of checklist assessments to determine how well we are doing. This could involve investigating how many times we pray and how many passages of Scripture we read each day, how many Bible texts we have memorized, how many pages of devotional material we read per week, how many pieces of literature we distribute, how many people we have been kind to, and how often we meet with our accountability partners. While all of these are useful as empirical information to quantify organizational effectiveness, in themselves they are not discipleship.

Yes, discipleship includes all of the above and more. However, it has more to do with attitudes or motives than actions. If our motives are not right, all the activities that we produce become an end unto themselves. Discipleship is a genuine lifestyle of faithfully imitating Christ's example. It gives us a sense that we are not the most important mortals on earth; we are simply followers of the most important Being in the universe.

In the Great Commission in Matthew 28:18–20 Jesus commanded His disciples to (1) go and make disciples, (2) baptize them, and (3) teach them. Furthermore, in Matthew 4:19 He said, "Follow me, and I will make you fish for people" (NRSV). This is an actual command that came directly from His lips. It was and still is a command that all of His believers must apply to their personal life experience. When church members faithfully carry out this command, the result is the dynamic and sustained growth of the kingdom of God here on earth and the preparation of believers to live in the kingdom of glory.

In His discourse on love in John 15, Jesus reinforced His call to making disciples with the use of the metaphor of a fruit-bearing tree: "You did not choose Me, but I chose you and appointed you that you should go and bear fruit and that your fruit should abide, so that whatever you ask the Father in My name, He may give it to you. These things I command you, so that you will love one another" (v. 16, 17). When Jesus said: "Follow me, and I will make you fish for people," those words referred to far more than just walking in His physical presence. Rather, Christ intended that by following Him, believers would become like Him in their lifestyle and influence others to follow His example. As He thus reproduces His teachings among believers, the church achieves sustained growth as its members demonstrate a genuine, kingdom-focused attitude.

His disciples are like Him in their lifestyle, attitude, conduct and vocation and bear like passion for the redemptive mission. "As Jesus was walking beside the Sea of Galilee, He saw two brothers, Simon called Peter and his brother Andrew. They were casting a net into the lake, for they were fishermen. Come, follow me, and I will make you fishers of men. At once they left their nets and followed Him Going on from there, He saw two other brothers, James son of Zebedee and his brother John. They were in a boat with their father Zebedee, preparing their nets. Jesus called them, and immediately they left the boat and their father and followed him" Matthew 4:18-22. Those who actually followed Him were from varied circumstances and included more than the twelve. All those who are sympathetic and committed to Him, accept His teaching and embrace His lifestyle are His disciples. They acknowledge Him as their personal Savior and are members of the community of faith. "To the Jews who had believed Him, Jesus said, "If you hold to my teaching, you are really my disciples" John 8:31.

A Disciple is a Missionary

A missionary is a member of a religious group or organization that is involved in missions. The Latin *missionem*, which is the "act of sending" signifies "mission" in the English language. Before 1598 when the word "mission" originated among the Jesuits, Jesus had already instituted principle. He sent His followers to accomplish specific activities that would result in the transformation of life and the conditions of life for human beings (Luke 10: 1-12). Missionaries are sent with a specific mandate to proselytize and perform ministries of service. Spiritual and secular education, social justice, health care, economic development and literacy are just a few of the services that missionaries perform.

Since every member of the body of Christ is His disciple, every disciple is a missionary sent as active agents in advancing the kingdom of God. In this context, the terms *disciple* and missionary are *synonymous*. Ellen White said' "Every true disciple is born into the kingdom of God as a missionary. He who drinks of the living water becomes a fountain of life. The receiver becomes a giver. The grace of Christ in the soul is like a spring in the desert, welling up to refresh all, and making those who are ready to perish eager to drink of the water of life".—The Desire of Ages, 195. In Matthew 25:35, 36 Jesus described the *missionary* function of a disciple: "For I was hungry, and you fed me. I was thirsty, and you gave me a drink. I was a stranger, and you invited me into your home. I was naked, and you gave me clothing. I was sick, and you cared for me. I was in prison, and you visited me" (NLT).

Some Specific Activities of Missionaries

Christs' disciples fulfill the five core values through varying missionary activities. Some are listed below.

- Missionaries engage in intercessory prayers on behalf of others and in the name of Jesus, pray for healing of the sick. They also teach others how to pray.
- They actively participate in initiatives to evangelize people of villages, towns and cities.
- They study the scriptures with people and teach them varying methods to study the word of God and apply it to their personal lives.
- They are involved in compassionate activities that touch the lives of people who suffer socially, emotionally, physically and are otherwise in need of help.
- They encourage others to accept Christ as their Savior and become members of the body of Christ.
- They help people to accomplish personal feats and develop relevant skills to become independent.

"Were every one of you a living missionary, the message for this time would speedily be proclaimed in all countries, to every people and nation and tongue".—Testimonies for the Church 6:438.

The Five Core Values of a Disciple

True disciples of Jesus enjoy worshipping and spiritually communing with the Lord and other members of the church. We call that *devotion*. This takes place in both personal and corporate settings. Through the empowerment of the Holy Spirit, disciples share the gospel of Jesus— the good news of salvation—with others. We call that *evangelism*. They engage in various forms of social interaction within the community of faith. We call that *fellowship*. They also address material, social, and other needs of individuals in the surrounding community. We call that *outreach*. They consider all the gifts, talents, and other resources in their possession to be a trust that belongs to God, which is to be used wisely and appropriately to meet personal necessities, to further the cause of Christ, and to bless others. We call that *stewardship*. All five of these core values of discipleship can be seen in Jesus' relationship with the twelve disciples. He invested Himself in them as He taught them; spent precious, relational time with them; and sent them to proclaim the gospel. He equipped them so that through their example, He could lead others to Himself.

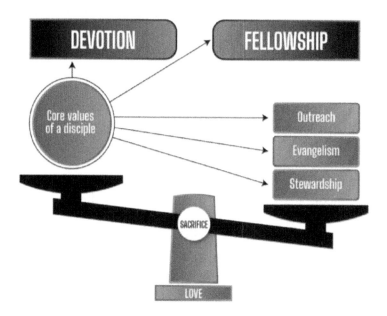

The Necessity of Sacrifice

Sacrifice is a key component in order for these core values to become a reality in the life of the disciple. The multitude of tasks that we have to get done and the various interests that beckon for our attention day and night are more than sufficient to eclipse our attention and deter us from finding time for *devotion*. We must be intentional in making it a priority, and this requires *sacrifice*. Likewise, to share the gospel with others through evangelism, we must find time to study the Word, to learn the art of explaining it, and to go out and meet individuals and share with them. We must *sacrifice* in order to budget time for these activities; and, irrespective of other attractions and urgencies, we must go forward and make evangelism happen.

God created us as social beings with a need for community and interpersonal contact through *fellowship*. Studies have shown that sharing with others on a social level significantly lowers stress levels, maximizing joy and minimizing or even eliminating pain, disappointments, and sorrow. Rates of suicide, mental illness, and alcoholism decrease significantly when people feel a sense of belonging. People who are socially involved may even have fewer colds, lower blood pressure, lower heart rates, and longer life expectancy. However, we can easily become so preoccupied with our careers, responsibilities, and ambitions that we neglect time for social interaction. In order to experience the benefits of fellowship, we must make a *sacrifice*, putting aside the distractions that vie for our attention so that we can dedicate time and energy to connect with others.

In Matthew 25:35 and 36 Jesus described the *outreach* ministry of a disciple: "For I was hungry, and you fed Me. I was thirsty, and you gave Me a drink. I was a stranger, and you invited Me into your home. I was naked, and you gave Me clothing. I was sick, and you cared for Me. I was in prison, and you visited Me" (NLT). Outreach includes all these compassionate services along with other activities that relieve human suffering and satisfy human needs. Thus, Christ's disciples must make intentional *sacrifices* in order to perform outreach.

All human beings are endowed with time, talents, spiritual gifts, and other resources. God is the Owner who commits this trust to our *stewardship*, and we are to administer these resources wisely for Him.

Time is our most valuable asset, which God gave to us as a special endowment. All of His disciples are expected to serve Him faithfully through the proper use of their allotted time (John 9:4; Eph. 5:15, 16). "Our time belongs to God. Every moment is His, and we are under the most solemn obligation to improve it to His glory. Of no talent He has given will He require a more strict account than of our time." (*Christ's Object Lessons*, chap. 25, p. 342).

Talents and abilities are God's gifts to His children, which are to be used for His glory and to fulfill His mission (1 Pet 4:10). Each disciple is expected to use these gifts and talents to perform a unique function in the body of Christ and society in general. God has also given various resources to each person that He intends for them to manage faithfully for Him. These resources include the body temple (Rom. 12:1; 1 Cor. 6:19–20) and finances. Faithfulness in stewardship requires sacrifice.

Implementing a Discipleship Program in the Local Church

First, the church should develop a discipleship vision statement, identifying exactly what is desired at the end of each discipleship-training period. An example of such a vision statement could be: "For every believer to live a consistent Christian life; attend church services regularly; support the cause of the Lord with time, talents, gifts, influence, and other resources; and seek opportunities to share their faith." A primary objective of every discipleship-training program should be to help new members assimilate into the life of the community of believers.

After formulating the vision statement, it is time to choose discipleship leaders. These leaders should be individuals who love the Lord deeply and have demonstrated genuine growth in their personal relationship with Him. They should have a desire to see transformation in the lives of believers and be willing to use their spiritual gifts to work for others. They must demonstrate a positive Christ-like attitude characterized by patience, kindness, and nonjudgmental acceptance. It is also important for them to enjoy working with people and be flexible and trainable. These leaders will receive training in how to assist members in the development of the core values of discipleship.

Organize the church members into discipleship teams or small groups, and determine the necessary growth areas for group members. Give special attention to the growth needs of new believers, and be sure to provide them with the necessary resources to develop all of the core values of discipleship. Establish a time frame for developing competencies in these values among the group members. Each member, particularly new believers, should have a coach who helps them to expand their vision, build confidence, and take practical steps to establish a lifestyle in which devotion, evangelism, stewardship, fellowship, and outreach become instinctive. This coaching focuses on personal growth; it concentrates on developing skills and strengths rather than on overcoming weaknesses.

Ultimately, discipleship depends on personal commitment and self-discipline. It is therefore essential for each disciple to develop and follow their own personal spiritual-growth plan. The following principles provide orientation for developing such a plan:

1. Make room for God to fill and transform your life through the Holy Spirit.
2. Be attentive to the sacred Word of God.
3. Recognize the value of edifying music.
4. "Pray without ceasing" (1 Thess. 5:17).
5. Spend time alone with God.
6. Be conscious of your personal spiritual-growth needs.
7. Strive to be like Christ.
8. Go and make disciples for Him.

Review and Discussion

- *Who is a disciple? Name four biblical and three extrabiblical disciples that you are familiar with.*
- *What are four Bible texts that extend a call to discipleship?*
- *Identify and define the five core values of discipleship.*
- *Explain how sacrifice is a key component of each core value of discipleship.*
- *What are some of the necessary steps to effectively implement a discipleship program in the local church?*
- *List six elements that you consider important in the lifestyle of a disciple.*
- *Develop a complete, ready-to-implement spiritual-growth plan for discipleship.*

20
How to Effectively Nurture New Believers

THE OBJECTIVE of evangelism could be summarized as "seeking the lost and keeping the found." Reflecting this dual focus, the Seventh-day Adventist Church identifies its mission as "to make disciples of all people, communicating the everlasting gospel in the context of the three angels' messages of Revelation 14:6–12, leading them to accept Jesus as personal Savior and unite with His remnant church, discipling them to serve Him as Lord and preparing them for His soon return."[1]

This discipleship and preparation process involves intentional nurturing. "The new converts will need to be instructed by faithful teachers of God's Word, that they may increase in a knowledge and love of the truth, and may grow to the full stature men and women in Christ Jesus" (*Evangelism*, sec. 10, p. 337).

---

5. "Mission Statement of the Seventh-day Adventist Church," General Conference of Seventhday Adventists, October 13, 2009, http://www.adventist.org/information/official-statements/statements/ article/go/0/mission-statement-of-the-seventh-day-adventist-church/6/.

Nurturing New Members

Nurturing individuals for the Second Advent is more than just a program. It is a way of life in which church members live out their salvation through joy, hope, peace, and love so that others become attracted to Christ. As Christians, we demonstrate in our daily lives that we are "a chosen race, a royal priesthood, a holy nation, a people for [God's] own possession, that[we] may proclaim the excellencies of Him who called [us] out of darkness into His marvelous light" (1 Pet. 2:9).

Jesus emphasized relationships between believers as a key component of permanence in the faith: "This is My commandment, that you love one another as I have loved you. Greater love has no one than this, that someone lay down his life for his friends. You are My friends if you do what I command you.... You did not choose Me, but I chose you and appointed you that you should go and bear fruit and that your fruit should abide, so that whatever you ask the Father in My name, He may give it to you. These things I command you, so that you will love one another" (John 15:12–17). "In Christ we are all members of one family. God is our Father, and He expects us to take an interest in the members of His household, not a casual interest, but a decided, continual interest" (*Evangelism*, sec. 10, p. 352).

Nurturing is important in order to preserve and perpetuate the doctrinal beliefs, heritage, and distinctiveness of the Seventh-day Adventist Church in the lives of church members, thus fortifying each one's individual commitment to the kingdom of God. One of the major concerns of the Seventh-day Adventist Church is for those who join the church to remain as active disciples who are deeply committed to the kingdom of God. This objective requires a conscious effort to nurture all members.

The following quotations from the Spirit of Prophecy emphasize the importance of nurturing new converts:

> After individuals have been converted to the truth, they need to be looked after. The zeal of many ministers seems to fail as soon as a measure of success attends their efforts. They do not realize that these newly converted ones need nursing—watchful attention, help, and encouragement. These should not be left alone, a prey to Satan's most powerful temptations; they need to be educated in regard to their

duties, to be kindly dealt with, to be led along, and to be visited and prayed with. These souls need the meat apportioned to every man in due season.

No wonder that some become discouraged, linger by the way, and are left for wolves to devour. Satan is upon the track of all. He sends his agents forth to gather back to his ranks the souls he has lost. There should be more fathers and mothers to take these babes in the truth to their hearts, and to encourage them and pray for them, that their faith be not confused. (*Testimonies for the Church,* vol. 4, chap. 7, pp. 68, 69)

Those who have newly come to the faith should be patiently and tenderly dealt with, and it is the duty of the older members of the church to devise ways and means to provide help and sympathy and instruction for those who have conscientiously withdrawn from other churches for the truth's sake, and thus cut themselves off from the pastoral labor to which they have been accustomed. The church has a special responsibility laid upon her to attend to these souls who have followed the first rays of light they have received; and if the members of the church neglect this duty, they will be unfaithful to the trust that God has given them. (Evangelism, sec. 10, p. 351)

The Need for an Intentional Nurturing Strategy

As the church places great emphasis on soul winning and receives a large influx of new members, intentional efforts must be made to conserve these gains. Research indicates that people leave the faith for social and relational reasons far more often than because of doctrinal disagreements. In fact, many who leave maintain the beliefs and even some of the practices of the church. A lack of meaningful relationships and belonging within the local congregation is one of the most frequently cited reasons for new members leaving the church. Leaders, therefore, must take specific action to counteract this problem.

Make sure to educate all of the members about the church's nurturing and conservation program. It is important to train both leaders and members for this essential spiritual activity. A selection of nurturing and conservation initiatives must be available in each congregation. As soon as new members accept the faith, these initiatives must be implemented. There must also be an appropriate evaluation mechanism in place to ensure that the objectives of the program are being fulfilled and that new believers are enjoying their new life in Christ.

In 2006, the General Conference committee voted that while the specific strategy for conserving members will vary from place to place and will reflect the cultural diversity of the global church family, certain principles are universal. These universal principles include the following:

1. Members must feed their spiritual life through Bible study and prayer.
2. They must be able to articulate their beliefs.
3. They must have friends within the congregation.
4. They must engage in a personally meaningful ministry.
5. They must have a sense of belonging and identity.
6. They must use their spiritual gifts in the advancement of the church's mission.

Five Phases of the New-Believer Experience

New members enter a spiritual warfare that they have never before encountered, and they need both human and divine aid to carry them through. The decision to commit one's life to the Lord and embrace the Adventist faith entails significant struggles. While many are frustrated with the lifestyle of the world and long for a new way of life, often they have become accustomed to the status quo and are resistant to change. Furthermore, many new members become discouraged when they observe the reality of failure and unfaithfulness among those who profess the Adventist lifestyle. The devil actively employs such circumstances to deter many from abandoning their previous life and becoming Christians.

Regardless of an individual's background and circumstances, change is difficult, and becoming a Christian requires change. The good news is that the gospel contains the necessary empowerment that brings about change in human lives. However, this change comes about through several phases. When individuals reach the point of making the decision to accept Christ and become Christians, they usually become *passionate* about this decision. Unfortunately, they often enter the church with that passion only to become *disillusioned*. At this point, many fall away from the faith. If they survive the disillusionment phase, they progress through the phases of *acceptance, integration,* and *commitment*

Figure 1: Phases in the New-Believer Experience

The Passionate Phase

This is the period in which new believers experience satisfaction as a result of their decision to accept Christ and become members of the church. During this phase, they tend to feel that if Jesus should come immediately, they would be ready for translation. It is in this stage that they experience unusually strong emotions of love for the Lord, as well as for the church, its members, and its mission.

During this phase, new members are willing to go anywhere and do anything that the Lord requires. Their attitude resembles the innocence of a newborn baby. They accept the church and its leaders as the voice of God. They are curious and eager to know and learn more about their new faith. They will make any possible sacrifice of their time, talents, and material resources. They are ready to work, to share their faith, and to participate in the various services and activities of the church. Both the pastor and the church members should do everything possible to nurture this passion.

The Disillusionment Phase

As new members continue to interact with other church members, the passionate phase often gives way to disillusionment. Through conversing and listening, observing and experiencing, they begin to discover that the realties of imperfect human nature exist within the church as well. At the same time, they often find themselves struggling with personal problems, spiritual challenges, and other discouraging factors. As a result, they begin to have doubts that cause them to question their faith. To make matters worse, the reactions of other church members to these doubts—in addition to the influence of their non-Adventist family and friends— may not be encouraging.

As new members find it difficult to adjust to their new lifestyle, they develop a fear of failure. They may experience feelings of rejection or receive criticism from both inside and outside the church. Feelings of frustration, depression, apathy, and isolation follow. As a result, they begin to miss the comfort of the status quo that they previously enjoyed.

Nurturing is especially important during this stage. There should be an intentional guardianship plan in which spiritual-support guides are assigned to new members in order to help them navigate this critical period.

The Acceptance Phase

Acceptance takes place when new members overcome disillusionment. The love, attention, and care of their spiritual-support guides, the empowerment of the Holy Spirit, and the relationships they have developed with the Lord and with other church members have helped them to reach this point. They have seen, heard, and experienced a lot and now understand that being a Christian comes as a package of emotions, realities, and experiences. They accept that the wheat and tares must grow together until the harvest. They have become able to withstand ridicule through the grace of the Lord. Their prayer and study lives improve, and they learn to trust more in Jesus.

They are now able to turn everything over to the Lord and trust Him to carry them through. Whether it is a situation they find difficult or impossible to control, a personality trait that is hard to change, or an emotion that overwhelms them, they are able to move forward. They minimize the questioning that can leave them powerless, and they choose to accept the reality of their new life. They are conscious of their own strengths and weaknesses and recognize that others have strengths and weaknesses as well. They take control of their actions and focus on the broader picture.

At this stage, they start asking questions about how things are done in the church and why they are done that way. They want to understand correctly and do things right. As a result, they are sensitive about their mistakes and concerned about what people think about them.

The Integration Phase

This is the phase in which new members wholeheartedly embrace the faith. They are now able to perceive exciting new opportunities in the church. Their views now transcend the mere earthly benefits of church membership as they learn to focus on eternal benefits. At this point they have come to recognize the interdependence that exists between members of the faith, and they understand the roles and functions of the pastor, elders, church officers, and members. As they develop a desire to participate in the activities of the church, they attend the services regularly and look for ways to be involved.

The Commitment Phase

In the commitment phase, new converts have arrived at a point of satisfaction in their maturing relationship with the Lord and the church. They have modified their beliefs and lifestyle to conform to the doctrinal positions, practices, and culture of the church. They understand the basic teachings of the faith and are actively witnessing to others, assuming leadership roles in the church, and using their time, talents, and other resources for the fulfillment of the church's mission. They do not need to be coerced by anyone to participate in this mission. Rather, they have a sense of belonging, claim ownership of their faith, and are joyful. With the Apostle Paul they can say, "I am not ashamed of the gospel, for it is the power of God for salvation to everyone who believes" (Rom. 1:16). In addition, they are not ashamed to be called Seventh-day Adventist Christians.

Four Immediate Needs of New Believers

When new converts are baptized, they give up relationships with some friends and associates, long-standing connections with certain organizations, vital support structures, and other things that they love dearly. They now face unknown experiences and harbor doubts about the decision they have made. Recognizing these realities, the church should address their needs for *affirmation, love, assurance* *and* *support.*

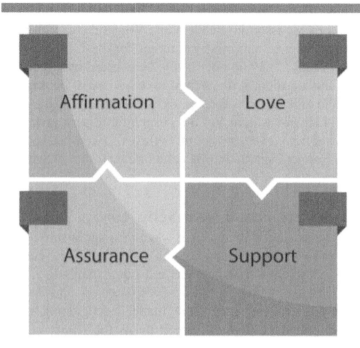

Affirmation

The decision to be baptized invariably attracts the darts of the devil. New members will be bombarded with all kinds of temptations, and the enemy will try to convince them that they made the wrong decision. He attacks them like Pharaoh, who after allowing the Israelites to leave Egypt, pursued them, expecting to catch them defenseless in the wilderness, conquer them, and force their return to Egypt (Exod. 14:1–9).

New converts need verbal affirmation that they made the right decision in accepting Christ and becoming members of the church. Tell them something that you admire about them, no matter how minor or insignificant it may seem. Make them feel special. Talk to them about the benefits of church membership for both this life and eternity. To help them overcome their doubts, tell them how happy you are that they made this decision. Talk to them about the global nature of the church that they are now members of, and share mission stories with them that will build their confidence, commitment, enthusiasm, imagination, and motivation.

Love

The Apostle John said, "Beloved, let us love one another, for love is from God, and whoever loves has been born of God and knows God" (1 John 4:7). New believers have given up the love of the world for a greater love. John 3:16 identifies the source of this greater love: "For God so loved the world, that He gave His only Son, that whoever believes in Him should not perish but have eternal life." Similarly, Romans 5:8 declares that "God shows his love for us in that while we were still sinners, Christ died for us." Believers must demonstrate to new members that they can find the love of Christ within the church. However, lip service is not enough. They need more than theory at this point. They want to experience love in action. "Stephen Covey points out that in all the great literature, love is a verb rather than a noun. Love is something you do, the sacrifices you make and the giving of yourself to others."[2]

The following are some suggested ways that church members can actively demonstrate love to new converts:
- Greet them and welcome them to the worship services at the church.
- Know and use their names.
- Establish an environment for them that reflects care, respect, and concern and that will influence them to engage with the people and agenda of the church.
- Help them to experience positive emotions at the services and social activities of the church.
- Help them to get involved in the activities and programs of the church.
- When necessary, demonstrate forgiveness toward them and others so that they can understand and embrace this fundamental Christian virtue.
- Listen to and try to understand them.

---

6. Richard L. Daft, The Leadership Experience (5th ed.; Mason, OH: South-Western Cengage Learning, 2011), 155.

- Avoid doing or saying things that will embarrass them.
- Acknowledge special qualities and virtues that you see in them.
- Look for and take notice of their loving and genuine intentions.
- Tell them the truth, even when it is hard or difficult, but always with compassion.
- Encourage independent thinking and open-mindedness rather than mere conformity.
- Prepare their favorite food for them as a surprise.
- Take them to a special place to enjoy a wholesome and uplifting activity.
- Offer to help them with something they are working on.
- When they are feeling upset, frustrated, or down, make yourself available to talk to them.
- Be confidential. When they speak, listen and don't spread their private business all around the church or the Internet.
- Introduce them to people in your life and show how proud you are of them.
- Tell them and demonstrate to them that they are welcome in the church family.
- Make room for them in your various activities.
- Accompany them on errands like shopping or take them to a sports event.
- Accept their invitations to do things with them.
- Teach them how to do something that you love and let them teach you how to do things that they love.
- Show patience toward them.
- Remind them that the church loves them and that the Lord wants more than anything for them to be faithful to Him.
- When necessary and possible, give them gifts that they will appreciate.

Assurance

Assurance is given through positive words that inspire confidence and provide encouragement. New members need the assurance that their God is the same God who came to the defense of the Israelites in the wilderness. They need the assurance of Matthew 28:20—"And behold, I am with you always, to the end of the age"—Jeremiah 29:11—"For I know the plans I have for you, plans for welfare and not for evil, to give you a future and a hope"—and Philippians 4:19—"And my God will supply every need of yours according to his riches in glory in Christ Jesus." Share personal experiences with them of how the Lord has led you and others in the past. Assure them that God still holds all power and that He will come through for them.

Support

It is important to provide support to new members by meeting their needs through acts of service. Help them discover their talents and spiritual gifts and learn to utilize them (see chapter 5). Help them to study the Bible, Sabbath School lesson, and Spirit of Prophecy writings. Offer to be their prayer partner. Explain things about the church and the gospel to them. Help meet some of their material needs. Are they in need of clothes, shelter, a job, food, or anything else? Can you help, or can you find someone who can help? Can you teach them any new skills, or do you know someone who could?

A Nurturing Program for the Local Church

The following program has been tested and proven to be very effective in nurturing new believers in the faith when applied appropriately. In a test case, it was found that over 90% of more than 240 newly baptized members were still in the faith two years after their baptism.

1. Hold a fellowship reception as early as possible after the baptism to welcome new members into the church socially.
2. Organize all the newly baptized members into their own new believers Sabbath School class, which should last for at least one quarter.
    a. For at least the first twelve weeks of this Sabbath School class, concentrate on a specially designed Bible study program that will cover the essential doctrines of the church and the principles of discipleship.

b. If using this Bible study program during Sabbath School time, take ten minutes each week to review the regular Sabbath School lesson before beginning the special Bible study topic.

c. At the end of each study, give a short quiz. This will serve the purpose of providing motivation and assessing the impact of the program.

d. Record the names of the class members each week. This record will enable the leaders to know how many of the doctrines each person has already studied. It will also indicate which members are getting weak and need special attention.

3. Assign each new member to a spiritual-support guide, who will look after the new member's wellbeing. This guide should:
   a. Visit, call, encourage, and assist the new member in order to help them adjust as quickly as possible to church life.
   b. Make sure that other church members invite the new member to dinner each week for at least the first three months after they have accepted the faith.
   c. Learn what talents and interests the new member has and work with the leaders of the various departments and ministries to find ways that the new member can utilize these talents and interests in the programs and services of the church.

4. Incorporate new believers into small groups and witnessing teams, in which they will unite with other church members in witnessing initiatives.

5. Organize a new-converts day at least once each quarter, giving new members the opportunity to participate in various aspects of the church service.

6. Other opportunities for new converts to participate in the church may include:
   a. Conducting a new-converts Sabbath School program.
   b. Leading out in a new-converts youth program.
   c. Being facilitators in a new-converts Bible study class.

d. Conducting a new-converts prayer meeting.

   e. Participating in a new-converts choir.

7. Encourage new members to study the following topics. Provide them with the book *Bible Readings for the Home* or another useful Bible study resource, such as *What We Believe* from the Inter-American Division Publishing Association (IADPA) or *Seventh-day Adventists Believe* from the General Conference Ministerial Association.

   a. The sacred Scriptures

   b. The character and attributes of God

   c. The Holy Spirit and His work

   d. Confession and forgiveness

   e. The kingdoms of grace and glory

   f. Satan's warfare against the church

   g. Making an image to the beast

   h. The moral and ceremonial laws

   i. Reasons for Sabbath-keeping

   j. Support of the ministry and freewill offerings

   k. Christ's second coming

   l. The two resurrections

   m. Enduring hardship and persecution

   n. How to be a ready witness

   o. How to defend your faith

   p. Ellen White and the Seventh-day Adventist Church

   q. Structure and organization of the Seventh-day Adventist Church

   r. Being a disciple of Jesus

   s. The sanctuary

A Discipleship Paradigm in the Retention of New Members

The Objectives
1. To nurture the new members in the faith
2. To address the needs of new members
3. To enable new members to actively share their faith

Introduction
The mandate of Jesus to his disciples is found in Matthew 28:19-20; "Go therefore and make *disciples* of all the nations, baptizing them in the name of the Father and of the Son and of the Holy Spirit, teaching them to observe all things that I have commanded you; and lo, I am with you always, even to the end of the age."

Based on this text, discipleship making is the core responsibility of the Church. Five of the core values of Jesus' disciples are; Devotion, Fellowship, Outreach, Evangelism and stewardship. The design of this program is to engage each new believer within the church to grow in these five primary areas as faithful disciples and stewards of Jesus (See chapter on discipleship).

Organization
The church appoints a nurturing committee comprised of persons who:

1. Are committed to the holistic growth of the new members
2. Are able to dedicate time to direct the nurturing program
3. Are committed to the fundamental principles and practices of the Seventh-day Adventist Church
4. Can guide the new members to grow in the six universal principles of retention established by the General Conference of Seventhday Adventists and which are embedded in the five core values of discipleship in this book.
5. Will study and understand the five phases and four immediate needs of new members.
6. Will execute the nurturing program for the local Church.

7. Will ensure that the orientation interview is done between the Pastor/Elder of the Church and each new member as outlined in the chapter for new members.
8. Will instruct all the new members based on the content of chapter that deals with the new members.

Suggested activities for each core value of the discipleship program:

I. Discipleship Core Value – Devotion

Under this value, the new members will be encouraged to:
- Attend weekly worship services
- Study their Sabbath School lesson
- Enhance their personal prayer life through ongoing prayer initiatives.
- Have daily worship or family worship (if applicable)
- Read their bible that will inspire and motivate them to develop a personal bible reading routine that will help them to increase their bible knowledge and apply the word of God to their personal life.
- Encourage the members to enhance their knowledge of the ministry and counsels of Ellen White and to make personal applications to their lives and ministry.
- Support and participate in the various spiritual programs and initiatives of the church.
- Be engaged in any other initiative relevant to grow their spiritual life.

II. Discipleship Core Value – Fellowship

Under this value, the new members will be encouraged to:
- Develop contacts and relationships with others on a social level that leads to friendly relations, engaging in various forms of social interaction with individuals both within and outside the Church community.
- Be involved in one-to-one contact with others within the church through organized social activities or personal encounters.

- Help both members and non-members to deal with their social, physical and emotional issues.
- To have at least two persons in social relations at all times. One should be a member of the Church; the other should be a non-member who is a prospect for church membership.
- Learn how to attract the attention of other individuals as mentioned above and build friendly relations with them.
- Participate in specific social activities organized by the church or a small group to get them connecting with each other, building strong bonds and enjoy the Christian community.

III. Discipleship Core Value – Evangelism

Under this value, the new members will be encouraged to:
- Share their faith and the gospel of Jesus—the good news of salvation—with others.
- Work with a team or a partner in sharing of the gospel to others.
- Determine the most appropriate time to be involved in faith-sharing activities.
- Participate in the menu of faith-sharing activities that is determined by the group.
- Learn how to attract the interest and attention of non-Adventists and conduct bible studies with them (See Appendix G).

IV. Discipleship Core Value – Outreach

This value deals with addressing material, social, and other needs of individuals in the surrounding community. Under this value, the new members will be encouraged to:
- Participate in organized outreach ministries of the church or personal outreach endeavors.
- Address material, social, and other needs of individuals in the surrounding community (See chapter on Field Preparation).
- Matthew 25:35 and 36 Jesus described the *outreach* ministry of a disciple: "For I was hungry, and you fed Me. I was thirsty, and you gave Me a drink. I was a stranger, and you invited Me into your home. I was naked, and you gave Me clothing. I was sick, and you cared for Me. I was in prison, and you visited Me" (NLT).

- Participate in organized Outreach that includes all these compassionate services
- Participate in other activities that relieve human suffering and satisfy human needs.
- Participate in relevant surveys within the church and the wider community to determine social and other needs and work to address such deficiencies.

V. Discipleship Core Value – Stewardship

This core value deals with all the gifts, talents, and other resources in our possession that are given to us in trust and belongs to God. The members are encouraged to use them wisely and appropriately to meet personal necessities, to further the cause of Christ, and to bless others. The new members are encouraged to:
- Sacrifice at least 8 hours weekly to participate in organized fellowship and outreach activities of the church
- Spend at least 45 minutes daily in prayer, lesson study, bible study and other inspirational reading
- Return their tithe and offering faithfully.
- Identify their talents and spiritual gifts and be encouraged to use them within the Church
- Live a life of faithfulness to the Lord in the way they manage their talents, time, resources and body temple and serve the church and others.

Organizational Worksheet for Retention of New Members

I. Name, of chair for Retention program:_____

II. Names of other members of the retention committee:

_____   _____
_____   _____
_____   _____
_____   _____

III. Names of new members   Names of Spiritual Mentors

_____   _____
_____   _____
_____   _____
_____   _____
_____   _____
_____   _____
_____   _____

Names of Coordinators for each Core Values

Devotion Coordinator _____

Fellowship Coordinator _____

Evangelism Coordinator _____

Outreach Coordinator _____

Stewardship Coordinator _____

Evangelism Coordinator _____

1. Name four specific Devotion initiatives that the new members will do.

_____
_____
_____
_____

2. Name four specific Fellowship initiatives that the new members will do.

_____

_____

_____

_____

_____

3. Name four specific Evangelism initiatives that the new members will do.

_____

_____

_____

_____

4. Name four specific Outreach initiatives that the new members will do.

_____

_____

_____

_____

_____

5. Name four specific Stewardship initiatives that the new members will do.

_____

_____

_____

Review and Discussion
- *How does Ellen White confirm the need for such a strategy?*
- *In what way does the mission statement of the Seventh-day Adventist Church refer to the need for a spiritual-nurturing strategy in each church?*
- *Identify three factors that are essential for nurturing new members in their faith, and explain how the church can help make these factors a reality.*
- *Name and describe the five phases of the new-believer experience.*
- *How would you meet the four immediate needs of new believers?*
- *Draft a twelve-week plan that you could implement to nurture new converts in the faith.*
- *What are the seven most important doctrinal topics that you would explain to a new member who had no prior association with the Seventh-day Adventist Church before their conversion experience?*

21
For the New Believer

YOU ARE NOW a Seventh-day Adventist Christian—welcome! Through baptism, you have given public expression to your faith in Jesus and have begun your new life in Him (Rom. 6:3, 4). Baptism can be thought of as a gateway into the church and as a spiritual marriage with Christ (Rom. 7:2–4). It is a manifestation of your decision to break your allegiance to the world and become a member of the body of Christ, and it is a significant step in your salvation experience. In fact, it is the most important decision you will ever make, and it brings the assurance of a secured future in Christ.

Becoming a Christian is a journey, not a destination. The kingdom of heaven is the destination, and on this journey you will have both desirable and undesirable experiences. Like any other journey, you will pass over both smooth and rough terrain. There will be days when you feel excited and motivated about your faith, and there will be days when you question whether you made the right decision.

However, as you receive help from the Holy Spirit and guidance from the Word of God, you will discover that every day with Jesus inspires new hope and confidence. The instructions that follow will help you to minimize some of the difficulties along the way, making your adjustment to your new faith positive and satisfying.

Biblical Assurance for New Converts

As a new member of the church, it is essential for you to be aware that your salvation is based entirely upon the grace of Jesus Christ, whom by faith you accept as your Lord and Savior. "For by grace you have been saved through faith. And this is not your own doing;

it is the gift of God, not a result of works, so that no one may boast" (Eph. 2:8–9). This assurance of salvation does not depend upon your feelings. There will be times when you will feel bright, happy, and assured, but there will be other times when you feel the opposite. Just remember that the Lord will never abandon you, regardless of how you feel. He has promised, "I will never leave you nor forsake you" (Heb. 13:5). In your newfound relationship with Christ, you live each day not by what you can see but by faith and confidence in the Lord. The Apostle Paul expresses this with the following words: "We walk by faith, not by sight" (2 Cor. 5:7).

The Bible contains this precious promise from the Lord: "If you confess with your mouth that Jesus is Lord and believe in your heart that God raised Him from the dead, you will be saved" (Rom. 10:9). You have made such a confession, and that is why you are a member of the body of Christ today. Whenever the devil attacks you with doubt and tells you that you are not really saved or that you are not as good as other Christians, just remember this text and let it encourage your spirit.

The Scriptures teach that as human beings we are born with a sinful nature that separates us from God. This nature results in eternal death. However, Jesus came and suffered the consequences of sin so that He could transform our nature. He died as your Substitute, and now that you have accepted His death on your behalf, He has forgiven you of your sins and made you a partaker of His spiritual nature (2 Pet. 1:4). "If we confess our sins, He is faithful and just to forgive us our sins and to cleanse us from all unrighteousness" (1 John 1:9).

As a Christian, you will make mistakes; however, the blood of Christ has cleansed you and given you a new life, and the Holy Spirit will enable you to live that life constantly. "I have been crucified with Christ. It is no longer I who live, but Christ who lives in me. And the life I now live in the flesh I live by faith in the Son of God, who loved me and gave Himself for me" (Gal. 2:20). He has washed you, and through His empowerment, you can continue to follow Him with the assurance that you are not condemned. "There is therefore now no condemnation for those who are in Christ Jesus" (Rom. 8:1).

Remember also that the moment you accepted Jesus as your Savior, the Holy Spirit began to dwell in your heart. "Do you not know that your body is a temple of the Holy Spirit within you, whom you have from God?" (1 Cor. 6:19). You did not merely become a better person at your conversion. Rather, you were born again as a spiritual person, and the Holy Spirit now lives within you. You are now an entirely new person. "Therefore, if anyone is in Christ, he is a new creation. The old has passed away; behold, the new has come" (2 Cor. 5:17). This cannot be explained humanly, for it is a divine mystery.

Because you have accepted Christ as your Savior, God gives you eternal life as a free gift. Eventually, after your physical body dies, God will give you a new body at the first resurrection, and you will live with Him in His kingdom for all eternity. Jesus promised, "Let not your hearts be troubled. Believe in God; believe also in Me. In My Father's house are many rooms. If it were not so, would I have told you that I go to prepare a place for you? And if I go and prepare a place for you, I will come again and will take you to Myself, that where I am you may be also" (John 14:1–3).

Your continued relationship with Him matters, for He is the One who keeps you spiritually alive. You cannot do this yourself, but as the Apostle Paul says, "I can do all things through Him who strengthens me" (Phil. 4:13). You will not stagnate or decline in your relationship with Him as long as you surrender to His leading. Instead you will grow in faith and become spiritually stronger as you walk with Him. "But grow in the grace and knowledge of our Lord and Savior Jesus Christ" (2 Pet. 3:18).

Do not drift away from Christ's leading because of discouragements, temptations, or trials. He is the One who gives you salvation, so if you depart from Him, you also leave behind your salvation. For this reason, the Apostle Paul urged all believers to "continue in the faith, stable and steadfast, not shifting from the hope of the gospel that you heard" (Col. 1:23).

Hebrews 10:25 urges believers to support each other, "not neglecting to meet together, as is the habit of some, but encouraging one another." This text serves as a great reminder of the importance of attending church regularly. When you worship with like-minded believers, you will grow spiritually and socially as a Christian, and your faith will be strengthened by the messages preached from the Word of God, the study of Bible doctrines, corporate prayer, and fellowship with other members. Worship services also provide you with the opportunity to express your love, faithfulness, and gratitude to God. Do not be absent from church without valid reasons. Don't follow feelings that make you want to stay away sometimes, even if it's just a day here or a Sabbath there. When you are absent one week, the devil is delighted and uses that one absence to encourage other absences until he eventually discourages you from attending. The Bible tells you to resist the devil: "Submit yourselves therefore to God. Resist the devil, and he will flee from you" (James 4:7).

Prayer is an essential part of your daily spiritual life. The Lord wants to have daily fellowship with you, and prayer forms an important part of that fellowship. God promises to answer your prayers, and He loves to hear your voice. In Jeremiah 33:3, He says, "Call to Me and I will answer you, and will tell you great and hidden things that you have not known." The Apostle Paul says that we should "pray without ceasing" (1 Thess. 5:17).

Paul counseled Timothy, "Do your best to present yourself to God as one approved, rightly handling the word of truth (2 Tim. 2:15). This counsel applies to you too; when you diligently study the Word of God, you become approved by Him. The psalmist David said, "Your word is a lamp to my feet and a light to my path" (Ps. 119:105).

As you grow in your relationship with the Lord, He will give you more and more power to overcome sinful behaviors and habits. "Since we have these promises, beloved, let us cleanse ourselves from every defilement of body and spirit, bringing holiness to completion in the fear of God" (2 Cor. 7:1). Through the power of the Holy Spirit, you can obtain victory over the corruption of the world.

The Bible says that the Holy Spirit immerses you with special power for service, which enables you to give a convincing testimony through a genuine Christian life and to be bold in your witness to the supremacy of Christ. "But you will receive power when the Holy Spirit has come upon you, and you will be My witnesses in Jerusalem and in all Judea and Samaria, and to the end of the earth" (Acts 1:8). As a believer in Christ, you must tell others about Him. Do not keep it a secret. Jesus declares, "So everyone who acknowledges Me before men, I also will acknowledge before My Father who is in heaven, but whoever denies Me before men, I also will deny before My Father who is in heaven" (Matt. 10:32, 33).

Nurturing Your Personal Spiritual Life

Prayer

Endeavor to develop and intensify your personal prayer life. Talk to the Lord as frequently as possible every day, and cultivate both a spirit and a habit of prayer. When you wake up each morning, make prayer your first concern. You can pray wherever you are. You do not have to stand, kneel, or sit; you can pray to the Lord while walking or lying down. You may assume different postures according to circumstances; however, kneeling is one of the best ways to approach the Lord in prayer. It is good to demonstrate this attitude of humility as often as possible while talking to God.

The community of the church provides opportunities for corporate prayer, and you should make these opportunities a fundamental part of your prayer life. Your church may have special prayer groups that you may join. You should also attend the weekly prayer meeting. In addition, the worship service on Sabbath is an opportunity that you should anticipate for uniting with the entire church family in prayer.

Personal Study

Develop a Bible study routine in order to expand your knowledge of the Word of God, hear God's voice speaking to you, and feed your spiritual life. Do this daily or as often as possible throughout the week. Try to read the entire Bible, from Genesis to Revelation. There are various study guides and methods from which you may choose according to what fits best into your time and situation. Your spiritual-support guide or other church members can help you identify some of these methods.

Other helpful spiritual resources include the Sabbath School Bible study guide, a daily devotional, and a hymnal. The book *Bible Readings for the Home* will answer many of your questions about the Bible, and the writings of Ellen G. White provide important and valuable counsels that will nurture your faith and help you develop positive lifestyle practices in diet, health, social relationships, and entertainment.

You should explore the doctrines of the church and learn the basic differences between your new faith and your former faith. The books *What We Believe*—available from the Inter-American Division Publishing Association (IADPA)—and *Seventh-day Adventists Believe*—from the General Conference Ministerial Association—will help you become familiar with the following twenty-eight fundamental beliefs of the Seventh-day Adventist Church:

1. The Holy Scriptures
2. The Trinity
3. The Father
4. The Son
5. The Holy Spirit
6. Creation
7. The nature of man
8. The great controversy
9. The life, death, and resurrection of Christ
10. The experience of salvation
11. Growing in Christ
12. The church
13. The remnant and its mission
14. Unity in the body of Christ
15. Baptism
16. The Lord's supper
17. Spiritual gifts and ministries
18. he gift of prophecy

19. The law of God
20. The Sabbath
21. Stewardship
22. Christian behavior
23. Marriage and the family
24. Christ's ministry in the heavenly sanctuary
25. The second coming of Christ
26. Death and resurrection
27. The millennium and the end of sin
28. The new earth

Family Worship

It is essential to set aside a time for all the members of the household to come together for worship and devotion. You can sing a song, pray, and study a passage of Scripture, the Sabbath School lesson, or some other inspirational material. This should be a daily exercise. It will be very helpful to make it the first activity in the home every day. When it is impossible for all members of the family to meet together for worship in the morning, they should do so in the evening. It is even better to have both morning and evening worship with your family if possible. Even if you are the only one in your family, embracing the practice of morning and evening worship is an excellent way to build and nurture your faith.

Welcoming the Sabbath

The Sabbath is a special time in the life of every Seventh-day Adventist. Since in Creation the days began in the evening, the Sabbath, which was the seventh day of Creation, begins at sunset on Friday and ends at sunset on Saturday, the seventh day of the week (Gen. 1:5, 8, 13, 19, 23, 31; Lev. 23:32; Neh. 13:19). Make sure to complete all your secular work, shopping, secular pleasure, entertainment, and Sabbath preparation before the sun sets each Friday so that you can meet with your family to welcome the Sabbath.

The following are some of the activities that you may choose from to welcome the Sabbath: singing special hymns and gospel songs, including hymns about the Sabbath; praying as a family; studying passages from Scripture; reviewing the week's Sabbath School lesson; playing Bible games; reading inspirational stories; and sharing how the Lord provided blessings, guidance, and protection throughout the week. Keep this vespers service short but meaningful. After a long week of work and other activities, the members of the family are no doubt tired, and they will not want to be bored with lengthy speeches and presentations. Play soothing gospel music in the background to set the tone for a peaceful and spiritual atmosphere. You could invite some friends to join your family to welcome the Sabbath or join other families for this special occasion.

Church Services

Attending church every Sabbath is of utmost importance to help you nurture your faith, build relationships with others within the church, and become integrated into the life of your new faith. The Sabbath services will augment the Christian life you live throughout the week. Some churches have Sabbath School, divine service, a Bible study time, an Adventist Youth meeting, and a vespers service every Sabbath. All of these services have their own particular nurturing function and value, and they will aid you in your spiritual development.

Sabbath School

The Sabbath School lesson is the official Bible study guide of the church. Seventh-day Adventists around the world study this lesson each week. There is a study guide for each age group. Make sure that you have the study guide for each quarter, and study the designated section every day. Thus when you go to the Sabbath School class on Sabbath morning, you will be able to participate in the lesson discussion, get answers to questions that occurred to you while studying the lesson, and share some of the ideas and insights that you found.

The Lord's Supper

Each local congregation celebrates the Lord's Supper, also known as the communion service, at least once each quarter. It is open to all who believe in and accept Jesus as their Savior. It serves as a tangible reminder of our Lord's death and resurrection and the hope of His glorious return in the future. This service also provides you with an opportunity to consecrate and recommit yourself to the Lord. Before partaking of the emblems, you take part in the ordinance of humility, in which participants wash each other's feet. This is like a miniature baptism that represents cleansing from the sins we have committed. You then partake of the bread, which symbolizes Christ's death on the cross in your place, and the wine, which is a symbol of the blood He shed for the remission of your sins (Matthew 26:26–30). This service is a necessary part of your spiritual experience, and you should participate as often as it is served.

Exploring Your Church

Learn as much as you can about your church, what it teaches, what it believes, how it operates, and what your rights, privileges, and responsibilities are. As you explore, do not depend on what others do or say. Find out for yourself, and when necessary, get biblical support for what you learn. Be involved, have an open mind, be ready to learn, and get to know your church!

Orientation Interview

Within one or two weeks of your baptism, you should have an interview with your pastor and church elder. As a new member, make sure that this meeting takes place. Your spiritual-support guide can help you to get it scheduled. When you meet with the pastor, be ready to share about yourself and ask questions. Here are a few suggested questions and ideas that will help you to get the most out of your orientation.

1. "What are your expectations of me as a new member?"
2. "What resources or support does the church provide to help me grow in the faith?"

3. "Is there anything in particular that you think I should know as a new member of this church?"
4. Tell the pastor about your experience of faith before joining the Seventh-day Adventist Church and share how you came to know this church.
5. Share about your family, work, and hobbies.
6. If you desire, share a little about your health.
7. Talk about your strengths and weaknesses and how these may be utilized or developed in the church.
8. If there are personal issues that you think the pastor should know about, feel free to share them.

The Structure of the Seventh-day Adventist Organization

The worldwide organizational structure of the Seventh-day Adventist Church is very unique. You are a member of a local congregation, which has a pastor who leads as the shepherd of the flock. The pastor, along with the members of the church board and other church officers, is responsible for the administration of your congregation. The Church Manual establishes the guidelines that govern the operation of the local church.

The members elect all of the church officers and members of the church board either annually or biannually. The church officers—including the elders, deacons, deaconesses, church clerk, treasurer, and the leaders of the various ministries—make up the church board. You should learn about the church board and its function, as well as that of the church business meeting. Find out when the church business meeting is held, and endeavor to attend.

Your pastor may be responsible for a district of more than one local congregation. The pastor is an employee of the Seventh-day Adventist organization who is assigned by the local conference. The conference has administrative authority over a group of churches that are organized into pastoral districts within a defined geographical area. A group of local conferences within a larger geographical area forms a union conference. Similarly, groups of union conferences are organized into divisions of the General Conference.

The General Conference is the worldwide governing body of the church. Its headquarters is located in Silver Spring, Maryland in the United States of America. In order to provide effective leadership for the global church, the General Conference consists of thirteen regional divisions. As new churches, conferences, and unions are formed, the General Conference may make adjustments to the divisions in order to ensure effective administration of the world field.

It is good for you to understand the relationship between your local church and the local conference, union, division, and the General Conference itself. You should know the names of your conference, union, and division, as well as where their main offices are located. It would also be beneficial to know the names of the president, executive secretary, treasurer, and departmental leaders at all of these levels of the church. Whenever the opportunity presents itself, it would good for you to meet and know these leaders in person.

Educational and Health Services

The global educational and health care systems of the church are among the largest such faith-based systems in the world. The church operates thousands of kindergarten, elementary, and secondary schools, as well as many colleges and universities. These institutions complement the church and the home in nurturing your faith and that of your children. If applicable to you, endeavor to pursue the educational opportunities made available through the church's institutions. It is a great blessing to receive academic training that complements your Christian faith. Similarly, you may obtain medical attention through the church's medical institutions. Get information on how you may access the services of these institutions if you have such needs. Be aware that the educational and medical services that the church provides do involve financial cost.

Local Church Ministries

The church has various ministries that provide spiritual nurture to you and your family and give you the opportunity to participate in the life of the congregation, utilizing your talents and spiritual gifts to build up the body of Christ. These include Sabbath School and Personal Ministries, Community Services, Communication, Stewardship Ministries, Children's Ministries, Youth Ministries, Women's Ministries, Adventist Men, Family Ministries, Publishing Ministries, Health Ministries, Education, Trust Services, and Religious Liberty. Small groups also provide an excellent opportunity for spiritual growth and participation. Try to determine in which areas the Lord has gifted you to contribute, and contact the leaders of the appropriate ministries to find out what services they provide and how you can be involved.

Clubs and Other Church Activities

If you are a parent, or if you are in any of the age groups listed below, make use of the opportunities that your congregation provides to train you or your children. The church has the Eager Beaver Club for children who are 1–5 years of age, the Adventurer Club for those 6–9 years of age, the Pathfinder Club for those 10–15 years of age, and the Ambassador Club for the 16–21 age group. Young Adults is for those who are 22–31+ years old, and the Master Guide program is for those who are 16 years and older.

You may also become a member of any of the other clubs that the church may have, such as a marriage club, singles club, or drama club. In addition, the various activities of the church, such as camp meetings, youth congresses, Pathfinder camporees, youth rallies, conventions, seminars, retreats, and socials, are excellent ways to become better acquainted with your church and enrich your spiritual and social life.

Church Membership

Value and appreciate your church membership, which provides you with all the rights and privileges to participate in the life and ministry of the church. As a member, you are entitled to hold church offices and leadership positions, which enable you to represent the church both inside and outside the faith. For this reason, you should allow the Lord to help you to know, understand, and live up to the high standards of Christian living of the Seventh-day Adventist faith. In your baptismal vows, you committed to observe these standards and practices. Resist every temptation to violate your conscience, jeopardize your future in Christ, compromise moral and ethical standards, or damage the good name of the church.

Your church membership resides in the local congregation that received you into fellowship; however, as a baptized Seventh-day Adventist, you are a member of a worldwide body of believers. Wherever you go around the world, seek out a Seventh-day Adventist church as one of your first orders of business and join the members in worship and fellowship.

If you transfer your residence from one place to another, request that your membership be sent to the new church in which you will be worshipping and finding satisfaction for your social and spiritual needs. You may no longer be in contact with your former church family, so it is best to formalize your relationship with the new congregation so that the members of the former congregation do not have to be concerned about your whereabouts. Furthermore, in order to hold a leadership position in the new church, your membership should be in that congregation.

A church can only transfer your membership to another Seventhday Adventist church. You can request to have your membership transferred to any Seventh-day Adventist congregation in the world, and it is unnecessary to be baptized again to become a member of that local church.

Loss of Church Membership

It is possible to lose your membership in the Seventh-day Adventist Church. The Church Manual describes the conditions under which this may take place. Some of these include participating in divisive movements, failing to observe the seventh day of the week as the Sabbath, committing adultery or fornication, bringing public reproach upon the church, and refusing to abide by properly constituted authority within the church. If your name is removed from the membership record of the church, you will no longer be able to hold leadership positions in the local congregation or represent the church in any capacity. In order to regain church membership, you will need to be baptized again after showing signs of repentance. While your membership is removed, if you choose to go to another Seventh-day Adventist congregation, you will have no membership to transfer and will need to be rebaptized in order to receive membership in that church.

Financial Stewardship

Returning tithe and offering is a part of your obligation and spiritual responsibility to the Lord (Lev. 27:30; Mal. 3:8–10). Tithe is one tenth of your earnings or one tenth of the increase of your investments. Your offering is based on your own free will, but it is nonetheless an essential component of your Christian stewardship. Both tithe and offering should be returned to your local church as soon as you receive it. It is never a good idea to store your tithe and offering for accumulation before giving it to the church, neither should you borrow it for personal use or lend it to others with the intention of returning it at a future date. Always resist such temptations. The Lord knows your earnings and the intentions of your heart, so return your tithe and offering as early as possible. The church uses the tithe for the expansion of the gospel around the world and for the support of those who are dedicated to full-time ministry. Offering is used for the operation of the local church and for certain mission projects.

Witnessing and Service

Look for ways to share your faith with others. The Lord has commanded you, as well as all other believers, to make disciples for Him (Matt. 28:18– 20). Tell them of the great things the Lord and the church have done for you, and invite them to take their stand for the Lord.

The church provides a variety of opportunities to witness through organized group initiatives or personal endeavors. You may serve as a lay preacher or Bible instructor or witness in many other ways. Spend some time with others in the faith who have more experience, or get some training in soul winning. This will help you to be more effective and will enable you to handle any opposition you may face while witnessing. The other chapters of this book will also help you to serve as an effective witness for the Lord.

Serving as a Literature Evangelist

Through literature evangelism, you can both witness and secure a financial income. Literature evangelists are self-supporting church workers who dedicate their service to the Lord by selling literature that contains the Seventh-day Adventist message. Their source of livelihood is the proceeds of these sales. You can become either a full-time or parttime literature evangelist. Many who are working full time in pastoral ministry today, as well as many with other careers, acquired funding for their secondary and university education through literature evangelism.

Volunteering as a Missionary

The Adventist Volunteer Service provides opportunities for church members to go as missionaries to other parts of the world. Based on your passion, talents, and skills, you may volunteer in many different ways, including teaching a foreign language, planting new churches, providing medical or dental care, and serving in areas such as education, construction, and evangelism. You may serve as a missionary for one or more years, depending on your availability and the nature of the volunteer project you would be involved in. You must be able to serve without financial compensation, except for a small stipend in some cases.

Representing Christ

Always remember that the most important witness you can give to the world is the daily life that you live for the Lord. Let your speech, actions, and conduct in business transactions and social relationships demonstrate that you are a child of God. Be honest, upright, fair, agreeable, kind, humble, loving, and trustworthy in all your dealings so that others can see the character of God reflected in your life.

In Closing . . .

The Seventh-day Adventist Church is happy to receive you as a member and affirms you for the decision you have made to become a part of this global body of believers who are preparing for the second coming of Christ. As a member of this church, you have enrolled in a university that will teach you about the science of salvation. This is a subject that we will continue learning about until Jesus comes, and when we reach the kingdom of heaven, we will simply enter another phase of learning and exploration.

Your best days are yet ahead. As you grow in grace and apply the counsels provided in these pages, the Spirit of the Lord will establish you in Christ, and you will find immeasurable joy in living and sharing your faith.

Review and Discussion

- *What are five biblical assurances for new believers?*
- *Identify eight practical steps that new believers can take to nurture their faith.*
- *What are some questions that a new member should ask the pastor in the orientation interview?*
- *Differentiate between local and global church membership.*
- *What does the Bible say about returning tithe and offering, and how important is stewardship for the spiritual life of the new believer?*
- *Identify some specific spiritual resource materials that new converts should acquire and utilize.*
- *How can new members discover their spiritual gifts, and how might they use particular spiritual gifts in specific ministries of the church? See chapter 5.*
- *Name the twenty-eight fundamental doctrines of the Seventh-day Adventist Church with which each new member should become familiar.*
- *Develop an eight-week, ready-to-implement plan to use for family worship.*
- *Name the various levels of the Seventh-day Adventist Church and explain the relation between each level.*
- *Who are the president, executive secretary, and treasurer at each of the levels of the church that is relevant to your geographical area?*

Appendix A Planting New Churches

IN ORDER TO FULFILL Christ's command in Matthew 28:18–20, Christians must go into new areas to establish communities of believers. When such a community grows, it should secure a place to assemble for worship, fulfill the duties of Christian stewardship, and provide for nurture, fellowship, outreach, and evangelism. Thus a new congregation is established.

Planting a new church is an ambitious endeavor, and as such, it requires strong commitment and thorough preparation. We must endeavor to plant churches that will thrive and grow rather than stagnate. For this reason, it is essential to perform a needs assessment to determine the growth potential of the church plant in the selected territory.

Six Phases of Church Planting

1. *Urgency*—It is necessary to create a sense of urgency and promote the church-planting initiative among church members. To this end, conduct a needs assessment of the territory and present the results to the church, showing how the initiative could make an impact in the community in question.
2. *Team*—A capable and devoted team that is committed to meeting the identified needs of the community should be recruited for this church-planting initiative. This team should consist of church members who are willing, interested, and available to be involved in the project as church-planting collaborators.
3. *Empowerment*—A vital aspect of preparation for this endeavor is equipping the team to function effectively. In addition to learning specific skills and methods, team members must develop habits of critical thinking in order to choose,

contextualize, and implement strategies that are appropriate for the designated territory. 4. *Strategy*—The team must develop a strategy that addresses all the aspects of establishing a vibrant new community of believers.

These include the vision, objectives, how to achieve the objectives, personnel, responsibilities, time frames, and resources.

5. *Implementation*—In this stage, the team puts the strategy into action, from implementing community-service initiatives to organizing the new church.
6. *Evaluation*—In order to obtain the desired outcome, evaluation should take place throughout the entire church-planting process to determine if and when to intensify efforts or shift the focus.

Practical Steps for Planting a New Church

1. Appoint a church-planting committee. The pastor or one of the elders should serve as chairperson of this committee, which is responsible for recruiting the church-planting collaborators and overseeing the initiative throughout the six phases of the church-planting process.
2. Choose a church-planting leader. This could be the chairperson or secretary of the church-planting committee. The church-planting leader directs the team of collaborators and reports to the committee regarding all matters related to the initiative.
3. Begin with prayer, presenting the project to the Lord with prayer and fasting.
4. Determine where to plant the new church.
5. Conduct a needs assessment and survey as explained in chapter 3 to gather information about the territory in which the church will be planted.
6. After analyzing the results of the survey, select and train the church planting collaborators. These should be individuals who are able to work with the needs and opportunities of the territory.

7. Discuss possible collaboration with community leaders.
8. Find an accessible venue to establish a community-service center.
9. Make a major announcement to commence the implementation of this community ministry. Use modern technology and social media to promote this program, and invite civic and other community leaders to participate if possible.
10. Begin providing services to the community based on the growth areas and needs that were identified through discussions with community leaders and the results of the needs survey.
11. Where possible, begin by providing services in collaboration with reputable businesses, organizations, or charities in the area. Important foci that can attract attention include child care, health, family life, parenting, money management, skills training, neighborhood safety, drug-dependency rehabilitation, professional counseling services, Vacation Bible School, animal care, senior care, healthy cooking, homeless care, weight management, exercise, coaching in sports activities, etc.
12. Open and close every activity with prayer.
13. Develop a church-planting prayer list with the names and addresses of the recipients of the ministry's services.
14. Appoint a church-planting prayer team to pray for the individuals included on this list.
15. Assign trained church-planting collaborators to establish contact with these individuals by either visiting them personally or calling them on the phone.
16. After developing a number of prospects, organize a half-hour weekly or biweekly prayer meeting and invite individuals in the community to attend. Each church-planting collaborator should bring at least one prospect to these prayer meetings.
17. As interest grows, increase these meetings to one hour to give time for sharing personal testimonies.
18. Begin Bible Studies with those who are interested.

19. When the time is right, organize a worship service on one Sabbath every month.
20. Continue to initiate activities that will grow the church progressively until it is organized. Have a major celebration at the organization and give special recognition to church-planting collaborators, civic and community leaders, others who facilitated the planting of the new church, and those who first accepted the gospel through the ministry of the church plant. After the organization, continue the evangelism process in order to ensure the continued growth and sustainability of the new church.

Appendix B Reaching Non-Christians

THE MISSION OF EVANGELISM includes witnessing about our faith to those who are not Christians. This may take place in a one-to-one encounter, in small groups, or in a large gathering. Whatever form it takes, evangelizing non-Christians requires careful attention to method and a clear and concise knowledge of the message of the gospel. Reaching non-Christians is a cross-cultural form of evangelism. The following suggestions may be applied to such cross-cultural evangelistic interactions.

1. Determine the ethnicity of the people group that you want to reach.

Once you have made this determination, go on a discovery tour. Find out as much as possible about that people group. This should include knowing about the language, culture, and symbols that unite them as a group. How do they think? What is their lifestyle? What are their main beliefs? What are their special customs, food, clothing, likes, and dislikes?

2. Determine your competencies and support system.

Can you communicate in their language? If not, how will you create understanding? Who are the best persons to help you in reaching them? What do you have in common with them? What are the differences between your religion and theirs?

3. Determine the message to share and the method to use.

Once you have determined the message to share, you must choose a method of transmission that takes into account both the common points and differences between the two faiths. Begin with common points, and emphasize humanitarian and ethical concepts before engaging in discussion about beliefs or doctrines. When evangelizing across cultures, take care not to rush to secure quick results. This can encroach on traditions and practices that are deeply rooted in cultural worldviews, creating dissonance that impedes interest and mutual understanding. It could even close the door to future dialogue and decision making.

4. Meet their needs.

Before Jesus began His ministry, He spent many years among the people in a cross-cultural learning environment. He developed a knowledge of their needs, understood their language, and became acquainted with their heartaches and joys. He mingled with them until He had won their affections, and as a result, they followed Him in great numbers.

It is necessary to win the confidence of the people, demonstrating love, care, and compassion. Develop personal relationships with them and win their trust. Identify their needs and work with them to address those needs. To this end, the community-action strategies suggested in chapters 9–15 may be adapted to the cultural needs of the identified ethnic groups.

The church could secure an appropriate venue to establish a ministry for addressing the material and social needs of the identified ethnic group. It would be good to find people from that culture to provide needed services to members of their ethnic community. For example, the church could organize a Jewish health clinic to provide health screening for Jews, enlisting the help of Jewish medical professionals to deliver the best service possible.

5. Share the message.

After determining the targeted ethnicity, learning about the culture, determining available resources, and meeting the needs of the people, it is time to address differences of faith with the hope of securing acceptance of the gospel message. Present the message to those you have been interacting with, engaging them in Bible studies, praying with them, and most of all, presenting Christ as their Savior. Show the difference between Christ and all the other deities that world religions revere.

When working with people of other faiths, always be aware that they are probably satisfied and content with their religion. It is the reality that they are most familiar and comfortable with. In order to be receptive to changes in their beliefs and practices, they must first develop cognitive dissonance with their religion, causing them to experience discomfort and a thirst for something that is more satisfying. To effect this process, we must intentionally use the elements of persuasion—ethos, pathos, and logos (see chapter 4)—working under the guidance of the Holy Spirit to influence them to accept Christianity.

As you present Christian doctrinal concepts, call for appropriate decisions at each step. Once the person has gained an understanding of the fundamental doctrines of the Christian faith, ask them to commit to Jesus, accepting Him as their Savior and being baptized into the Sabbath-keeping faith. We should then help them to adjust to the significant life changes that come with their new faith. Be patient in this process, remembering that only the Lord of the harvest can reach the unreached, open their minds to greater truth, and establish them in a Christian worldview.

As Christians, we are God's fellow workers. He loves all people and understands their needs and cultural backgrounds. He will provide the necessary enabling to all who commit themselves to cross-cultural witnessing. It is the Holy Spirit who wins souls, and He is working with people of other cultures as well as those in the Christian culture. We are commanded to preach the gospel to the whole world (Matt. 28:18–20). As a global community of Christians, we must consider the millions of people who fall outside our traditional evangelistic audience, acting decisively to develop strategies to reach them with the eternal gospel of Jesus.

Appendix C Prayer Breakfast for Ex-Adventists

The Challenge:

IN MANY COMMUNITIES there are as many former members of the church as there are current members. Some desire to return to the faith but they do not feel that they will find acceptance.

Our Mandate:

To restore to the fellowship of the Seventh-day Adventist Church all former members and to nurture them to live in readiness for Christ's Second Advent (Rev. 2:4–5).

Initiative: A prayer breakfast for ex-Adventists

Objectives:
- To demonstrate the love of Christ to former members of the church and introduce them to a caring, compassionate church that is praying for them.
- To assure ex-Adventists that prayer works and that the Lord is ready to work miracles for them.
- To provide a forum for the development of personal relationships between current and former members of the Seventh-day Adventist Church.

Executing the Initiative:

1. Choose a team to be responsible for organizing and promoting the program.
2. Determine the method for obtaining resources to execute the initiative.
3. Select prayer counselors to lead the group discussions.
4. Every member is to invite at least one former member of the church and bring or accompany that individual to the breakfast.

Suggested Format for Prayer Breakfast

Introduction—10 minutes
1. Call to order
2. Welcome
3. Song
4. Prayer

Food and fellowship—40 Minutes
1. Serve breakfast
2. Eat
3. Meet and greet attendees

Spiritual equipping—10 Minutes
1. Prayer tips
2. Biblical nugget
3. Experiences of answered prayer
4. Prayer challenge for the day (a prayer topic or issue to discuss)

Interactive session—15 Minutes
1. Divide into groups with prayer counselors
2. Discuss the prayer challenge within the group
3. Share personal prayer requests within the group

Prayer—8 Minutes
1. Pray in groups

2. Pray specifically for the requests that were shared

Closing—5 Minutes
1. Reassemble
2. Closing announcements and invitations
3. Closing song
4. Closing prayer
5. Prayer hug
6. Dismissal

Appendix D Fund-Raising for Evangelism

THE FOLLOWING are suggestions for obtaining funds for evangelistic initiatives.

1. *Contributions through letters.* Send letters to selected individuals explaining the cause and requesting a special donation. Be sure to mention the benefits of the campaign to individuals, families, the local community, and society at large.

2. *Online evangelism-support initiative.* Design a website to solicit funds through an online evangelism-support initiative. Collect the email addresses of family, friends, coworkers, church members, teammates, etc. Send them the link to the website and provide regular updates about your efforts. Collect donations through credit card, PayPal, or other electronic means.

3. *Fund-raising websites.* There are numerous reputable websites that allow individuals to raise money for projects and charities. For example, there are Facebook platforms for fundraising, which have an extensive reach and will give high visibility for building networks of friends and donors.

4. *Evangelistic–fund-raising event.* Invite people from far and near to attend. Have musicians and special, well-known guests to do ministry at the program.

5. *Percentage contribution.* Ask businesses and companies to set aside percentages of proceeds from special products and events to go toward the evangelistic cause.

6. *Evangelism sponsorships.* Ask residents of the community, members of the church, or persons of various social classes to serve as sponsors of the campaign. Some can sponsor the cost of transportation, music, seats, food products, etc.

7. *Fund-raising walkathon.* The pathfinders and other uniformed groups within the church can participate in this event, obtaining sponsors to contribute to the evangelistic initiative.

8. *Team fund-raising.* Divide the members into teams and give each team a financial target. Through pledges, solicitation, and fundraising projects such as banquets, luncheons, etc., each team will endeavor to realize its financial goals.

Appendix E Bible Surfing

BIBLE SURFING is a program through which young people and other church members prepare to share their faith with others. In this method, individuals challenge themselves to open their Bibles, read a passage, look for the main characters of the passage, and then dig into the passage through critical thinking in order to discover its meaning. They look up cross-references, examine maps, or reflect upon Bible stories that highlight a particular point in Scripture. They may utilize other relevant resources, such as Spirit of Prophecy writings, Bible commentaries, and other inspirational writings to confirm their conclusions.

Through Bible Surfing, each participant studies and learns to explain specific doctrinal topics from the Scriptures. The Bible Surfing experience includes memorizing the names of each of the twenty-eight fundamental beliefs of the Seventh-day Adventist Church, as well as a study of the topics that surfers will present when they go out to share their faith with prospects in their evangelistic endeavors.

If Bible Surfing forms part of an Adventist Youth meeting or small group initiative, the special feature for the program may be designated for Bible surfing on selected topics at least twice per month. This study could encourage small group participation that enhances the learning process of each participant.

Witnessing-Practice Exercises

In order to build confidence for witnessing to others, each member who participates in the Bible Surfing experience may be involved in witnessing-practice exercises, in which they share with other members of the church the doctrines and topics they have learned during the Bible Surfing experience. This should include sharing personal experiences and expressing praises to the Lord for His goodness. Participants should endeavor to utilize their spiritual gifts to perfect their witnessing ministry. The Bible Surfing and witnessing-practice exercises will help participants to develop confidence in utilizing their spiritual gifts and Bible knowledge to contact others, sharing with them the gospel story of God's love and the faith of Jesus.

Appendix F Bible Search Engines

What is Bible Search Engines?
BIBLE SEARCH ENGINES is an exercise in which individuals are challenged to see how many Bible stories they can learn within a specified period of time.

What Is Its Purpose?

The purpose of Bible Search Engines is to encourage members of the church or group to find joy, pleasure, and interest in Bible study.

How Does It Work?

The Bible consists of sixty-six interconnected books of relevant information that is never outdated, and these books function like search engines on the Internet.

The Challenge

The exercise begins with a challenge to participants to know as many Bible stories as possible, learn how many search engines have the same Bible stories, and identify differences in how the stories are presented in different search engines. If they so wish, participants may use computer tools and social media to aid them in their search.

The challenge may be presented in any of the following ways:
- An individual challenges himself/herself.
- A small group leader challenges their group.
- A departmental leader challenges their team.
- The pastor challenges the church.

- The leader of a Bible class in the church challenges the class members.

At the appropriate time, participants will relate the number of Bible stories learned and what they have learned from their study. The Bible Search Engines leader may direct this sharing session according to the example given below.

Leader: Brother Brown *[Brother Brown stands or acknowledges]*, what search engine are you in?

Brother Brown: I am in the search engine of Genesis.

Leader: How many stories have you found?

Brother Brown: I have found two stories.

Leader: What are the titles of the stories?

Brother Brown: Cain and Abel, and Sodom and Gomorrah.

Leader: Have you found those stories in other search engines?

Brother Brown answers yes or no as appropriate. If the answer is yes, the leader will ask him if he observed any differences in how the stories were presented in the different search engines. Brother Brown would then describe those differences. If time is available, the leader may also ask him to give a synopsis of the stories.

Bible Search Engines leaders may also give specific challenges like the following examples:

1. Do a search on the sanctuary system.
2. Do a search on all the stories in the search engine of 1 Kings.
3. Do a search on the prophet Zechariah.
4. Do a search on ten stories in the search engine of Ezekiel.

Participants may work individually or in groups. They may prepare a special Bible Search Engines chart in which the columns are labeled with the names of the search engines (the books of the Bible) and the rows are labeled with the names of the participating individuals or groups. The Bible Search Engines leader will record the number of Bible stories that each individual or group knows from each search engine, writing the number under the search engine that the story came from.

Appendix G Other Bible Study Methods

The Vasteras Method

THE VASTERAS METHOD gets its name from a Swedish pas- tor, who designed it to encourage more Bible study and participation among the members of his church. The most important aspect of this method is the participation of each member.

How to use this method:

1. Divide the participants into small groups and choose a leader for each group.
2. Read the assigned passage together, assigning a few verses to each participant.
3. Allow ten minutes for meditation so that the participants can review the passage and mark the text with the following symbols:
    a. + at the verses in which they find new truths or thoughts.
    b. ? at the verses they find difficult to understand.
    c. ! at verses that moved their heart or stirred their conscience.
    d.* at verses they would like to memorize.

---

7. *These methods are taken from the book A, B, C . . . Z *for Youth Ministries* (Silver Spring, MD: Church Ministries Department of the General Conference of Seventh-day Adventists, 1986), vol. 1, pp. 66–69.

On a separate sheet of paper, each participant should mark the three verses that they found to be most outstanding and explain their reason for choosing these verses.

The Silence Method

After the group director presents the passage to be studied, participants go by themselves to a quiet place and, using a study guide given to them beforehand, answer several questions about the passage. After a specified period of time, they come back together to share their answers with each other and discuss their findings.

The Answer-in-a-Circle Method

The small group sits together in a circle and reads the passage to be dis- cussed. Then one by one around the circle, each participant gives their opinion on the passage. If they have nothing to share when their turn comes, they can pass the opportunity to the next person.

The Dissertation Method

In this method, one speaker presents and explains the topic. This method is the least advisable for youth, who may find it too preachy. If it is to be used, the speaker should provide an outline to participants, use visual aids, and encourage participants to interrupt and ask questions. The speaker must also encourage the participants to read the texts.

Deepness Method

This method consists of going over the same portion of scripture several times and answering different questions. Questions to be asked include the following:
- What does this text tell the world?
- What problem does it address?
- Which questions does it answer?
- What is its purpose?
- What is its application?

The Bible Verse Method

In this method, the study concentrates on a particular Bible verse. Participants will read the verse several times and then meditate on it and try to answer the following questions individually:
- What personal message do I find here?
- Are there any promises from God for me here?
- Is there a command that I need to obey?
- Is there a warning for me here?
- Is there any comfort for me here?

Each person will try to find other verses that address the same issues or that present a contrast with this verse. They will then discuss their findings as a group. The objective is for all to contribute to this discussion. To this end, participants should be encouraged to ask questions and give opinions.

The Bible-Rewrite Method

The purpose of this method is to discover the message for today in a particular Bible passage. For example, examine Ephesians 3:7–13 and re- write it for our time. This method takes some thought and is best for creative people.

Step 1: Take the passage and read it aloud and then silently to yourself.

Step 2: Fill out the following information about the text:
- This text tells me to: _____
- This text must have been written when Paul was: _____
- The main point of the message is: _____

Step 3: Share your responses to this passage to see whether you understood it properly.

Step 4: This is the hard part. Rewrite the text in your own words for your time and place. Be creative, be interesting, use modern language, and use modern people and places. You might begin, "I was walking down the street in front of the church when I had this thought."

Step 5: Read to the group what each member has written. See which version best tells the story of the text.

The Theology Method

The purpose of this method is to study the Bible in a theological or doctrinal way and to clearly understand its message for you personally. For example, examine Ephesians 1–3 with the purpose of identifying the theological and doctrinal information in the text. Assign two people to each chapter and complete the following steps:

>Step 1: What is the main point of the chapter? Finish these sentences:

- The main purpose of Ephesians 1 is _____
- The main purpose of Ephesians 2 is _____
- The main purpose of Ephesians 3 is _____

Step 2: Give a name to each paragraph and fill out the following: (This maybe done by the same pairs that worked on the chapters.)
Text Name
1. Eph. 1:1, 2 <u>Example: Saying "hi" to the church</u>
2. Eph. 1:3–14 _____
3. Eph. 1:15–23 _____
4. Eph. 2:2–10 _____
5. Eph. 2:11–22 _____
6. Eph. 3:1–13 _____
7. Eph. 3:14–19 _____
8. Eph. 3:20, 21 _____

Step 3: Take six minutes to talk to one another about why each text is relevant and important to you as believers in the twenty-first century.

Step 4. Take five minutes to discuss what your group or you as an individual need to do in response to what you have found.

Step 5. As a group, identify the most inspirational kernel of truth in this passage and write it out for everyone to see.

The Devotional Method

The purpose of this method is to understand the Bible in a devotional way and to be inspired by God's word. For example, examine Ephesians 2 with the purpose of identifying the devotional material in the text.

Step 1: Read the text to yourself and take note of the most outstanding points that are helpful for your spiritual life. Find one or two that you think really make you feel good about God and what He has done for you in Christ.

1. Verse _____ tells me: _____
2. Verse _____ tells me: _____

Step 2: Pool the verses and statements that each member of the group has chosen and vote to choose the best three. Rewrite these verses to express what they mean to you and your group.

1. Verse _____ says _____
2. Verse _____ says _____
3. Verse _____ says _____

The "What it Means to Me" Method

The purpose of this method is to help participants learn how to discover the personal meaning of Scripture. For example, examine John 5:1–18 and determine what this story has to say to us today. Here are some practical steps to understand the passage:

Step 1: Pray and ask God to direct your group to the truth of His Word so that you can all apply it to your lives.

Step 2: Read John 5:1–18 together aloud. Then take three minutes to read it silently to yourselves.

Step 3: Fill in the following outline from the information you have learned:

Chapter 1
   a. _____
   b. _____
   c. _____

Chapter 2
   a. _____
   b. _____
   c. _____

Step 4: List the three most important truths about Jesus or God that your study provided.

1. _____
2. _____
3. _____

Selected Bibliography

Bible texts are from the New King James Version, unless otherwise noted

Achtemeier, Paul J., ed. *Harper's Bible Dictionary.* San Francisco: Harper & Row, 1985.

Barker, Steve. *Good Things Come in Small Groups: The Dynamics of Good Group Life.* Downers Grove, IL: InterVarsity, 1997.

Block, Peter. *Flawless Consulting: A Guide to Getting Your Expertise Used,* 2nd ed. San Francisco: Pfeiffer, 2000.

Bruce, A. B. (1889). *The Training of the Twelve; or Passages out of the Gospels, Exhibiting the Twelve Disciples of Jesus under Discipline for the Apostleship* (p. 99). New York: A. C. Armstrong and Son.

Burrill, Russell. *Creating Healthy Adventist Churches through Natural Church Development.* Berrien Springs, MI: North American Division Evangelism Institute, 2003.

Church Ministries Department of the General Conference of Seventh-day Adventists A, B, C . . . Z *for Youth Ministries.* Silver Spring, MD: Church Ministries Department of the General Conference of Seventh-day Adventists, 1986.

Daft, Richard L. *The Leadership Experience,* 5th ed. Mason, OH: South-Western Ce gage Learning, 2011.

Day, A. Colin. Collins *Thesaurus of the Bible*, rev. ed. London: Collins, 2003.

Dockery, D. S., Butler, T. C., Church, C. L., et. al, (1992). *Holman Bible Handbook* (684). Nashville, TN: Holman Bible Publishers

Dunn, James D. G. *The Epistles to the Colossians and to Philemon: A Commentary on the Greek Text.* Grand Rapids, MI: William B. Eerdmans, 1996.

Eckman, James P. *Exploring Church History.* Wheaton, IL: Crossway, 2002.

Elwell, Walter A., and Barry J. Beitzel, eds. Baker *Encyclopedia of the Bible.* Grand Rapids, MI: Baker, 1988.

Flowers, Karen, and Ron Flowers. *Family Evangelism: Bringing Jesus to the Family Circle* Silver Spring, MD: Family Ministries Department of the General Conference of Seventh-day Adventists, 2003.

Galli, Mark, and Ted Olsen. 131 *Christians Everyone Should Know.* Nashville: Broad man & Holman, 2000.

Handy, Charles B. *Beyond Certainty: The Changing Worlds of Organizations.* London: Hutchinson, 1995.

Helm, P. (1988). Disciple. In *Baker encyclopedia of the Bible* (Vol. 1, p. 629). Grand Rapids, MI: Baker Book House

Jacobs, Edward E., Robert L. Masson, and Riley L. Harvill. *Group Counseling: Strategies and Skills,* 3rd ed. Pacific Grove, CA: Brooks/Cole, 1998.

Janzen, Waldemar. *Exodus.* Believers Church Bible Commentary. Scottdale, PA: Herald, 2000.

Kim Parker; Pew Research Center, (2012). *Yes, the Rich Are Different.* https://www.
pewsocialtrends.org/2012/08/27/yes-the-rich-are-different/

Laurie, George. "Making the Invitation Compelling." I *Growing Your Church through Evangelism and Outreach,* edited by Marshall Shelley, 137–142. Nashville: Moorings, 1996.

Linthicum, R. (2005). *Building a people of power: Equipping churches to transform their communities.* Seattle, WA: World Vision Press.

MacArthur, John (2011). *Evangelism: How to Share The Gospel Faithfully.* Thomas Nelson Inc. Nashville Tennessee, USA.

Mark E. Denver, (2007) *What is a Healthy Church.* Wheaton, IL. Good News Publishers.

Manser, Martin H. *Dictionary of Bible Themes: The Accessible and Comprehensive Tool for Topical Studies.* London: Martin Manser, 2009. Logos Bible Software.

Maxwell, John. *"The Potential around You."* Growing Your Church through Training and Motivation: 30 Strategies to Transform Your Ministry, edited by Marshall Shelley, 4:18–19. Minneapolis: Bethany House, 1997.

McKenna, David L. Isaiah 1–39. *The Preacher's Commentary,* vol. 17. Nashville: Thomas Nelson, 1993.

Merrill, Dean and Marshall Shelley, eds. *Fresh Ideas for Discipleship & Nurture.* Carol Stream, IL: Christianity Today, 1984.

Neufeld, Thomas R. Y. Ephesians. *Believers Church Bible Commentary.* Scottdale, PA: Herald, 2001.

Newton, Gary C. *Growing toward Spiritual Maturity.* Wheaton, IL: Crossway, 2004 Packer, James I. *Growing in Christ.* Wheaton, IL: Crossway, 1994.

Patton, M.Q. (1987). *Qualitative Research Evaluation Methods.* Thousand Oaks, CA: Sage Publishers.

Powell, K., Mulder, J. & Griffin, B. (2016). *Growing Young: Six Essential Strategies to Help Young People Discover and Love Your Church.* Baker publishing Group, Grand Rapids, Michigan, USA.

Prime, Derek. *Opening up 1 Corinthians.* Leominster, UK: Day One, 2005.

Rainer, Thom S. *Surprising Insights From The Unchurched and Proven Ways to Reach Them.* Grand Rapids, MI: Zondervan, 2001.

Richards, Larry O. *The Bible Reader's Companion.* Wheaton, IL: Victor Books, 1991.

Sabbath School and Personal Ministries Department of the General Conference of Seventh-day Adventists. "Cool Tools for Sabbath School Action Units." Silver Spring, MD: Sabbath School and Personal Ministries Department of the General Conference of Seventh-day Adventists, 2009. http://www. sabbathschool personalministries.org/site/1/leaflets/Action%20Units.pdf.

Sam Chan, (2018). *Evangelism in a Skeptical World. How to Make the Unbelievable* News about Jesus More Believable. HarperCollins Publishing, USA.

Sahlin, Monte. "Net Results." *Adventist Review,* September 7, 2000. http://archives. *adventistreview.org*/2000-1541/1541story1-3.html.

Schwarz, Christian A. *Natural Church Development: A Guide to Eight Essential Qualities of Healthy Churches,* 6th ed. Carol Stream, IL: ChurchSmart, 2003. Charles, Illinois.

Spence-Jones, H. D. M., and Joseph S. Exell, eds. *Isaiah,* vol. 1. The Pulpit Commentary. New York: Funk & Wagnalls, 1910.

Spoon, Jerry and John W. Schell. "Aligning Student Learning Styles with Instructor Teaching Styles." *Journal of Industrial Teacher Education* 35, no. 2 (1998): 41–56.

Susan A. Ostrander (1986). *Women of the Upper Class.* Temple University Press. Philadelphia, PA.

Sweet, Leonard, Brian D. McLaren, and Jerry Haselmayer. (2003). *A is for abductive: the language of the emerging church.* Grand Rapids: Zondervan

Tracy, Brian. *Eat That Frog: 21 Great Ways to Stop Procrastinating and Get More Done in Less Time.* San Francisco: Berrett-Koehler, 2001.

Utley, R. J. (1998). Vol. Volume 5: *The Gospel according to Paul: Romans.* Study Guide Commentary Series (Ro 12:2). Marshall, Texas: Bible Lessons International

Weeden, Larry. K., ed. *The Magnetic Fellowship: Reaching and Keeping People.* Carol Stream, IL: Christianity Today, 1988.

White, E. G. (1890). *Christian Temperance and Bible Hygiene.* Battle Creek, MI: Good Health Publishing Co.
The Adventist Home. Washington, DC: Review and Herald, 1952.

———. *Christian Service.* Washington, DC: Review and Herald, 1925.

———. *Christ's Object Lessons.* Battle Creek, MI: Review and Herald, 1900.

——— (1903). *Education.* Pacific Press Publishing Association.

———. *Evangelism.* Washington, DC: Review and Herald, 1946.

———, eds. *Fresh Ideas for Preaching, Worship & Evangelism.* Carol Stream, IL: Christianity Today, 1984.

———. *Pastoral Ministry.* Silver Spring, MD: Ministerial Association of the General Conference of Seventh-day Adventists, 1995.

———. *The Desire of Ages.* Mountain View, CA: Pacific Press, 1898.

———. *The Ministry of Healing.* Mountain View, CA: Pacific Press, 1905.

———. *Welfare Ministry.* Washington, DC: Review and Herald, 1952.

Wilson, Jaye L. Fresh Start Devotionals. Fresno, CA: Willow City Press, 2009.

Made in the USA
Middletown, DE
08 July 2022